Praise for Anna Bennett's Debutante Diaries series

When You Wish Upon a Rogue

"Expertly tugs at the heartstrings." —*Publishers Weekly*

"Readers who love a grumpy-to-smitten hero will swoon."
—*Kirkus Reviews*

"A dashing Regency romance featuring a wounded earl and an unyielding heroine with strong convictions."
—*Library Journal*

The Duke Is But a Dream

"The pace of their story is steady and the flow is smooth, with plenty of chemistry and passion . . . A deeply satisfying tale of love persevering despite social constraints."
—*Publishers Weekly*

"In this story of finding yourself, it's the family the central characters create together that's the most satisfying discovery of all." —*BookPage*

"Again she creates relatable heroines similar in force and tone to those created by her sister historical romance authors Tessa Dare and Sophie Jordan." —*Booklist*

"A wonderful read, one that is hard to put down."
—*Affaire de Coeur*

"Anna Bennett is a fantastic storyteller . . . A delight of a read with characters you will love and subplots that add to the fascinating tale of old memories, new beginnings, and a happily-ever-after that made me smile."

—*Fresh Fiction*

"A finely crafted historical romance novel and a wonderfully entertaining read from cover to cover."

—*Midwest Book Review*

First Earl I See Tonight

"A kind, funny heroine is the perfect match for a stoic, brooding hero in Bennett's delightful first Debutante Diaries Regency romance. Sexy, clever . . . will bring smiles to its readers."

—*Publishers Weekly* (starred review)

"We love a heroine who doesn't wait to be rescued, so thank you, Anna Bennett! . . . A crumbling estate, mysterious letters, and a villain hiding among friends add a dash of intrigue to this tantalizing Regency adventure."

—*Apple Books Review*
(Apple Books Best of the Month)

Praise for the Wayward Wallflowers series

The Rogue Is Back in Town

"Fans of Regency romance authors Eloisa James, Tessa Dare, and Mary Jo Putney will go wild for the final installment of Bennett's Wayward Wallflowers trilogy."

—*Booklist* (starred review)

"Bennett's gift for writing a page-turner of a plot is on full display . . . a solid Regency story of true love."
—*Kirkus Reviews*

"Entertaining . . . [offers] plenty to satisfy Regency fans."
—*Publishers Weekly*

I Dared the Duke

"Sharply drawn characters, clever dialogue, simmering sensuality, and a dash of mystery make this well-crafted Regency thoroughly delightful."
—*Library Journal*

"Readers will enjoy this sassy Regency take on the classic *Beauty and the Beast* tale." —*Booklist*

"A captivating page-turner that will become a new favorite among romance enthusiasts!" —*BookPage*

"Bennett brings new life to traditional Regency stories and characters." —*Kirkus Reviews*

"Scrumptious . . . I devoured every word! A hot and wounded hero, a heroine you wish could be your friend in real life, and witty scenes that sparkle with life . . . The Wayward Wallflowers just keep getting better!"
—Laura Lee Guhrke,
New York Times bestselling author

One Duke Down

ANNA BENNETT

St. Martin's Paperbacks

First published in the United States by St. Martin's Paperbacks, an imprint of St. Martin's Publishing Group

ONE DUKE DOWN

Copyright © 2023 by Anna Bennett.
Excerpt from *It Takes a Rake* copyright © 2023 by Anna Bennett.

All rights reserved.

For information, address St. Martin's Publishing Group, 120 Broadway, New York, NY 10271.

www.stmartins.com

ISBN: 978-1-250-79393-5

Our books may be purchased in bulk for promotional, educational, or business use. Please contact your local bookseller or the Macmillan Corporate and Premium Sales Department at 1-800-221-7945, ext. 5442, or by email at MacmillanSpecialMarkets@macmillan.com.

Printed in the United States of America

St. Martin's Paperbacks edition / February 2023

10 9 8 7 6 5 4 3 2 1

*To the SIL party of 34
and the good times on Gower Street.*

Chapter 1

Miss Poppy Summers was accustomed to finding odd, unwanted objects tangled in her fishing nets: clumps of seaweed, discarded rum bottles, even the occasional clay pipe. But until that sun-soaked June morning, she had never, in the course of all her twenty-three years, had the misfortune of catching a *man*.

A strapping, half-dressed, unconscious man, at that.

Perched on the seat of her small rowboat several yards offshore, she raised a hand to her forehead and shielded her eyes from the glare in order to have a proper look at him.

He was sprawled facedown on the beach, his head turned to one side, long legs akimbo in the frothy, lapping waves. Raven hair covered his eyes, and sand salted the dark stubble along his jaw. Beneath the remains of his shirt—little more than a few scraps of lawn—he had the broad shoulders of a swimmer and the trim waist of a boxer. His trousers were plastered to thick thighs, and his bare feet were nearly the size of oar blades.

Zounds.

He must have stumbled out of the surf and collapsed on the beach. *Her* beach. To make matters worse, one corner of the net that she'd strategically placed in the deepest part of the cove was now wrapped around his left ankle, all but dashing her hopes for a good day's catch.

Disappointment sank onto her chest like a rusty anchor. The only time Papa smiled lately was when Poppy came home with news of a bountiful haul, but there'd been precious little cause for celebration lately. A devastating uptick in cod worm meant a third of the fish she caught weren't fit to eat, and the healthy ones tended to be younger, smaller fish that didn't bring nearly as good a price.

She'd weathered tough seasons before, but this summer was different. Her poor father rarely left his bed since taking ill over the winter, and her brother, Dane, had been spending more time in London of late. Perhaps that was for the best, though, since he had an infuriating habit of gambling away the meager earnings from the family's business—a business that she was now single-handedly trying to keep afloat.

Still, she supposed an empty net was the least of her problems. The stranger passed out on the sand could be a smuggler, a pirate, or worse. Good heavens, for all she knew, he could be . . . *dead*.

"Hullo!" She cupped her hands around her mouth and shouted over the *whoosh* of the waves. "Can you hear me?"

He didn't flinch.

She hesitated, then started rowing ashore. Approaching the man was risky to be sure, but he was clearly in need of help. Besides, no one could accuse her of being naïve or sheltered. She had a fillet knife strapped to her calf, and if necessary, would resort to using an oar as a bludgeon.

But she rather hoped it didn't come to that.

With a few easy strokes, she turned the bow into the waves and maneuvered her boat onto the shore. "Hullo!" she called again. She hopped lightly onto the sand, resting the oar on one shoulder like a cricket bat. "Are you injured?"

The man remained ominously still and silent.

Warily, she circled him, set down her oar, and knelt beside his head. The ocean breeze riffled his hair, revealing a wicked gash at his temple. The dark slash of an eyebrow was caked with dried blood, but his color was good, and his lips weren't blue.

On the contrary, they were full and slightly parted. Quite perfectly formed, in fact. Despite his rugged, dangerous air—or perhaps *because* of it—she had to admit that the man was devilishly handsome.

And most definitely *not* from Bellehaven Bay.

Which was no doubt for the best. All Poppy needed to do was rouse him, send him on his merry way, and cast her nets back into the water. He'd be erased from her memory as quickly as a drawing in the sand.

Tentatively, she poked at his shoulder, startled to find it much harder than her own. "Wake up," she urged. "You don't want to be lounging about when the tide comes in, do you?"

No response, but the subtle rise and fall of his back told her he was still breathing. At least for now.

She nudged his arm, harder this time. "Come on then," she said, deliberately brusque. "I have fish to catch, and I'm guessing you have brandy to smuggle. Or ships to commandeer. It matters little to me, really. All I ask is that you conduct your shady business on another beach."

When he failed to reply, she stood, planted her hands on hips, and sighed. "Not the cooperative sort, are you? I suppose I'll need to fetch Dr. Gladwell." She lifted her chin and gazed at the pink and blue horizon, mentally rearranging her day. Thanks to the mysterious man, there would be no fish to salt and dry, no reason to drive her cart to market, and no coins to put in her pocket. She swallowed, determined to ignore the familiar panic prickling the back of her neck.

She *would* find a way to keep food on the table and purchase the tinctures that relieved Papa's aches.

But first, she had to make sure that this man didn't drown in the surf. Not on her beach.

"I'm going to roll you onto your back," she said conversationally, on the off chance some hazy corner of his brain was listening.

Fortunately—or perhaps *un*fortunately—she had some experience dealing with large, unresponsive men. At least once a month the barkeep at the Salty Mermaid summoned her to retrieve her drunk-as-a-wheelbarrow brother from the pub. Her current situation wasn't terribly different. It simply required a combination of physical strength, patience, and finesse.

Using her body for leverage, she pushed the man's shoulder until he flipped over, belly up. She stepped back, waiting a moment to see if the movement woke him, but he was just as still as before.

She took a moment to study him, and her gaze was naturally drawn to the swaths of skin visible through the shreds of his shirt: the sprinkling of hair near his sternum, the defined contours of his chest, and the fuzzy ridges of his abdomen. He certainly didn't have the paunch of a man who drank six pints a night. But it was not going to be easy to drag a man his size ten yards up the beach.

"We're headed for that spot of shade at the base of the cliffs," she said as she wedged her hands beneath his shoulders. "Ready? Here we go."

Summoning every ounce of strength, she lifted him, raising his upper body a few inches off the sand. But his heavy head listed to the side, making him too unwieldy, so she gently lowered him to the ground again.

Already panting from her efforts, she quickly gathered the hem of her skirt and knotted it at her knees before wading into the water toward the man's feet. "Maybe we'll have better luck at this end."

She lifted one of his legs, freed it from her net, then pulled, slowly rotating him so that his feet were pointing in the direction she needed to move him. He must have weighed close to fourteen stone, but she propped his ankles on her hips and trudged backward, dragging him inch by inch across the beach.

Sweat trickled down her nape and her forearms quivered, but she managed to relocate him out of the waves' reach. Her chest heaved as she collapsed onto the soft sand beside him.

"We did it," she gasped, as if he deserved some of the credit. In truth, he hadn't shown any signs of consciousness—and that worried her.

The man looked even more disheveled now, if that were possible. The remnants of his shirt had rolled up around his neck, and his trousers had bunched above his knees. His muscular arms were coated in fine, gritty sand, and his hair resembled a dark mop. Most alarming, however, were the fresh crimson drops forming on his head wound.

She retrieved her bag from the boat, pulled out her canteen, and took several gulps of cool water. Then she knelt beside the man and poured a little water on the angry gash above his eye.

"I don't have a proper bandage," she said, frowning. "But I shall lend you my scarf." She slipped the triangle of fabric off her head, releasing a riot of strawberry curls around her shoulders in the process. She folded the large triangle into a long, thin strip and wrapped it around his head, securing it over one ear. He looked even more like a pirate now.

There. She'd made him as comfortable as she possibly could, and she simply had to hope he stayed alive until she returned with Dr. Gladwell. She'd hurry back to her family's small stable, take her cart into town, and return to the beach in an hour or two.

She slipped on the old pair of shoes she kept in her bag and placed the canteen next to the man in case he regained consciousness while she was gone. "No need to thank me," she quipped. "But if you should wake and aren't in a terrible hurry to return to your life of looting and pillaging, you could always cast my net back where you found it."

True to form, he did not respond. But those lips of his did look rather parched, so, on an impulse, she knelt, picked up the canteen, and trickled some water into his mouth. That went well enough, so she poured a bit more.

A sputtering sound erupted from his throat. Then a violent cough. *Gads*.

She dropped the canteen and rolled him onto his side.

His hand shot out, clasping her wrist in a vise-like grip.

She jerked back, trying to pull free, but he squeezed tighter.

Oh God. Her fingers turned numb. Her heart pounded in her ears.

Instinct kicked in, and she reached for her knife.

Keane woke with a jolt, immediately coming to grips with three disturbing facts. Someone had tried to choke him. His head hurt like the very devil. And the cool blade of a knife was pressed to his throat.

"Let. Go." The voice at his ear, husky and lethal, belonged to a woman.

For a split second, he didn't know what she was talking about. Then he looked down to find his own fingers clamped around a delicate wrist. He cursed and released her arm like it was a hot iron.

"Don't move," she said evenly. She held the knife firmly against his neck as she leaned over him.

He squinted up at her, wondering if it was possible she'd been the one who attacked him last night. But she didn't look like any other criminal he'd encountered.

Her long, wild curls were the fiery hue of the sky at dusk. Her smooth cheeks were tanned and freckled. Her pink lips were plump—and ominously unsmiling.

"Who are you?" she demanded.

Damn, but his tongue felt thick and dry. "Andrew Keane," he rasped. "Duke of Hawking."

She bared even, white teeth, and the point of her blade pinched his neck.

"I'm not amused," she said, as if that weren't painfully obvious. "What is your name?"

"My friends call me Keane."

"And everyone else?"

"Duke, mostly."

"You're delusional," she said, her expression a mix of pity and disgust. "The lump on your head must be to blame."

"I might be a bit foggy," he admitted, "but I'm not delusional."

"A duke." Her shrewd gaze flicked to his tattered shirt. "Your cravat and waistcoat have gone missing, *Your Grace*." The last two words dripped with the sort of disdain typically reserved for pesky vermin and tax collectors.

"I suspect the rest of my clothes are in the same place as my boots." Along with his jacket, money, and pocket watch.

She narrowed her turquoise eyes. "You don't look like a gentleman. More important, you lack the manners of one."

He swallowed guiltily. "I'm sorry I grabbed your wrist. I thought you were . . . someone else. You have nothing to fear from me."

One auburn brow lifted, and the pressure of the knife decreased ever so slightly. "What happened to you?" she asked.

"I'm not sure."

Someone—perhaps more than one person—had jumped him after he left the pub last night. What occurred after that was a blur, and he didn't trust anyone, including the woman who currently held him at knifepoint. "All I know is that my head aches and the ground is spinning." He winced and fought back a wave of nausea. "I promise I'm no threat. Maybe you could lower the knife?"

She glanced down at her weapon like she'd forgotten she held it, slowly pulled it away, and sat back on her heels.

"Thank you." He exhaled, tried to lift his head, and immediately regretted it. "What's your name?"

She scowled as if the question was an affront. "There are only two facts pertinent to your situation. First, you're on my beach. Second, I will not abide illegal activity. No smuggling, no carousing. As soon as you can walk, you must leave and rejoin your swashbuckling friends."

"Swashbuckling?" He blinked. "I'm not a pirate. I'm a *duke*."

She polished her blade with the hem of her skirt and nodded as though she were listening to an oft-repeated, rather tedious story. "So you've said. I was just about to fetch the doctor when you woke. Let us hope he has a remedy for your muddled head."

"No." He rolled onto his side and propped himself on his elbow, grimacing. "No doctor."

She clucked her tongue. "Clearly, you require medical attention."

Maybe. But the fewer people who knew he was there—wherever *there* happened to be—the better. Unless he was mistaken, last night was not an ordinary burglary. Someone had tried to kill him and had come bloody close to succeeding.

He scoffed and pressed his fingertips to the bandaged, throbbing knot on his head. "This? It's naught but a wee bump, and apparently, you've already dressed it. I'll rest for a spell, and in a few hours, I'll be fit as a . . ." He closed his eyes, searching for the word. "Er, I'll be right as . . ."

She cocked an ear and arched a brow as if he were proving her point.

"I just need to sleep," he said, exhaling.

"I don't know," she mused. She glanced over her shoulder at a tangled net near the shoreline.

"Is that yours?" He gestured at the net, hoping to distract her. "And the boat, too?"

She raised her chin a notch. "I was fishing when I found you."

That would account for her sun-kissed skin and unexpected strength. "I don't want to keep you from your work."

"You already have," she said without malice as she stood and paced in front of him. "Worse, I fear your presence here could attract more nefarious activity."

"Nefarious?" He chuckled in spite of the pounding in his brain.

She shrugged, unapologetic. "By the look of that gash

on your head, I'd say you're embroiled in unsavory business. Surely, someone will come looking for you."

Diggs, his valet and loyal friend, might. He was the only person who'd traveled with him from London. But Diggs had been staying at the Bluffs' Brew Inn and probably didn't have an inkling of what had occurred last night. Bellehaven Bay was a fashionable resort town, and Keane had traveled there from London to escape a bit of drama. It certainly wasn't the sort of place one expected to be attacked on the street.

"No one will look for me," Keane said earnestly. "Not a soul in the world knows I'm here, and clearly, we'd both prefer to keep it that way. Allow me to rest here for a few hours and regain my strength. I'll be gone before nightfall."

For several seconds she said nothing, but he could almost see the battle playing out in her mind. At last, she strode back to him, picked up the canteen, and thrust it at him. "There's a little water left in here. You should drink it."

He tipped back the canteen and gulped the last swallows. "Thank you."

"I'll return at dusk. If you're still here, I *will* fetch the doctor, word will spread, and by breakfast tomorrow, all of Bellehaven will be buzzing about the Delusional Duke. This"—she traced a circle in the air around him—"is but a short reprieve, so don't become too comfortable."

Gingerly, he lowered his head to the soft sand. "I wouldn't dream of it," he said solemnly. His eyelids grew heavy, and the ocean breeze tickled his face, taking the edge off his pain. "What will you do now?" he murmured, even though he knew the question was likely to annoy her.

"What I always do." She twirled her knife in her palm, watching the silver blade glint in the sun before lifting her hem and smoothly sliding the weapon into the leather sheath strapped to her lithe leg. "Work . . . and read. Farewell, Keane."

If his tongue had been more cooperative, he might have asked what she liked to read. He might have asked who had taught her to fish or whether she'd lived in Bellehaven her whole life or whether she was aware that her irises were precisely the same vivid blue-green as the sea.

Instead, he watched through half-closed eyes as she gathered her net, scooped up her things, and waded into the surf like a fiery-haired Aphrodite. He admired the graceful, efficient movements of her limbs as she climbed into her boat, took up her oars, and disappeared over the crest of a wave.

Leaving him alone to ponder the target on his back.

He could think of half a dozen people who despised him—and a few who might even want him dead. But for the sake of the woman who'd rescued him, he fervently hoped that no one had followed him. That no one would disturb the tranquility of her cove.

He reached for a rough, fist-sized rock at the base of the cliff, clutched it in his palm, and hid it beneath his chest, just in case.

The next time someone tried to attack him, he'd be ready.

Chapter 2

"How's your father faring?"

Poppy blinked, snapping her attention back to Hazel, the headmistress of Bellehaven Academy and her dear friend. Poppy had come to town after pulling the stranger out of the surf, determined to salvage the rest of the day in spite of the odd encounter with him.

She'd intended to banish him from her thoughts while she went about her usual errands, but he trespassed into her head in much the same way he'd trespassed onto her beach. Vexing, that he should affect her so, but understandable. It wasn't every morning that she brandished her knife at a devilishly handsome rogue.

Poppy shook her head in a futile attempt to clear it and mustered a smile for Hazel. "Papa's about the same. The willow bark seems to ease his aching joints. I'm going to stop at the apothecary on my way home and pick up some more."

"You must let me know if I can help in any way," Hazel said earnestly. Her brown hair was swept into its usual tidy knot, but one rebellious chestnut curl above her forehead fluttered in the breeze coming from her office window.

"You've done far too much already," Poppy said, setting the small stack of books that she'd borrowed from

Hazel on her desk. "Thank you for sending Kitty over with the basket. The oranges are delicious, and I was able to coax Papa into eating a few bites of the stew."

"It was nothing," Hazel said, waving a dismissive hand. "You know Kitty is always grateful for the chance to see you."

"I was happy to see her, too. It's been too long since we Belles were all together." Poppy, Hazel, and Kitty had formed a special bond the previous summer after discovering they were each still grappling with the grief of losing their mothers far too soon. Kitty, the youngest of their trio, had started out as Hazel's most troublesome student. But since Hazel married Kitty's uncle and guardian, the Earl of Bladenton, last summer, they'd formed a family that included Kitty and two other orphaned students—Lucy and Clara. Now Hazel, her smitten husband, Blade, and all the girls were living in a spacious suite of rooms in the center of Bellehaven while they began construction on a grand house on the outskirts of town.

"Blade brought more books from London," Hazel said excitedly, turning to pluck several from the shelves behind her desk. "I stayed up late several evenings reading this one."

Poppy chuckled as she flipped through the gothic novel that Hazel handed her, along with a few other books. "Thank you. I am sure I shall enjoy it, too." Indeed, it seemed reading was the one bright spot in her dreary existence, her only escape from worrying about Papa, missing her mother, and struggling to keep food on the table.

As if she could sense Poppy's melancholy, Hazel rounded her desk and gently squeezed her shoulders. "Why don't you come visit on Saturday? You, Kitty, and I could take a picnic to the beach, do a little shopping in town, and spend the whole day together."

"I'd love that . . ." Truly, she would. "But I don't like to leave Papa for too long." Besides, she'd lost a whole morning of fishing, thanks to the virile stranger on her beach. She hesitated a moment, then asked, "Did anything unusual happen in town last night?"

Hazel arched a brow. "Unusual in what sense?"

"I don't know," Poppy said with a shrug. "I just wondered if there was talk this morning of any strange goings-on, any rumors involving prominent tourists in Bellehaven?"

"Poppy Summers." Hazel narrowed her eyes, suspicious. "Is there something you'd like to tell me?"

"No." Her face heated. "Let's just say that the source of my information is extremely unreliable. Hardly worth sparing a second thought."

"Hmm," Hazel murmured, clearly unconvinced. "I won't press you further, but I will say this: Whatever might be going on, have a care. I have not heard any gossip, but I do know that the tourists who flock to our little town sometimes imagine that they're in another world where the rules of society don't apply. After a few days of carousing, they hop into their fancy carriages and return to their elegant London town houses or country estates. And it's left to the good folk of Bellehaven to clean up the messes they leave behind."

"That is true," Poppy said sadly.

She fervently hoped that the man—Keane, he'd said his name was—wouldn't leave a mess behind. That he'd keep his promise and be gone by dusk, before she or her family were swept up in any unsavory business. That he'd vanish from her life just as quickly as he'd dropped into it, long before she could possibly have the misfortune of falling prey to those rakish good looks and stray-puppy eyes.

Her life was difficult enough as it was. The last thing

she needed was for a man to muck it up—and remind her that she'd once wished for something more.

As the sun began to set, Keane realized he'd made a gross miscalculation. Despite all the assurances he'd given his fiery-haired rescuer earlier, he was in no physical condition to walk to town. The first time he tried to stand, his legs gave out, and he ate a mouthful of sand. On his second try, he staggered several feet, fell onto all fours, and heaved up the meager contents of his stomach.

His pulse raced, his head ached, and his throat was parched. But he had to make it as far from the beach as he possibly could. Not only because he'd promised the young woman, but also because the seed of a plan had begun to sprout in his mind. And it required him to stay out of sight.

So, he followed the shoreline west, alternately stumbling and crawling through the surf. His progress was woefully slow, but when he found one of his boots washed up near the rocks, he dragged it along and kept a keen eye out for the other.

When darkness fell and he was too weak to take another step, he stumbled to the foot of a cliff, sank onto the pebbled sand, and leaned his back against the cool, mossy rock. He only wanted to catch his breath and rest his eyes for a bit. He wasn't going to sleep—or dream of an expressive, freckled face framed by fiery tendrils that danced in the ocean breeze.

"Keane." He recognized the sensuously husky, slightly irritated voice at once and pried one eye open. She stood a yard away, holding a lantern in the space between them. The thick auburn braid that hung over her shoulder glowed like a gemstone, and her simple cotton dress was the color of springtime grass.

"Let me guess," he said wryly. "This is your beach, too."

"No." She tossed a scuffed, water-logged boot onto the ground beside him. "But I found this tangled in my net. I thought you might need it."

"How'd you know where to find me?"

"It was hard to miss your trail. It looks as though someone dragged you across the beach by your hair."

"I may not have been entirely upright," he admitted. "But I managed to make it here on my own."

"You must be very proud." Her eyes flicked to his forehead, and she frowned as she set the lantern on the sand and slipped the bag off her shoulder. "How's your wound?"

"Perfect," he quipped. "Not grave enough to kill me. Just deep enough to leave a dashing scar. The kind that's sure to drive the ladies wild."

She pursed her lips, skeptical. "One can hope."

He chuckled. "Thank you for bringing my boot . . . and for your earlier kindness."

She arched a brow. "I held you at knifepoint."

"And almost drowned me."

That elicited a smile so sly and so sweet that it landed in the vicinity of his groin.

"I did, didn't I?" She reached into her bag, pulled out the canteen, and handed it to him.

He raised it in a mock toast, took a few glorious swigs, and wiped his mouth with a tattered sleeve. "Thank you—again."

She sank to the sand beside him. "I still think you are in need of a doctor's attention."

He shook his head firmly. "No."

"And you intend to stay here tonight?"

"Just until my fellow pirates send the dinghy for me."

"Fair enough." She opened her bag again, and this time withdrew a small, wrapped parcel. "It's a sandwich—in case you grow hungry before your mates are able to retrieve you," she said, only half joking.

His belly rumbled at the mention of food. "I'm going to repay you someday. But it would help if I knew your name."

"You don't need to repay me," she said simply. "In Bellehaven we're kind to everyone. Even strangers."

He gazed at her, thoughtful, as he sank his teeth into the savory chicken sandwich. "What if I said I'd still like to know your name?"

"What if I said I'd like to be queen of England?" she countered. "We don't always get what we want."

He grinned at her. "True, but sometimes we do."

"Maybe *you* do," she mused. "Some of us aren't so fortunate." Her reply was snappy, but there was a heaviness to her words. A truth that punched him like a right hook.

"Fishing must be difficult work."

"It's more than work. It's both a science and an art."

"How so?" He wanted to know. Wanted her to keep talking. About anything.

She tucked her knees to her chest and gazed out at the ocean. "A good angler listens to the caw of seabirds, studies the patterns of the currents, and predicts which way the fish are moving. She can row a boat on the surface without disturbing a school below. She knows when a fish in her net is too small to keep and how to quickly free it. With one sniff of the air, she senses when it's time to pick up her nets, return to shore, and secure the boat in advance of a storm."

As she spoke, her blue-green eyes sparkled in the moonlight. A few loose tendrils fluttered around the graceful column of her throat. Keane stared, mesmerized. "You love fishing."

"Not really," she said softly. "I love providing for my

family. I don't mind the hard work, but the truth is I detest being at the mercy of the weather and the seasons and the whims of nature."

He nodded, debating how to best ask the question bouncing around inside his head. "Is it entirely up to you? Providing for your family, I mean."

She hesitated, then exhaled. "At the moment. My father is bedridden and my brother . . . He's been going through a difficult time."

"I'm sorry." Keane meant it, but a part of him was relieved that she hadn't mentioned a husband. An idea he'd had earlier took root, and before he could change his mind, he looked into her eyes. "But I may be able to help."

She smiled ruefully. "Forgive me for saying so, but you're scarcely able to stand. You're in no position to help me—or anyone, for that matter."

"You're right. I need a little more time to recover. A spot to sleep. Someone to bring me food and water. I could pay you handsomely."

"You haven't two pennies to rub together."

"Perhaps not *with* me," Keane said. "But I am a duke—and in possession of a considerable fortune."

She sighed and pressed a hand to her forehead. "And here I thought we'd progressed beyond fantastic tales."

"I'm the Duke of Hawking," he said, adamant. "And if you give me the chance, I can prove it."

Chapter 3

"This must be highly diverting for you," Poppy said dryly.

"What do you mean?" Keane asked innocently. He seemed completely oblivious to the absurdity of his claim. *Duke, indeed.*

"I can't fault you for having a bit of fun at my expense." She stood and shook the sand from her skirts, cursing herself for lingering on the beach with the virile stranger, who looked even more disreputable with his day-old beard. She'd only meant to check on him, to be certain he hadn't bled to death or blistered in the sun. She hadn't intended to share anything personal, and she definitely hadn't wanted him to think she required his charity.

But it had been nice to have someone besides the Belles to talk to. She adored chatting with Hazel and Kitty, but her conversation with Keane had an altogether different feel. He looked at her with a mixture of wonder and curiosity—as if he truly believed she was destined for more than a lifetime of repairing gill nets and drying fish.

For a few moments she'd felt lighter—free of the responsibilities that tied her to the cottage by the sea. But then he'd gone and spoiled the evening by claiming, once again, that he was a down-on-his-luck duke.

He tossed her a roguish half smile—the sort that had

undoubtedly charmed barmaids in every port from Plymouth to Dover. "Do you want to know what I think?" he drawled.

"I feel certain you shall tell me, regardless of my answer."

"I think you're afraid that I *am* telling the truth."

She scoffed. "Why would I be afraid to discover I'm harboring a duke?"

He shrugged his broad shoulders and searched her face. "An excellent question. Why don't you tell me?"

Her spine prickled. He was only engaging in a bit of banter. He couldn't possibly know that he'd touched a nerve.

"Very well. Against my better judgment, I shall play along." She heaved an exasperated sigh and crossed her arms. "Pray tell, how do you intend to prove you are a duke? And please don't insult me by producing some tarnished signet ring that you likely found in a pawn shop."

"I wouldn't dream of it," he said, sitting up a little straighter. "I have something better than a ring: a witness. My valet."

"A valet, you say?" Poppy craned her neck up and down the beach. "Is he polishing your boots behind the rocks? Organizing your cufflinks in the cove?"

"He's in town. If you're willing to help, I'll send for him."

"In case it wasn't perfectly clear, I'm trying to rid the beach of strange men, not add to their numbers."

"Diggs wouldn't stay. I'd only let him know I'm safe and ask him to bring me a few things—including money to pay you."

Poppy narrowed her eyes. "What, precisely, would you be paying me for?"

"Room and board while I recover," he answered. "I

don't require much. Meals twice a day, a few blankets here on the beach, and, most important, your secrecy."

"I don't understand. If your valet is in town, surely he could arrange for more comfortable lodgings."

"Yes," Keane conceded, "but then everyone would know I'm alive."

She blinked. "You want them to think you're *dead*?"

"Not everyone," he said. "Just the person who tried to kill me."

"Why?"

"Because it will be easier to discover who wants me dead if they believe they've succeeded."

"And do you have a long list of mortal enemies?" she quipped.

"Just two or three," he said smugly, as if he should be congratulated on the low number.

"I had no idea that being a duke was such a hazardous business." She sat beside him again, close enough to look into his eyes. "Let us suppose for a moment that I was stupid enough to agree to such a ridiculous plan. How much would you be willing to pay me?"

The sum he named exceeded an entire summer's worth of fishing profits, and she gaped at him, stunned. She reminded herself that he'd suffered a terrible blow to the head. That he probably didn't possess that much money. That he might not even know who he really was.

But she was tempted, nonetheless.

If not for the cod shortage or Papa's illness or the bills piling up, she might have ordered him right off her beach. But if there was any chance that he could afford to pay the sum he'd quoted, she didn't have the luxury of refusing him.

Apparently mistaking her silence for disinterest, he said, "Fine. I'll double my offer."

The cavalier manner in which he threw around such numbers made her wonder if he truly *was* a duke. "I would be exposing my family to potential danger," she said.

"Have you told anyone that I'm here?"

"No."

"Then there is no risk of discovery."

"You want to involve your valet," she countered.

"I trust him with my life," Keane said solemnly.

"And you expect me to trust him with mine?"

His eyes flicked across her face, then stared straight into her soul. "Is it so difficult for you to trust?"

Blast. It just so happened he'd touched another nerve, and she felt her hackles rise. "Trust has to be earned."

He held her gaze till heat crept up her neck. "I trust you—and I don't even know your name," he said, clearly baiting her.

She'd always had the devil of a time resisting a challenge.

"My name is Poppy Summers," she said, matter of fact.

His mouth curled into a heart-stopping grin. "Consider this, Miss Summers. If you agree to help me, you stand to gain more than a few extra coins in your pocket. You'll have a bit of adventure and intrigue. You might even make a friend."

She stared at him, keeping her face impassive. "I have enough friends. But I will consider your offer and give you my decision when I return tomorrow."

"Must you leave already?"

"You should rest." She took a folded quilt out of her bag and set it next to him. "I have chores to do in the morning but will be back here by midday. Until then, do try to avoid further trouble or injury."

He chuckled, tucked the blanket behind his head, and

leaned back. "I know you still don't believe me," he said. "But I think you want to."

She left the canteen next to him, slung her bag over her shoulder, and scooped up the lantern. "Good night, Keane."

"Sleep well, Miss Summers."

Poppy left him sitting at the base of the cliffs, wondering if that would be the last she saw of him. Only time would tell if his outlandish claims were true. He could be rich as a king or poor as a church mouse. He could be an esteemed member of the nobility or the chief cook in a ship's galley. His silver tongue and rakish charm did not sway her—much.

But he had been correct about one thing: She did long for adventure and intrigue. She did wish to escape to a world free from salted eels, fish intestines, and blistered palms. Which was why, as usual, she did not go directly home.

Despite the late hour, she followed the well-worn trail to her private sanctuary. No one except Hazel and Kitty had ever been there—not even her father or brother. She'd needed a place that was just for her and her books. A place where she could spend an hour or two when her work for the day was done.

She'd built the rustic lean-to a couple of years ago in a clearing between two large trees. Using wooden floorboards from old boats, discarded scraps of canvas, and extra pieces of rope, she'd managed to create a surprisingly sturdy and comfortable shelter. Mother Nature had embellished her refuge with verdant moss, trailing vines, and colorful wildflowers, giving it the charm of an illustration straight out of Grimm's fairy tales.

Poppy wound her way up the path till she reached the

faded blue quilt hanging in the doorway of the shelter, then slipped off her shoes and went inside. She set her lantern on an upside-down crate next to a bottle filled with stems of fragrant lavender, sank onto a large pillow, and opened her book.

She might not have a closetful of ball gowns or invitations to soirees or box seats at the theater. But she had her refuge, a vivid imagination . . . and stories.

Poppy placed a kettle on the stove the next morning and began her routine, which included tidying the cottage and preparing breakfast. The alternating rumble and hiss of Papa's snoring floated into the living area from his small, adjoining bedroom, so she was careful not to clatter the dishes as she made a tray for him.

Since he wasn't fond of the taste of willow bark tea, she'd resorted to bribing him to drink it—promising a pastry from the tea shop if he finished every drop. The blueberry tarts were an extravagance they could ill afford, but what was the point of toiling day in and day out if she couldn't spoil her dear Papa a little? Besides, if she didn't spend the money on tarts, her brother was sure to squander it on brandy.

Dane had been spending an increasing amount of time in London of late, claiming he could make more money taking odd jobs on the docks than he could fishing with Poppy. But he sometimes disappeared for weeks on end, and when he did return to Bellehaven, he certainly didn't come home with full pockets.

By all rights, she should be furious with him—but deep down he wasn't the selfish rogue everyone assumed him to be. Indeed, there was a time not so long ago when she'd idolized him. He'd been hard-working, generous, and quick with a smile. He'd taught her to fish, declared himself her protector, and surprised her with a book on her eighth birthday.

But that was before Mama became sick. Before bitterness and resentment snuffed out the light inside him.

Poppy understood all too well how anger and grief could change a person.

"Poppy, my dear," Papa called groggily.

She picked up his tray and swept aside the curtain that served as the door to his room. "You're awake early," she said with a smile.

He gestured toward the tiny open window above his bed. "There's a storm coming. I feel it in my joints." He sat up and winced as he flexed swollen, gnarled fingers.

She set the tray beside him and gazed out at the brilliant pink sky and the glass-like surface of the water. "You could be right."

"Of course I'm right," he said, mildly offended. "If you must take the boat out today, stay close to shore."

"Don't worry about me, Papa." She fluffed a pillow behind his back and handed him a mug of tea. "This will help your aches."

He took a sip, grimaced, and stared longingly out the window. "This is not how things are supposed to be. I should be casting my nets right now. You should be spending your days at that school in town. Your mother wanted that for you—clever friends, a fine education, a bright future."

"Don't be silly," she said, ignoring the pang she always felt at the mention of Mama. "I have everything I could possibly want: dear friends, diverting books, and a father whom I adore. I'll see you at dinner." She planted a perfunctory kiss on his cheek, walked to the doorway, then called over her shoulder, "Don't touch that pastry until your tea is gone!"

He grumbled under his breath, but Poppy smiled to herself as she fastened a scarf around her head. She quickly gathered a few supplies before heading out the door.

There was no use dwelling on the dangerously handsome stranger on her beach or the exorbitant amount of money he'd offered for her help.

If she was going to keep Papa supplied in tarts, she had work to do.

After a few productive hours of fishing, Poppy hooked their sweet old mule, Calypso, to the cart, loaded the back with baskets of fresh cod, and drove into town. She made the rounds to her usual customers, selling or trading the fish for goods at each stop.

As Poppy was hoisting a bag of flour in her cart, her friend Hazel breezed out of the milliner's shop, laden with packages. "I was hoping I'd see you again today," she called. A couple of older ladies standing nearby arched their brows at the sight of the strikingly beautiful countess approaching Poppy and her fishing cart. They were the same women who thought nothing of spending a small fortune at the modiste but refused to let their servants pay market price for fresh fish. Hazel, dear friend that she was, seemed oblivious to their disapproving glances.

"A welcome surprise, seeing you two days in a row," Poppy said sincerely. "But why aren't you at the school?"

"Jane is teaching today's lesson, and I didn't want her to feel like I was peering over her shoulder. Besides, it seemed like a fine day to do some shopping." She handed Poppy a small round box. "For you."

Poppy opened her mouth to protest, but Hazel held up her palm. "It's just a simple straw bonnet trimmed in bluebells—a nod to the Belles, of course. I bought matching ones for Kitty and myself. You know how Kitty adores secret society rituals. Perhaps the bonnets will prevent us from having to take a blood oath at our next meeting."

Experience had taught Poppy that attempts to refuse the generous gift would be a waste of her breath. "Thank you."

"It's my pleasure," Hazel said, beaming. "But that's not the only reason I'd hoped to see you." She stepped closer and lowered her voice. "Yesterday you asked whether I'd heard rumors regarding prominent tourists."

"Yes. I suppose it was a silly question."

Hazel's eyes narrowed shrewdly. "I overheard something in the tea shop this morning that might be of interest."

Gooseflesh covered Poppy's arms, but she managed a wry smile. "There's never any shortage of gossip in Bellehaven, is there?"

"Lady Rufflebum was saying that the Duke of Hawking was in town two days ago . . . and that he hasn't been seen since."

Poppy swallowed. "How odd."

"I thought so, too. Apparently, his valet made discreet inquiries with the countess's staff." Hazel pursed her lips, pensive. "Anyway, I thought you'd want to know."

"Always good to be informed," Poppy said briskly. "Thank you again for the bonnet. I should head home. Papa says a storm is on the way, and I feel it, too."

"I'm glad I saw you." Hazel smiled softly. "If only to remind you that if you should need anything—or find yourself caught up in any sort of trouble—you can come to me."

Poppy nodded gratefully. Hazel was loyal and generous to a fault. Which was precisely why Poppy wouldn't dream of involving her, Blade, and their sweet girls in a potential scandal. "I'm accustomed to taking care of myself. Don't waste your worrying on me," she said with a wink. "Save it for any man who dares to cross me."

Chapter 4

Keane woke in a cold sweat, his heart beating out of his chest. The sun was high in the sky, and it took him a moment to recall where he was.

In Bellehaven Bay. On Poppy Summers's beach.

He'd dreamt of the night he'd been attacked, and some of the details had come into focus.

A high-stakes game of vingt-et-un.

An obscene amount of brandy.

A midnight walk on a pier.

And a teeth-jarring blow to the head.

His attacker had snuck up from behind and clocked him with something heavy, maybe a fire iron or crowbar. Keane had staggered a few steps and teetered on the edge of the dock before he was shoved head-first into the water.

He could only recall snippets after that. Sinking into the darkness. Needing to breathe. Wrestling out of his jacket as he kicked to the surface. And, finally, sputtering and gasping for air.

But he hadn't been able to see anything. Hadn't even been able to properly command his arms and legs. So he'd floated with the current, drifting in and out of consciousness till he'd awoken, tangled in a bloody fishing net.

Then the feisty, flame-haired Poppy Summers had found him on the beach. And he'd been there ever since.

Hoping to slow his racing pulse, he focused on the calming sights and sounds of the cove: the gently lapping water, the towering cliffs, the moody gray sky. After a few minutes, he felt more like himself—physically, at least.

Sleep had done wonders for his head. He felt stronger, too. After another day or two of rest, he'd be quite capable of packing up his things and returning to London and his duties. But the truth was that he was in no hurry to leave this beach.

Which probably proved that his father had been right about him. Maybe he *was* a lazy idiot and a pathetic excuse for a future duke. But in the end, it didn't matter what the former, formidable, great Duke of Hawking had thought, because despite his grumblings that he'd be stuck with running the estate till he reached ninety years of age, his heart had unexpectedly given out when he was but fifty.

And, two years ago, Keane had been left with the daunting task of filling his father's boots. Why should Keane care if his father had never thought him worthy of the title or capable of performing his duties? Like it or not, Keane *was* the duke now.

He stretched his aching limbs, drank the remaining water in the canteen, and tried sitting again, pleased to find his head wasn't as heavy as it had been yesterday. He sniffed the front of his shirt and ran a hand over his scratchy beard, longing for a hot bath and a shave. But since neither was possible, he supposed he'd have to settle for a swim.

He peeled off the remnants of his shirt and trousers, tossed them onto the sand, and waded naked into the surf.

* * *

The wind was already picking up as Poppy followed the trail to the beach. Dark clouds gathered in the western sky, and whitecaps dotted the inky blue sea.

Now that she knew Keane really was a duke, she was prepared to negotiate the terms of a deal. He'd been correct about a couple of things. She *did* need the money, and she *did* long for adventure. But this arrangement with him would be nothing more than a business deal.

If he could afford to pay her an exorbitant amount for a place to sleep and a few sandwiches, well then, who was she to—

Zounds.

She drew up short, stunned to see Keane, waist-deep in the water. His clothes were in a pile on the beach. And he was . . . magnificent.

Granted, it wasn't the first time that Poppy had seen a naked man—in books or in real life. But it was the first time the sight had taken her breath away.

She hesitated near the bottom of the cliff, a potent mix of curiosity and wantonness rooting her slippers in the sand. Water sluiced between his tanned shoulder blades, and his biceps flexed as he scrubbed his face. The pale strip of skin where the waistband of his trousers should have been and the tantalizing indent at the base of his spine left her feeling decidedly dizzy.

Sweet Jesus. All things considered, the best course of action would be to turn around immediately. Before Keane saw her and realized that she'd seen him. Yes, that would spare them both from undue embarrassment. She'd simply take a leisurely stroll, return in half an hour, and pray that he was decent by then.

As she turned to go, thunder crackled, raising the hairs on the backs of her arms and putting her on notice.

Apparently, the storm was not in agreement with her plan. In fact, it showed a complete disregard for both Keane's lack of clothing and her abject humiliation.

"Miss Summers," he called, his deep voice laced with amusement. "I fear you've caught me at an inopportune time."

"So it would seem," she shouted back, averting her eyes as she slowly spun toward him. "Trust me, I had no intention of disturbing your swim. But you—that is, *we*—should not be on the beach when the storm hits."

While he swiveled his head to look at the angry clouds, she peeked at the water surging and retreating around his hips.

"You're quite right," he said affably. "I'll come ashore at once."

He took one stride toward the beach, and she held up a palm. "Wait!"

He froze and blinked innocently. "You'd rather I stay here, then?"

She reached into her bag and produced the clean shirt and trousers that she'd swiped from Dane's loft. "I've brought some clothes for you," she said, tossing them onto the ground. "I shall turn around while you come ashore and dress."

"I have nothing to hide." He gave her a cheeky shrug. "But suit yourself."

"You may inform me when you're done dressing."

"An excellent plan." His lopsided grin made her belly flutter.

She took one last lingering look before facing the cliffs and doing her best *not* to imagine the view behind her. But the splash of the surf conjured vivid images of a chiseled abdomen, thick thighs, and—heaven help her—even more shocking things.

While she waited, her skirt snapped in the wind. Thunder boomed again, so loud this time that she felt the echoes of it in her chest.

"It's safe to open your eyes," he teased.

She whirled to face him. "I never closed them."

He chuckled, and the sound was unexpectedly sensuous—like the caress of a fingertip down her spine. He stood a few yards away, the worn cotton shirt clinging to his damp chest as he rubbed his hair dry with the corner of the quilt she'd given him.

"Thank you for the clothes. I will pay you for them as soon as I'm able."

"They belonged to my brother, but he outgrew them when he started drinking more and fishing less. They're not the sort of garments you'd typically find in a duke's wardrobe, but since your valet's not here at the moment . . ."

He arched a dark brow at that. "You believe me?"

"Let's just say we have much to discuss." The first drops of icy cold rain pelted her cheeks. "But not here. Gather your things and follow me."

She led him up the cliff and along the trail toward her sanctuary. The decision to bring him to her refuge had not been an easy one. In many ways, it was akin to letting him read the pages of her diary. Her shelter was held together by more than pieces of twine and clumps of clay. She'd fashioned it from secret hopes and precious dreams. From the simple but radical belief that she deserved her own beautiful little corner of the world.

Part of her feared Keane would look down his aristocratic nose at it. That he'd mock the low, slanted ceilings and the sparse, rustic furnishings. But she reminded herself that it didn't really matter what he thought of it. He was going to pay her to stay there—enough to carry her family all the way through the winter.

Lightning illuminated the sky like fireworks, and rain fell in buckets by the time they reached the clearing. Her dress was soaked, and her heavy braid was dripping as she swept aside the blanket at the doorway of the shelter. "Here we are," she shouted over the pounding rain and rumbling thunder. "Leave your boots there"—she pointed to a small area under a canvas awning—"and make yourself at home."

He ducked through the entrance, moved to the back of the shelter, and sat beneath the small round window opposite the door. Poppy pulled the blanket shut behind her, set down her bag, and knelt on the quilt-covered wood floor.

"You live here?" he asked, sounding rather awestruck.

"No." She lit the lantern on the overturned crate and sat facing him. "My family has a cottage nearby. I come here to be alone and read. Only my dearest friends know about this place—and now, you."

"Here," he said, offering her the quilt that had been rolled under one of his arms. "It's only a little damp. Wrap it around your shoulders so you don't take a chill."

She blinked at him, so he leaned closer and slid the quilt around her back.

"That's better," he said, satisfied.

Warmth blossomed in her chest. To him, it may have been an insignificant gesture, but in that moment, she'd felt less like a fisherman's daughter and more like . . . a princess.

He ran a hand along one of the ceiling beams and whistled. "Did you build this place?"

She nodded.

"It has all the best parts of a childhood hideaway and a cozy cottage. Thank you for sharing it with me," he said sincerely.

She used a corner of the quilt to squeeze her braid dry while Keane gazed around the interior. "How is your head?" she asked.

"Improving, I think. As you have already observed, I'm able to walk without falling down. That's considerable progress."

"The wound is still red and swollen." She inspected the angry-looking gash on his forehead, doing her level best to ignore his open shirt collar and the patch of bronzed skin it revealed at the base of his throat. "I brought some strips of cloth to dress it, along with food and drink. You must be famished."

He nodded and pressed a hand to his impressively flat abdomen. "Do you mind if I eat while we talk?"

"Please do." She handed him a sack containing an apple, cheese, crusty bread, and some sliced ham.

"Thank you." He dug into the sack with gusto and held out the apple. "Will you join me?"

"No." She shook her head, adamant. The soothing patter of rain and the fragrant scent of lilacs would not lull her into thinking this was a friendly picnic. "I was in town this morning. Your valet is looking for you."

Keane frowned. "I hope Diggs hasn't raised the alarm yet."

"I don't think he has. But he might soon."

"I need to let him know I'm here and that I'm all right."

"Agreed. I've decided I'm willing to help with your plan—under a few conditions."

He sandwiched ham and cheese between two chunks of bread and cast her a wary look. "What conditions?"

"First, you must remain hidden. Only your valet may know you're here. If someone sees you on our property, I will say you are trespassing and deny that I've ever met you."

He raised his eyebrows. "Seems a bit harsh, but fine. What else?"

"Second, if I determine that your activities pose a threat to my family or friends, you will leave at once."

"Fair enough."

"And pay me in full."

He choked on a bite of his sandwich, pounded a fist into his chest, and composed himself. "You are a rather ruthless negotiator," he grumbled. "But I'll agree to those terms. Is there anything else?"

"Yes, one more condition," she said soberly. "For the duration of your stay here, you will refrain from prying into my personal affairs. You will not ask me anything of a private nature."

"Why not?"

Why, indeed? She couldn't very well tell him the truth—that his probing questions only reminded her of all the hopes she'd had for herself and all the ways in which she'd settled for less. That she'd learned a painful lesson about the chasm between working-class folk and the nobility at a young, vulnerable age. "The particulars of my life are none of your concern."

"Perhaps not." He set down his food and met her gaze. "But we will, out of necessity, be spending a great deal of time together. You've made it clear that you're not interested in friendship, and I respect that. But shouldn't we at least understand each other?"

Poppy blinked at him, disbelieving. "*This* is the condition you take issue with? You've no qualms about cutting off contact with the outside world or paying me an obscene amount of money, even if I kick you off my beach. And yet, my simple request for privacy sticks in your craw?"

He stared at her as though she were a horrifyingly complex math problem that he was intent on solving. "I'm not

certain why, but it does. I suppose I can't help being curious about you."

She blew out a long breath. Bargaining with the duke
would be vastly easier if the flickering light from the lantern didn't illuminate every handsome angle of his face.
If he didn't smell of rain and cotton and the sea. But she
was determined to hold her ground. "Then I believe we are
at an impasse, Your Grace."

"I did not take you for someone who would give up so
easily."

"I am not the party who walked away from the deal,"
she countered.

His green eyes flashed with satisfaction. "Perhaps we
can agree to a compromise."

"What, exactly, do you propose?"

"That you allow me to ask the occasional question." He
rubbed the stubble on his jaw, thoughtful. "Whether or not
you answer it—that shall be up to you. But at least I can
look forward to the possibility, however remote, of learning more about you. What do you say, Miss Summers? Do
we have a deal?"

Chapter 5

Rain pattered steadily on the roof and thunder rumbled in the distance as Keane waited for Poppy Summers to respond to his only request: that he be permitted to ask her the occasional question.

She searched his face in a blatant and valiant attempt to ascertain if he was bluffing.

He was not.

He was intensely curious about her, and not solely because she was beautiful, although there *was* that. Far more intriguing to him were her confidence, her honesty, and her passion. He needed to find the sources of those traits within her. Maybe then he'd have a shot of finding them within himself.

Unlikely, that. But even if he was a lost cause, probing Miss Summers's mind would give him something to look forward to each day.

She sat on a pillow opposite him with her feet tucked under her, her knees only inches from his. The strands of her thick braid glowed like red-hot embers in the light of the lantern. After the space of several heartbeats, she met his gaze, her face impassive.

"Is this all a lark to you?"

He shook his head, bewildered. "A lark?"

"A game. You've decided a holiday is in order—to give you respite from the weighty demands of running a dukedom." Her tone was dry, with a distinct note of sarcasm. "You have time and money to spare, so you've elected to waste away the summer, doing nothing more than lounging in the sun and baiting me for your amusement."

He shook his head. "Do you think so little of me?"

For the space of several breaths, she stared at him. "Let us just say that I'm well acquainted with your type."

That stung. More than it should have. "You don't know me, Miss Summers. Not yet."

"Perhaps not. Fortunately for you, it's not necessary for us to like or trust each other in order to do business. I am prepared to agree to your terms if you can adhere to mine."

She extended her hand, and he took it in his, sealing their deal. He felt the calluses on her palms and the strength in her fingers, but he felt something else, too. A crackling of awareness, a jolt of anticipation—as if they were standing side by side at the edge of the cliff, preparing to leap into the ocean together.

They sat there, hands clasped, for longer than was strictly necessary, and her cheeks pinkened. "Now then," she said, letting go at last. "How do you propose that we contact your valet?"

"I have a plan." Keane shot her a grin. "But I'll need your help to execute it."

Poppy prepared an early dinner for Papa, read him a chapter of his favorite mystery, and made sure he was tucked into bed before she headed to town in her cart. The rain had pushed off to the east and the sun was slowly setting, leaving a burnt-orange sky glowing in its wake. In short, it was an ideal evening for a bit of subterfuge.

The note Keane had written was tucked in the pocket of the old cloak she wore. She knew precisely where to go, knew exactly what to do. The trick was to accomplish the task without being seen.

She walked into the Salty Mermaid at a quarter past nine, scanning the hazy room from the ancient bar in the front to the dark booths in the back. Locals and tourists alike clinked glasses of ale, shared boisterous tales, and smoked cheroots while holding fans of playing cards. She waved to a few of the familiar patrons, wound her way through the crowd to the bar, and sat on a stool across from the barkeep, who was drying and stacking pint glasses as he chatted with customers.

"Poppy Summers." The burly bartender slung a towel over his shoulder and shot her a friendly smile. "Always a pleasure to see you. How's your father?"

"He's well, thank you, Nathan." She glanced at the men on either side of her, leaned across the bar, and, in a lower voice said, "I don't suppose you've seen Dane lately?"

"Afraid not, lass. I haven't seen your brother since . . ." He rubbed the back of his neck and stared at the ceiling as if he were consulting a calendar—giving her just enough time to take the note out of her pocket and slide it onto the bar in front of the bespectacled older gentleman on her right.

Meeting her gaze again, Nathan said, "Last time I saw Dane was the night I helped you load him into the back of your cart."

Poppy heaved a sigh. Not because the news surprised her, but because it was what the barkeep expected her to do. "Thank you. If he should happen to make an appearance, will you tell him I was looking for him?"

"I will." Nathan gave her a wink. "In the meantime, be

sure to call on me if there's anything you or your father need."

She thanked him, turned, and left. She felt a little guilty for deceiving Nathan, but she'd also felt a rather heady rush when she'd slipped Keane's valet the note. Now she simply had to hope that Diggs read it in private and didn't inadvertently inform the entire pub that the Duke of Hawking was living on her beach.

Now that the excitement was behind her, she looked forward to climbing into her loft and laying her head on her pillow. But she had one more stop to make first. She'd promised Keane that she'd go to the hideaway and tell him about her visit to the Salty Mermaid.

Despite her weariness, she looked forward to seeing him again. Probably more than she should have.

She found him sitting on a broad, flat rock outside the shelter, staring out at the moonlit sea. "This is a favorite spot of mine," she said, climbing onto the rock and sitting beside him.

"It's easy to see why." He leaned back on his palms, his long legs stretched in front of him. "It seems like London is a million miles away."

"Only one hundred. But it feels much farther on nights like this."

He chuckled, and a warm breeze rustled the curls that fell over his bandage. "How was your trip to the Salty Mermaid?"

"I am pleased to report that the mission has been accomplished," she said, making a mock salute. "Your valet was precisely where you said he'd be. The task could not have been any easier."

"Then we shall think of something more challenging next time," he teased. More seriously, he added, "You needn't worry. Diggs will follow the instructions we laid out. He'll be at the meeting spot tomorrow morning—and he'll come alone."

Keane's casual use of the word *we* made her skin tingle. With one simple handshake, they'd embarked on a journey of sorts, and she wasn't at all certain of the destination. "How long has Diggs been your valet?" she asked.

"Since my father died," he said flatly. "Two years ago."

"I'm sorry," she said sincerely.

He shrugged. "I knew Diggs long before that. He was a footman in our household when I was a lad, and he eventually married my nanny."

"How sweet," Poppy mused.

"Yes," he said, swallowing hard, "but she passed away during childbirth. Their baby didn't survive, either. I'm the closest thing Diggs has to family now—and vice versa."

She checked the sudden and unexpected impulse to reach out and squeeze his hand. To tell him that she understood loneliness and loss. She longed to ask him what had happened to his mother but bit her tongue—mostly because she was not prepared to answer similar questions about her own mother.

"Then I'm glad Diggs knows you're safe," Poppy said sincerely. "He was probably worried sick, scouring all of Bellehaven looking for you."

Keane chuckled. "I'm afraid he's accustomed to my misadventures. But yes, I'm happy we could put his mind at ease"—he turned and shot her a lopsided grin—"thanks to you."

She ignored the warmth blossoming in her chest, sat up straight, and brushed her palms together. "I shall leave you to rest. You should be comfortable enough."

"After two nights sleeping on the cold, hard ground,

your shelter is going to feel like a palace. I already vastly prefer it to my room at the Bluffs' Brew."

"That's good, because you're paying me a considerably higher rate," she said, hopping off the large rock. "I'll see you tomorrow, Keane."

"Wait."

Blast, she'd been *so* close to making her escape. "What is it?" she said dryly. "Did you need me to tell you a story? Tuck you into your bed?"

"I wouldn't mind either of those things, truth be told, but no. I wanted to ask you a question."

"By all means," she said, extending an arm in invitation. "Fire away." She kept her tone breezy and her expression slightly amused. But her belly turned somersaults as she waited to hear what he'd ask.

He jumped off the rock and walked toward her until they stood toe-to-toe. Moonlight painted the clearing in silver and gray, tall grass tickled their legs, and salty air swirled around them. For several heartbeats he held her gaze, as if choosing a question was a matter that required deep deliberation. Meanwhile, the flips in her belly grew more vigorous.

At last, his mouth curled into a slow, wry smile. "Miss Poppy Summers," he drawled, "if you found yourself injured and stranded on a remote beach, and you could only contact one person in the world, who would that person be?"

She didn't even have to think about her answer. "My friend Hazel."

"And who is she?" Keane asked. "How did you become acquainted?"

Poppy arched a brow. "Those are two additional questions—and they will have to wait for another day."

"Fair enough." His low chuckle rumbled through her, settling in the vicinity of her belly.

She was about to do the prudent thing—namely, to turn and go—when her curiosity prevailed over good sense. "What about you?" she asked. "Is there someone who you are missing while you are isolated here? Someone in London, perhaps?"

"Miss Summers," he said teasingly. "If I didn't know better, I'd think you were doing a different sort of fishing."

Heat bloomed in her cheeks, and she was grateful for the cover of darkness. "Do not flatter yourself. It was simply a question. One I find I'm already regretting."

"Come, now." He shot her a knowing look. "You're not the least bit interested in knowing if I am romantically involved with a woman?"

She rolled her eyes. "Good night, Your Grace."

She'd taken two steps toward the path when he said, "Wait. Please."

She froze but did not turn around.

"Forgive me," he said. "I was only having a bit of fun. You asked a straightforward question. If you give me another chance, I promise to answer truthfully."

She remained rooted to her spot in the sand.

"Please. I . . . like talking with you."

The sincerity in his voice thawed her resolve. Slowly, she faced him. "I'm listening."

He quickly retrieved a quilt from the shelter, spread it on the ground, and waited for her to sit before he sat opposite her and continued.

"The person I miss is my cousin, Teddy. We grew up together, close as brothers. I spent more time at his home than I did my own, and I liked it that way. We climbed trees, swam in the river, and learned to ride together. When I was twelve, Teddy and I snuck into his father's study, drank a decanter of brandy between us, and passed out beneath the desk. No one knew where we were, and when night fell, my uncle was so worried that he and the rest of the staff scoured the estate in search of us. We finally awoke and staggered into the breakfast room the next morning, our clothes reeking of spirits. My uncle was understandably irate."

"Oh dear." Poppy clucked her tongue. "Was your punishment severe?"

Keane shook his head. "Teddy told his father that the brandy had been his idea. Later, when I asked why he'd taken the fall for me, he said there was no sense in both of us enduring my uncle's wrath."

"He sounds like a good friend. It's no wonder you're close."

He gazed toward the sea, oddly wistful. "Lately, we haven't seen each other as frequently as I'd like. We both reside in London, but our schedules rarely align. I suppose we've become preoccupied with adult matters."

"It happens," Poppy said with a shrug. "Life carries us along like we're fish swept up in a current. But if you keep swimming, eventually you'll find your way back to the people who matter most. When you see Teddy again, you'll probably pick up precisely where you left off. Let's hope it's not in a drunken stupor on the floor of a study."

Keane laughed. "I can think of worse things."

Poppy arched a brow. "I don't doubt it."

She stayed on the beach talking with Keane longer than she should have.

And not nearly long enough.

Chapter 6

"You must be Miss Summers." A barrel-chested man with salt-and-pepper hair shuffled toward her the next morning, a large satchel in each hand. "Homer Diggs at your service," he said, breathing heavily. "Pleased to make your acquaintance."

"Likewise, Mr. Diggs. Have you walked all the way from town carrying those heavy bags?"

"No, no. I had the coach drop me at the side of the road about a half mile back." The valet set down the satchels, pulled a handkerchief from the pocket of his jacket, and mopped his furrowed brow. "The duke's note emphasized the need for discretion. Are you quite certain he's well? I must say, the plan he laid out in his note sounds rather . . . odd."

"I agree about the plan. But he is recovering quite nicely from his injuries, as you'll soon see for yourself. It's a short walk from here." Poppy pointed at one of the bags. "Shall I carry this?"

"Absolutely not," he said gallantly. "The duke is already indebted to you for your generosity. If you would be so kind as to lead the way, I will take care of these." He grunted as he picked up the bags and fell in step behind her.

"You must have packed the duke's entire wardrobe into

those satchels," Poppy joked. "But I fear he'll have little use for evening jackets and top hats on the beach. Ball invitations are few and far between around here."

"I find it best to be prepared for every eventuality," Diggs said quite seriously. That was the precise moment that Poppy decided she liked him.

They followed a narrow path through the grass, chatting along the way. Poppy answered Diggs's questions about where and how she'd found Keane, doing her best to relay the particulars of that morning without distressing the valet.

She glanced over her shoulder at him. "Do you know why anyone would want to hurt the duke?"

Diggs frowned. "Not exactly. But I do know that very few people understand him. If they did, well . . . they wouldn't judge him so harshly."

She pondered that for a moment, resisting the urge to probe further.

"The duke is fortunate to have you on his side," Poppy said sincerely. She paused and pointed down the trail. "Follow the path until you reach a little clearing. You'll find him there."

"Thank you, Miss Summers." Diggs bowed graciously, as if she were a duchess instead of an angler. "And may I say that the duke is equally fortunate to have you on his side?"

"I appreciate the sentiment," she said soberly, "but I have not taken a side—and I don't intend to. I am prepared to uphold my end of the deal. I expect the duke to do the same."

"Well, of course," Diggs said, tripping over his words in his haste to reassure her. "He is a man of his word. A gentleman."

"You say that as if one necessarily goes with the other.

I happen to know that honor has nothing to do with one's social status." She handed the valet a sack containing sandwiches, nuts, and fruit. "Please inform your employer that I shall return with his second meal this evening. Good day, Mr. Diggs."

Keane had never been so happy to see Diggs. Sweat beaded on the valet's clean-shaven upper lip, and he shouldered his way through the tall grass at the edge of the clearing as if he were pushing through a crowd at Vauxhall Gardens. "This certainly is a remote location," he said, with impressive diplomacy.

Keane slapped him on the shoulder and grabbed one of the bags. "Why does it look like you've packed for a month-long house party?"

"I took the liberty of adding a few items to your list—your shaving kit, for one." He cast a horrified glance at Keane's stubble, and added, "Which we should put to good use immediately."

"We'll see," he replied with a chuckle. "But come sit first. Tell me what the gossips are saying about me in Bellehaven Bay."

They set the bags next to the shelter and brought the sack of food to the large flat rock overlooking the sea. "I suppose I can see the charm of this place," Diggs admitted, awkwardly climbing onto the massive stone. "But I cannot understand why you wish to stay when you could return to the comforts of London."

"I have unfinished business here." Keane unwrapped a sandwich and handed half to Diggs.

He bit into it with obvious relish. "Would the unfinished business have anything to do with Miss Summers?"

"Don't be ridiculous," Keane muttered.

"She's a kind, beautiful lass. Fiery, too."

Keane growled in response. "Flirtation is the last thing on my mind, Diggs. I'm here to track down the coward who snuck up on me, cracked open my head, and threw me into the bay."

"And you intend to do that by letting your assailant believe they've succeeded in killing you?"

"That's part of the plan."

Diggs heaved an exasperated sigh. "Have you considered that your supposed death will spark a host of other, less desirable events—not the least of which are your funeral and the passage of your title?"

"I won't be quite *that* dead, Diggs."

"Just a little, then." He pinched the bridge of his nose as if he felt the devil of a headache coming on.

"The title cannot pass without proof of my death. There are no witnesses and no body."

"Not yet," Diggs said dryly. "Who knows? If you stay here another month, perhaps your luck will change."

Keane grinned. "Worried about me, old chap?"

The valet scoffed. "Given your propensity for finding trouble, I probably should be. But no, I am not worried. I suspect, however, that your uncle and cousin *will* be. Perhaps we should let them in on your plan."

"No," Keane said, adamant. "I trust them, of course. Teddy might know even more of my secrets than you do. But I promised Miss Summers that I wouldn't tell anyone else I'm staying here. I intend to keep my word."

"Good," Diggs said, approvingly. "The last thing we'd want to do is make her life more difficult."

"Agreed." Keane leaned forward and rubbed his hands together. "Now, what have you overheard at the pub?"

"When it comes to your whereabouts, there is no shortage of theories. Initially, most people assumed that when you left the Salty Mermaid you were too foxed to find your way to the inn and that you passed out some-where."

He scoffed, insulted. "After a few pints?"

Diggs shot him a wry smile. "Others speculated that you had spent the night in the company of a lady and were reluctant to leave her."

"Slightly more believable," Keane conceded.

"Still others wondered if you'd impulsively returned to London."

"Without my valet, driver, or coach?" he asked, incred-ulous.

Diggs shrugged. "They thought that perhaps you'd en-countered another gentleman from Town, commiserated about missing the social whirl, and made the sudden de-cision to travel back with him."

"I wouldn't abandon you, Diggs—not even for a week's worth of bloody soirees."

"Yes, well, the residents of Bellehaven don't know you like I do."

"True." Keane stroked his jaw. "And we might as well use that to our advantage."

Diggs leaned forward. "I'm all ears, Your Grace. Tell me how I can help."

Keane was halfway up a tree when Poppy Summers arrived with dinner.

"What are you doing?" she asked warily.

He scooted along the branch, shimmied down the trunk, and hopped to the ground. "Just making a few repairs. The wind from yesterday's storm damaged part of the roof, so I patched it up."

She wrinkled her nose, drawing his attention to a charming smattering of freckles. "I don't think someone with a head injury should be balancing on a tree branch twelve feet high."

"Miss Summers," he teased, crossing his arms. "You're afraid I'll fall and re-injure myself."

"On the contrary. I'm afraid you'll fall and leave an ox-sized hole in my roof."

Damn, but he'd missed her. "Tell me about your day," he said. "Did you fish again this morning?"

"Aye." She thrust a warm pot toward him. "And afterward I made a stew. It's nothing fancy, but I thought you could use a hot meal."

The savory scent tickled his nostrils. "It smells delicious. Thank you."

"You're welcome." Her gaze flicked over his clean shirt, buckskin trousers, and polished boots. "I suppose I can see how you're able to pass for a duke."

"I *am* a duke. Remember?"

"As if you'd let me forget."

He shot her a grin. "Diggs wanted me to shave, but I thought the beard could prove useful if I need to disguise myself."

She shrugged her slender shoulders, nonchalant. "That is between you and your valet."

"Diggs is fond of you," Keane said.

"You are lucky to have such a loyal friend. For his sake and for mine, I hope you know what you are doing." With that, she spun on her heel to go.

"Wait," he called.

She turned and arched an auburn brow.

"I was hoping to tell you about my plans and elicit your opinion."

"I'm fairly certain I don't need to hear the plans in order to render an opinion." She hesitated, then pursed her lips, thoughtful. "But I suppose I can spare half an hour."

"Good." He set down the pot, fetched a quilt, and spread it on the ground. "Would you care to sit?"

She inclined her head and sank onto one end of the quilt, tucking her feet under her skirts. He stretched out on the other end of the quilt, propped himself on an elbow, and looked into her cerulean eyes. A few wisps of hair escaped her braid and fluttered around the column of her neck. Damned distracting, that.

"So, how do you plan to find your attacker?" she asked, snapping him back to attention.

"I thought I'd begin by tracking down the three people who have reason to hate me," he said.

"*Hate* is a strong word," she mused. "How can you be certain it wasn't simply a robbery? Maybe someone at the Salty Mermaid was deep in his cups and looking for a few easy pounds."

"I'd been playing cards all night, and I don't think I won a single round. Everyone in the pub knew I was leaving with empty pockets."

"Maybe the perpetrator mistook you for someone else."

Keane shook his head. "Just before he shoved me off the dock, he said something."

She leaned forward slightly. "What?"

"'Damn you to hell, Hawking.'"

She blew out a long breath. "Maybe *hate* is apropos after all. Very well. Who is the first person you suspect, and what on earth did you do to anger him?"

Keane swallowed. He'd known that she would ask the question and that she deserved to hear the truth. But until that very moment, he hadn't realized how much her opinion of him mattered.

He didn't give a damn if he was vilified in London

drawing rooms or smeared in the gossip rags. The ton could say whatever they would about him, and some of it would be true.

But he did *not* want Poppy Summers to think of him as a heartless, depraved blackguard.

"First of all," he said haltingly, "you should know that I'm not proud of my behavior. If I could go back, I'd do things differently—or not at all."

"This conversation grows more interesting by the second," she said. "I confess I'm intrigued."

"The truth is that I didn't come to Bellehaven Bay for a holiday at the shore. I left London in order to put some distance between me and the Marquess of Camden."

"And why is that?"

Keane swallowed a curse and met her gaze. "Because he found me in bed with his wife."

Chapter 7

Poppy blinked at Keane. "The marquess found you in bed with this wife?" she repeated, incredulous.

He rubbed the back of his neck. "I know. It sounds horrible."

"It does indeed." She gazed at the puffy pink clouds in the sky so that he wouldn't see how disappointed she was. He was a rich, handsome duke, after all. She was a fool to think for even one second that he might be different. But it was an excellent reminder to stay in her shell. To shore up the high seawalls around her heart, no matter what.

Keeping her face impassive, she added, "I can understand why the marquess would be a bit cross with you."

"As can I," Keane admitted. "But in my defense, there's more to the story."

"You needn't share the particulars with me." Her belly was already winding itself in knots, and she didn't think she could stomach either feeble excuses or torrid details. "You had a tryst with a married woman," she said, matter of fact. "I believe I can fill in the gaps."

"I didn't know she was married." His voice held a mix of exasperation and embarrassment.

"Then you must not have been very well acquainted."

He hung his head. "I know you must think poorly of me.

I don't blame you. But I'm hoping you'll still be willing to help me."

"In what way?" she asked, wary.

"Come to London with me. Tomorrow."

"I beg your pardon?" she said, incredulous.

"If we leave at dawn, we should be able to return before nightfall. We'll make a few inquiries. Find out where the marquess was on the evening I was attacked. If we can prove he was in Bellehaven"—Keane paused to shoot her a triumphant smile—"mystery solved."

She inhaled deeply, briefly imagining what such a trip might entail. A chance to rumble over cobblestone streets, peer into the windows of the most fashionable shops, and sample treats from Gunter's Tea Shop. She might even have the opportunity to seek out her brother and ensure he was all right.

The prospect was tempting, to be sure. Until she recalled that it also involved hours spent in the cozy confines of a coach. With the devilishly handsome duke.

"I feel certain you're capable of making inquiries without my assistance," she said, resolute. "And I have work to do here."

"But I need you." His boyish, crestfallen expression softened the edges of her resolve.

"Whatever for?"

"I can't go knocking on doors or walking down the street without being recognized. But you can. You can ask the questions. You can be my eyes and ears."

"Ah, yes. The perks of being a nobody," she said wryly.

His expression turned deadly serious. "You are not a nobody, Poppy Summers. Anyone with half a brain could see that." He swallowed and looked away—as if he'd inadvertently revealed too much. "Besides, I thought you might enjoy a day in London."

She *would* enjoy a trip to Town. With him. More than she cared to admit. But that didn't mean such a thing was prudent—or even possible.

"I don't like to leave my father for long stretches of time," she said.

"Perhaps you could ask a neighbor or friend to check on him."

She lifted her gaze to the softly glowing horizon. "It's not that simple."

He sat up and looked at her earnestly. "Forgive me. I don't mean to badger you. I understand why you'd hesitate to spend the day with me."

"It's not personal, Keane. I have responsibilities. I am not free to gallivant around the countryside."

He nodded, contrite. "I won't press you further, except to say this. If you should change your mind, I'll be waiting near the main road at sunrise, in my coach."

"Your coach?" she repeated. "I assume it's decorated with your ducal crest. Part of our bargain was that no one would know you're here, but now you're involving your driver."

He grinned at that. "True, but the driver is Diggs, and I asked him to bring an unmarked coach."

"Your valet is also your driver?"

"He wields the reins even better than he does a razor."

"Fascinating," she mused. "Does he cook, too?"

"Absolutely not. I doubt he could find his way to the kitchen, much less boil water for a pot of tea."

The mention of tea made Poppy think of willow bark—and Papa. "I should go, and you should eat your stew while it's still warm."

He quickly stood and offered a hand to help her up. It was a polite, perfectly proper gesture, but the moment her fingers landed in his warm palm, her body tingled all over. His breath hitched in his throat—as if he felt it, too.

And he didn't let go.

They stood toe-to-toe, gazing into each other's eyes. "Are you ready for your question?" he asked, his voice so deep that it seeped beneath her skin.

She'd almost forgotten that part of their deal. Keane, of course, had not.

"Suppose you could go anywhere you liked in London," he said. "The opera, Vauxhall Gardens, the theater, the shops on Bond Street . . . Where would you most like to go?"

"I think I would enjoy all of those things, but if I could pick truly anything . . ."

"Yes," he urged. "Anything."

"I would go to a masquerade ball," she said dreamily. "Colorful costumes, graceful dancing, plentiful champagne. Yes, I'd definitely choose a masquerade—if only for the chance to be someone else for an evening."

"I can't imagine why you would want to be anyone else," he said softly. "But I'm glad you told me."

She took one step back, and her fingertips slid from his hand. "Good luck with your sleuthing tomorrow."

"Sleep well, Miss Summers."

He chuckled softly as she walked away. As if he had an inkling that she'd lie awake into the wee hours of the morning, recounting all the reasons that going to London with the duke was a horrid idea.

"Ready?" Diggs called from the driver's seat. The brim of his worn brown cap was pulled low, and his sleeves were rolled to the elbows. The horses at the ends of his reins shuffled their hooves, as if they, too, were impatient to be on their way.

"Almost." Keane stood outside the coach in the golden glow of a new day, scanning the long, empty stretch of road ahead. He threw his bag onto a rack at the rear of the cab and took his time buckling the straps to secure it.

Granted, the odds of Poppy Summers strolling up the path were slight, but a one in one hundred chance was still a chance. So he searched the tall grass, hoping for a glimpse of her auburn braid, faded calico dress, or freckled face. "Five more minutes," he said to Diggs. "And then we'll go."

The words had barely left his mouth when the grass at the side of the road rustled and a woman emerged. Her stylish straw bonnet shielded her face, and a simple, pale-blue gown subtly skimmed the curves of her slender frame.

Keane's heart skipped a beat. Because while the woman approaching bore little resemblance to the angler who'd rescued him a few days earlier, she moved with a familiar grace and athleticism.

And he was willing to wager that beneath the skirts of her pretty dress she had a knife strapped to her leg.

"We should be going, sir," Diggs muttered, clearly trying to avoid an awkward encounter with a strange woman.

"Where are your manners, Diggs?"

"Begging your pardon?"

"Good morning, Miss Summers." Keane strode toward her, feeling ridiculously happy. "You came."

"Against my better judgment." She gazed up at him, the dark fringe of her lashes framing clear blue-green eyes. A few fiery tendrils danced around her shoulders and skimmed the smooth skin at the hollow of her throat. The neckline of her gown dipped across the swells of her breasts, unexpectedly setting his blood on fire.

As though completely unaware of her effect on him, she breezed past and gave Diggs a friendly wave.

"Apologies, Miss Summers," he said, tipping his cap. "I didn't recognize you in your bonnet. Delighted to have you along with us today."

"Beautiful day for a drive," she replied cheerfully. Keane tamped down an unexpected pang of jealousy. He'd gotten a caustic barb, and Diggs had gotten the blinding smile.

She climbed into the carriage and placed her small port-manteau on the seat beside her—leaving him no choice but to sit across from her. Which suited him perfectly. From his vantage point, it was easier to study her. To read her expression beneath the wide brim of her bonnet.

As the coach started rolling, he met her gaze. "Why did you decide to come?"

"Two reasons." A faint blush stained her cheeks. "First, I realized it could be ages before I have another opportu-nity to visit London."

"When were you last there?"

The light in her eyes dimmed. "Several years ago. I was just a girl."

"We'll make certain this trip is one to remember then," he promised. "What's the other reason you came?"

She exhaled tremulously. "Time permitting, I thought I might be able to persuade you to help me locate my brother. He's been working as a dockhand."

"We can make some inquiries," he said. "But it's a bit like searching for a needle in a haystack. Do you have a clue as to his whereabouts?"

She reached into her bag and produced a small, folded paper. "The address of his favorite pub. Dane is constantly on the move, but if I can give my father some assurance that he's all right, it would be a great comfort to him."

"Then we'll do our best to find him." Keane stared out the window at the green hills and golden horizon, thoughtful. He wanted to ask if all the responsibility fell on her shoulders and whether anyone was looking after her. But he suspected he already knew the answers. She was accustomed to taking care of herself. "Your brother and father are fortunate to have you."

"Dane had a plan," she said, as if she felt the need to defend him. "He thought if he made a decent wage at the docks, we wouldn't be at the mercy of the fishing business. And when we started to see more sick fish in our nets, it seemed like the right time for him to make the move to London."

"But you're still working every day," Keane said. "By yourself."

"It's only been a couple of months."

"And taking care of your father, too."

"I was worried about leaving him alone today," she explained, "so I was up late, cooking and cleaning. At least now I know he'll be relatively comfortable and well fed."

"It sounds like you could use some rest. Fortunately, we have about three hours before we reach London. Plenty of time for a nap."

"Perhaps I will close my eyes." She stifled a yawn, removed her bonnet, and leaned her head against the side of the coach.

As the carriage rumbled down the road, he tried to focus on the green fields and golden sky, but they couldn't complete with her pink lips and satin skin. He'd never seen her so relaxed, so unguarded . . . so soft.

Until one of the coach's wheels hit a rut—and the cab suddenly lurched. Her head bumped the frame of the window, and she frowned as she rubbed one cheek.

"Are you all right?" he asked.

"Mmm," she said sleepily. She settled her head against

the window and closed her eyes just before the coach rocked again. "Oww," she murmured.

"May I make a suggestion?" he asked.

She squinted at him with one open eye. "By all means."

He moved her portmanteau to the floor, sat on the bench beside her, and patted the shoulder of his jacket. "Lean on me," he said. "It will be softer."

"I'm not so sure about that," she said, but she tentatively rested her cheek on his shoulder . . . and promptly fell asleep.

He listened to her even breathing. Savored the weight of her body pressed against his. Didn't even mind a bit of drool on his favorite jacket.

With every mile they traveled, she sank into him further, snuggling against his chest and nestling her head in the in crook of his elbow. By the time the coach rolled through St. James's Square, she was curled up on the velvet squabs of the bench with her cheek resting on his thigh.

It was too soon to know if they'd have any luck tracking down the marquess or Poppy's brother, but Keane was glad that he'd come.

And he was even happier that Poppy was with him.

Chapter 8

Determined to steal two more minutes of sleep, Poppy snuggled into her pillow.

It seemed to have lost all its feathers, but no matter. Her bed rocked softly from side to side. A breeze tickled her cheek. Her limbs felt loose and relaxed.

But then the rocking abruptly stopped.

Which made no sense, when she stopped to ponder it. A straw-stuffed pallet in a cottage loft should *not* be rocking.

She opened her bleary eyes, blinked at the plush interior of a coach, and muttered a curse.

It was bad enough that she'd slept in front of the duke. But by the looks of it, she'd also slept *on* the duke.

"Good morning, sunshine," he said, vexingly cheerful. "I hope you're feeling more chipper."

Poppy lifted her head off Keane's lap, dismayed to find that half her hair had escaped her pins. "You should have awoken me."

"You needed to rest," he said sincerely. "I'm glad you did."

She scowled and attempted to wrestle her curls into some semblance of a knot. "I didn't want to sleep the entire morning."

"I wish I'd known," he drawled. "If I'd woken you an hour ago, maybe I'd still be able to feel my leg."

"How gallant of you to mention it." She surreptitiously wiped the corners of her mouth. "Where are we?"

"Mayfair."

She peered across the street at an elegant house boasting enough columns to rival a Greek temple. "The Marquess of Camden's residence?"

"Precisely," he said frowning. "The question is, how do we determine his whereabouts on the night I was attacked?"

Poppy gaped at him. "I thought you had a plan."

"I did. My plan was to come here, with you, and figure out what to do."

"Very well," she said, blowing out a breath. "Let's start by listing the places the marquess typically visits here in London. Does he belong to a gentleman's club?"

Keane nodded. "White's."

"That's good. Maybe we can ask some of the members if he was there that night."

"I can't show my face in White's, and even with a disguise, you wouldn't get past the front door."

"Then it's fortunate I have no desire to smoke cheroots and swill brandy."

Keane clucked his tongue. "You have no idea what you're missing."

"What other places would the marquess frequent?"

"Social events." He was still sitting next to her. Close enough that she could see the mossy flecks in his eyes. "Soirees, balls, and the like."

"Are you generally invited to the same types of parties?"

"Sometimes." His mouth curled into a slow, sly smile. "Excellent idea. I can ask Diggs to retrieve the post from my house for the last two weeks. You and I can sort through the invitations to figure out what social events occurred on the day I was attacked."

"Perfect," Poppy mused. "A few invitations would give me something to work with."

Keane opened the door of the carriage and briefly conferred with Diggs, then they set off again, rumbling over wide streets and through stately squares.

"It's only a short ride to Hawking House. In case you were thinking about napping," he added with a knee-melting grin.

She shot him a disingenuous smile. "I'm quite refreshed, thank you."

"I should hope so." He chuckled as he drew the shades on his side of the cab, then reached across her to cover the windows on the opposite side.

"What are you doing?"

"Diggs is going to park the carriage a block from my house. I'm trying to keep us out of sight."

"Oh." The interior of the coach had felt cozy before; now it was indisputably intimate. The scarlet shades that covered the windows distilled the bright sunlight into a dim, rosy glow.

The sounds of clopping hooves and clacking wheels faded into a low, distant beat.

She didn't mind the close quarters nearly as much as she should have. Indeed, it was no hardship sitting next to a strong, sinfully handsome man in snug buckskin trousers and rolled-up shirtsleeves.

In fact, she had to remind herself that Keane was a duke. That this excursion was naught but a lark for him. He was looking for answers and a bit of adventure, but he'd grow tired of the game soon enough. Eventually, he was going to return to his world . . . and Poppy was going to stay in hers.

So she might as well enjoy the experience while it lasted.

As the carriage rolled to a stop, Keane angled his body toward hers, propped an elbow on the seat back, and gazed into her eyes. "Tell me what you are thinking, Miss Summers."

She exhaled. "I am thinking you should call me Poppy."

His brooding stare morphed into a blinding smile. "Poppy," he repeated, testing it out. "Thank you."

"Don't think this makes you special," she said brusquely. "I'd do the same for anyone who allowed me to use their lap as a pillow."

"Understood," he said, but he clearly struggled to wipe the satisfied expression from his face.

"Is Hawking House where you spend most of your time?" she asked.

His gaze flicked to the floor. "I've lived here for the last two years, since becoming duke. Before that I kept an apartment but spent most of my time going from one scandalous house party to another."

"Were you close to your family?"

He hesitated. "My cousin Teddy was like my brother. Every happy memory from my childhood includes him."

"What about your parents?"

"My mother was rarely home," he said succinctly. "I was a constant source of disappointment to my father. I learned early on that the best course of action was to stay away."

"That is so sad," she said softly.

He arched a brow, as if that thought had never occurred to him. "I suppose it is—especially for someone like you."

"What does that mean?"

"You obviously care deeply about your family. Surely, they care about you, too. They're the center of your world, but not all families are like that. It's never been that way for me."

"Why not?" she asked, her expression troubled.

"It's a dull, tedious tale. Not even worth telling." He forced a smile. "Speaking of family, I thought we'd visit the pub your brother frequents later, once most of the dockhands have finished work for the day."

The abrupt subject change wasn't lost on her. "You don't have to tell me about your family if you'd rather not," she said, "but as long as we're here, I'd love to have a peek at Hawking House."

"Of course." He lifted one corner of the shade next to him and pointed. "Do you see the black gabled roof?"

"No. I don't have a good angle." She slid closer to Keane and leaned across, inadvertently brushing an arm against the solid wall of his chest. Heat rushed to her cheeks.

"How about now?" His breath was warm on her ear, and the deep timbre of his voice sent a delicious tremor through her body.

"Your shoulder is in the way."

"Here," he said. "I'll switch places with you."

"Very well."

He slid to his left while she attempted to step over him, but the toe of her slipper caught in the handle of her bag, and she felt herself falling—

But then Keane's large hands circled her waist. She grasped his shoulders to steady herself and found herself face to face with him, the tips of their noses nearly touching.

His palms were warm against her belly. Her thigh was nestled between his knees. She knew she should move. That she should do *something* to break the spell, but she didn't want to. And the heat in his eyes said he didn't, either.

"Poppy," he murmured.

Her skin tingled with anticipation, and beneath her bodice, her nipples tightened. His breath hitched, and his gaze dropped to her lips.

Knock. A loud rap on the carriage door startled them like a spray of cold water.

He muttered a curse and smoothly guided her onto the seat beside him. "Diggs can be vexingly efficient."

As Keane opened the door and spoke to his friend, Poppy did her best to look composed and positively uninterested in kissing anyone. Particularly the duke.

Fortunately, Diggs seemed unaware of any tension inside the carriage. He handed Keane a pile of invitations and a basket full of food and wine before closing the door and leaving them alone once more.

Keane rubbed the back of his neck and looked at her, his expression earnest. "Poppy, I didn't mean . . ." He searched for words she wasn't at all certain she wanted to hear.

"Why don't we forget that happened?" she said casually.

"*Almost* happened," he corrected.

"Right." She should be thankful that they'd been interrupted. Before they did something foolish and irreversible.

Besides, they wouldn't even be in London at that moment if he hadn't been discovered in bed with a married woman—a fact Poppy would do well to remember. She took a deep breath as the carriage started to roll down the road. "Where are we headed now?"

"Hyde Park. I thought we could find a remote spot and enjoy a picnic before resuming our mission."

"Very well. But we'll need to eat quickly," she said, sifting through the dozen invitations Diggs had brought them. "If this plan of ours is going to work, I'll need to be in the right place at precisely the right time."

"I have faith in you," he said, his voice uncharacteristically tender.

She ignored the warmth that blossomed in her chest and arched a cynical brow. "Maybe that's because you don't have any other choice."

Less than an hour later, Poppy peered through the carriage window as a pretty young woman wearing a serviceable gray gown and a cap left the marquess's house and hurried down the pavement.

Poppy grabbed her reticule and headed for the door of the cab. "I'll return as soon as I can," she told Keane. "Stay here and stay out of sight."

He made a mock salute, then, turning sober, added, "Be careful."

She alighted from the carriage and set off after the maid, trailing several yards behind as she walked away from the square down a bustling road lined with fashionable shops. After a few blocks, the maid stopped in front of an elegant modiste shop with a huge picture window and a dainty hanging sign that read *Madame Fontaine's*. She went inside, and Poppy followed, pretending to peruse a book of fashion plates at one end of a long counter.

"Good afternoon," the maid said to a stylish woman pulling a bolt of silk from a cubby along the back wall. "The marchioness sent me to fetch her gown."

The dark-eyed shop owner tucked the bolt under one arm. "Madame Camden, no?"

"That's correct," the maid answered nervously. "She needs it for a ball this evening. I do hope it's ready."

"One of the girls is finishing it now, *ma chérie*. Please, make yourself comfortable, and you shall have the gown in a trice." With that, Madame Fontaine disappeared behind a curtain, and the maid began pacing.

As she walked by, Poppy smiled warmly. "Pardon me. I wondered if I might ask your opinion."

The maid's forehead creased. "Mine?"

Poppy nodded. "My employer has asked me to alter one of her older gowns to make it appear more fashionable." She pointed at a fashion plate on the counter. "Do you think this neckline would suit a rather buxom woman with slender shoulders?"

The maid studied the sketch thoughtfully. "Perhaps. But you should ask the modiste."

"Forgive my poor manners. I neglected to introduce myself." Poppy extended a hand. "Miss Winters, companion to Lady Slattery. We're visiting from Brighton."

The maid tentatively shook her hand. "I'm Louise. I'm just a lady's maid."

"Then I daresay you know as much about fashion as any modiste," Poppy replied in a conspiratorial whisper. "Besides, my employer is rather frugal. As long she has a companion who is perfectly handy with a needle, she 'cannot see the wisdom of paying for the services of a seamstress.'" She idly flipped the page of the book. "Who did you say your employer was?"

"Lady Catherine, Marchioness of Camden."

Poppy pressed a hand to her chest. "Heavens, I don't think I've ever met a marchioness before. I wonder if she's been at any of the social events I've attended with Lady Slattery in the last two weeks."

"I suppose it's possible."

Poppy tapped a fingertip against her bottom lip. "How exciting. Let's see, we made an appearance at the Countess of Everton's soiree last week. Was the marchioness there, perchance?"

"No," Louise said, looking anxiously toward the back of the shop. "She and the marquess had another engagement that evening."

"Oh? Here in town?" Poppy probed.

The maid hesitated as if she were trying to recall that particular night, then nodded. "The Rutherford ball. She and the marquess had a public row. You may have read about it in the *Hearsay*."

"No. I confess I don't often read the gossip rags."

"Just as well. They're wrong more often than not."

"Were they wrong in this case?"

Louise shook her head. "The fight was real, but the reason behind it . . . well, there's always more to the story, isn't there?"

Madame Fontaine swept into the room carrying a large flat box on outstretched arms. "Here we are—a stunning new gown for the marchioness, as promised." She leaned closer and whispered, "I even included a golden apple. It shall be the *pièce de résistance* of her ensemble."

"Thank you, Madame." Louise took the box and smiled at Poppy. "I should be on my way. Enjoy your stay in Town."

"A visitor to London?" The shop owner turned to Poppy, clearly intrigued. "How may I be of service?"

"I was just admiring your lovely fashion plates, but I'm afraid I must go and meet my employer in Hyde Park."

"Perhaps you will return one day soon," Madame Fontaine mused. "I have a turquoise satin that would be the perfect complement to that fiery hair of yours."

"*Merci!*" Poppy waved as she hurried out the door.

Louise was already half a block away, her brisk strides taking her in the direction of the marquess's house.

Poppy had the proof she needed. A public argument between the marquess and his wife at a London ball meant the marquess couldn't have possibly been in Bellehaven on the night Keane was attacked. And yet, Louise's words echoed in her head. There was always more to the story.

Poppy lifted the front of her skirts and hurried after the maid. "Louise!"

The maid spun around, and Poppy caught up to her, breathless. "I don't mean to be a nuisance, but I'm going to the park and since you seem to be headed in the same direction . . . shall we walk together?"

Louise blinked at her, then said, "Please don't take offense, Miss Winters. Maybe things are done differently in Brighton, but here in Town, lady's maids and companions don't typically socialize with each another."

"That seems rather silly," Poppy said, falling into step beside her. "Besides, I am an outsider. Certainly not a member of the social elite. I have no friends here in Town, and I could use someone to talk to."

Louise sighed, relenting. "What would you like to talk about?"

"Earlier, you hinted that there was more to the row between the marquess and his wife than the *Hearsay* reported."

"Aye."

"How so?"

The maid looked around before responding. "According to the gossip pages, they were arguing because the marchioness had an affair with a duke."

Poppy frowned. "Did she?"

"Yes," Louise said with a shrug. "They were caught *in flagrante*. I'd be willing to wager that was the marchioness's goal all along."

"She wanted to be caught?"

"She was trying to make her husband jealous—and she succeeded." Louise clucked her tongue. "The poor duke she slept with was just a pawn."

"But willing enough, I presume," Poppy replied, unable to hide the trace of censure in her voice.

"I'm not certain about that. The duke wasn't in possession of all the facts." Louise stopped in front of the marquess's house.

"What facts?"

"I've already said too much. Besides, I must go." She inclined her head toward the dress box. "The marchioness is eager to try this on."

"Thanks for your company," Poppy said, wishing the walk could have lasted for one more block. "It was a pleasure."

"Likewise." Louise smiled over her shoulder as she headed toward the back of the house.

Poppy took a circuitous route to the carriage in case anyone had noticed her talking outside of the marquess's residence. She walked along the edge of the park in dappled sunlight, pondering the information that Louise had shared.

By all accounts, Poppy's mission had been a success. She could confidently tell Keane that the marquess had not been in Bellehaven on the night he was attacked, thereby eliminating him as a suspect. But the conversation with Louise had raised vexing new questions in Poppy's mind.

She'd assumed the duke was a depraved, heartless rogue who'd seduced a married woman.

But it seemed there *was* more to the story.

Maybe there was more to Keane, too.

Chapter 9

"This is it," Keane said.

Poppy looked out the window as the carriage rolled to a stop. A rickety sign hanging from the eve of the ancient pub declared it *The Barking Barnacle*, and the sun had just begun to sink behind its sagging roofline.

"I'll only be a few minutes," she said, sliding toward the door.

"I'm coming, too," he said, adamant.

She shook her head. "Someone might recognize you."

"Not likely in this part of town. I'll borrow Diggs's cap."

She debated arguing with him, but the set of his jaw said he wouldn't be easily swayed. "Very well," she said, not bothering to hide her exasperation.

"You might try to muster a little more enthusiasm," he said dryly. "Besides, you've had all the fun today. I deserve a turn."

"You'll need to keep your distance from me," she continued. "If my brother or his friends are in there, they mustn't realize that we're together. It would raise a whole host of questions, and Dane can be a bit . . . protective."

"I would be, too." He hesitated, then more soberly added, "You should know that this place isn't like any establishment in Bellehaven. It will make the Salty Mermaid look more genteel than a duchess's drawing room."

"The Mermaid isn't *that* tame. Have you forgotten you were almost murdered outside of our quaint little pub?"

"I have not," he said with a chuckle. "Just promise me you'll be careful in there."

"I'm perfectly capable of taking care of myself. Wait five minutes before you follow," she said sternly, punctuating her order with a slam of the door.

She took a deep breath of cool evening air, entered the pub, and lingered near the door while she surveyed her surroundings. The interior of the pub was as dingy as the exterior, and it reeked of whiskey, smoke, and sweat. Sailors and dockhands hulked over tables, while barmaids carried mugs with ale sloshing over the rims.

She felt every pair of eyes in the Barnacle tracking her as she strode toward the bar. If she'd been wearing her working clothes, she would have blended in a bit more. Instead, her silvery blue gown suggested she was a lady, the sort of woman drunken patrons might mistake for easy prey. She almost relished the prospect of proving them wrong.

Assorted leers and ribald suggestions were thrown her way as she navigated her way through the crowd, but she managed to keep her chin raised and her expression impassive. She skirted a group of burly men, approached the counter, and signaled to the ruddy-faced barkeep, who was replacing a barrel beneath the counter.

While she waited for him, she spotted Keane making his way to the opposite end of the bar. He had not waited five minutes. Two, perhaps, if she was being generous. But it was difficult to be vexed with him when he was clearly battling the urge to flatten the men staring at her. He gripped the edge of the counter as if it was the only thing preventing him from leaping onto the bar and announcing to the entire pub that she was under his protection.

No, she could not be cross with him. Especially when his shirtsleeves were rolled, revealing sinewy forearms, and his eyes had a wolfish, possessive glow. She met his gaze and her body shimmered with heat.

As the barkeep approached, she reminded herself of the task at hand. When she asked about Dane, he frowned and began wiping the counter in front of her. "I don't keep track of customers. Don't interfere in their personal affairs."

She nodded. "I understand. I just want to know if my brother is well."

He muttered a curse and flipped his towel so it hung over one shoulder. "I can't tell you much." But the barkeep did share what he knew, and it was enough to give Poppy some peace of mind.

She thanked him and began making her way toward the exit. She was halfway there when an ox-sized man with a missing front tooth grabbed his crotch and thrust his hips behind her. "How about you come sit on my lap, milady?"

She ignored him. Didn't flinch when he scrambled in front of her, blocking her path.

"Move," she said evenly.

He cackled, raising the hairs on the backs of her arms.

His mouth curled into a sinister grin.

Her fingers went numb.

He lunged for her wrist.

She ducked, unsheathed her knife, and brandished it in front of his chest. "Step away," she said, her calm tone at odds with the hammering of her heart. "Permit me to pass."

He held up his palms, gave a nervous gap-toothed smirk, and slowly took a step backward.

Keane approached the bully with clenched fists and a

look on his face that could only be described as murderous. Poppy shot Keane a surreptitious look and shook her head as she glided past the brute. There was no need to spoil the night with a brawl. Besides, the sea of burly bodies was already parting, allowing her to make her way out the door.

She heard Keane grumble behind her, and she smiled to herself as they walked out of the Barnacle.

Two minutes later, they were back in the carriage, sitting across from each other as they rolled down the road.

"Are you all right?" Keane searched Poppy's face, willing his heart to stop pounding.

She lifted her hem and sheathed her knife. "Why wouldn't I be?"

"Why, indeed?" he muttered, dragging a hand down his face. "I'm glad that miscreant didn't upset you. I, on the other hand, am in need of a very large glass of brandy."

She shot him a saucy smirk. "Clearly, you are overcome. Shall I fetch the smelling salts?"

He snorted in response. She'd accused him of treating their bargain as a lark. But *she* was the one who had taken unnecessary risks, who had blithely placed herself in jeopardy. He stared out the window, but in his mind, all he could see was that hulking oaf, making obscene gestures at Poppy.

After a prolonged silence, she asked, "Are you truly bothered?"

"Do you have any idea how difficult it was for me to watch a man threaten you? To stand by and do nothing while a brute twice your size attempted to place his filthy hands on you?"

She gazed at him, thoughtful. "What did you want to do?"

"Pulverize him."

For several heartbeats, she was silent. Then, she said, "Thank you."

He scoffed. "For doing nothing?"

"For caring." Her sea-green eyes met his, and some of the tension drained out of him. "Would you like to hear a secret?" she asked, leaning toward him.

He nodded soberly. "I want to know all your secrets, Poppy Summers."

"I *was* a bit nervous about visiting the Barking Barnacle," she admitted. "But I could sense you were there, and that gave me courage. Made me feel safe. In the back of my head, I knew that if I was truly in peril, you'd come to my rescue."

"Of course I would." He rubbed an odd ache located in the center of his chest and tried for a light tone. "It's the least I could do after you pulled me out of the sea." He leaned his elbows on his knees, taking a beat to compose himself. "Did you learn anything about your brother?"

"He was at the pub yesterday," she said brightly, and the relief on her face made the summer evening feel like Christmas morning. "The barkeep couldn't say where in Town Dane has been staying, but at least I know he's alive and well. Papa will be glad to hear it."

"We could try a few nearby pubs if you'd like. We might be lucky enough to find him."

She shook her head. "I asked the barkeep to give him a message next time he's at the Barnacle. That's comfort enough for now." She sighed, as if a weight had been lifted from her shoulders. "Are we headed back to Bellehaven?"

"Not yet. It's still early, so I figured we have time for one more stop."

Her eyes sparkled like emeralds. "Do tell."

"And spoil the surprise? Wouldn't dream of it."

She shrugged, crossed her arms, and tapped the toe of one slipper as if she was only vaguely interested in their destination. But he caught her stealing glances out the windows at the various storefronts. He could almost see her mind at work, trying to guess where they were headed.

A short time later, the carriage rolled to a stop across the street from Gunter's, and her face lit up.

"Ice cream?" she asked hopefully.

"Of course. And an assortment of other treats. I asked Diggs to bring us one of everything. I would take you into the shop if I could, but since I can't, the least I can do is let you sample to your heart's content."

She narrowed her eyes at him. "If you are attempting to ply me with sweets, I feel obliged to inform you that it just might work."

Half an hour later, Diggs parked the carriage in Hyde Park. They watched the moonlight dance on the Serpentine while they feasted on sorbet, mincemeats, caramels, and biscuits.

When Poppy tasted a spoonful of vanilla mousse, her eyes fluttered shut, her expression turned rapturous, and she moaned softly—all of which naturally made Keane think of other sensual pleasures.

He could see her lying on silk sheets, her fiery hair loose and wild. He could feel her smooth skin beneath his palm and hear her soft cries of ecstasy. Cursing to himself, he shifted in his seat and attempted to turn his thoughts to safer, if drier, subjects like the price of sheep.

"This has been a good day," Poppy said between bites. "One I won't soon forget."

"Nor will I." Too stuffed to eat another bite, Keane rifled through the stack of invitations Diggs had brought them earlier. Dinner party, soiree, ball . . . masquerade. And an admittedly mad thought entered his head.

Elegant script on fine vellum provided all the pertinent details. The party was being hosted by Lady Aurora. Costumes were absolutely required. Guests were to arrive at nine o'clock. And the date was that very night.

Keane tapped the invitation against his palm. "What if I told you that the day didn't have to end quite yet?"

Poppy leaned against the velvet squabs, looking sated. "I'd say it's late, and we have a long drive ahead of us."

"That is true. If you wish, we can leave now and be back in Bellehaven in a few hours. Or"—he handed her the invitation—"we could put in an appearance at Lady Aurora's."

"Lady Aurora's," she repeated. Her gaze flicked over the calligraphy, and she sat up straight. "A masquerade?"

"I think we should go and fulfill your wish. We could stay for a couple of hours and slip out before the unmasking at midnight."

"It's a lovely thought, but I don't see how we could possibly attend. You'd need a foolproof disguise—a costume that would completely hide your identity. And we don't have anything to work with."

"Between you, me, and Diggs, I feel certain we could round up something." He leaned forward and looked at her earnestly. "You're in London, and you're holding an invitation to a masquerade. When will you have this opportunity again?"

She bit her bottom lip, clearly tempted. "We wouldn't be able to stay long."

He shot her a rakish grin. "Long enough to drink some of Lady Aurora's champagne."

"Very well," she said with an impish smile. "Who shall we be tonight?"

Less than an hour later, after making a few brief stops, Diggs ushered Poppy and Keane through the door of a modest flat. "My brother and his wife are visiting his family in Bristol," he explained. "You can dress for the masquerade here. I was able to find a couple of sheets, masks, and accessories. Not the most elaborate of costumes, but no one will guess your identity."

Poppy's pulse quickened as she accepted the small bundle Diggs gave her and headed into a bedchamber to change. Agreeing to go to the masquerade with Keane may have been foolhardy, but he'd been correct about one thing. A fisherman's daughter didn't receive many invitations to London balls—and she resolved to take full advantage of the evening.

She unwrapped the bundle, spread the contents on the bed, and stripped off every stitch of her clothing. Then, she folded a satin sheet, tucked one end under her arm, and wrapped it around her body, knotting it artfully over one shoulder. The whisper-soft fabric clung to her curves and grazed the tops of her knees, caressing her skin as she moved. Never before had she worn anything so daring in public, and she wasn't at all certain that it was appropriate for Lady Aurora's ball.

The members of the ton were bound to be curious about her. She wasn't one of them, and they could sniff out an interloper as easily as they could a three-day-old fish.

But, as she checked her reflection in a looking glass, she suppressed the urge to make over the toga into a longer, more modest version. The goddess of the hunt would not tolerate a long, bothersome skirt when tracking her prey. Neither would Poppy.

The half mask that Diggs had purchased at a pawn shop was made of dark-green felt embellished with sparkling green sequins. She held it over her eyes, testing the fit. With the bow and a quiver of arrows, she could pass as Artemis.

And yet the woman who stared back at her had not been entirely transformed. She was still too mortal-like, too tame.

But perhaps there was an easy remedy for that. She pulled every last pin from her hair, freeing her tresses from their tidy knot. She shook out her long auburn curls and let them run wild.

She gazed into the mirror once more, only now she didn't see herself.

All she saw was the Moon Goddess.

By the time she gathered her clothes and emerged from the bedroom, Keane had transformed himself as well. His long, loose toga was stuffed with a pillow, hiding his trim torso and taut abdomen, which was admittedly dis-appointing. But he still looked the part of a handsome Greek god. His fierce black mask, long fake beard, and grape leaf crown made him unrecognizable.

"Dionysus," she said, grinning. "Well done."

But he didn't smile back. His mouth gaped, and behind his mask, his eyes blinked at her.

Diggs shuffled his feet. "I'll be waiting outside," he said, scurrying off. The door closed behind him, and she looked at Keane, waiting for him to say something.

"Do I have a tear in my sheet?" she asked nervously.

"Poppy," he said, sounding a little breathless.

"Artemis, actually."

"You're . . ." He swallowed and started again. "That is, you look like . . . well, like a goddess."

"That was the goal. I've never attended a party such as

this," she said earnestly. "So you must tell me if my costume won't pass muster. Do you think I'll blend in sufficiently with the other female guests?"

He let out a low, sensuous chuckle, the sort that felt like a downy feather tickling the back of her neck. "Blend in? I think not. But trust me when I say that your costume is perfect in every way."

Her cheeks heated, and beneath her satin toga, her nipples tightened to hard little buds.

He offered her an arm. "Ready?"

She curled her fingers around a hard biceps and exhaled. "I'm ready."

Chapter 10

Keane had walked into Lady Aurora's ballroom on other occasions. But this time felt different, and not just due to the dance floor teeming with milkmaids and emperors, vestal virgins and goblins.

This time, he had Poppy Summers on his arm.

Every pair of eyes in the room seemed to be on them. Or, more precisely, *her.*

Ladies whispered behind their fans. Gentlemen cast appreciative glances. Poppy took it all in stride, responding to each curious greeting with a graceful nod or mysterious smile.

"Are you worried someone will recognize you?" she whispered as he escorted her around the perimeter of the ballroom.

"As long as I'm with you, I might as well be invisible," he joked. But it was true, and his costume was foolproof. Even some of his friends from the club looked past him, which was odd. He idly wondered if they'd missed him since he'd been hiding out in Bellehaven. Life in London certainly seemed to have gone on without him.

He and Poppy strolled past the refreshments table and picked up glasses of fizzy champagne.

"A toast," he said. "To the goddess of the hunt. May

your arrow always find its mark, and may you have all that you desire."

"To the god of wine," she replied. "May your cup always be full, and may your heart be even fuller."

He smiled at her naïveté. She couldn't know that love, for him, was always just beyond his grasp. The one person he should have been able to rely upon as a lad had scarcely been able to look at him, so Keane had convinced himself that his father's detachment was for the best. It had made him harder. Stronger. More independent.

But it had also left an ache in his chest—the sort that all the intervening years couldn't erase. It was a poison that surfaced now and again, an insidious voice that said he didn't deserve love or happiness. He knew it to be a ridiculous sentiment, and yet, the feeling persisted.

Determined not to dwell on the past, he tipped back his glass while gazing into the bright blue-green of her eyes. "What do you think of your first proper masquerade ball?"

"It's wonderful—and more than I imagined. More people, more noise, more frenzy."

"If you'd like some fresh air, we could go outside on the terrace for a while."

She nodded eagerly. "I'd love to escape the curious stares for a bit."

They slipped out the French doors at the rear of the ballroom and stepped into the balmy evening. Colorful lanterns hung from tree boughs, and lush scents wafted through the air. He and Poppy wandered down a path bordered by meticulously trimmed hedges and stopped in front of a huge urn overflowing with blooming vines.

She gazed up at the stars, her spiral curls glistening in the moonlight. "I'm glad we came."

He knew she was thinking that the evening was almost over. Maybe that was why every minute they had left felt precious. "Don't worry," he said as they strolled back toward the house. "I'll return you to Bellehaven well before dawn."

"I'm not worried, I just—" She stopped short and frowned. "Oh dear. My toga. It's snagged on a branch." She leaned over, carefully freed herself, and moved below a lantern to assess the damage. A long loop of thread dangled several inches below her hem.

"I can break that off for you," he offered.

She shook her head firmly. "Knowing my luck, the whole toga would unravel. It will be safer for me to knot it and snip off the excess. Perhaps I'll find a pair of sewing scissors in the ladies' retiring room."

"I can assure you the men's retiring room is not nearly as well equipped."

"I'm not surprised in the least," she said, wrinkling her nose.

"Why don't you go in first?" He gestured toward the French doors. "After you've repaired your toga, we can meet in the ballroom, near the potted palms."

"Yes sir, Your Grace." She snapped a salute, then blithely glided toward the house.

"Poppy," he called.

She paused and turned to face him, her expression inquiring.

"Be careful."

She shot him an amused smile. "Rest easy, Keane. I'm armed with a bow and arrow, after all. Besides, the ladies' retiring room is not nearly as perilous as the Barking Barnacle."

He grunted. "That's not what I've heard."

Poppy easily navigated her way around the dance floor and down an adjacent corridor to the makeshift ladies' lounge—a room nearly the size of her family's whole cottage. Several dressing screens in the rear afforded privacy, while the front of the room boasted a large looking glass and a table full of cosmetics, ribbons, and other frippery.

Only a few guests lingered, including a strikingly beautiful woman who stood barefooted on a stool while another woman—a maid or companion, perhaps—repaired the torn hem of her gown.

And a magnificent gown, it was. Yards of ivory silk embroidered with gold shimmered in the candlelight. A matching gold ribbon was woven into the woman's elaborately plaited blond hair. Her gilded mask was crusted with gems.

And in one hand, she held a golden apple.

The apple clearly signaled that she was the goddess Aphrodite. But it revealed something more to Poppy. The costume was the one that Louise had fetched from the modiste that morning.

Which meant that the beautiful woman was the marchioness—the one discovered in bed with Keane.

The marchioness's shrewd gaze flicked to Poppy's bow. "Artemis," she drawled, deftly tossing the apple and snatching it out of the air. "I must commend you on your costume. Rather simple and crude, but undeniably effective. It seems everyone is talking about the fresh-faced, red-haired goddess . . . and placing bets as to your identity."

"I'm certain Lady Aurora's guests have more titillating topics to discuss." Poppy set down her bow, found a sewing basket on the floor, and pulled out a pair of scissors, intent on returning to the ballroom as soon as possible. "And as far as costumes are concerned, mine cannot compare to yours."

"An admirable attempt to change the subject," the marchioness conceded. "I don't blame you for wanting to remain anonymous for as long as you can. A costume affords us women all sorts of freedoms we wouldn't otherwise have."

"I suppose that is true." Poppy carefully smoothed the skirt of her toga, knotted the loose threads, and snipped off the long ends. "Sometimes it's nice to be someone else."

"It is indeed. I'll tell you a secret, Artemis. I once pretended to be my own twin . . . and succeeded in luring a duke into my bed."

Poppy's heartbeat thudded in her ears. "A duke? He must have been quite gullible."

The marchioness shrugged. "It was an elaborate ruse. He and my sister were once fond of each other. I simply took advantage of his tender feelings."

Poppy's blood boiled, and she struggled to keep the anger from oozing out. "Why would you do that?"

From her perch, the marchioness barked a hollow laugh. "You said it yourself, my dear. Sometimes it's nice to be someone else."

"I must go." Poppy scooped up her bow and headed for the door before she could say or do something she'd regret. The marchioness's callousness took Poppy back to her childhood and the hard lesson she'd learned about members of the nobility. They thought only of their own well-being. Their own comfort and desires. They couldn't possibly understand the plight of those less fortunate.

"I'll look forward to making your acquaintance," the woman called out, "after the unmasking."

Her words were still echoing in Poppy's ears when she located Keane in the ballroom, and the prickling sensation at the back of her neck warned it was time to leave. She opened her mouth to suggest that they go, but then he reached for her hand. And a frisson of awareness shot through her limbs.

"Miss Summers," he whispered in her ear, "will you dance with me?"

He looked so dashing and sounded so solemn that in spite of her misgivings, she heard herself say, "Yes."

He took her bow and quiver, propped them next to a giant palm, and led her to the edge of the crowded dance floor.

"You should know that I'm not accustomed to waltzing," she said. "I'm only familiar with the steps because I once practiced with the girls at Bellehaven Academy."

He placed a reassuring palm on her back, positioned one of her hands on his shoulder, and squeezed the other in his. "We'll start off slowly," he promised, gazing intently into her eyes. "You tell me when you're ready for more."

His words lingered in the scant space between them, lighting up every nerve ending in her body. They were discussing dancing, and yet, a seductive current flowed below the surface of their conversation.

It beckoned, drawing her deeper.

And for once, she let it sweep her away.

The heat in his eyes was intimate. Intoxicating. The intensity of his gaze made it rather difficult to recall the steps of the waltz. But she mirrored his movements and followed the gentle pressure of his hands. Before she knew it, she was spinning across the ballroom, free as a butterfly.

They swayed in time to the music, and the melody wove a cozy cocoon around them. As the rest of the ballroom blurred, they moved together. Chest to chest, hip to hip they glided over the smooth dance floor, twirling as if it were only the two of them, frolicking on a moonlit beach.

Then the clock began to chime.

The music came to an abrupt halt.

"We'd better go." There was an urgency to Keane's voice that raised the hairs on the backs of her arms.

"My bow," she said, heading in the direction of the potted palms.

"There's no time." He tugged on her hand and led her toward the ballroom door. "We need to leave before the unmasking."

The frenzied crowd had begun counting down. "Nine . . . eight . . ."

Keane wound his way through the guests, walking so fast that Poppy had to jog to keep up with him. "Are you all right?" he called over his shoulder.

She nodded. "Hurry!"

". . . Six . . . five . . . four . . ."

Poppy ducked her head as they breezed past the marchioness.

"Artemis," she said slyly, "leaving so soon?"

"Don't take the bait," Keane warned, keeping his eyes straight ahead. "We're almost there."

". . . Two . . . one!"

As they raced down the grand staircase, Poppy could hear the excited shouts of revelers ripping off their masks and their gasps as mystery guests were revealed. But she and Keane kept moving until they finally burst through the front door of Lady Aurora's town house and spilled out onto the pavement, their chests heaving.

"The coach is waiting around the corner," he said, his fingers still laced with hers. "But we can rest here a moment if you'd like."

"No, let's go." She hurried toward the carriage and waved to Diggs in the driver's seat as she approached. He nonchalantly tipped his cap—as though it were perfectly normal for a couple to run through the streets of London hand in hand while wearing togas.

She and Keane dove inside the cab, pulled the door shut behind them, and leaned against the velvet squabs while they caught their breath. Her heart was still pounding when the wheels started rolling down the cobblestone street.

"You did it." He shot her a blinding grin. "You attended your first masquerade ball."

"*We* did it," she corrected. "And we managed to escape before anyone guessed your identity."

He untied his mask, peeled off his beard, pulled the pillow out of his toga, and tossed everything onto the floor of the cab. "I've been to at least a dozen masquerades, but this was the most enjoyable—by far."

"A night I won't soon forget," Poppy mused, adding her own mask to the pile.

She faced Keane and found him staring at her strangely.

"Did the mask leave a mark?" she asked, skimming her fingertips beneath her eyes.

"No, no." He looked away quickly, as though embarrassed.

"What is it, then?"

He shook his head. "I was just thinking that while you looked lovely in your costume, I missed your freckles. I missed your face."

"Oh." Her heart fluttered like a hummingbird's wings.

Keane cleared his throat, and in a blatant attempt to change the subject said, "Diggs is going to drive straight through to Bellehaven. Feel free to close your eyes if you'd like."

"I'm far too excited to sleep."

He chuckled softly and folded his arms across his broad chest, making himself comfortable. "Then maybe *I'll* sleep."

She gazed out the window at the city soaked in

moonlight, and as the storefronts flitted by, she recalled her conversation with the marchioness. It left her feeling unsettled—and a tad guilty.

"I think I owe you an apology," she said to Keane.

He cocked his head and arched a brow at her. "What for?"

"When you first told me you'd been caught in bed with the marquess's wife . . . Well, I assumed the worst."

He barked a laugh. "That I was a philandering rake who is completely without morals? Trust me, you're not far off the mark."

"Nevertheless, I shouldn't have jumped to conclusions," Poppy said. "I know that the marchioness tricked you. That she pretended to be her twin."

He winced. "Where did you hear about that?"

"The ladies' retiring room."

"Naturally," he said with a sardonic shrug.

"She shouldn't have deceived you."

He dragged his fingers through his hair and frowned. "I blame myself for letting her. Better to be a philandering rake than a gullible fool."

"I'm not so certain about that, and I don't think you're a fool." She hesitated, then asked, "Were you devastated when you learned the truth?"

"Devastated?" he repeated, scoffing. "Shocked is more like it. Her irate husband burst into the room, I scrambled to grab my shirt off the floor, and before I could button my trousers, he chased me out the front door with a fire poker."

"How awful."

Keane waved a dismissive hand. "He did me a favor. I would have figured out her ruse eventually, but thanks to her jealous husband, the relationship ended abruptly. Much better than a long and protracted demise."

"That's putting a good face on it." But she wondered if Keane's flippant façade was a cover. His affair with the marchioness had ended less than a fortnight ago, and Poppy suspected the pain was still fresh. Every bit as real as the cut on his forehead.

His generous mouth curled at one corner. "Would you like to hear something interesting?"

"Always," she replied.

"I didn't think about Catherine at all tonight," he said solemnly. "That is, I saw her, and I'm certain I *should* have had some sort of visceral response. Perhaps I should have felt anger or bitterness or pain. But I didn't, because I was too preoccupied. With you."

A delicious warmth blossomed in her chest. "I'm glad I was able to provide a distraction."

He angled his body toward hers and frowned slightly. "You are more than a distraction."

Heat crept up her neck, and she resisted the impulse to look away. "What am I, Keane?"

He gazed at her and rubbed his chin, as though he was seriously pondering the question. "You," he said at last, "are a beam of sunlight. A breath of air. A force of nature."

She gathered his words to her chest and tucked them away for safekeeping. Then she reminded herself of the difference in their stations. The impossibility of anything lasting coming out of their arrangement. No matter what, she had to protect her heart. "How much brandy did you imbibe tonight?" she quipped.

The corners of his eyes crinkled in amusement. But there was an intensity in his expression, too—a heat, a hunger. "I have not had any brandy," he said smoothly. "And I have not forgotten about our deal."

She narrowed her eyes. "What are you talking about?"

"Poppy Summers, are you ready for your question?"

Right. She must have been quite mad to agree to a daily interrogation, especially since he seemed to have a knack for finding her most vulnerable spots and poking at them. The day had been exhilarating but long, and she wasn't feeling strong enough to talk about the heartache of losing her mother or the hollowness she still felt inside. She wasn't feeling courageous enough to discuss the dreams that seemed to be wilting like flowers on a vine.

But a deal was a deal.

"I suppose I'm ready." She sat up, faced him, and blew out a long breath. "What would you like to know?"

"I'd like to know if I could kiss you."

Her belly flipped and her heart pounded. "Why?" she asked, incapable of articulating anything vaguely coherent.

"I've been wanting to for a while now. It's hard to think about anything else when I'm with you, and I know it might complicate things, but I suspect it will be worth—"

Before he could finish, Poppy leaned forward . . . and brushed her lips across his. "Yes," she whispered. "You can kiss me."

Chapter 11

Keane cupped Poppy's cheeks in his palms and smoothed his thumbs over her freckles, worshipping each and every one. The long, loose waves of her hair tumbled around her bare shoulders. Her bright eyes glowed in the moonlight. The brief, tantalizing taste of her lips left him wanting more.

But he always wanted more when he was with Poppy.

She'd seemed on guard at first, but when he leaned in again and covered her mouth with his, she softened. The tension that was usually bottled inside her drained away, and she melted into him, pressing her lush curves against his body.

He traced the seam of her lips with his tongue, and she opened to him. The kiss deepened, his blood caught fire, and desire swept his legs out from underneath him. She seemed caught up by it, too, splaying her fingers through the hair at his nape and sighing into his mouth.

Holding her felt like his first thrilling horse ride, his first daring plunge into the river, and first forbidden sip of brandy all rolled into one. His head spun and his heart pounded, as if his own body had difficulty believing she was letting him in. To her thoughts. Her life. Maybe even her heart.

As the carriage rolled along, he trailed kisses down the column of her neck and found a sensitive spot behind her ear. Surely, she had other such places, and he vowed, one day, to discover them all. But she seemed intent on exploring him, too. She pressed her lithe leg against his thigh and boldly skimmed a hand across his chest, filling his head with a dozen wicked ideas.

He knew exactly what he wanted to happen next. He'd strip off both their togas. Haul her onto his lap. Kiss every inch of her until she cried out in pleasure. He could see it in his mind's eye, and her sensuous sighs suggested that she wanted more as well.

But he was determined to earn her trust, and that meant going slowly. He wanted her to believe in him, to see that he was more than a rake concerned with slaking his own lust. Maybe he needed to prove it to himself, too.

He lowered the temperature of the kiss, pulled back slightly, and looked into her eyes. "That was, without a doubt, the best ending to the best night."

She blinked at him, dazed, and touched a finger to her swollen lips. "What you said before, about the kiss complicating things. It was true."

"I'd like to propose that we save that conversation for tomorrow when my head is less muddled."

Her gaze flicked to the cut above his eye, and her brow creased with concern. "Is your wound bothering you?"

"Not at all." But he was far too aroused to think clearly. The sight of her sitting beside him with her hair down and wearing nothing but a sheet was damned distracting. "It's just that we only have a few hours before dawn, and I figured we both could use some rest."

"You've been awake longer than I have. Why don't you take a turn sleeping? You can put your head on my lap."

He hazarded a glance at her thighs, and the hem of her toga skimming her knees.

And he could only conclude that Satan was toying with him. Taunting him. Testing the very limits of his self-control.

Keane scrubbed the back of his neck. "I don't think I should rest on your lap."

"Why not?"

Why, indeed? "For one thing, I have a very heavy head."

"I feel certain I can handle it."

"If anyone should lie down, it's you. You'll have to work and take care of your father tomorrow."

"Why are you being so stubborn?" She slid to one end of the bench, shot him a saucy smile, and patted her leg.

God help him, he caved. "Very well. But only if you'll let me help you fish tomorrow."

She hesitated, then said, "I suppose I can find something for you to do close to the beach."

"Good." He knew how protective she was of her family and her business. Her willingness to let him in—even a little bit—felt like victory.

He exhaled and prepared himself for the next bit. The trick was to imagine he was simply lying on a pillow. Slowly, warily, he lowered his head, facing away from her body and as close to her knees as possible.

"You can rest easy, Keane. This is my lap, not a guillotine."

"Either way, I'm at great risk of losing my head," he mumbled.

"Hmm?" She gently swept his hair back from his brow, and her touch was a balm to his soul. He relaxed and nestled his cheek against her supple thigh.

"Nothing," he said. "Are you certain I'm not crushing you?"

"I'm certain." Her fingers swirled in his hair, making his scalp tingle and his eyelids heavy. "Good night, Keane."

Poppy had been kissed before. But Keane's kiss was entirely different from anything she'd experienced—and not simply because they were in a carriage and wearing togas.

He made her *feel* things. Not only in the places where they touched, but all over.

He'd slanted his mouth across hers, and her toes curled in pleasure. He'd speared his fingers through her loose hair, and her nipples turned to hard buds. He'd whispered in her ear, and her core pulsed with desire.

She'd read about passion and seen it illustrated on the pages of a book. But until that night, she'd never truly felt it. Never understood why perfectly intelligent women risked their reputations for an illicit kiss—or more.

Poppy knew she had to proceed with caution. She would not make the mistake of confusing physical attraction for an emotional connection. On the contrary, she would guard her heart as fiercely as the Crown Jewels.

But she wasn't going to pass up this opportunity to know pleasure. This summer with Keane could well be her only chance to live the life she'd dreamed of, venturing outside the town limits of Bellehaven—and outside the bounds of proper behavior.

As their carriage rumbled over the country roads, his head rocked on her lap. One of his hands clasped her leg above the knee, and every so often he caressed her in his sleep, sending delicious shivers across her skin.

She stayed awake throughout the drive, partly because she needed the time to think, and partly because this was a golden opportunity to study him freely. His toga gave her an excellent view of the muscles in his shoulder and arm.

The seat was only long enough to hold his torso, so his long legs spilled onto the floor.

Best of all, his chiseled face looked softer in sleep. More vulnerable. And the sensuous smile that played about his lips made her quite certain that his dreams were far from innocent.

The drive passed quickly, and before she knew it, the carriage was rolling into Bellehaven, the eastern sky already beginning to glow pink.

But she didn't feel sad as she woke him, disembarked, and walked back to the cottage on stiff legs. Their first adventure may have ended, but another was just beginning, and it could prove far more perilous than the first.

The next chapter might not involve irate dockhands, drawn knives, or hidden identities, but there was plenty at stake. Namely, her heart.

"Thank you for checking on my father yesterday," Poppy said to Kitty. She'd taken the cart to town in order to purchase some supplies and intercepted Kitty as she left the office where she worked as an architect's apprentice. "Papa said that you read a few chapters of his book to him. That was very sweet of you."

"It was my pleasure. I'm happy to visit with him any time." Kitty held her sketchbook to her chest and narrowed her shrewd blue eyes. "Where did you say you were yesterday?"

Poppy grinned. "I did not. I made a quick trip to London in order to look for my brother."

"London?" Kitty sighed. "I wish I could have gone with you. Did you find Dane?"

"Not exactly. But I spoke to a barkeep who saw him recently. He said that Dane bought a round for the pub, so I'm guessing he's been able to find work."

"That's good." Kitty's golden hair gleamed in the afternoon sun, and she caught the attention of more than a few gentlemen who passed by. As usual, she seemed oblivious to their admiring glances. "At least you know he's staying out of trouble."

"I hope so." Poppy reached into her bag and pulled out a package. "For you. A small token of my thanks."

"You didn't need to do that," Kitty protested, but her face lit up with delight as she unwrapped a long thin box that Poppy had decorated with shells. "Oh, I adore it," she said breathlessly.

"I thought you could use it for your pencils."

"It's perfect. But I hope you know that friends don't expect gifts in return for simple favors."

"That is true, but your 'simple favor' meant a great deal to me." Poppy winked at her. "Besides, I'm a little too proud for my own good."

"Fair enough," Kitty conceded. "As it turns out, I'm shameless enough to accept your lovely gift."

Poppy grinned at her friend. "Are you headed home? Calypso and I can give you a ride if you'd like."

"Actually, I'm going back to the school. I promised one of the younger girls I'd give her drawing lessons. But I'd love a ride."

They climbed onto the wooden bench of the cart and headed east on Main Street toward Bellehaven Academy. As they passed the Bluffs' Brew Inn, Kitty subtly elbowed Poppy in the ribs. "Do you see that gentleman outside the inn?"

Poppy glanced at the impeccably dressed, broad-chested man with the familiar black and gray head of hair. Diggs. "Do you know him?" she asked.

"He's the Duke of Hawking's valet," Kitty whispered.

"And apparently he's been staying in Bellehaven for several days now."

"You don't say," Poppy said, striving for a breezy tone despite the fact that her heart was pounding. If townspeople were talking about Diggs, it was only a matter of time before someone asked the obvious question. Namely, where was the duke?

"Oddly enough, the duke—who's rumored to be *sinfully* handsome—hasn't been seen since the day they first arrived," Kitty continued with obvious relish. "And there's delicious speculation as to why."

Poppy steered the mule around the corner and hoped her cheeks weren't as red as they felt. "What are people saying?"

"One theory is that he took ill and has been staying at the inn while he recovers. But Dr. Gladwell hasn't been seen there, so it's difficult to know. Perhaps the duke is a rather private person," Kitty mused. "His valet is certainly tight-lipped."

"An illness could explain why the duke hasn't been seen," Poppy said.

"There is another theory," Kitty said, glancing around them. "That the duke was the victim of foul play."

"What sort of foul play?"

Kitty shrugged. "He was last seen playing cards at the Salty Mermaid—and apparently, he had a terrible losing streak. Maybe he owed someone money."

Poppy pulled on the reins and brought the cart to a stop in front of the school. "You can't believe everything you hear," she said to Kitty.

"I know," she replied, rolling her eyes. "But there's usually at least a kernel of truth to gossip, and I, for one, intend to be on the lookout for a dashing duke—just in case."

She shot Poppy a saucy smirk, hopped down from the cart, and waved goodbye as she strode toward the front door of the school.

During the drive home, Poppy contemplated her next steps. With each day that passed, the speculation as to Keane's whereabouts was bound to increase. More and more people were going to be looking for the missing duke. And, from what Kitty had shared, the rumors weren't far off the mark.

Poppy needed to talk to him about speeding up the investigation. They'd ruled out one of the three suspects, and it was time to take a look at the next one. As soon as she unloaded her cart, she was going to find Keane on the beach. And not simply because they needed to plan their next course of action.

They also needed to talk about their kiss. Even now, her lips tingled at the memory.

It had been one of the most ill-advised, foolhardy, and reckless things she'd ever done.

And yet, she was seriously contemplating doing it again.

After finishing up her chores and chatting with Papa, Poppy filled a pail with some leftover shepherd's pie, fruit, cheese, and nuts and headed to the hideaway.

Since Keane had insisted that she give him something to do, she'd left an old fishing net outside the shelter with instructions to untangle it. But since she'd tried herself on several occasions and given up each time, she didn't expect him to fare any better.

"I came as soon as I could," she called out as she approached the clearing. "I hope you're not too famish—" She drew up short and blinked at the scene before her.

Keane caught her eye first, for myriad reasons, not the least of which was that his thin lawn shirt was barely clinging to his broad shoulders. It gaped open at the front and revealed a wide swath of tanned skin, from his collarbone all the way to his waistband. In a half-hearted attempt to make himself presentable he hastily tugged at the collar and shoved his shirttail into his buckskin trousers. But it was too late. The knee-melting image was already burned into her mind.

When she finally managed to drag her eyes away from Keane, however, she noticed something else rather amazing: the old net she'd left for him. It hung neatly between two trees that were about ten yards apart, and there wasn't a single knot to be found.

"I wasn't sure I could salvage it," Keane said with a boyish grin. "I don't mind telling you that I was this close"—he held up a thumb and forefinger like a crab pincer—"to cutting it up to make a hammock."

"I wouldn't have blamed you if you did." She stepped closer to take a look at the holes he'd obviously repaired. "I'm impressed."

"I had to take a piece off one end and use the extra string to tie up the bigger gaps. It's not perfect," he admitted, "but it might last you another season."

She smiled and handed the pail to him. "You've earned your luncheon today."

"Thank you." He gestured toward the quilt spread on the grass. "Will you join me?"

"I ate earlier with Papa. But I do think we should talk," she added pointedly.

"Is this about my snoring last night?" he quipped. "I promise it's not nearly as bad when I have a proper pillow."

She arched a brow. "It *almost* sounded as though you were complaining about the sleeping arrangements just then."

The corner of his mouth lifted in wicked amusement. "Never."

"Good. Because one of us slept a great deal more than the other last night—and it wasn't me." She dragged the quilt into the shade of a tree and sank onto the soft patchwork. "We need to talk about what comes next."

"Next?" he repeated, stretching out beside her on the quilt and propping himself on an elbow. "More chores? All you must do is tell me. Make a list if you wish. I am yours to command, Poppy Summers."

His lazy smile and heavy-lidded gaze suggested he was offering more than just menial labor. She swallowed and resisted the urge to fan herself. "I appreciate your willingness to help, but that should not be your focus. We need to figure out who hurt you so you can return to London . . . and resume your real life."

A frown flicked across his face. "Are you so eager to be rid of me?"

"Not exactly. But I do worry that you'll be discovered here. I was in town earlier today, and there's already a great deal of speculation as to where you are. If you don't make a public appearance soon, word of your absence will spread to London. Perhaps it already has."

"I'm not ready to resume my real life," he said, his expression so earnest that it nearly broke her heart. "I do need to find out who tried to drown me and why. That's the reason I asked you to let me stay here. But I don't think I realized till today that there's another reason."

"What's that?"

"I need to be more than a duke—a man who sits behind a desk or relaxes at his club while his steward, solicitor, and staff do all the work. I want to roll up my sleeves and sweat, feel the earth between my fingers." He looked at the puffy white clouds as though he might find the words he searched for hidden among them. "I like it here, where I am not defined by my title."

She flicked her gaze toward the sea. The truth was that he couldn't run from his title, and neither could she. It mattered every bit as much there, overlooking the beach, as it mattered in London. His dukedom was the precise reason she—a poor fisherman's daughter—couldn't seriously consider a future with him. Moreover, it was the reason she could never, ever love him.

"It is a part of you that you can't deny," she said softly. "But it's not the whole."

"If my father had had his druthers, it *would* have been the whole of me." He kicked a pebble with the toe of his boot and smirked. "I was a grave disappointment, to say the least."

"How so?"

"I won't bore you with the particulars, but I failed to measure up to my father's expectations. My intellect, ambition, and decorum . . . All, apparently, are sorely lacking."

"That is not true," she said sincerely. "Perhaps your father saw great potential in you and merely wished to spur you on."

Keane scoffed. "He saw nothing of value in me. You can take me at my word on that."

She reached for his hand on the quilt between them. "I'm sorry." Her little family was imperfect, but it had always been loving and supportive. She sometimes forgot that not all families were like hers.

"My father had his reasons for resenting me, and I had mine for resenting him," he said with a shrug. "That was simply the way of it."

"Forgive me for speaking plainly, but that should *not* be the way of it. A boy needs his father."

"You might think me a monster for saying so, but I'm better off without mine."

"You're not a monster. You're wounded."

He shook his head as if she were mad. "I made my peace with it long ago. We shouldn't waste our breath talking about him."

Poppy had never seen this side of Keane. Though he appeared calm, she suspected he was hanging onto his composure by the thinnest of threads. "If you decide you do want to talk about your father, I am a good listener."

"You are good at many things." He shot her a rakish grin, effectively signaling a change in subject and making her belly flutter at the same time.

She leaned back on her palms. "I understand wanting a holiday from your responsibilities. I sometimes wish for a break from mine. Nevertheless, your time on this beach is limited, and you still have two more suspects to investigate. What do you intend to do next?"

He lifted her hand, turned it over, and pressed a kiss to the inside of her wrist. "Convince you to go on another excursion with me."

Her heart leapt and plummeted in the space of two breaths. "I wish I could. But I shouldn't leave my father again so soon."

His eyes clouded with disappointment. "I understand. It was probably selfish for me to ask, but I couldn't help myself." His lips skimmed across her forearm, making it rather difficult to think clearly.

"I'm glad you asked," she said sincerely. "And I would go if I could."

"It won't be nearly as much fun without you, but you can help me plan if you'd like."

"I would like that," she said eagerly. At least she

could be involved in some way. "Are you going back to London?"

"Not quite." His breath blew softly on her sensitive skin. "When you come back tonight, I'll tell you more."

Chapter 12

Later that afternoon, Diggs joined Keane on the pair of flat rocks that overlooked the bay. "It's growing more difficult to skirt questions regarding your whereabouts," the valet said. "I've become adept at changing the subject and avoiding people altogether, but there is an exceptional amount of curiosity about you."

Keane stroked the stubble along his jaw. "We want my attacker to think he succeeded in killing me. Everyone else can formulate whatever theories they wish, so the less you say, the better."

"Don't worry. I am nothing if not obtuse." Diggs shifted on the boulder and scowled, clearly wishing for a proper chair. "I am impervious to the inquires of matrons, ladies, and debutantes alike. For reasons I cannot quite fathom, you're something of a celebrity in Bellehaven."

Keane chuckled at the good-natured dig. "I'm sorry to have put you at the center of this, my friend. If you want to escape the questions and scrutiny of the townspeople, you could remove yourself to the country. Take the coach to Hawking Manor and hide out there until all of this is over."

"And forgo the chance to witness your hare-brained

scheme as it plays out? No, I prefer to keep my front-row seat for the drama that will undoubtedly ensue."

"I was hoping you'd say that," Keane admitted. "Because I could use your help for the next act."

Diggs lifted his chin and straightened his cravat. "I've become rather indispensable, haven't I?"

"I suppose," Keane said with a snort. "But don't let it go to your head. We still have far more questions than answers. Which brings me to our next suspect—the Earl of Tottenshire."

Diggs snarled. "Nasty bit of business."

"Indeed. And I happen to know exactly where he'll be two days from now."

"Wherever it is, I'm guessing we'll be there, too."

Keane shot his friend a grin. "You can bet on it."

It was dusk when Poppy glided into the clearing. Her loose white gown billowed around her legs and a satin green ribbon pulled her hair away from her sun-kissed cheeks. Keane's pulse quickened at the sight of her.

"What's all this?" she asked, gesturing at the pile of driftwood he'd collected that afternoon.

"It's for my next project," he said. "I'm going to try and make a chair so that Diggs will have a place to sit the next time he visits."

She nodded in approval. "It's the least you can do for Diggs."

"If it's not a complete disaster, I'll make another for you. In the meantime, I have a more traditional gift for you." He pulled the book he'd been hiding from behind his back and gave it to her.

"For me?" Her face beamed.

"A small thank-you for your help."

"This is lovely. Have you read it?"

"Me?" He scoffed. "I only read when it's an absolute necessity. I asked Diggs to select something with adventure and a bit of romance. And I firmly instructed him to steer clear of anything remotely stodgy."

"I detest stodgy books." Poppy hugged the gift to her chest. "Thank you."

"I also asked him to bring some wine," Keane said. "Care for a glass?"

She hesitated for a beat, then relented. "Perhaps a small one."

As he headed for the shelter to fetch the wine, a rogue raindrop hit his forehead. He paused, faced her, and felt a few more drops. "Would you like to come inside?"

She frowned at the sky and shrugged. "No sense in getting soaked."

He swept aside the curtain at the entrance while she went through, then followed her into the cozy lean-to. She lit the lantern while he uncorked the wine and poured a glass for each of them. They sat facing each other, her knees only inches from his.

They'd been in the shelter together once prior, but that was before half the space was filled with bags of clothes and other necessities. It was before he'd known her name. And it was definitely before he'd kissed her.

"A toast," he said, raising his glass. "To books that aren't boring . . . and to kisses that are unforgettable."

She flushed, clinked her glass to his, and tipped it to her lips. "I suppose we should talk about that, but first I am eager to hear what you have planned for your next excursion."

"A day at the Royal Ascot, in Berkshire. The day after next."

"The horse races?" Poppy's eyes sparked with excitement. "I once overheard Lady Rufflebum say it's a mad crush of ladies and gentlemen, dressed in their finest and behaving their worst."

Keane laughed. "It can be a raucous affair. Steep wagers will be placed, and a great deal of money will change hands. That's often a recipe for trouble."

"And your next suspect will be at the race?"

"Without a doubt. Tottenshire never misses an opportunity to gamble. In fact, he owes me quite a bit of money."

She sipped her wine, thoughtful. "You think he might have attacked you in order to avoid paying his debts?"

"Among other reasons." Keane idly swirled the liquid in his glass. There was no need to tell Poppy the whole of it, especially since he'd sworn to keep the scandal a secret. "Suffice it to say that the earl is not an honorable man."

"A dishonorable earl," she mused, her expression brooding. "I cannot claim to be surprised."

"You say that as if you've encountered a few."

She blinked at him, then looked away. "In my experience, the nobility do not always behave nobly."

A surprisingly fierce, primitive rage sparked inside him. "Did someone hurt you?"

"Not exactly," she said, slow and deliberate. "Not in the way you may think. But they did hurt someone I loved— and I'll never, ever forgive them for that." The quiet finality in her words was frightening in its intensity. For a moment, all the air seemed to have been sucked out of the shelter, and the only sound was the distant rumble of the surf below them.

At last, he said, "I don't know what you went through, but I'm sorry that your loved one suffered."

Her expression turned wistful. "So am I."

"Maybe someday you will tell me what happened."

"I don't think so," she said, uncharacteristically chilly.

"Someone like you . . . Even if you wanted to, you couldn't understand."

Her lack of faith in him stung. "That's not fair."

She scoffed. "Much in this life is not fair."

"But you haven't even given me a chance."

"I don't blame you, Keane. It's not your fault that you were born to be a future duke. But you can't begin to comprehend what it's like for the rest of us. A few weeks away from your elegant London town house and your sprawling country estate doesn't change that."

"True," he said. "But if you were to talk to me, maybe I could understand."

"I could confide in you, tell you everything there is to know about me. What I eat for breakfast, what songs I sing on my rowboat, and what I worry about at night. You might learn enough to know me here," she said, pointing to his head, "but you still wouldn't know me here." She placed a palm over his heart. "There's a difference, you know. Between understanding something logically and feeling it deep in your bones."

Damn. One of his guiding principles in life was to avoid anything deep. To run like hell in the opposite direction, actually. But he didn't want to run from Poppy. "Give me some time," he said. "Maybe I'll prove you wrong."

"I'm hardly ever wrong." The half smile she shot him seemed sadder than a full-fledged cry. "But if I am in this instance . . . well, just this once, I wouldn't mind."

Her words hung in the air for several heartbeats, challenging him. Daring him to rise to the occasion. And though he didn't know exactly what the test would be—how he'd prove to her that he understood her in the depths of his heart—he suspected he'd recognize the test when it presented itself. And whatever form it took, he planned on passing it.

At last, she took a sip of her wine. "Tell me more about Lord Tottenshire. How do you plan to discover if he was in Bellehaven on the night you were attacked?"

"Diggs and I will be going undercover. He's going to play the part of a wealthy bloke looking to wager his money on the horse races."

"And you?"

"I'll be a stablehand. Close enough to help Diggs if he should encounter trouble."

"A stablehand?" She nodded thoughtfully. "You did say you wanted to get your hands dirty. This should be a prime opportunity."

He smiled, smug. "I can shovel with the best of them."

"I'm certain you can." She rolled her eyes and took a long sip from her glass.

"Now," he drawled. "Let's talk about that kiss."

Poppy had rehearsed just what to say to Keane on the subject of kissing.

"Yes, the kiss." She'd intended to make several well-reasoned points, but the close quarters, the heady wine, and the pattering rain all seemed to conspire against her. She took a deep breath. "First of all, I think it's important to note that it wasn't a single kiss but rather a series of small kisses."

"I agree with that characterization," he said so seriously that she could only conclude he was jesting.

"The distinction is important because it demonstrates just how easy it is to become carried away in the moment."

"Once again, I find myself in complete agreement."

"Are you mocking me?"

"Not at all." He set his glass on the overturned crate, reached for her face, and brushed a thumb across her lower lip. Her whole body shimmered in response. "When I kiss you, Poppy Summers, I am at grave risk of being carried away. The pull I feel toward you . . . it's stronger than a riptide."

His words swirled around her, sweeping over her skin like a caress.

"That's why we must be careful," she murmured.

Reluctantly, he lowered his hand. "I want to kiss you again, but if you don't feel the same, I won't press you."

She swallowed. "Kissing you *is* akin to a riptide. But a dangerous current doesn't induce one to give up swimming entirely. The trick is to be aware when you are in peril and have a plan for escaping it."

His eyes turned dark, and his voice grew husky. "I see. And how, precisely, do you plan to escape the peril of our kisses?"

"Simple," she said, with more confidence than she felt. "I shall swim parallel to the shore."

His forehead creased adorably. "I'm not certain I follow."

"When we feel as though we're being swept away, we needn't struggle against the passion, but we needn't surrender to it, either. Rather, we shall slowly steer ourselves into safer waters." He still stared at her blankly, so she chuckled and said, "We can take a step back and gradually lower the temperature—until we're able to think with clear heads once again."

"I can see how your plan would work in theory," he said with a wickedly brooding glare. "But one never knows about these things until they're put into practice. Perhaps a test is in order."

It took several heartbeats for her to catch her breath, and in that short space of time, the shelter grew warmer, the rain fell steadier, and the air around them crackled with energy.

"Very well." Her belly flip-flopped as she placed her glass next to Keane's, sat back on her heels, and placed her palms on her thighs. He leaned forward and stared at her mouth, silently willing her to initiate the kiss.

And she reminded herself what was at stake.

This kiss was about proving that she was capable of touching him without completely losing her head. That she could enjoy the considerable physical attraction between them without forgetting who he was—and that their differences made a future with him nigh impossible.

So even though she longed to crash into him, to feel the rush of passion, she mustered every ounce of restraint she possessed and moved ever so slowly. Deliberately, she trailed her fingertips down the side of his face and across the stubble on his jaw. Tipped her forehead to his. Listened to the subtle hitch of his breath and savored the first sensuous melding of their mouths and tongues.

Despite all her good intentions and grand plans, her heart began beating triple-time. Her skin tingled like she'd taken a January dip in the ocean.

Everything Keane did seemed designed to please her. He speared his fingers through her loose hair. Brushed his lips along the column of her neck. Tangled his tongue with hers.

Indeed, given his level of expertise in these matters, it was no wonder her body responded by melting into a puddle of pure pleasure. His warm, sure hands caressed her upper arms, cruised down her back, and skimmed over her hips, drawing her closer. Making her dizzy with desire.

She would have loved nothing more than to throw caution to the wind. To let passion carry them where it would. But some remote corner of her mind was aware that now was the time to pull back. To resist the tide while they still could.

Reluctantly, she pressed a palm to his chest. Felt his heart beating as erratically as her own. "Keane."

He nipped at her lower lip, lingering for a few interminable seconds before sitting back. He blinked and shook his head as if waking from a dream. "You rescued me this time," he said with a knee-weakening grin. "Next time, I shall rescue you."

"Are you certain there shall be a next time?"

"I'm hopeful there will be. Call me an eternal optimist. Or an insufferable rake. Your choice."

She suppressed a smile and blew out a long breath. "I enjoyed the wine and the experiment, but I must go."

"Then I will bid you good night . . . after my one question."

Her heart tripped in her chest. "You are insatiable. But please, go on."

"Would you rather see a sky full of fireworks or a single shooting star?"

"Fireworks," she said firmly. "I've seen at least a half dozen shooting stars, and all my wishes have been in vain."

"Give them time," he said smoothly. "Your wishes might still come true."

She rolled her eyes, slipped her shawl over her head, and ducked through the doorway into the misty night.

Most old wives' tales were harmless, but not this one. Keane made her want to believe—and that was very dangerous indeed.

Chapter 13

The next morning Poppy jolted awake to the sound of pots banging. "Papa," she called from her loft. "What are you doing up? Go back to bed, and I'll bring you your tea and tart momentarily."

"He's still snoring," came a familiar, jocular voice. "And I'm making breakfast today."

She leaned over the edge of the loft and peered into the dimly lit kitchen. "Dane?"

He held out his arms and shot her a grin. "In the flesh."

"When did you—" she began in a stage whisper. "Never mind. Give me one minute, and I'll be right down."

"Take your time. I'm not going anywhere. Teapot's already on the stove."

Poppy shoved her arms into her robe, stuffed her feet into her slippers, and clambered down the ladder. Dane stood in the kitchen like a regular cook, simultaneously poaching a couple of eggs and frying some ham in a pan.

"Earl Grey tea for you," he said, sliding a cup toward her. "Coffee for me."

"Papa has been worried about you. I was, too." She sighed, exasperated and relieved at the same time. "When did you arrive home?"

"A little after midnight, on the last mail coach." He

flipped the slices of ham, and the savory aroma tickled her nose. "I didn't think I should wake you. Figured you could use your beauty sleep."

A tiny ember of resentment sparked between her shoulder blades. "I do need my rest," she said, taking a sip of steaming tea. "Rowing, hauling nets, and lugging baskets of cod is rather exhausting."

"I know," he said, chastened. "I'm sorry that you've had to work so hard. I shouldn't have left you to run the business on your own."

She exhaled, releasing most of her anger. Granted, apologies came easy to Dane. But she knew her brother almost as well as she knew herself, and the rawness in his voice revealed the weight he'd felt on his conscience.

"We've been managing surprisingly well," she said. "Papa's been following Dr. Gladwell's orders, and his pain seems to have subsided a bit. The fish have been plentiful, and business is brisk."

Of course, it helped that she'd had a windfall of sorts, thanks to Keane. He'd given her half of his room and board money up front, and that had allowed her to pay off a few debts, stock the cupboards, and replenish her fishing supplies. She'd hidden the small amount that was left under her mattress, but now that Dane was home, she was considering moving it to her shelter for safekeeping. Just in case.

Poppy was happy that her brother was home, truly she was. But his return did present a particular challenge at the moment. Dane had always respected the clearing with the lean-to as her private domain—primarily because the idea of a reading nook didn't interest him in the slightest. Now that Keane was staying there, though, it was more critical than ever that Dane steer clear of the shelter.

"I owe you a debt, Poppy. For taking care of Papa,

running the business, and keeping up the cottage. I shouldn't have left everything in your hands, but maybe I can make it up to you, starting now." He reached into the pocket of his trousers, pulled out a small sack, and plunked it onto the dining table.

"What's this?"

"My wages," he said gruffly. "From working on the docks. Use them to buy whatever you need around here."

She loosened the drawstring, peeked inside, and jingled the coins. It wasn't a fortune, by any means, but it was enough to keep Calypso in hay and apples for a few months. Besides, the amount of the offering wasn't nearly as significant as the gesture itself.

Dane could have stayed in London. Spent the coins on whiskey. Wagered them on cards.

But he'd put family first this time and come home. She knew better than to believe he'd turned over a new leaf, and it wasn't as though she could trust him completely, but it was a start.

"I know it's not much," he said, staring at the scuffed toes of his boots. "I owed a fellow . . . But the wages are good on the docks. Think of this as the first installment."

She cinched the drawstring, tucked the pouch in a cupboard, and smiled encouragingly. "This will help. Best of all, Papa will be delighted to see you. How long will you stay this time?"

Dane winced. "A couple of days is all I can spare. But for as long as I'm home, you're not touching a gill net, cod trap, or fillet knife. Let me take care of the business for a spell."

She opened her mouth to protest, then thought better of it. A respite would be lovely—and there was no telling when another opportunity would present itself. "Very well," she said. "I vow to stay away from the beach for the next two days, if you'll promise to stay away from my reading nook."

"You're not hiding a decanter of whiskey or a box of cigars in there, are you?"

"No," she said, scoffing.

"Then you won't catch me within one hundred yards of that place."

"Good. It's settled then. I shall gladly turn over the oars to you." Poppy plucked a cup from the shelf, filled it with hot water, and steeped Papa's willow bark tea.

"How have you been?" Dane's expression turned sober. "Any of the blokes in town been giving you trouble?"

"They wouldn't dare," she replied with a shrug.

"Been spending time with anyone special?" He arched a curious brow.

"Not that it's any concern of yours," she said pointedly, "but I've had neither the time nor the inclination."

"I don't mean to pry." He slid the ham slices onto a plate and turned his attention to the eggs. "But I worry about you. Don't you feel lonely?"

"Sometimes. This"—she waved a hand around the rustic kitchen—"isn't exactly the life I'd envisioned for myself, but after Mama . . . Well, everything changed."

"It did indeed. I don't know how, but she made this tumbledown cottage feel like a palace."

Poppy nodded, wistful. "Some days I can still hear the sound of her humming—those cheerful little melodies she sang while she cleaned the kitchen or sewed by the fire. The notes would float up to the loft while I lay in bed at night, and no matter how terrible the day had been, I'd feel better."

"What I miss most is the way that Papa was with her."

It was the first time Poppy could recall her brother reminiscing about Mama, and the catch in his voice made her own throat ache. "Even when he was in the foulest of moods," Dane continued, "Mama could make him laugh."

"She was the center of his world," Poppy said softly. "His North Star."

"Mine, too," Dane admitted. "It's why I can't stay here too long. There are pieces of her everywhere I look. This chipped teacup, the patchwork curtains, the overgrown garden . . . they're all painful reminders of the family we used to be."

"We're still that family," Poppy said firmly. "Perhaps we're a bit broken, but Mama would want us to pull together, to be there for each other."

"Family was everything to her, and yet, she couldn't rely on hers in the end, could she?" His nostrils flared.

"No," Poppy said. "I think it broke her heart."

His eyes turned to stone. "I'll never forgive them for the way they treated her—and you."

"You mustn't dwell on it," Poppy said, even though she was guilty of doing the same. "At least we aren't beholden to them. I humbled myself once to ask for help, but I won't make that mistake again. We don't require charity from anyone."

"She was their own flesh and blood, and they abandoned her when she needed them most."

Poppy raised a finger to her lips. "Quiet. You'll upset Papa."

"All I'm saying is that you should have a care when you choose the people you spend time with and the people you trust."

The hairs on the back of her arms stood up. Dane couldn't possibly know about Keane, and yet, he was giving voice to the worries in the corners of her mind. She narrowed her eyes at him. "What are you implying?"

"The headmistress you get your books from—Miss Lively, is it?"

Poppy felt her hackles rise. "Hazel is a dear friend."

Dane shrugged. "Maybe she was—before she married an earl. Just wait till she has her fancy house, a couple of babies, and all the comforts money can buy. She'll forget where she came from. Before long, she'll be just as haughty as Bladenton."

"No." Poppy frowned. "Blade's not like that, either."

But she had to admit that a tiny part of her had wondered the same thing. After all, Hazel was a countess now, and it would be natural for her to gravitate toward friends who were her social equals. People who attended the same sort of parties and mingled in the same circles. Hazel would never forget about the Belles—Poppy was certain of that—but as their trio grew older, the bond between them was bound to diminish.

And Poppy would be left with a gaping hole in her heart.

"Don't fool yourself," Dane continued. "They're *all* like that. They're not from our world, and they don't understand it. The truth is, they'd like to pretend that us commoners don't exist."

Poppy swallowed. She'd said something remarkably similar to Keane last night, but hearing her brother echo the sentiment was oddly disheartening.

Because she'd wanted to be wrong about Keane.

"What happened to Mama colored our view of the world, and we can't help that. But perhaps we shouldn't paint every member of the nobility with the same broad brush," she said diplomatically.

Dane snorted. "I don't have to personally meet every shark in the sea to know they have sharp teeth."

"Poppy, who's that you're talking to?" Papa called from his bedroom, his voice still thick with sleep. "It sounds like Dane."

"That's because it *is* me." He hurriedly added a poached egg to the breakfast tray, carried it into Papa's room, and placed it on his lap. "Surprise!"

Papa didn't even see the heaping plate of food. He circled his arms around Dane's neck, held on tight, and sobbed with sheer happiness. "Welcome home, son. Welcome home."

Keane rose at sunrise, took his usual morning swim, and sat on the flat rock overlooking the ocean, hoping to catch a glimpse of Poppy's rowboat bobbing on the waves. He was still thinking about their kiss last night—and wondering if she was thinking about it, too.

He couldn't wait to see her today and make the most of their time together before he left for Ascot.

Strange how he already anticipated missing her.

Odd how someone whom he hadn't even known a fortnight ago had become so familiar, so important to him.

The bright morning sun glinted off the turquoise-blue water, and the warm breeze riffled his damp hair. He held a hand level with his brow and looked east, to Poppy's fishing spot. Before long, her rowboat came into view—a bit farther from shore than usual.

He stared more intently, but without a telescope it was impossible to make out anything more than the shape of the boat. Still, there was something different about the way it moved today. It seemed to cut through the waves faster and with greater ease.

Someone other than Poppy was holding the oars.

"Keane," came the breathless voice behind him. And it was her.

"Is everything all right?" He hopped off the rock and reached for her hands.

Her cheeks turned a delightful shade of pink, and he belatedly realized he wasn't wearing a shirt. "I hadn't quite finished dressing," he said with a grin. "Allow me to remedy that."

"You needn't bother on my account." She smiled shyly. "Besides, I cannot stay. I only came to tell you two things."

"Someone commandeered your rowboat?" he asked, gesturing over his shoulder.

She nodded. "My brother is home for the next few days. I don't anticipate he'll come here, but you must stay close to the shelter and well out of sight."

"Right," he said frowning. "Maybe Diggs and I could leave for Ascot a day early and return after your brother is gone."

"You don't have to do that." A few strawberry curls fluttered around her freckled face. "In fact, I'd like to accompany you tomorrow . . . if the invitation still stands."

He lifted her hand, turned it over, and pressed a kiss to the palm. "Poppy Summers, you have an invitation to join me anytime. Anywhere. On any adventure you like."

"I'll remember that," she said coyly. "And hold you to it."

"Nothing would make me happier," he said. To her, it might have sounded like a bit of idle flirtation, but the moment the words left his mouth, he knew they were the God's honest truth.

"There is only one catch. I'll need to concoct an excuse—a believable reason for leaving Bellehaven." She nibbled her bottom lip. "I have an idea, but it involves my dear friend, Hazel."

"The countess?"

"Yes. I don't want to lie to her. I was thinking of confiding in her and wanted to see how you felt about that."

"You trust her?"

"Absolutely," she said, emphatic.

"Then I trust her, too."

She exhaled, clearly relieved. "I'll speak with her today while I'm running a few errands in town."

"Don't worry about bringing me food today. I have plenty left, and we don't want to make your brother suspicious."

She hesitated. "If you're certain."

"There's no chance of me starving. Thanks to you and Diggs, I have enough food here to host a dinner party for ten." He squeezed her hands and released them. "I'll see you at dawn tomorrow?"

"You will." Her gaze flicked over his face, lingered on his bare chest, and headed south, roving over the ridges of his abdomen. The naked heat in her eyes made his trousers tight.

She turned, headed toward the path, then paused and faced him. "I've a feeling I shall regret this, but apparently I am a glutton for punishment." She closed her eyes briefly and exhaled before she continued. "Since I won't see you later, would you like to ask your question now?"

"Indeed I would." His pulse raced, and though she stood several paces away, he felt a powerful, magnetic energy crackling between them.

She planted her hands on her hips, expectant.

He crossed his arms, thoughtful. There were dozens of questions swirling in his head, but one in particular haunted him. It rose to the top now.

"At night," he said, "when you are alone, lying in your bed in the dark . . . do you ever think of me?"

Her cheeks turned a deeper shade of pink. "I think of a great many things, Keane."

"You did not answer the question."

She raised her chin. "Yes. I think of you."

"I think of you, too," he said huskily. "Do you want to know what I think about?"

She swallowed and nodded, almost imperceptibly.

"I think about the sweet taste of your lips . . . the satin feel of your skin . . . and the lush sound of your laugh. And I wish that you were with me."

"When I first found you on the beach, I thought you were a pirate," she mused. "Now I find myself wondering if you're more of a poet."

"Hardly," he scoffed. "But when you live in a hut by the sea, you have plenty of time to ruminate."

"Well," she said slowly, "since you shared your thoughts, I will share a few of mine."

He gazed into her eyes, shamelessly hanging on her every word.

"Sometimes at night I think about how it feels to kiss you. Like I'm standing on a cliff with my toes curled over the edge, breathless and ready to dive into deep blue waters." A wistful smile played about her mouth, and she looked at him earnestly. "I wish I could bottle it up—the wonder, the pleasure, the closeness. Do you want to know why?"

He nodded wordlessly.

"Because in my heart I know it's impossible for something that feels so lovely to last."

He opened his mouth to reply, but she was already walking toward the edge of the clearing. Already making her way up the winding path through the tall grass.

Maybe she was right. Maybe their connection burned too bright to last.

But the fuse had been lit, and he intended to follow it.

Even if it dragged him feetfirst into a powder keg of heartache.

Chapter 14

Hazel's teacup clattered on its saucer. "You're going to the Royal Ascot with a *man*?" Her expression wasn't judgmental so much as shocked.

Poppy glanced at the door of her friend's elegant drawing room to be certain no one had overheard. "I know it must seem like the height of foolishness. Perhaps it is."

Hazel deliberately set her cup on the table in front of her and stood. "I think this conversation calls for something rather stronger than tea." She walked directly to the sideboard, poured two glasses of ratafia, and returned, handing one to Poppy. "I'm glad you came to me," she said. "Tell me about this man. Is he kind? Is he honorable? And, most importantly, do you care for him?"

"He is kind and honorable in his own way." Those questions were easy to answer, but as she pondered the third, her tongue became uncooperative—like an ornery mule walking in six inches of mud.

Hazel sipped the apricot-flavored liqueur, patiently awaiting Poppy's answer. When it became apparent that none was forthcoming, she ventured, "If you are seriously considering traveling to Ascot with him, accompanied by only his valet, I must assume that you have *some* feelings for him."

"I do have feelings," Poppy admitted. "But I cannot identify them with any degree of certainty. He can be obtuse and exasperating but also charming and thoughtful. We have very little in common, and yet I'm drawn to him. I believe he's drawn to me, too."

Hazel took another large gulp of wine. "If that is the case, why isn't he properly courting you? Why must everything be so secretive?"

"It's complicated," Poppy admitted. "I can understand why you might question his motives, but he has behaved like a gentleman. And he hasn't taken advantage of me in the slightest. We started out as strangers, then became business partners of sorts. But lately, our relationship seems to have taken something of a romantic turn."

"And that is something you wish to explore further?" Hazel had a knack for getting directly to the heart of the matter.

"Yes. I know it might seem foolhardy—especially since there is no chance for a future between us. But that is precisely why I can't pass up this trip to Ascot. It may well be my last chance to experience adventure and passion before I resign myself to a mind-numbingly ordinary life in Bellehaven." Poppy nervously twirled the stem of her glass. "Do you think me completely without morals?"

Hazel blinked, aghast. "Of course not. You're following your heart. I'd do the same thing if I were in your shoes. Actually, I *did* the same thing." She set down her glass and squeezed Poppy's hand. "If I seem less than enthused about the situation it's only because I worry about how all of this will end. I don't want to see you hurt."

"Thank you," Poppy said sincerely. "That is a distinct possibility, but it's a risk I'm willing to take."

"I trust your judgment," Hazel said, adamant. "What can I do to help?"

"You've already helped tremendously, just by allowing me to confide in you. But I would like to ask one other favor."

"Of course. Shall I look in on your father while you're gone?"

Poppy shook her head. "Dane is home for a bit and will tend to him. But they will be curious as to my whereabouts. Would you mind if I told them I was staying with you for a day or two?"

"Not at all. I will be your alibi," Hazel said, "as long as you promise me one thing."

"What is that?"

"That you leave yourself open to the possibility—however remote—of love."

Poppy balked. "I don't think you understand. Love is the furthest thing from K—" She stopped herself just short of speaking his name. "From his mind *and* mine."

"Perhaps it is," Hazel said with a noncommittal shrug. "Or perhaps your feelings are like water in a kettle—still heating up, only starting to boil. Eventually, all that steam will release, and the force of it may surprise you."

"Fine." Poppy barely refrained from rolling her eyes. "I will do as you ask. But you mustn't raise your hopes too high."

Hazel beamed and held up her glass. "To daring adventures with mysterious gentlemen."

They clinked glasses, and each took a ceremonious sip of ratafia.

"Now then," Hazel said with a conspiratorial smile. "I have never been to the races; however, I understand that it's customary for the ladies to wear frothy summer gowns and delightfully whimsical hats. If you are going to embark on this adventure, I must insist that you embrace this time-honored tradition."

"I'll wear my blue dress," Poppy said with a chuckle. It was simple, but it would suffice for a daytime, outdoor event. "And I shall top it off with the smart straw bonnet you gave me."

"A straw bonnet? That will never do." Hazel clucked her tongue, stood, and clasped Poppy's wrist. "Come with me."

Oh dear. She briefly considered making up an excuse about having chores to do at home. But Hazel had a look in her eye that said she was not to be trifled with. "Where are we going?" Poppy asked.

"To my dressing room so that we may find something special for you to wear," Hazel replied, her tone brooking no argument as she strode down the corridor, Poppy in tow.

"That's really not necessary," she said. "My dress is perfectly serviceable."

"Serviceable?" Hazel repeated. "Are you even listening to yourself?"

"It's fine," Poppy said with a chuckle. "Besides, I don't wish to draw attention."

Hazel stopped abruptly and spun around to face her. "Poppy Summers, there will be no muted colors, no modest necklines, no dull, tasteful hats for you when you visit Ascot. If you're going through with this, you may as well give it your whole heart."

Poppy hesitated a beat, then smiled in resignation. "As usual, you are right. It's one of our rules, after all. Belles *always* chase their dreams."

Hazel's gaze turned soft and suspiciously watery. "Yes, we do." She sniffled and shook off the sentimentality like it was chalk dust on her fingers. "Now then, let's see what we can find in my armoire. I have one of Clara's creations in mind."

Clara was Hazel and Blade's fourteen-year-old adopted daughter—one of the orphans who attended Bellehaven Academy—and she was devilishly talented with a needle. She'd started sewing complete wardrobes for her doll and the boardinghouse cat, and before long, she'd advanced to embellishing Hazel's old gowns. Each of Clara's creations was unique, clever, and breathtakingly lovely.

"She was in a hat phase last month," Hazel explained. "She experimented with a variety of trimmings—feathers, beads, lace. Even seashells."

Poppy's heart fluttered with happiness. Not due to the gowns and hats, although she *was* looking forward to wearing one of Clara's masterpieces. It was the closeness she felt with Hazel. The prospect of experiencing something new. The anticipation of spending time with Keane.

She wasn't certain how long she'd have with him. It could be as little as a few more days or as long as a few more weeks. All she knew was that it would eventually come to an end—and she intended to enjoy it while she could.

"I can't wait to see Clara's handiwork," Poppy said. "And I plan on wearing the most gloriously ostentatious bonnet in the bunch."

"A Belle through and through," Hazel replied proudly. "Let's go."

"You're looking very dapper, Diggs," Poppy said.

Keane's valet sat across from her in the coach, every inch the gentleman in his exquisitely tailored dove-gray jacket and burgundy waistcoat. The wool top hat in his lap had a dashing red feather tucked into the band. "Dapper enough to pass for a wealthy baron?"

"Absolutely," Poppy said, confident. Diggs had driven

the coach most of the way to Berkshire, but they'd stopped at an inn a couple of miles back so that he and Keane could change into their disguises. Keane, dressed as a humble stablemaster, was now in the driver's seat holding the reins, while Diggs and Poppy rode in the cab so they could review the details of their plan.

"Tottenshire's bound to be in one of the gaming tents or in the Royal Stand," Diggs said. "We'll find him and casually engage him in conversation."

"You are Lord Bonham, a wealthy widowed baron with a sprawling estate in Sussex," Poppy recited, committing the words to memory. "You're attending Ascot for the first time and are eager for any inside information regarding the horses."

Diggs nodded. "And you are Diana, my daughter—my only child—and the apple of my eye."

"We'll make sure Tottenshire always has a drink in his hand," Poppy said, arching a brow. "Once his tongue is loosened, we'll steer the conversation to Bellehaven Bay and see if he will admit to ever having visited."

"If we're unable to determine his whereabouts on the night of the attack, we'll reveal that we are acquainted with Lord Hawking and observe what response that elicits."

"Seems simple enough," Poppy said.

"Yes," Diggs agreed. "It's extremely unlikely that anyone at Ascot will recognize us, especially dressed as we are. But I would feel better if you stayed close to my side."

"I don't intend to wander off." Poppy shot him a reassuring smile. "And as much as I appreciate your concern, Diggs, no danger will befall me. I'm quite capable of taking care of myself."

"Perhaps," the valet said with a frown. "But Tottenshire can be quite devious. You should not be alone with him."

Keane had made it a point to say the same thing during the ride, and despite the warmth of the day, the hairs on the backs of Poppy's arms stood on end. But, hoping to allay Diggs's fears, she waved a dismissive hand. "We will be in a throng of people. The earl wouldn't dare try anything untoward."

"One would hope not," Diggs said, clearly unconvinced.

Before long, the coach was rolling into Ascot, and as Poppy gazed out the window, her pulse quickened. The large racetrack was flanked by three elevated stands, with the center being the most prominent. A dozen large tents covered the adjacent field, and swarms of gaily dressed spectators strolled around the grounds. Ladies twirled their parasols; gentlemen tipped their hats. Performers on stilts towered above the crowds, and small bands of minstrels entertained onlookers with their merry songs.

The coach slowed, then stopped, and Diggs smiled at Poppy. "Ready, Diana?"

She put on her hat—a velvet peacock-blue creation embellished with sea-green beads and ivory shells—and hastily secured it with pins. "Ready, Lord Bonham," she said with a wink. "Or rather, *Papa.*"

The coach door opened, and Keane stood outside. His trousers were worn, his boots scuffed. His brown jacket stretched tightly across his shoulders and chest, and his threadbare shirt was loose at the collar, exposing a small but enticing glimpse of tanned skin. His rumpled tweed cap, which was pulled low over his forehead, was unable to contain the longish dark curls at his nape. But even his humble clothes couldn't hide his confidence and virility. Indeed, it only heightened it, and the sight of him made Poppy's knees wobble.

When he met her gaze, his full lips curled into a wicked smile. He held out a hand, and as he helped her hop to the ground, he whispered, "Your hat is the same unique color as your eyes. It will help me locate you when you're in the crowd."

"You don't need to worry. Diggs will look after me and I shall look after him."

"I know," he said, mildly chastened. "But I still wish I could be with you."

Ignoring the pitter-patter of her heart, she replied matter-of-factly. "I'll see you at the end of the day. In the meantime, you are the one who needs to have a care. If someone recognizes you, it will be difficult to explain why the Duke of Hawking is dressed as a stablehand."

He grinned. "I can think of a few people who would pay to see me mucking out the stables." He glanced around and surreptitiously raised her hand to his lips. "Enjoy the races. Enjoy the day. I'll be counting the minutes till we're together again."

With that, he released her hand, jumped back into the driver's seat, and clucked his tongue to urge the horses into a trot.

Poppy watched as the coach rolled away, then joined Diggs, who waited patiently in the shade of a nearby tree. He offered her his arm and shot her a droll smile. "Come along, Diana. We're off to the races."

Chapter 15

Poppy and Diggs soaked in the sights and sounds of the racetrack as they strolled across the grounds. Horses, led around the track by jockeys wearing jewel-colored riding costumes, whinnied and clopped their hooves. Gentlemen dressed in bright-green velvet jackets greeted passersby and steered tipsy spectators off the course. The crowd milled in and out of the large tents while chatting animatedly.

"What's happening under the tents?" Poppy asked.

"Rather more primitive entertainments," Diggs replied. "Cockfights, boxing matches, carnival shows. Would you care to see any of them?"

"No. I'd rather focus on finding Tottenshire."

"He could be in the gaming tent," Diggs said. "Shall we wander through and see if we can spot him?"

She nodded. "What does he look like?"

"Tall, fair-haired, about the same age as Hawking—and fashionably good-looking, I'm afraid."

Poppy scanned the half-dozen tables for a man matching that description. There were plenty of young gentlemen with light hair, none of whom she considered handsome. She idly wondered if Keane had spoiled her for all other men. "Do you see him?" she whispered.

"He's not here."

"Shall we check the other tents? I'm certain there are plenty of wagers being placed elsewhere."

Diggs pulled out his pocket watch and glanced at the face. "The main race will be starting within the hour. I think we should proceed to the Royal Stand. If he isn't there already, he will be soon."

They made their way to the tallest grandstand and climbed the steps leading to a large, covered platform overlooking the course. Ladies and gentlemen with fancy accents sipped bubbly champagne and exchanged witty repartee. Footmen in gold livery circulated among the guests while balancing trays of delicate watercress sandwiches and sliced fruits. Poppy swallowed and fought back a sudden wave of panic.

"Act as though you belong here," Diggs whispered.

"It's a far cry from my rowboat," she admitted. "But I shall do my best."

"There he is." Diggs faced her. "Over my left shoulder, wearing the plum-colored top hat."

Poppy flicked her gaze in that direction and found Tottenshire. He stood half a head above the crowd, flashing icy blue eyes and a wide charming smile at a trio of admiring women. "I'll lead the way."

She withdrew a fan from the reticule on her wrist as she weaved her way through the throng. When she was within earshot of Tottenshire, she began waving her fan dramatically. "I shall be *fine,* Papa. I only require a bit of space and . . ." She paused directly in front of the earl, swayed, and let her eyes flutter shut. "Oh my."

"Whoa, there." Tottenshire grasped her shoulders and held her upright. "No swooning is permitted in the Royal Stand," he quipped.

"Thank you, kind sir," Diggs said. "I've got her now."

Poppy blinked as though she didn't know quite where she was. "Papa?" she moaned.

"Right here, darling. Let's move to the railing where you'll be able to feel the breeze."

"Allow me to assist you," Tottenshire insisted. Even with her eyes half closed, she could feel the earl's gaze on her.

He and Diggs escorted her to the rear of the stand where the crowd was thinner and eased her onto a cushioned stool. "Oh," she exclaimed, fanning herself. "Forgive me for making such a spectacle. I am positively mortified."

"How many times must I tell you," Diggs said with fatherly exasperation, "that you mustn't overexert yourself?"

"Please don't fuss, Papa. Especially not in front of this fine gentleman." She looked up at Tottenshire. "I am in your debt, er . . . ?"

"Charles Draven, Earl of Tottenshire, at your service." His eyes roved over her face and lingered on her chest a tad too long.

"Lord Tottenshire," she said demurely. "You have my utmost thanks."

"Think nothing of it, Miss . . . ?"

"Miss Diana Cadbury," Diggs interjected, extending his hand. "I'm her father."

"My *doting* father," Poppy said affectionately. "Lord Bonham."

Tottenshire arched a blond brow and shook Diggs's hand. "A pleasure to meet you both. You're not from London, are you? I'm certain I would have remembered Miss Cadbury if our paths had crossed before."

"You're quite right," Diggs confirmed. "We're a bit out of our element I'm afraid. I have a small estate in Sussex."

"Papa, you're being far too modest," Poppy scolded. To

Tottenshire, she said, "He owns seven hundred acres of fertile soil, including the most productive farms in all the county. His profits doubled over last year."

Diggs chuckled nervously. "Diana, dear, it's not polite to discuss such matters in public." He shot Tottenshire an apologetic smile and said, "I fear I've involved my daughter in my business affairs more than I should. Ever since my wife passed—God rest her soul—I have allowed Diana to assist me with my accounting ledgers."

Tottenshire held up a palm, magnanimous. "There's no need to apologize, Bonham. I admire a young woman with a keen mind and an appreciation for numbers." His bold stare suggested he was equally impressed with her physical attributes.

Poppy raised her chin as though vindicated. "Thank you, my lord. It's refreshing to hear such an enlightened view."

"Is this your first time to Ascot?" the earl asked.

"It is. Papa says I may place a bet, but I don't know which horse to choose. Perhaps you could be so good as to advise me?"

Tottenshire's eyes gleamed. "I'd be happy to. In fact, why don't you and your father join me in my private box?" He hesitated, then added, "If you're feeling better, that is."

"I'm quite improved," Poppy said. "But we would not wish to impose."

"It's no imposition at all, and you'll have an excellent view of the race from there."

"Quite good of you," Diggs said. "I shall join you after I fetch a lemonade for Diana. Can I interest you in something stronger?"

"You can indeed." Tottenshire turned to Poppy and offered her his arm. "Shall we?"

She fluttered her eyelashes like a shy debutante as she

placed her hand in the crook of his elbow. "I should be delighted."

The earl escorted her to his box and introduced her to his two companions—a full-bellied squire and an inebriated viscount. Thankfully, neither of the men asked her many questions. Tottenshire seated her on his right so that she was unable to easily converse with the men, who were on his left.

As Poppy pretended to smooth her skirts, she ran a hand over the inside of her calf—just to make sure her knife was still there. Though it was unlikely Tottenshire would try anything in public, she had met plenty of men like him. She needed to keep her wits about her.

"Do you see the brown horse with the white markings on his nose and feet?" he said, pointing at the racetrack. "That's the aptly named Gunpowder. He's the popular favorite. The gray gelding behind him is Gladiator, who won the Gold Cup last year. Most people say he's lost a step, but make no mistake, he'll be a contender again today."

"They're both magnificent creatures," Poppy mused. "Which would you recommend I place my wager on?"

Tottenshire leaned close to her ear. "Neither," he said in a conspiratorial whisper. "My money is on the white filly with the gray mane—Discord. The odds are against her, but she's nimble, fiery, and unpredictable. I like her chances."

The earl was so close, she could feel his hot breath on her neck. A sinister shiver stole over her skin, and she understood why Keane had warned her about him. Indeed, she wondered if Keane was watching her now—and what he would think to see Tottenshire taking such liberties.

"If you advise me to place a wager on Discord, then that is what I shall do," she said, resolute.

"There are no assurances she'll win." He rested his elbow on the arm of her chair, crowding her to the opposite side of her seat. "But I can guarantee you that the filly will enjoy the ride."

Poppy suppressed a shudder and smiled sweetly as she handed him a ten-pound note. "Perhaps you could help me place my bet?"

The earl chuckled, took the money, marked up a card, and signaled to a lad in a blue jacket and cap. As the boy scurried away with the card and the note, Tottenshire said, "He'll register your wager and return with the receipt. Then we must hope that the filly doesn't disappoint."

"How exciting," Poppy said. "Just being here at Ascot is a thrill. It's not often that Papa and I travel outside of Sussex."

"No?" the earl drawled. "Are you so very sheltered, then?"

"I would not say that. I have been fortunate enough to visit some lovely, if somewhat provincial, locales."

"And what was your favorite, my fair Diana?"

She arched a brow but let his impertinence slide because he'd given her the perfect opening. "My favorite destination is a picturesque seaside town called Bellehaven Bay. Have you ever been there?"

Poppy studied Tottenshire's face, looking for the slightest reaction. "Bellehaven," he repeated, stroking his jaw. "I've heard of it. It's west of Brighton."

"Yes. Their annual regatta and cricket match are great fun. Papa and I stayed for a couple of weeks last summer. They had a pub with a whimsical, nautical name." She tapped a finger to her lips and pretended to search for the name. "The *Salty* something."

Tottenshire nodded, thoughtful. "The Salty Sandbar?"

"No," she said, frowning.

"The Salty Sailor?" he guessed.

"That's not it, either." The earl didn't seem to be lying. If he knew the name of the pub where Keane had been on the night he was attacked, his face gave no indication, and certainly no hint of guilt. But there was always the possibility that the earl lacked a conscience altogether.

"Ah, there's your father," Tottenshire said, sounding vaguely disappointed.

Diggs shuffled into the earl's box, turned to the footman behind him, and took a pair of drinks from the silver tray he held. "A lemonade for you," he said, handing Poppy a glass, "and a brandy for you," he continued, offering a snifter to Tottenshire.

"You must join me, Bonham," the earl cajoled.

Diggs hesitated, then relented, and helped himself to a large glass of brandy.

"Papa, the earl and I were just discussing Bellehaven Bay," Poppy said conversationally. "I was telling him about our trip there last summer."

"Delightful place," Diggs said. "I'm sure you've been."

"Can't say that I have," Tottenshire replied with an amused smile. "However, if you and Miss Cadbury plan a return trip this summer, I may have to add a visit to my schedule."

"Your calendar must be very full," Poppy said, feigning envy. "I wouldn't be surprised to hear you've already attended two house parties this summer."

"Only one, so far," Tottenshire said. "I was there a fortnight ago, but the festivities ended abruptly during a fox hunt when our host tumbled off his horse."

"Terrible," Diggs said, clucking his tongue.

"The marquess will survive, thank goodness," Tottenshire said with a shrug. "Luckily for Rutherford, he only bruised his backside—and his pride."

Poppy nodded sympathetically but made a mental note. If they could verify Tottenshire's story about the house party, he had an alibi on the night Keane was attacked.

Which meant that she and Diggs had the information they came for—and that there was no need for them to remain in the company of the earl where they risked being exposed. Besides, she was already counting the minutes until she could find Keane.

She met Diggs's gaze, and he nodded almost imperceptibly. "Diana, my dear," he said, "I had not realized the earl was entertaining friends. We should leave these gentlemen to their own devices."

"You can't leave now," Tottenshire balked. "The race starts within the hour. And you haven't even finished your brandy."

"Well, I suppose we could stay for one drink," Diggs said, obediently taking a large gulp.

Poppy wriggled to one side of her seat in an attempt to put more space between her and the earl. "When you're done, Papa, I think I would like to stretch my legs."

"There's no need to wait. I'll take you for a stroll around the tents." Tottenshire proffered his arm, and alarms sounded in Poppy's head.

"I should stay with Papa," she said. "He doesn't like me to wander off, especially in a crowd such as this."

"But you won't be alone," the earl said with a feral grin. "You'll be under my protection."

Despite her valiant efforts to remain agreeable, Poppy bristled. "I am under my *father's* protection."

"And I am certain your father trusts me," Tottenshire said. "You should, too."

She didn't reply, but merely pasted on a smile and pretended to soak in the view. In truth, she was plotting how she and Diggs could escape the box without making a scene.

"Have you placed your bet yet, Bonham?" the earl called to Diggs.

"Er, not yet."

"I'll go with you, Papa," Poppy offered.

Tottenshire narrowed his eyes at her. "If I didn't know better, I'd think you were suddenly eager to be rid of me."

"Not at all," she assured him. "I simply wish to accompany my father."

Diggs threw back the rest of his brandy and set down his glass. "Excellent. Let's be off, my dear."

"I shall escort you both there," Tottenshire said. "So there's no chance of you getting lost."

Diggs protested, but it was clear that the earl would not be deterred.

Poppy exchanged a helpless look with Diggs and allowed Tottenshire to walk them toward the betting window.

Keane set down a pail at the edge of the racetrack, took the handkerchief from his pocket, and patted the back of his neck. He'd left one set of stables under the pretense of bringing grain to another. Fortunately, the scene was so chaotic that no one questioned him or gave him specific orders.

And that left him free to search for Poppy.

He had an inkling that she and Diggs would eventually find their way to the Royal Stand, and that's where he caught a glimpse of the green beads on her hat sparkling in sunlight. She was seated near a railing overlooking the track. And the tall, blond-haired man beside her had to be Tottenshire.

The sight of him so close to her raised the hairs on the backs of Keane's arms. He reminded himself that Poppy was far from defenseless, and that Diggs was bound to be nearby. But Tottenshire was ruthless and crafty. Like a wolf circling a stray sheep, he'd be patient. He'd wait till she was unsuspecting and alone. Then he'd pounce.

As Keane watched from afar, his unease only grew. And when it appeared that Poppy was leaving her seat—with Tottenshire by her side—some instinct would not let him wait there, watching and hoping that all would be well.

He muttered a curse, pulled down the brim of his cap, and left his pail behind as he strode toward the Royal Stand.

In that moment, his world came into sharp focus, as if he'd rotated the eyepiece on a telescope and was finally able to see everything clearly.

He didn't care if he was discovered masquerading as a stablehand.

He didn't care if the earl had, in fact, almost murdered him.

All he cared about was keeping Poppy safe.

Chapter 16

Poppy eyed the large crowd in front of the betting window with dismay. Men jostled their way toward the front, eager to place their wagers before the bell sounded. "Could we have someone else place the bet for Papa? A footman, perhaps?" she asked Tottenshire.

"I suspect all of them have been called upon to place bets for others. Unfortunate, that." Ironically, he didn't sound regretful in the least. "Never fear. I'll remain here with you while your father wades into the fray. There's no sense in subjecting you to the mad crush."

"Quite right," Diggs said, a bit warily. "At least the line is moving quickly. Stay right here, and I'll return in a trice."

"Take your time, Bonham," Tottenshire drawled. "Your daughter is in good hands."

Poppy opened her mouth to tell the earl he would be wise to keep his hands to himself, but thought better of it and sighed. She supposed a few more minutes in his company wouldn't kill her.

But as she and Tottenshire watched Diggs forge his way into the crowd, a footman approached him and clapped him on the back. "By God, Diggs—it *is* you!"

Diggs cast a nervous glance in Poppy's direction. "I'm afraid you must be mis—"

"Haven't seen you in Town for a few weeks, and here you are wearing a bloody top hat, looking like some toff," he said, his booming voice carrying.

Poppy sensed the earl tense beside her.

"What the devil is going on here?" His ominous whisper made her stomach drop through her knees.

"Clearly, Papa resembles someone else," she replied, striving for a breezy tone. "The man he's talking to must be well into his cups."

"I don't think so."

Suddenly, the footman was joined by a pair of others—both of whom seemed quite familiar with him.

"Excuse me for a moment," she said smoothly. "I shall go over there and sort out this case of mistaken identity."

Tottenshire clasped his hand around her upper arm like a vise. "He's no baron," the earl said. "And he's probably not your papa, either."

"You are out of order, sir. Release me," she said through her teeth. "Or I shall cause a scene."

"And risk exposing your partner in crime? The authorities don't look favorably on servants who impersonate members of the nobility." He yanked her toward the exit. "You're coming with me."

She glanced back at Diggs, touched by the alarm on his face. "Diana!" he called out.

She schooled her expression, hoping to reassure him that she'd be fine. She'd dealt with plenty of overbearing men, and she intended to escape the earl's clutches at the first opportunity.

And, if all else failed, she had her knife.

"What were you intending to do?" Tottenshire mumbled

as he whisked her toward the back of the tents where the crowd was sparse. "Pick my pockets? Attempt to seduce me?"

"My, but you have a vivid imagination, my lord." She looked behind her, but there was no sign of Diggs, who must have lost sight of her in the tussle.

The earl dragged her behind a rickety cart holding a couple of goats and roughly backed her up against it. "Why don't you tell me who you really are," he demanded, bracing an arm on either side of her head.

"Step aside and allow me to pass," she said icily.

He leaned closer, his breath hot on her neck. "You needn't rush off on my account. In spite of your lies—or perhaps because of them—I find myself intrigued by you, *Diana*."

"You presume too much, sir." She turned her cheek to avoid his encroaching lips. "Back away at once, or—"

"Or what?" he interjected snidely.

"Or I'll do this." She jerked a knee up between his legs. Hard.

He grunted and collapsed forward, pinning her to the goat cart with his body.

She shoved at his chest, but he wouldn't budge, and in between his anguished moans, he uttered nasty threats.

Blast. She should have lunged for her knife while she had a chance. Now, she was trapped. And the earl was enraged.

She opened her mouth to scream, but he clamped a sweaty palm over her mouth.

Her heart thumped in her rib cage; panic clawed at her spine. Behind her, the goats bleated, as if they, too, realized the peril she was in.

But she would not be easily overpowered. She was prepared to fight. To bite, thrash, kick, and claw.

And then, the earl was suddenly yanked backward. Someone grabbed him by the jacket and spun him around.

"Hawking?" Tottenshire spat.

"In the flesh," Keane said, seething. Her knees wobbled with relief.

The earl sneered. "Always interfering in my trysts. Was it not enough that you absconded with my gover—"

Bam. Keane's fist connected with his mouth, and Tottenshire was laid out cold.

Keane stepped over him and reached her in two strides. He cupped her cheeks in his palms and searched her face. "Are you hurt?"

"No," she assured him, warmed by the naked concern in his eyes. "But we should find Diggs and leave at once. I last saw him in line at the betting window."

"I found him before I found you," Keane said. "I told him to meet us at the coach."

"I didn't listen." Diggs emerged from the other side of the goat cart, breathless, as if he'd been running. "I couldn't abandon Miss Summers. Or you," he added hastily.

"Thank you, Diggs. I'm fine. And, as you can see, the earl got what he deserved."

The valet scowled at Tottenshire and sniffed. "Indeed."

"The Gold Cup is about to start, and all eyes will be on the track. It's a good time to make our escape." Keane cast a questioning glance at Poppy. "Unless you'd like to stay and see the outcome of the race?"

"I think I've seen more than enough of Ascot," she said with a weak smile.

"I'm sorry I put you in danger," he said soberly.

"You didn't. It was my choice. And thanks to you, I escaped without harm." She linked an arm through Keane's as they walked in the direction of the coach, with

Diggs several paces in front of them. "It wasn't him, by the way."

He cocked his head. "What do you mean?"

"It wasn't Tottenshire who attacked you in Bellehaven."

"Poppy," he said, anguished. "Do you honestly think that I care about that right now?"

"It's why we came," she said. "I just thought you should know that we've eliminated another suspect."

"Yes," he said tightly. "I suppose we have."

Keane was mostly silent for the rest of the walk. When they finally reached the coach, he called to Diggs. "I'll drive for a while—at least until we find a spot where we can stop for dinner."

"Are you certain?" Diggs took off his top hat and stuck a finger between his neck and cravat to loosen it.

"Aye," Keane responded. "I'm in need of the fresh air."

Poppy's chest ached as she climbed into the coach. She'd thought Keane would want to spend time with her. That he'd be as eager to be alone with her as she was with him. But he was oddly distant. Uncharacteristically brooding.

Nevertheless, it was a relief to be done with the charade. She took off her hat and leaned back against the plush squabs as the coach started to roll.

As if privy to her thoughts, Diggs, who was seated across from her, clucked his tongue. "He's not cross with you. Just a bit shaken is all. Especially after what happened with the governess."

Poppy leaned forward. "The earl's governess?"

Diggs grimaced and rubbed the back of his neck. "I should not have mentioned it."

"Now that you *have* mentioned it, you must elaborate, Diggs."

He sighed and nodded, relenting. "Shortly after Tottenshire became earl, he began making unwanted overtures toward his half brother's governess."

"That's not at all difficult to imagine," Poppy said with a shudder.

"No." Diggs scowled, as if the story conjured a bad taste in his mouth. "When the governess gave her notice, he threatened to tell everyone that he'd fired her. He said that without a good reference, she'd never work in London again."

"What a monster," Poppy murmured.

"The governess is a dear friend of the duke's housekeeper and turned to her for help. The housekeeper relayed the dilemma to Hawking, and he intervened."

"How?" Poppy asked, curious about the fate of the governess—but also about any involvement Keane may have had with her.

"He found her another position. In the countryside, where Tottenshire cannot torment her. That is why the earl is so irate. He's been looking all over London for the governess, claiming that it's naught but a misunderstanding. He's begged Hawking to reveal where she is, but he, of course, refused," Diggs said with obvious pride.

Poppy pondered this for a few moments, then asked, "Why didn't he tell me?"

"The governess did not wish for her name to be printed in *The London Hearsay* or whispered as drawing room gossip. She asked him not to expose Tottenshire's depravity because she would also be exposed as his victim."

"I can understand that," Poppy murmured.

"In short, the earl is a sorry excuse for a human being," Diggs said. "But he's *not* the cretin who dumped Hawking into Bellehaven Bay."

"No, but we're getting closer and closer to the truth."

Poppy crossed her arms, more determined than ever. "I can feel it."

Shortly after sunset, Keane left the highway and pulled the coach to a stop in front of a quaint-looking inn with ancient stone walls, a thatched roof, and a trio of chimneys with smoke plumes curling above them. He hopped off the driver's seat, helped Poppy disembark, and set her portmanteau on the ground. "Are you certain you don't want to drive through the night? I can have you back in Bellehaven before morning if you'd like."

"I'm sure." Her blue-green eyes shone in the dusky light, reassuring him that in spite of her harrowing ordeal, all was well.

He nodded, turned to Diggs, and slapped several notes into his palm. "Take their best rooms and ask the innkeeper to send up dinners and hot baths. I'll tend to the horses and meet you in the taproom." He clasped the valet's shoulder, then jumped back onto the bench and picked up the reins.

A short time later, Keane walked into the inn's taproom covered in sweat, straw, and road dust. He couldn't wait to quench his thirst, wash off the grime, and slip into bed—where he'd be free to dream of Poppy.

After a quick scan of the noisy, crowded room, he found Diggs nursing a pint at a bench in the corner and took the seat opposite, where a full glass of ale awaited him. Keane took a greedy gulp, swiped his mouth with the back of his sleeve, and sighed gratefully. "You're a good man, Diggs."

The valet shifted in his seat. "Er, there's been a slight problem, Your Grace."

Keane froze, his glass halfway to his mouth. "What sort of problem?"

"There were only two rooms available."

"Bloody hell," Keane grumbled.

"My sentiments exactly, sir."

"Looks like we'll be bunking together, Diggs."

"That was my suggestion, but Miss Summers wouldn't hear of it."

Keane arched a questioning brow.

"She insists upon sharing a room with you."

Keane hesitated a beat while that sank in. "Probably because she doesn't want you sleeping in the stables."

"Perhaps," Diggs said, staring at the ring of foam in his glass. "But I don't think so."

"I'll go speak to her." He blew out a long breath. "And let her know that if anyone will be sleeping in the stables tonight, it will be me. After all, I'm the one who's dressed for it."

"Good luck, Your Grace."

Keane pressed his palms to the tabletop and stood. "Why would I need luck, Diggs?"

The valet sipped his ale, the picture of innocence. "No reason."

Chapter 17

Keane strode down the second-story hallway, paused outside the last door on the left, and knocked. "Poppy?"

"Come in," she called.

He swung open the door and stepped inside. "I appreciate your offer, but there's absolutely no way that you and I—" He halted abruptly and blinked.

Sweet Jesus. Poppy was sitting in a steaming bathtub, her glorious red curls piled high atop her head, and her satin skin glistening in the light of a candle. Whatever thought had been in his mind left it; his words dried up on his tongue. All he could do was stammer while his body responded, rather predictably, to the vision before him.

"Would you mind closing the door behind you?" she said smoothly.

"Right." He practically tripped over his own feet but managed to shut the door and drop his small leather bag on the floor. "What . . ." He raked a hand through his hair, half wondering if he was dreaming. "What are you doing?"

"I thought I'd make use of the bath until you arrived." She slid a soapy cloth down the length of one arm, lathering her skin from shoulder to wrist. "I hope you don't mind."

"Mind?" he repeated dumbly.

"The tub looked too inviting to pass up."

"No, I . . . I understand." Despite a valiant attempt to refrain from gawking, his gaze lingered on the graceful column of her neck and the round swells of her breasts. His cock grew even harder. "I probably shouldn't be here right now."

"I asked you to come in," she reminded him. "Besides, I was hoping you could help me rinse." She gestured toward a large, steaming pitcher of water at the foot of the tub.

Even if he'd wanted to, he couldn't refuse her.

He knelt behind her, lifted the pitcher, and poured a thin trickle over her shoulder. "Is it too hot?"

"No, it feels heavenly." She leaned forward and hugged her knees to her chest. "Will you rinse my back?"

Rendered mute by the nip of her waist and the subtle flare of her hips, he tipped the pitcher, watching as the water streamed down her spine, all the way to the indent at the small of her back. "How's that?" he murmured.

"Perfect." She sighed and eased herself backward, letting her neck rest on the edge of the tub. "Now the front."

"Poppy," he whispered.

"Please," she said, closing her eyes and resting her arms on the sides of the tub. "I can't remember the last time I've been so pampered."

He swallowed, wondering what he'd done to deserve such exquisite torture. "Very well." Carefully, he poured a ribbon of water over her delicate collarbone, between the fullness of her breasts, and across their taut, rosy tips. The citrus-scented lather slid off her body, revealing freshly scrubbed, freckled skin.

"You . . . are . . . beautiful," he choked out.

Her eyes fluttered open, and she smiled at him like he'd slain a dragon. "Hand me the towel?"

As he did, she rose from the tub, standing gloriously naked before him, rivulets running down her body.

"Now it's your turn," she said, gracefully wrapping herself in the towel and tucking a corner beneath her arms to secure it. He held her hand as she stepped out, and even after she was seated on a small stool, he found himself reluctant to let go. "You'll need to take off your clothes now," she said, an amused smile playing about her sensuous mouth.

"While you watch?" he rasped.

She shrugged slender shoulders. "I've seen you naked before—that morning when you were swimming in the surf."

"True enough," he said, unceremoniously tossing aside his cap, wrestling off his jacket, and hauling his shirt over his head. "But you might be seeing more of me today."

"Oh?" she arched a strawberry brow. "I confess I am intrigued. But we should not waste time talking. The water will grow cold."

A little cold water might have helped matters, actually, but he had nothing to hide. He tucked his thumbs inside his waistband and shot her a warning look. "Here goes."

"I shall try not to swoon," she quipped.

But when he shoved his trousers over his hips and let them drop to the floor, she did stare. And she blushed before quickly regaining her composure. "Into the tub," she ordered, pulling up the stool behind him.

He sank into the warm water and sluiced handfuls over his chest and arms—until he felt her soft palms settle on his shoulders. "Lie back and relax," she said, her breath puffing softly against his earlobe. "Let me do this."

He did as she asked, closing his eyes as she poured water

over his head and massaged his scalp till it tingled. When his hair was washed and rinsed, she used a soft cloth to clean his face and neck. She hummed softly while she tended to the rest of him. With deliberate strokes, she lathered the planes of his chest and the ridges of his abdomen. She kneaded the muscles of his back and shoulders and brushed her lips across his nape.

"Poppy," he groaned. "I came up here to tell you that you don't have to share your bed with me. I can bunk with Diggs."

"Wouldn't you rather stay here with me?" she asked simply.

He turned and faced her. "I'd rather be here with you than any other place on this earth," he said solemnly. "But I don't want either one of us to get hurt."

"Hurt is inevitable," she whispered. "I would hurt if you left me tonight. I will hurt when you leave me tomorrow. Or the week after that. But we have tonight."

He hesitated, and her words hung in the air around them. "I'll stay with you tonight," he said soberly. "Hell, I'll stay with you as long as you let me. You make it sound as though I'm the one who will eventually walk away from this—from us—but I don't think that's true."

"No?" She slowly slid the washcloth up his torso, over his shoulders, and down his back.

"No," he repeated, refusing to be distracted. "I think you'll push me away. That no matter how much I try to weasel my way into your heart, you'll lock me out."

"You're here now." She wrung out the cloth, picked up the pitcher, and poured the last of the warm water over his body. "And I'm not pushing you away."

Keane looked into her eyes, gripped the sides of the tub, and slowly rose.

Poppy tried very hard to maintain her composure, but this was much different from the time that she'd seen him naked on the beach. Now, he was close. So close that she could see the subtle flexing of muscles in his chest, forearms, and abdomen.

And that was not all she saw. Her gaze slid south, over narrow hips, taut buttocks, and his long, hard—

"Hand me a towel?" His wicked grin suggested he knew the direction of her thoughts—and didn't mind her curiosity in the slightest.

While she looked for another bath sheet, he casually stepped out of the tub, dripping all over the floor. "You could always give me yours," he teased.

"We have a spare." Her cheeks heated as she tossed it to him. He used one corner to scrub his hair dry, then slung the towel around his hips. Between the dark stubble on his jaw and the cut above his brow, he looked far too rugged to be a duke. With a helmet and spear, he could have easily passed for a Roman gladiator.

And the sight of him left her breathless.

He stood facing her, a question in his eyes.

"I'm glad you're here," she said.

"I am, too." He took a step closer and cupped her cheek in his palm. "This is much better than the stables."

"I think I misjudged you. Again," she admitted.

His forehead creased. "How so?"

"I assumed that the animosity between you and Lord Tottenshire stemmed from something trivial—like a gaming debt or some imagined slight. But Diggs told me about his governess . . . and what you did for her."

He scoffed. "She was the courageous one. I only helped to find her another position. It's what any gentleman would have done."

"Not any gentleman," she protested, very aware that

they were separated by nothing more than their towels. "You helped protect her from Tottenshire. And this afternoon, you did the same for me."

"When he cornered you and refused to let you pass . . ." He cursed under his breath. "I thought my head would explode with rage."

She brushed a damp lock away from his forehead. "I wish I'd reached for my knife earlier," she said. "But no harm came to me, and the earl got what he deserved."

"He's lucky to be alive," Keane grumbled.

She smiled, touched by his protective streak. "You displayed admirable restraint."

"I did." His eyes turned dark, and he tipped his forehead to hers. "But that was nothing compared to the restraint I'm showing right now."

"What if you could do anything you wanted?" she murmured. "What would you do?"

"That's easy. I'd start by kissing you."

She circled her arms around his neck. "Then do it."

The words were scarcely out of her mouth before his lips descended on hers in a kiss that was hungry. Primitive. Wild.

All the passion they'd been bottling up overflowed, carrying them along for the ride.

His fingers tangled in her hair. Her nails raked down his back.

Their bodies collided in a tempest of desire, longing, and bliss.

The connection between them was improbable, powerful, and utterly inevitable. She'd tried to resist the pull; so had he. But now that she was in his arms, she realized how perfectly they fit—physically *and* emotionally. Keane may not have been the sort of man she'd dreamed of, but he was proving to be exactly the man she needed.

His tongue plundered her mouth, and his hands roved over her bottom, melding her hips to his. "Poppy," he murmured. "I'm hopeless with words and even worse when it comes to feelings. But I am rather good at other things." He traced a small circle at her nape, leaving no doubt in her mind as to his area of expertise. "I want to show you what you mean to me."

"I don't need poetry," she said, gazing into his eyes. "I don't want flowery declarations. I just need you to hold me tonight . . . while I hold onto you."

With a low growl, he scooped her into his arms, crushed her against his warm, naked chest, and strode toward the bed as if she weighed no more than the towel that covered her. Carefully, he deposited her on the soft mattress, resting her head on a plump feather pillow. She shifted to one side, making room for him, and he stretched out beside her.

They lay there, face to face, for several heartbeats, their breath mingling sweetly in the scant space between them. His broad shoulders and muscled torso were burnished by the dim lamplight, and the shadows accentuated the sharp angles of his face. He was strength, masculinity, and power personified.

But more than anything, it was the surprising softness in his eyes that captivated her. He gazed at her as though he knew her inside and out—and adored her just as she was. At the same time, his face was completely unguarded, as if he was inviting her in for a rare and unexpected tour of his soul.

That vulnerable look in his eyes melted her heart. Shifted her world.

And she suspected she'd never be quite the same.

At last, he brushed a kiss across her lips and trailed a wicked fingertip along the curve of her shoulder. "I have a confession. I'd like this towel better if it were anywhere else."

She smiled, tugged it loose, and let it fall away. "No more hiding, at least for tonight."

He sucked in a breath and froze as if he were momentarily stunned. "No more hiding," he repeated in a gravelly voice. "We've come a long way, haven't we? I can recall a not-so-distant time when you wouldn't even tell me your name."

"Look at us now," she said breathlessly.

His deep, low chuckle made her belly flutter. "I could look at you forever, Poppy Summers."

She placed a palm on his chest and felt his heart thumping as fast as hers. Her gaze dropped to his mouth, and all she could think of was that she wanted him to kiss her.

As if he knew, he hauled her close and pressed his lips to hers, sparking a tempest. She'd known it was a powerful thing—the attraction between them. But she'd assumed she'd be able to control it. That she could play at the edges without letting it consume her.

She'd been quite mistaken.

Every lingering kiss, every sensual caress dragged her deeper into the vortex and left her craving more. More skin on skin. More tangling of tongues. More of *him*.

Greedily, she ran her hands over his shoulders and down his back, savoring the subtle flex of his muscles beneath her fingers. He may have been a duke, but underneath his expensive clothes he was pure man. And tonight, he was hers.

He trailed kisses down her neck and lower, his damp hair feather-soft against her chest. When she arched toward him, he cupped her breast and took the taut tip in his mouth, sucking till she shimmered with pleasure.

His hips rocked against hers, sparking a sweet, insistent pulsing in her core. She clung to him as he caressed the inside of her thigh, moaned as he circled the sensitive spot between her legs. And when he finally touched her, she trembled with desire.

Keane was able to read her like a map, his hands and mouth traveling over the terrain of her body as if he meant to discover all her secrets.

As if he intended to explore every square inch of her heart.

He gazed at her with heavy-lidded eyes and nibbled a course down her belly, around her navel, and lower. She had an inkling of what he was about to do, having once seen it depicted in a book, and she shivered in anticipation.

But she was wholly unprepared for the intense pleasure that shot through her with the first touch of his tongue. Her hips lifted off the mattress and her fists gripped the sheets. Tiny whimpers erupted from her throat as need and desire spiraled in her core.

Keane stayed with her. Dedicated himself to pleasing her. Urged her to give into the bliss that beckoned. And when it all became too much, she did.

All the feelings she'd been denying, all the emotion she'd been holding back crashed ashore like a tidal wave . . . and it carried her away. Delicious tremors pulsed through her, lifting her higher and higher till there was nowhere else to go. She shattered into a million droplets, light and free as a sea spray mist.

When Keane laid beside her and pulled her to his chest, she knew she'd found a safe harbor. At least for that night.

"Are you all right?" he murmured into her hair.

Heavens. "I will be, once I recover sufficiently to move my limbs." More seriously, she added, "That was rather like a dream."

"A good dream, I hope?"

"The best." She glanced down at the towel still draped across his waist, saw the evidence of his arousal beneath it, and tugged on the loose knot near his hip.

"Poppy," he said, his voice ragged.

She pressed a kiss to the hollow of his throat. "May I?"

He made a sound that was half chuckle, half groan. "Yes. The answer is always *yes*."

Chapter 18

Poppy's nimble fingers made short work of the knot in Keane's towel, and when it fell away, she flashed a smile that was both sensual and triumphant. That look alone would have made his cock go hard—if it wasn't already.

She slid a supple thigh between his legs and tentatively curled her fingers around his shaft. He sucked in a breath. Tried to maintain a shred of control.

But it wasn't easy. Not when she was unabashedly stroking him, exploring his body, and writhing against him. Not when she was nipping at his shoulder, licking his ear, and sucking his lower lip. With every soft moan, with every touch, she was demanding more, and he was more than happy to oblige.

This was a side of Poppy he'd never seen. Tonight, there was no hesitation, no reservation, no running away. It was as if she was finally discovering what he'd suspected all along—that they would be amazing together.

She slid her hand up and down his length, bringing him to the brink. Blood pounded through his veins and every muscle in his body coiled tight, primed for release. And then she licked a path down his torso. Flicked her tongue over the ridges of his abdomen. Took him into her warm mouth.

He growled. Felt his eyes roll back in his head. Said her name over and over. And when he couldn't hold back any longer, he pulled away, spending himself on the towel.

While he tried to catch his breath, she searched his face, uncharacteristically unsure.

"Was that . . . ?"

"Perfect in every way." He gazed into her eyes, trying to convey a measure of what he felt for her. "Now I'm the one who can barely move."

"Good." She smiled smugly. "Since neither of us is capable of leaving this bed, I suppose we'll have to stay here all night."

"I can think of worse fates." He closed his eyes for a couple of minutes, trying to tattoo the memory on his heart. The perfection of her body nestled against his. The sweetness of their breath mingling as they talked. The sublime satisfaction of knowing he'd made her happy.

"I confess there is one reason I am tempted to venture out of bed."

"What is that?"

"Food." She sat up, a riot of auburn curls framing her face. "I'm famished. The dinner tray is still sitting on the table by the door."

"Easily remedied." He leaped out of bed, fetched the tray, and placed it on the mattress beside her. "It might be a little cold. Shall I ask for a new plate?"

"I don't mind cold shepherd's pie, and there's plenty here for us to share." She savored a bite, then offered him a forkful of minced meat and potatoes smothered in gravy.

They took turns feeding each other until there wasn't a morsel left on the plate, and they washed it down with a glass of ale.

"I confess I've never eaten dinner naked before." She patted her lips primly with a napkin. "I'm quite certain that the Bellehaven Academy of Deportment frowns upon this sort of thing."

"No doubt," he said. "That's what makes it fun."

She laughed and rubbed the tops of her arms.

"Are you chilled? I have a clean shirt you could sleep in." He rummaged through his bag, handed her the shirt, and relished the sight of her slipping it over her head. Her petite frame swam in the white lawn, covering her from chin to mid-thigh.

"Thank you. It's so soft that I don't mind looking a bit ridiculous."

"You could not be more beautiful," he said sincerely. "Not if you were dressed in a ball gown meant for a princess." He tidied the room, turned the lamp low, and slid into bed beside her. Raucous laughter and music from the taproom below drifted up through the window as they snuggled beneath the covers. "It's been a long day. Are you tired?"

"A little." The corner of her mouth curled into a soft smile. "But I don't really want to sleep, because then morning will come too soon."

"Then we'll stay awake all night and talk."

"We could do other things." She ran her palms down his chest and kissed the side of his neck.

His body, very much in favor of the suggestion, responded immediately and enthusiastically. But he was recalling the night on the beach when they'd kissed. "Do you remember what you told me that night in the shelter," he asked, "about escaping the riptide?"

"I do," she said with a resigned sigh. "We said we'd take things slowly."

"I wouldn't change a thing about tonight, but perhaps we should tread water for a while."

"I don't regret anything, either." She laced her fingers

through his. "But I think you are probably right. We should content ourselves with this." She closed her eyes and wriggled close to him, resting her head in the crook of his arm while he ran his fingers through her hair.

Gradually, her breathing slowed and her limbs grew heavy.

"Poppy Summers," he whispered.

She didn't respond right away, and he feared she was already asleep. But then she stirred. "Yes?" she asked groggily.

"It's time for your question."

"Mmm." She yawned. "Very well."

"One day, when all of this is over, will you introduce me to your family?"

She propped herself on one elbow and gazed into his eyes. Something in their blue-green depths told him that he wasn't going to like her answer. "Why?"

"Because I'd like to meet the people who are closest to you." He was going to add that he'd like to tell her father his intentions, but given her hesitation, it made more sense to proceed slowly. "Unless there's a reason you don't want them to meet me?"

She went very still. "It's rather complicated," she said. "My father and brother are very protective. They don't want to see me hurt."

"I understand that. I respect that. And I would never want to hurt you," he said firmly.

"I believe you." Her eyes shone with regret. "But it would be difficult to convince them."

"This has to do with the incident you mentioned earlier. When a member of the nobility mistreated someone you love?"

She tensed as if he'd crossed an invisible but distinct line. "Yes."

"Maybe if you explained it to me, I'd be able to allay their fears—and yours."

"I want to confide in you," she said, swallowing. "But it's difficult for me to talk about. I'm not certain it's the right time."

Her whole body shivered as if she'd taken a sudden chill, and he pulled the quilt tightly over her. "I know you're still worried that I won't understand—at least not with my heart. But I'm going to win you over, Poppy. I'll prove you can trust me with your pain as well as your joy."

She said nothing but nodded, rubbing her smooth cheek against his chest, wetting it with silent tears.

The next day, Keane was back on the beach, sweating in the afternoon sun as he worked on the chairs he was building from driftwood and rope. The tripod bases were sturdy, but the seats still needed to be planed and sanded before they'd be functional.

He would have liked to comb the beach for more wood, but since Poppy had asked him to stay close to the shelter, he was searching the area around the clearing and just off the path that led to the road. He walked several yards into the tall grass, bent over to pick up a large stick, and froze at the sound of a low whistle that was growing louder by the second.

Someone was walking down the path. Poppy had planned to have tea with her friends, and Diggs wasn't a whistler, so Keane continued crouching in the reeds, trying to stay out of sight.

A young, burly man sauntered closer. He hauled a large oilskin sack over one shoulder and held a basket against the opposite hip. His work clothes were worn and stained, and his cap was faded from the sun. The hair at his temples was brown, with a hint of red. And his skin, though tanned, was as freckled as Poppy's.

He had to be her older brother, and Keane was intensely curious about him.

He looked like the sort of bloke one could enjoy a glass of ale with. The sort who could spin a riveting tale, dance a drunken jig, and win a brawling pub fight—all in one night.

Suddenly, the breeze shifted, a seabird cawed overhead, and the whistling stopped. The man halted only a few yards away, set the basket on the ground, and looked around warily.

Keane held his breath and prepared to be discovered. He had no idea what he'd say to Poppy's brother. How he'd explain his presence on the beach without implicating her.

The man muttered something under his breath and swiped his brow with the back of his wrist, which had a vivid red handkerchief knotted around it.

Keane had the eeriest sensation that he'd seen that handkerchief before.

His spine tingled like he'd trod on a grave—and that grave was his own.

A series of memories flickered through his mind like snippets from a waking dream.

The distant sounds of the pub mingling with the roar of the ocean.

The shuffle of boots approaching from behind.

A beefy forearm clamped around his neck, crushing his windpipe.

And on the wrist that was wedged beneath his chin—a red handkerchief.

He jabbed his right elbow hard into the side of his attacker. Heard the crack of a rib and an oath. Thought he might be able to overpower the brute.

But then searing pain ripped into his skull. Everything went black.

Holy hell.

Poppy's brother was the man who had tried to kill him.

"I can hardly believe it, but Papa's shown marked improvement since Dane returned home." Poppy sat at a corner table in the Bellehaven Tea Shoppe talking with Hazel and Kitty. "He's even felt strong enough to venture outside a few times. Dane said Papa walked halfway to the beach yesterday and is determined to make it to the ocean by week's end."

"How wonderful." Hazel brushed aside the errant curl dangling in front of her forehead. "Walking on the beach always restores me and makes me feel better somehow."

"Will Dane be staying long?" Kitty asked. She'd piled her blond curls high atop her head, making her look like a more sophisticated, stylish version of herself.

"No. He's returning to the London docks in a couple of days. He can earn much more as a dockhand than he can catching fish." Poppy took a sip of hot tea and attempted a breezy tone. She didn't want to dampen the sunny mood by dwelling on her struggles. Diseased fish. Falling market prices. The struggle of running the business on her own. "It's probably for the best. This way I'll be blissfully ignorant of all the trouble he's getting into."

Hazel's shrewd gaze saw through the façade. "It cannot be easy being the sole caretaker for your father while you earn a living with your nets. I have the utmost admiration for you, Poppy, but I do wish you'd let Blade and me offer some assistance. You and your father are both welcome in our home."

"What a grand idea!" Kitty said, beaming. "Three Belles under one roof. Think of it. We could braid each other's hair, gossip about handsome gentlemen, and have fantastic rows over gowns—just like proper sisters do."

Poppy smiled, deeply touched. "I adore you both for your kind offer, but Papa's too proud to leave his cottage. Besides, it's where he feels closest to Mama. He says she had hands as busy as the ocean and a smile as warm as the sunrise."

"Beautiful," Kitty said with a sigh. "I hope that one day I shall inspire that sort of devotion in a man."

"I've no doubt you will—but not for a few years," Hazel added pointedly. Turning to Poppy, she said, "What about you? You always have a slew of gentlemen vying for your attention. Has any man succeeded in capturing your affections?"

She hesitated then exhaled. "Perhaps."

Kitty gasped and clattered her teacup. "Who?"

Poppy's face heated. "You are not acquainted with him, but his identity does not matter, as there is no chance of a future with him."

Kitty leaned forward and whispered, "Is he married?"

"No!" Poppy replied, aghast.

Kitty frowned, then placed a palm over her chest. "Is he on his deathbed?"

"What? No."

"Then I'm afraid I don't understand the problem," Kitty said with a shrug. "If he is fond of you and you are fond of him, you should be together."

"Matters of the heart aren't always so simple," Hazel said, sympathetic. "Even when they should be."

Poppy fiddled with the handle of her teacup. How could she explain to her friends that trusting Keane with her heart would make her feel as though she was betraying the memory of her mother? She'd vowed that she'd never again place herself or her family at the mercy of the ton.

That she'd never again subject herself to the pain and humiliation of being summarily dismissed, brushed aside as if she wasn't worthy of basic human kindness.

And yet, Keane had given her no reason to mistrust him.

He'd asked to meet her family, and she could think of no reason why he would want to do that. Unless . . .

"Well, if you want to know my advice," Kitty said, sounding surprisingly sage, "a man who is worth his salt will fight for you."

"And when you reach an impasse, where it appears that the two of you have no future," Hazel added, "he'll stand by your side and help you find a way forward. Together, you'll clear a path. You'll carve out the one that was meant to be."

Poppy wavered. "If I told you his name, you'd understand the impossibility of a match."

They stared at her, expectant.

"Andrew Keane," she said, swallowing. "The Duke of Hawking."

Chapter 19

"Let us hope you never have to make your living as a carpenter," Diggs said wryly. He cast a critical eye at one of the chairs Keane had made, then lowered himself onto the seat as if he feared it would swallow him whole.

"You're welcome to sit on the ground if you prefer," Keane said. "But then you'd have to deal with the crabs."

Diggs cautiously leaned back, crossed his ankles, and nodded, mildly impressed. "It's more comfortable than it looks," he admitted. "Which isn't saying much."

Keane chuckled and sat in the chair across from him. "I can always count on you to be brutally honest," he said. "Which is why I need to speak with you."

His friend arched a brow. "Sounds serious."

"It can't leave this beach," Keane said soberly.

"Understood."

Keane hesitated a beat, oddly reluctant to speak the words. But failing to say them wouldn't make them any less true. "I figured out who attacked me," he started.

Diggs's nostrils flared, his hands fisted. "Who?"

Keane exhaled. "Dane Summers—Poppy's brother."

Diggs blinked like someone had poured a bucket of cold water over his head. "No."

The dismay in his voice mirrored Keane's own. "Yes."

His friend's gaze flicked to the ground between them, and his forehead creased as he struggled to make sense of the news. "Are you certain?"

Keane nodded. "I saw him as he walked to the beach this morning. It was him."

"Why? Why would he do it?"

It was the question that Keane had been asking himself all day. "I don't know."

"You're not going to like what I'm about to say." Diggs dragged a hand down his face. "Hell, I can barely bring myself to say it."

"Go on," Keane said, bracing himself.

"I think we must consider the possibility, however repugnant, that Dane and Poppy Summers are involved in some sort of nefarious scheme."

Keane shook his head firmly. "Maybe Dane, but not Poppy."

"Think about it," Diggs urged. "Her brother bashes your head, and just a few hours later, she discovers you on the beach."

Keane scoffed. "To what end?"

"Clearly, their family is in need of funds. Perhaps they were desperate enough to kidnap you."

"Ridiculous. They didn't even attempt to ask for ransom."

"They didn't have to." Diggs rubbed the back of his neck and waved a hand at the shelter behind them. "You offered Miss Summers a large sum of money for room and board."

"No." Keane stood and started to pace. "She didn't even want me here in the beginning. She didn't believe I was a duke."

"The truth is that I am very fond of Miss Summers. I

abhor the notion that she and her brother might have concocted a plot to . . ." His voice trailed off.

"To what?" Keane demanded.

Diggs met his gaze, his expression regretful. "To swindle you."

His skin prickled, as if his whole body rejected the very idea.

"Poppy would never do that—to me or to anyone," he said, brimming with a potent mix of conviction and outrage.

Diggs leaned his elbows on his knees and proceeded with due caution. "You must admit it's a rather extraordinary set of circumstances that led you to your current predicament. You have no doubt that her brother was the one who attacked you?"

"None. He has a handkerchief tied around his wrist. It's distinctive. Worn, but with a bright red floral pattern. As soon as I saw it, I recalled seeing it on the arm of my attacker."

Diggs rubbed his head, skeptical. "Perhaps the handkerchief is more common than you think."

"I doubt it's a typical fashion choice among dock workers weighing eighteen stone," Keane reasoned. "Besides, I watched him fishing earlier. He was favoring his right side as he cast his nets."

Diggs shrugged. "I don't follow."

"I fought back the night I was attacked. My right elbow cracked his rib."

"But you still can't recall exactly how you came to be washed up on the beach?"

Keane shook his head.

"Then it seems an unlikely coincidence that Miss Summers found you." Diggs pulled a small flask out of his chest pocket, took a swig, and offered it to Keane.

He tipped back the flask, letting the brandy burn a trail down his throat and into his chest. But it wasn't strong enough to numb the ache that had taken up residence there.

"Forgive me for saying this," Diggs continued, "but perhaps you don't know her quite as well as you imagine."

"I know her," Keane said, adamant. Granted, she seemed intent on guarding a few secrets from him. And she *was* reluctant to have him meet her family, but she must have a good reason. She'd confide in him one day, and then it would all make sense.

He stalked across the clearing and stared at the ocean, where the turbulent waves mirrored the churning in his stomach. But he refused to accept that Poppy was anyone other than the woman he knew.

The woman who had pulled him out of the surf and bandaged his head with her own scarf.

Who'd run through the streets of London with him while they wore makeshift togas.

Who'd kissed him in her shelter while a storm raged outside and who'd murmured his name in her sleep.

He knew Poppy Summers—she was the woman he *loved*.

With that sudden, unexpected realization, all his doubts receded, his demons quieted.

He loved Poppy, and he trusted her. With his life. With his heart.

Diggs walked up from behind and clasped his shoulder. "Are you all right?"

Keane shot him a half smile. "I'm not contemplating flinging myself off the cliff, if that's what you're wondering."

"Glad to hear it. I'm sorry if I spoke too candidly."

"You didn't," Keane scoffed. "I came to you because I knew you'd be frank with me. Thank you."

"You're welcome," Diggs said gruffly.

"But you're dead wrong about Poppy," Keane said. "She wasn't involved in the attack, and she's not a part of any scheme. I'll wager someone hired Dane to knock me out and throw me in the bay."

"You could be right," Diggs said with a wry chuckle. "Fortunately, there's an easy way to resolve the matter. We confront Dane Summers and demand answers."

Keane crossed his arms and faced his friend. "No."

Diggs's bushy brows bounced halfway up his forehead. "Pardon?"

"Poppy's family means everything to her. I don't want to create any strife between me and her brother."

"Strife?" Diggs repeated, incredulous. "He almost killed you! You cannot allow such a heinous act to go unpunished. He must be handed over to the authorities at once."

"It's not subject to debate," Keane said evenly. "I won't confront him or notify the magistrate until I know the full story. Poppy respects her brother, which means he must have had good cause for what he did."

"What he did was to try to send you to an early grave." Diggs rolled his eyes heavenward and took another swig from his flask.

"I need to figure out why he attacked me. Who hired him."

"It would be infinitely easier to obtain those answers if you'd allow me to have a heart-to-heart chat with him." Diggs flexed his fingers, cracking a few knuckles and leaving no doubt as to the nature of the chat he had in mind.

"I'll find out another way," Keane said. "The truth will come to light." He just hoped that when it did, it wouldn't destroy his hopes for a future with Poppy.

"Did Dane see you this morning?"

"I don't think so. Poppy said he'd be in Bellehaven for a few days but will be returning to London soon. Perhaps as soon as tonight."

"That's good," Diggs said. "The last thing we want is for him to discover you're still alive."

"Actually, I think I'm ready to rejoin the land of the living."

"Now, of all times?" Diggs sputtered. "Are you mad?"

"I'll spend one more night here in the shelter," Keane said. "Then I'll move back into a room at the Bluffs' Brew."

Diggs scratched his head. "How will you explain your prolonged absence?"

"I'll say I was visiting a friend in the country for a few weeks. We can make it sound like it's an eccentric tendency of mine to disappear for days on end without informing anyone."

"Whoever hired Dane—assuming that someone did—is bound to hear that you're very much alive. What if they send someone else to finish the job?"

"He won't catch me off guard this time," Keane said. "Regardless, I'm through hiding. Maybe the best way to identify the culprit is to lure him with bait."

"And *you're* the bait?" Diggs asked, clearly skeptical.

"Right," Keane said. "With a little patience, we'll catch ourselves the big fish."

The moon was high in the sky by the time Poppy was able to go to Keane. After spending the better part of two days with him, she'd become rather accustomed to having him near. She'd missed him. There'd been a shift last night—something that transcended the physical. And she couldn't wait to see if he'd felt it, too.

But in addition to her usual chores, she'd had to say

goodbye to Dane, who was returning to London on the mail coach, and Papa had been especially talkative, so it had taken her a bit longer to surreptitiously prepare a basket of food to bring Keane.

The path to the clearing was so familiar to her that she had no difficulty navigating it, even in the dark. When she emerged into the clearing, Keane was waiting for her.

He swept her into his arms, basket and all, and spun her around as though he hadn't seen her in a fortnight. She couldn't recall a time when her heart had ever felt so light. So free.

"This welcome leads me to believe you've been anxiously awaiting your dinner," she quipped.

"I've been anxiously awaiting *you*." Reluctantly, he set her feet on the ground and presented her with a huge bouquet of pink sweet peas, golden wildflowers, and feathery reeds bound with a bow fashioned from long shoots of grass. "The best I could do, given the current circumstances," he said, apologetic.

She buried her nose in the fragrant blossoms. "I couldn't love them more."

He shot her a lopsided grin. "Then I shan't bother with hothouse flowers in the future."

"Here you are," she said, handing him the dinner basket. "It's a few slices of roast along with potatoes, carrots, and leeks. You should eat before it grows cold."

"I'll save it for later." He set the basket near the door of the shelter and took her by the hand. "There's something I want to discuss with you tonight."

"What do you mean?"

"Shall we sit on the big rocks?" he suggested.

A frisson of foreboding stole over her skin. "If you'd like."

He scooped up a lantern, led her to the boulders, and

helped her climb onto the flat surface. He clambered up beside her and gazed out at the inky infinity of the sea.

"My brother is on his way back to London," she said in a desperate and blatant attempt to avoid weightier topics.

Keane hesitated a beat, then said, "Were you sad to see him go?"

"Papa was delighted to have him home, and I liked having his help. But we both knew he was only visiting. He's promised to be a better correspondent, but we'll be lucky if he writes a three-sentence missive once a month." She chuckled to herself. "He's not much of a writer, but he has a good heart."

Keane's gaze flicked away. "I hope you and your father won't have to wait too long before he visits again."

"At least it makes things less complicated where you're concerned. Now that he's gone, we needn't worry that he'll happen upon you here or on the beach. And it's easier for me to slip out of the cottage and bring the things you need."

"As it happens, that is what I wanted to talk to you about," he said slowly.

"There's something else you need?"

"No." He reached for her hand and laced his fingers with hers. "I think the time has come for me to leave your beach."

She stared at him, dumbfounded. She'd known this day would come, of course. It was inevitable. And yet, it felt as though a six-foot wave had unexpectedly slammed into her back and knocked her to her knees.

He could have mentioned something during their trip to Ascot. He could have given her some warning.

"I don't understand. What about your plan?" She croaked out.

"Plans change," he said with a philosophical shrug.

"Are you going to give up on finding your attacker?" she asked. But what she truly wanted to know was: *Are you going to give up on us?*

"No, but it's time I took a different tack. If I come out of hiding, perhaps the facts will come to light."

"Why now?"

He glanced away, as if the question had touched a nerve. Almost as if he was hiding something from her.

At last, he said, "I would stay here if I could, but I have imposed on you for too long. You've had to keep the truth from your friends, your family. You've had to juggle taking care of me with all your other chores. But it wasn't until your brother unexpectedly came home that I realized just how risky this situation is for you. That's why I have to go."

He released her hand, reached into his jacket pocket, and placed a heavy pouch on her palm. "It's the rest of the money I owe you, along with some extra to repay you for your help in London and in Ascot."

She dropped the pouch on the rock, and the clink of the coins grated like the scrape of fingernails across a slate. "You don't need to pay me extra," she said. "It was my choice to travel with you on those days."

He shook his head. "I know, but I kept you from working. The least I can do is replace your lost profits."

She swallowed, wondering if this was how it was going to end. Diggs would come to retrieve him and all his things from her shelter. They'd drive away and, in time, she'd be little more to him than a name in his accounting ledger. A woman to whom he'd paid a considerable sum. A woman with whom he'd spent an amusing summer.

But this wasn't really about money, and she wouldn't let him reduce their relationship to a series of payments. "Will you be returning to London?"

"I thought I'd stay in Bellehaven for a while."

Her pulse quickened. "So that you may pursue your attacker?"

He lifted her hand and pressed a kiss to the back. "So I may pursue *you*."

His words reverberated in her head, giving wings to the hope that cowered in her heart. "Then why have you decided to leave, Keane? Why now?"

"Because as long as I'm hiding here, I cannot publicly court you—and that is what I intend to do."

She gaped, as if his words would make more sense once they sank in. But they did not.

"You must know that is impossible."

"Not at all," he said wryly. "Despite some indications to the contrary, I'm quite capable of behaving like a gentleman. I'll admit that the start of our relationship was unconventional, but there's nothing preventing us from furthering our acquaintance in the more traditional way."

"You seem to have forgotten that I am not a lady," she said, lifting her chin. "And I've no desire to be one."

He gazed at her, earnest. "I would never want you to be anyone other than who you are."

Her hackles lowered a fraction. "Most of the ton would shun a fisherman's daughter—and they'd shun you for associating with me."

"I've no wish to associate with anyone that narrow-minded," he said with a casualness that, ironically, could only stem from the fact that he'd been destined for a dukedom from before he took his first breath.

"Perhaps not, but those are your peers. That is your world. It isn't mine."

He heaved a sigh. "I won't deny we're from separate worlds, but I think you dwell on it far too much."

In the blink of an eye, she was back on the doorstep

of the woman who was her aunt—at least by blood—shivering in the chilly rain, begging for an ounce of compassion. And when her aristocratic relatives refused to grant Poppy an audience, she'd huddled next to the steps with her knees tucked against her chest. She'd stayed awake all night, partly because her fingers and toes were numb and partly because she could still hear Mama's fevered cries—the ones where she called out for her older sister.

That was the reason Poppy was acutely aware of the vast divide between a fisherwoman and a duke. She'd have as much luck bridging that divide as she would swimming across the English Channel.

"You are right," she conceded. "The differences between us are never far from my mind. Suffice it to say I have my reasons."

"I don't doubt it," he said soberly. "And one day, you'll trust me enough to confide in me." He paused, clearly hopeful that today would be that day. Alas, it was not.

She *wanted* to tell him everything. To open her heart to him and see if he'd do the same. But his decision to leave the shelter seemed so abrupt. She couldn't help feeling as though he was hiding something of import from her.

They stared at the ocean for several moments, letting the low roar of the waves fill the silence between them.

"Please don't give up on us," he whispered. "Because I certainly have not."

"I don't know how we move forward from here."

"Slowly," he said. "One day at a time. I'll be staying at the Bluffs' Brew. Maybe we'll have a chance meeting while shopping in town or walking on the beach. We can go for a cup of tea or watch a cricket match together."

"After all we've been through, it seems as though we'd be taking a step backward."

"I don't see it that way," he said. "For the last few weeks, our relationship has been like a rosebush in a hothouse, growing and thriving in this perfect, private sanctuary. But now it's time to venture outside."

"What if we can't survive out there?"

"We will," he said with impressive confidence. "As long as we don't sabotage things ourselves."

She nodded mutely. It seemed Keane knew her better than she knew herself. She *was* tempted to sabotage their relationship. To blow it up like a keg of gunpowder rather than witness its slow and tortuous demise.

"I'm not suggesting it will be easy," he continued. "But we're strong enough to do this."

He sounded so sure, so impassioned that it nearly broke her heart. He truly had no idea of the scorn they'd face. He probably hadn't even considered the fact that she knew next to nothing about being a duchess. She'd never even attended a proper dinner party, much less hosted one.

And yet, she couldn't bring herself to break things off with him. She owed it to him—and to herself—to see their relationship through to the inevitable, bitter end.

"Will you leave tonight?" she asked.

"Diggs is planning to come at dawn. Do you think you can tolerate me for one more night?" he asked with a grin.

"I suppose so," she said with a grudging smile.

"Thank you," he said, cupping her cheek in his warm palm. "For saving my life and sharing this special place."

She tipped her forehead to his and wrapped her arms around his neck. "What would you like to do on your last night here?"

He brushed his lips across hers in a kiss that was clearly meant to whet her appetite—and it did. "I was thinking—hoping, that is—that we could go for a midnight swim." He gazed at her with heavy-lidded eyes. "What do you say?"

"I say . . ." She nibbled her lip in mock indecision. ". . . I'll race you to the beach!"

She was halfway down the path before Keane had even climbed off the rock.

Chapter 20

Keane sprinted after Poppy, jumping over the stray articles of clothing that she'd dropped in his path. A slipper at one bend, a stocking in another, till he reached a puddle of her cast-off clothes on the beach.

She was standing in the surf, waist-deep in the gently lapping waves, her long auburn curls fluttering around her shoulders as if she'd walked straight out of a Botticelli painting. Moonlight limned the curves of her face and body, giving her an angelic glow completely at odds with the devilish gleam in her eyes. "I thought you'd never arrive," she teased.

He almost tripped over his own legs in his haste to pull off his boots. While he dispensed with his trousers and shirt, he kept his gaze fixed on her, fearing that if he looked away, she'd vanish like an apparition.

But she floated on her back as she waited for him. Her sultry laughter carried in the evening breeze, guiding him to her like a siren's call. He waded into the water, dove beneath a breaking wave, and surfaced right in front of her.

She gasped in surprise, then stood and placed her palms flat on his chest. "Your time on the beach has changed you," she mused. "You're practically a merman. Indeed, all you're missing is a trident."

"I *have* changed since I came here, and in more ways than you think." He slid his hands around her waist, pulling her close. "I'm going to prove it to you, Poppy."

"You realize this is madness," she rasped.

He shook his head, sending droplets flying. "Madness would be letting you slip away."

They collided in a kiss that was primal and fierce, timeless and true. The seawater swirling around them had felt cool only moments before; now, their passion burned hot enough to warm the entire ocean.

She wrapped her lithe legs around his hips and pressed her full breasts to his torso. He grasped her bottom, rocking against her till they were both breathless with desire. Till they both writhed with need.

"I want you, Keane," she said. "Before you go, I want all of you."

"I want you, too," he murmured against her salty skin. "And not just for tonight."

She froze briefly, then relaxed. "Let's treasure this— however long or short it may be." There was a thread of doubt in her voice that niggled at the back of his brain, but now didn't seem the proper time to dwell on it.

So he scooped her into his arms, spun her around, and carried her toward the shore. She playfully kicked, spraying an arc of water droplets over their heads. Her laughter seeped beneath his skin, making him hopeful. Making him whole.

Once they were back on the beach, he carefully deposited her on a smooth rock, and she wrapped her arms around her body, shivering. "Here," he said, handing her the shirt he'd discarded in the sand. "Put this on."

She shot him a grateful smile as she stuffed her arms into the sleeves.

"Do you want to go back to the shelter?" he asked.

"I think we should stay here." She tipped her face to the starlit sky. "In our cove."

Maybe it was the way she'd said *our,* or the way she looked wearing nothing but his shirt, or both, but his chest felt like it could burst. "I'll run back to the shelter to fetch some towels and a quilt. Will you be all right here for a couple of minutes?"

"I shall be fine," she assured him with a saucy smile. "I don't anticipate any more strange men will be washing ashore."

"If one does, I doubt he'll be as handsome as me." He held his arms akimbo and made a slow turn, giving her one last eyeful before he strode toward the path.

"Perhaps not," she called after him. "But there's every likelihood he'll be more humble."

True to his word, Keane returned to the beach a few minutes later wearing a towel around his waist and carrying a heap of supplies: another towel, two thick quilts, a lantern, the basket she'd brought filled with his dinner, and a bottle of wine. While Poppy dried off, he spread one of the quilts on the sand, wisely choosing a nook near the base of the cliffs that would protect them from the wind and afford them privacy.

They sank onto the quilt, and he pulled her close, planting a kiss on her shoulder. "Have I mentioned how much I adore the sight of you wearing my shirt?"

"I don't recall you mentioning it," she said, a bit breathless.

"Allow me to rectify the situation." He cleared his throat, indicating the import of what he was about to say. "Imagine a gown made by the most sought-after modiste in all of Paris."

"Very well," she said, indulging him.

"This gown is her greatest masterpiece," he continued dramatically. "Her finest creation."

Poppy smiled. "It sounds quite lovely."

"No doubt about it," he agreed. "What color do you think it is?"

She shrugged. "How should I know?"

"I asked you to imagine it." He clucked his tongue, feigning disappointment. "I did not think this would prove so difficult."

"Blue," she said, playing along. "The gown is blue."

He nodded approvingly. "The modiste has decided that you are the only woman in England who is beautiful enough to wear the gown, and she gives it to you."

"I am honored," Poppy said. "Will she mind if I wear it to the beach?"

"Not in the least," he said. "In fact, she requests that you pose for a portrait in the dress. Right here. With the sea behind you and moonlight shining on your hair."

"I suppose it's the least I can do."

"She hires the most talented artist in all of Europe to paint you in that gown, and when he finally sets down his brush, he hurls himself into the sea."

"Seems a bit dramatic."

"Not at all," Keane said soberly. "You see, he knows he shall never create anything so lovely ever again."

She scooted closer to him, touching the tip of her nose to his. "What does this have to do with your shirt?"

"I'm glad you asked," he said smugly. "The modiste offers me the portrait, and I, of course, am very keen to have it. It's worth thousands of pounds, after all. But there is a catch."

"Oh?"

"If I want to keep the portrait, I must agree to allow a witch to erase a memory from my mind."

She arched a sardonic brow. "The story has taken quite the turn."

"Mmm," he murmured dramatically. "Indeed. Because the memory the witch intends to erase is the one we're making right now. The vision of you, with your hair loose around your shoulders, wearing my shirt."

"I begin to understand your dilemma," she quipped, though it was difficult to follow the thread of the story when he was sitting so close and wearing nothing more than a towel. "It seems you have a difficult decision to make."

"It's the easiest choice I shall ever make," he said solemnly. "I choose this moment. I'd choose it over a hundred portraits, over a thousand other happy memories. I choose now . . . with you."

"I choose you, too," she breathed. "I choose this night. To be the memory I keep with me always."

His forehead creased so briefly she might have imagined it. "We're going to make plenty more memories, Poppy."

"Perhaps." She wished that she could be as confident as Keane, that she held the same unshakable conviction that their connection was strong enough to withstand the forces conspiring to pull them apart. But those forces had ravaged her family, devastating them at their most vulnerable moment.

"How can I make you believe?" he rasped.

"Give me time." She brushed her lips across his. "But first, give me tonight."

"That, I can do." He cradled her head in his palm and slanted his mouth across hers.

She closed her eyes and forgot about everything but the way Keane made her feel. The steady pressure of his fingers on her skin. The subtle warmth of his breath on her cheek. The deep timbre of his voice thrumming through her limbs.

This was a slice of paradise, a taste of happiness. And she intended to savor every moment.

She ran her hands over the chiseled contours of his face and torso, reveling in the contrasts—from the abrasive stubble on his jaw to the peach-like fuzz below his navel. His body, so different from her own, seemed to have been made just for her.

His hand slipped beneath the hem of the shirt she wore, then cruised over her hip and up her side, lightly stroking her rib cage. The tips of her breasts tightened, and when she leaned into his open palms, he growled approvingly.

They stretched out on the quilt and removed the last remaining barriers between them—her shirt, his towel. And they set about the infinitely pleasurable task of exploring each other.

He traced a fingertip around the pale birthmark on her belly; she brushed her lips across a pink scar on his chest. He nibbled on her earlobe; she gave the taut muscles of his backside a playful smack.

So much of this was new to her, and yet, she was not nervous in the slightest. She trusted Keane to respect her. Knew he'd be a generous lover—and she was right. He ran his hands over her body, lingering in the most sensitive areas: the crook of her neck, the base of her spine, the arches of her feet.

And he kissed her everywhere. She loved the rasp of his tongue and the way his damp hair tickled her skin. She loved the moans that escaped his throat as she stroked the hard, thick length of his arousal. But most of all, she loved having him all to herself.

He rolled on top of her, ravaging her mouth and rocking

his hips against hers until they were both gasping with longing. Aching for more.

She reached between them, guiding him to her entrance, and he touched his forehead to hers. "You're everything I want, Poppy."

She wrapped her legs around his thighs and arched toward him. "I'm yours," she breathed. "For tonight, I'm yours."

He gazed into her eyes as he eased inside her, searching her face for any sign of pain. "Are you all right?"

"Yes." She speared her fingers through his hair. "This feels like . . ."

He froze mid-thrust and shot her a knee-melting grin. "What does it feel like?"

Honestly, it felt like a promise. A sacred, solemn promise. But she couldn't say the words aloud in case it proved to be a promise that she couldn't keep.

So she told him a slightly different version of the truth. "This feels like it was meant to be." *Even if it can't be forever.*

They moved together, faster, harder, till she could think of nothing but the insistent pulsing between her legs and the potent desire spiraling inside her.

"You're right," he murmured in her ear without breaking stride. "This *is* meant to be. Don't fight it anymore. Come with me, Poppy . . . *now.*"

Before the plea had even left his lips, her body began to unfurl. Pleasure beckoned, and Keane pushed her along, nudging her closer and closer to release—until her body surrendered to the bliss. Her cries mingled with the roar of the ocean and her climax rolled through her like thunder. Distant at first, then turning powerful, almost deafening in its intensity. It overtook her, lighting up every nerve, from the roots of her hair to the tips of her toes, before slowly, sweetly receding.

But Keane was still with her, and just as she started to catch her breath, he closed his eyes and groaned—reigniting the embers of pleasure still glowing inside her. This time, they found their release together, and hers was all the sweeter for it.

But at the last minute, he pulled back and rolled over, panting as he spent himself on the sand. She placed a palm on his back and felt his muscles tense for several seconds before they relaxed. When he faced her again, his gaze was soft and sated.

"I thought it best," he said, gesturing over his shoulder.

"Yes." She nodded, emphatic. "We probably should have discussed that beforehand."

"There could still be a babe," he said slowly.

She lay back, gazed up at the stars, and allowed herself to ponder the possibility for approximately six seconds. A baby. With Keane. Her heart broke into an unexpected, joyful dance.

Which she promptly interrupted by shaking her head. "No, the timing works in our favor."

With a winsome smile, he leaned forward, kissed her on the nose, and pulled the spare quilt on top of them. She nestled her head against his chest and listened to the waves crashing on the shore while he trailed his fingers up and down her back.

Her eyelids were growing heavy when she heard him whisper in her ear. "I know our deal is officially over. You've met your obligations and I've met mine."

She frowned and lifted her chin. "Why do you mention it now?"

"Because I have a favor to ask," he said soberly. "Even

though you owe me nothing, I was hoping that you would grant me one last question tonight."

"Oh," she said with a smile. "I suppose that is the least I could do. What would you like to ask, Your Grace?"

"It's a simple question." He brushed the pad of his thumb over her lower lip. "Could you ever love someone like me?"

She swallowed hard. "If you'd asked me a month ago, I would have said no, without hesitation. Now . . . I'm not so certain."

He stroked his chin, thoughtful. "So your answer is maybe?"

"I won't deny you've changed me, Keane. I'd hazard to guess that I've changed you, too. But we're each still the same at our core. I don't know if small changes around the edges will be enough. That's why I can't give you a resounding yes, and it's why my answer is maybe."

He sighed contentedly. "It's not precisely what I wanted to hear, but even you must admit that this is progress."

"Infinitesimal perhaps, but I suppose it is." She sniffled and surreptitiously swiped away a tear.

"Never underestimate the power of incremental change." He propped himself on an elbow, glanced around, and reached for something in the sand behind him. "Do you know where this came from?"

"It's a bit of sea glass." She ran the pad of her thumb over the smooth frosted green stone, remarkably similar to the color of his eyes. "Probably from an old whiskey bottle. Pieces like this wash up on shore all the time."

"Mmm," he mused. "That whiskey bottle might have been thrown overboard by a drunken sailor. Or maybe it was aboard a ship that wrecked off the coast. And it broke into a dozen rough, jagged shards."

"Not a very auspicious beginning," she said.

"Beginnings rarely are," he said sagely. "But it launched that broken piece of glass on its journey. Decades—maybe even a century—of tumbling in the ocean, grinding against rocks, and rolling across the sand took away the sharp edges and smoothed out the imperfections. All before fate brought it to us and placed it in your hand."

She turned the pristine stone over in her palm, trying to imagine how it had looked at the start. Maybe Keane was right. Sometimes things had to break before they could become what they were meant to be. There was only one problem.

"I don't have a century to try to make this work."

He chuckled softly. "Our transformation doesn't have to be finished. We'll just tumble through the ocean, together."

She set the sea glass on the quilt and gazed into his eyes. "I like the sound of that, but I cannot make any promises."

"I understand." He cradled her face in his hands and kissed her softly. "I can live with maybe. Actually, I'm pretty damned ecstatic about maybe."

"You're an insufferable romantic," she teased.

"If I am," he said with a yawn, "it's entirely your fault."

She nestled against his chest and let the sounds of his heartbeat and the ocean fill her head until she drifted off to sleep.

When she woke in the middle of the night, her back was flush against the wall of his torso and his arm was wrapped around her waist as if he feared she'd slip away while he slept. She gazed up at the diamond-filled sky and blinked as a comet shot across the black velvet curtain of night.

"Keane," she whispered loudly. "Are you awake?"

"I am now," he grumbled.

"I saw a shooting star."

He pressed his lips to her shoulder. "I know your feelings regarding shooting stars. Did you bother to make a wish?"

"Yes." She'd wished that Keane would be safe when he came out of hiding. And that the horrible, no-good cretin who'd tried to kill him would pay dearly for his crime.

"Don't tell me," he said, "or it won't come to pass."

"You should make one, too."

"I didn't see the shooting star. But it doesn't matter." He slid his palm up her belly and cupped her breast, gently pinching the taut peak. "My wish is already coming true."

Before long, she was arching her back, pressing her bottom against his hard length. His fingers were sliding up the insides of her thighs, touching the folds at her entrance, finding her most sensitive spot.

They made love again, and this time it was so slow, so sweet, that it could have been a dream. And after they found their release together, Poppy dozed off once more, sated and secure in his arms.

The next time she stirred, pale gold beams were peeking over the cliffs; Keane snored softly beside her. She slid out from beneath the quilt, hastily gathered her clothes, and dressed.

If he hadn't looked so peaceful, she might have woken him, but perhaps it was better this way. Last night, under the stars, they'd had their perfect goodbye, and there was nothing left to say. So, she knelt beside him and dropped a kiss on his forehead before heading back to the cottage.

An hour later, when Keane awoke, he stretched contentedly and reached for Poppy. Only, she wasn't there. He called for her, just in case she was still close, but he sensed in his gut that she was gone.

All that was left on the quilt beside him was a piece of smooth, green sea glass, glowing in the morning sun.

Chapter 21

Two days later, Lady Rufflebum made a beeline for Poppy and Hazel as they exited the bakery on Main Street. "The Duke of Hawking has mysteriously reappeared," she said, glancing over her shoulder as if there might be a French spy lurking around the corner.

The mention of Keane's name made Poppy's heart flutter. She hadn't seen or heard from him since the night they'd spent on the beach. "Perhaps that will put an end to all the speculation about him," she ventured.

"Hardly." The countess laughed as if this were the most diverting tidbit she'd heard in an age. "He was missing for weeks before he was finally spotted at the Bluffs' Brew Inn. Ever since then, he and his man have been making inquiries around town."

"What sorts of inquiries?" Hazel asked the countess.

"Vague questions regarding an unfortunate incident at the pub some weeks ago." Lady Rufflebum leaned closer. "No one knows precisely what happened, but it seems that the duke recently acquired a dashing scar above one eye."

"Perhaps it was more than an unfortunate incident," Hazel mused, shooting Poppy a pointed look.

The countess made an indelicate snort. "I dislike the notion of a Londoner implying that there was nefarious activity at one of our fine establishments. For all we know, his scar is a result of him swimming too close to the rocks."

Poppy suppressed a smile. First, because the countess had dubbed the Salty Mermaid "a fine establishment," and second, because she seemed to have forgotten that she herself resided in London for half the year.

"Perhaps the duke is simply gathering information," Poppy said. "We cannot fault him for that."

"I suppose not," Lady Rufflebum conceded. "And we cannot fault his looks, either. He's devilishly handsome." Jabbing Hazel with an elbow, she added, "Too bad you've already snared yourself a husband."

Hazel cast a sympathetic glance at Poppy because she, too, had gleaned the countess's underlying message: that while Hazel, a headmistress, might have once had an outside chance at marrying a duke, Poppy, a fisherman's daughter, was in no way a suitable candidate. Indeed, she was not even worthy of consideration.

Poppy wasn't surprised by Lady Rufflebum's unintentional slight. A month ago she would have shrugged it off without a second thought, but now it stung as surely as a jellyfish's tentacles.

Hazel, dear friend that she was, responded to the countess with the same forthright, patient tone Poppy had heard her use when talking with her students. "I can assure you that there was no ensnaring on either my part or the earl's. Moreover," she said, linking her arm with Poppy's, "if Lord Hawking happens to be looking for a partner in Bellehaven Bay, there are plenty of eligible young ladies here, not the least of which is—"

Poppy squeezed Hazel's forearm and interjected, "Pardon me for interrupting, but isn't that Kitty coming out of Mr. Sandford's office?"

As Kitty made her way toward their group, Lady Rufflebum clucked her tongue. "I cannot fathom why a beautiful young heiress would waste her time learning the business of architecture."

Hazel blinked and opened her mouth to respond, but halted, focusing on a spot over Poppy's shoulder. "Don't look now, but Kitty isn't the only one strolling through Bellehaven this morning."

A tingle slid up Poppy's spine, and she arched a questioning brow at her friend.

"The duke himself," Hazel confirmed. "And I do believe he's coming this way."

Kitty joined the circle, sketchbook tucked under one arm, and greeted everyone with a sunny smile. "Good morning, all." She cast a curious glance at Lady Rufflebum, who was patting her hair and pinching her cheeks. Leaning close to Poppy, she whispered, "Have I missed something? A bit of gossip, perhaps?"

Poppy exhaled shakily. "No, but stay where you are. I've a feeling you won't be disappointed."

The words were barely out of her mouth when Keane's deep voice called out, "Lovely day, isn't it, ladies?"

All four women turned to face him, as synchronized as a ballet troupe, and he made a gallant bow.

"Indeed it is, Duke." The countess twirled her parasol, blushing like a debutante. "Then again, it's always beautiful here in Bellehaven. Even the rain cannot dampen its splendor."

"I am learning that this town has much to recommend it, Lady Rufflebum. Not the least of which are the charming residents." He shot the countess a blinding smile. "Perhaps you'd be so good as to introduce me to a few more?"

"But of course," she replied, all too happy to oblige. "This is Lady Bladenton, her niece, Miss Kitty Beckett, and . . . uh, Miss Poppy Summers. Ladies, this is the Duke of Hawking, on holiday from London."

"Welcome to Bellehaven," Hazel said warmly.

"It's a pleasure," added Kitty.

He smiled politely at each of them, then gazed at Poppy, expectant. A casual observer would not have suspected that he and Poppy had been lovers, but his eyes sparked with emotion, and his throat swallowed unspoken words.

She inclined her head. "Your Grace," she managed.

Lady Rufflebum watched the exchange with a mixture of confusion and relief. As if she'd been worried Poppy would seize the moment to try to sell him cod out of the back of her cart.

"Miss Summers," he said softly. "I'm delighted to make your acquaintance."

"In any event," the countess said smoothly, "I am grateful for this fortuitous meeting, Duke, as I wished to extend an invitation. I could have sent round a note, but I prefer the personal touch when possible."

"You've a reputation for being a most gracious hostess," he replied.

Lady Rufflebum fanned herself. Vigorously. "I'm having a dinner party tomorrow night," she said. "I do hope you will be able to come. Lady Bladenton, you and that handsome earl of yours must join us—and Miss Beckett, too."

"How very kind of you," Hazel began stiffly, "but I'm afraid I already have plans . . . with Poppy."

Lady Rufflebum's fan came to an abrupt halt. "I see. Well, no matter," she said, obviously mildly affronted. "We shall have plenty of other guests to entertain His Grace."

Keane flashed a dimple at the countess, and Poppy almost pitied her. The poor woman didn't stand a chance.

"Now that we've all met, it seems a shame that I won't

be able to further my acquaintance with these ladies, and the situation is easily remedied, is it not?"

Lady Rufflebum's brow creased. "I'm not certain I follow."

"Am I correct in assuming that your dining table can accommodate one more?" He flicked his gaze meaningfully to Poppy.

Poppy wasn't certain if she wanted to hug Keane or clamp her hand over his mouth.

"Of course it can," the countess replied, mildly affronted.

"Then I'd like to propose that Miss Summers join us as well."

"Miss Summers?" she repeated, seemingly baffled by the suggestion.

"What a lovely idea!" Hazel exclaimed.

"Inspired," Kitty chimed.

"Well then, I guess it's settled. I shall look forward to the evening with great anticipation." Keane placed a hand over his heart as he tipped his hat. "Good day, ladies." Looking directly at Poppy, he added, "Until tomorrow."

Keane waited impatiently in Lady Rufflebum's drawing room, swirling his brandy while he chatted with Gladwell, Bellehaven's good-natured doctor, and Dunmire, a pompous viscount who was in town for the summer. A few other guests, all dressed in their finest, milled around the countess's pink and silver drawing room.

The room was decorated with dour-faced portraits, superfluous trinkets, and the sort of furniture that required you to sit at attention—all of which seemed contrived to impress visitors and establish that Lady Rufflebum had an excess of money and taste.

The thought would not have crossed Keane's mind

before he met Poppy, but he'd begun to see the world through her eyes. Now that he'd had a glimpse, he wasn't at all certain that she'd make an appearance at tonight's dinner party. Not that she lacked the courage. It was more a matter of pride. And she had every right to rebuff Lady Rufflebum after her abominable behavior the day before.

But he was hoping that the connection he and Poppy shared would be enough to convince her to come in spite of her obvious reservations. That she'd step out of her idyllic cove and into the countess's elegant drawing room for his sake—and for theirs.

"The annual regatta is only a week away," Dr. Gladwell remarked to Keane. "It's a spectacle not to be missed."

Dunmire threw back the contents of his glass and winced as the brandy traveled down his throat. "I hope to make a better showing this year," he said, puffing out his chest. "Last year was an aberration."

"An aberration?" Keane repeated, sensing a story. "In what way?"

Just as the viscount opened his mouth to respond, the room fell silent, save for a few gasps and surprised murmurs.

"In *that* way," the doctor replied, gesturing toward the door, his expression softening. "Miss Poppy Summers was the aberration. She and Miss Beckett took home the silver cup last year. I confess I never imagined I'd see them here."

Keane made a mental note to ask Poppy about the regatta as he turned to face her.

But as soon as he did, every thought fled. It hadn't been long since they'd seen each other, but he drank in the sight of her like he'd been staggering through the desert the whole time.

Her simple gown was striking—and utterly stunning.

Her tanned, freckled skin glowed against the soft white silk, and while most of her hair was gathered in a knot at her crown, a few loose strawberry curls cascaded over her shoulders. She kept her chin high and her gaze direct as she and the rest of her party glided into the drawing room and greeted Lady Rufflebum.

The countess appeared momentarily confused when they approached, but quickly recovered, smiling at Poppy with sincere, if grudging, admiration. "I will admit you have a knack for surprising me, Miss Summers—and at my age, surprises are a rare and welcome occurrence."

Poppy made a graceful curtsey. "Thank you, Lady Rufflebum. I confess that I sometimes surprise even myself."

Keane set down his brandy and strode toward them. "I, for one, find predictability to be vastly overrated," he said, bowing in Poppy's direction.

"Then you have come to the right town, Your Grace," she countered. "Things are rarely as they seem here in Bellehaven. Surprises lurk around every corner—and in every cove."

"That's hardly news to the duke," Dunmire said, leering at Poppy and slapping Keane on the back. "If the scar on his forehead is any indication, I'd say he's already encountered a surprise or two. Care to tell us how you came by the souvenir, Hawking?"

Keane glared at the viscount but kept his tone friendly. "I think not. I'd hate to squash the speculation when there are so many interesting stories being bandied about, including one theory that I was on the losing end of an encounter with a rather ornery seagull. A rumor which I can neither confirm nor deny."

"Notoriously impudent birds." Lady Rufflebum pressed a hand to her chest and shuddered. "Shall we make our way through to the dining room?"

Keane automatically looked for Poppy, but the countess was already reaching for his arm, expecting him to adhere to the usual social rules. And he couldn't flout them without causing a scene that would likely embarrass Poppy.

He had little choice but to endure four courses of dinner and banal conversation near the head of the table, when he longed to be near Poppy, who was seated at the opposite end. But every so often, she glanced at him over the rim of her wine glass with those sea-green eyes. She didn't smile coyly or bat her lashes, but there was a softness to her expression that made his chest ache.

And it made him think that maybe she missed him as much as he missed her.

After dinner, Lady Rufflebum persuaded Kitty to sing a few songs while Hazel accompanied her on the pianoforte. Poppy sat with the rest of the women, admiring Kitty's clear, lyrical voice and Hazel's nimble, skilled fingers. The countess didn't press Poppy to perform, which was just as well. She did not play any instruments, and the songs she knew were the sort sung in unsavory pubs rather than sophisticated drawing rooms.

Keane had remained in the dining room to enjoy an after-dinner drink with the other gentlemen: Dr. Gladwell, Lord Dunmire, and Hazel's dashing husband, Blade. Poppy was enjoying herself, but her eyes flicked to the door searching for a familiar pair of broad shoulders more often than she cared to admit.

When at last the men filed in, Lady Rufflebum cleared her throat. "Excellent. Now that the gentlemen have joined us, we may begin a proper game of charades."

Keane and Blade exchanged mildly alarmed looks. "I wonder if we might delay the start of the game for a while," Blade said smoothly. "I'd hoped to escort my wife and niece on a stroll through your beautiful garden."

"Very well," the countess relented. "We will play charades when you return. While you're in the garden, be sure to take notice of my award-winning roses."

"We would not dream of missing them." Blade shot her a smile that ensured he was already forgiven for thwarting her after-dinner plans.

"Miss Summers." Keane stood so close that the timbre of his voice seeped beneath her skin. "Shall we join the others for a walk in the garden?"

Lady Rufflebum gasped, but Keane didn't flinch. Neither did Poppy. "I should like that," she said, taking the arm he offered. She ignored the stares of the rest of the guests as Keane escorted her to the French doors leading to the terrace.

Since Hazel, Kitty, and Blade were already outside, walking a bit ahead of them, they were not alone.

But for the first time all evening, Poppy was not under the watchful eyes of Lady Rufflebum and the other guests.

For a few precious moments at least, she'd have Keane all to herself.

Chapter 22

"I'd say the dinner party's going rather well so far," Keane ventured, as he and Poppy strolled down the pebbled path in Lady Rufflebum's lush garden. A few lanterns hung from tree boughs, lighting their way, and a sultry summer breeze ruffled the tendrils at Poppy's nape. "Wouldn't you agree?"

"I suppose that depends on the goal you're trying to achieve," she replied. "What *do* you hope to accomplish?"

He chuckled and shot her a look so intimate, so hungry that it took her right back to the night they'd lain together on the beach. "My goal is to spend time with you, in the company of others, so that no one will think it odd when I begin to openly court you."

"They're going to think it odd, regardless," she said.

He shrugged. "Then let them. The only opinions that truly matter to me are yours and your family's."

She glanced at his handsome profile. He looked quite ducal in his fine jacket and freshly trimmed hair. "And what of *your* family's opinion?"

"My uncle would be pleased—and a bit relieved, I suspect—to learn that I've found someone who makes me happy. I've no doubt your courage and wit will win him over. Say the word, and I'll arrange a meeting," he said, arching a brow.

"I think we would do better to focus on successfully navigating this evening's festivities." She paused to admire a large topiary trimmed in the shape of a dolphin. "Have you made any more progress with your investigation?"

He hesitated for a beat, then said, "Not really. I'm still not certain who wanted me dead or why."

"But you have some leads that you're pursuing?"

"Nothing definitive," he said vaguely. "Now that I'm out of hiding, perhaps my nemesis will try again."

Poppy shivered. "What if he succeeds this time?"

"He won't," Keane said, confident. "If he makes a reappearance, I'll be ready for him."

"I hope so." But she still had an uneasy feeling. Not only that he was still in danger, but that he was reluctant to share all the details, to tell her everything he knew.

After all they'd endured together, it hurt to think he was keeping something from her. But there were topics she avoided, too, and he'd been patient with her. She could do the same for him.

On the path ahead of them, Hazel, Blade, and Kitty strolled along, chatting and laughing like a proper little family. Poppy loved seeing her friends so happy, but she felt a pang of longing, too. She'd known that sense of belonging once, but now it seemed forever out of reach.

Keane faced her, clasped her hand, and lifted it to his lips. "I've missed you," he said softly.

"I've missed you, too." She sighed. "Everything is different now that you're gone from the beach."

"How is your father?" he asked, and though it might have sounded like a polite inquiry to anyone who overheard it, the concern in his eyes touched her.

"He's been trying to walk a bit each day, and he's gradually getting stronger. The recent visit from my brother seems to have benefited Papa more than the medicinal tea I give him. Whatever the reason for his improvement, I'm grateful for it."

"Do not discount everything you do for your father," Keane said sincerely. "You've devoted most of your life to caring for him, and that is admirable. But you deserve the chance to chase your dreams also."

"I'm beginning to believe that," she admitted. "I know I want more than the life I'm living now, but sometimes when I'm dressed like this"—she swept a gloved hand down the lovely gown she'd borrowed from Hazel—"I feel like an impostor. Like an actress playing the part of someone I'll never be."

"I feel like that too sometimes," he confessed. "I wish we were still free to swim in the ocean and sleep under the stars."

"We could be there now . . . if you hadn't left."

He laced his fingers through hers and searched her face, as if willing her to understand. "We couldn't hide there forever, Poppy. And I wasn't going to be satisfied with another day or another week. I want a lifetime with you."

His words wrapped around her like an embrace, burrowing their way into her chest. Still, she couldn't help but point out the obvious. "I was not born into this life." She waved an arm around the elegant garden. "I fear it would take the life out of me."

"I'm not asking you to change. I'm only asking you to envision a future with me in it. We can sort out the details as we go."

"I want to say yes, but I can't risk losing myself in the process."

He nodded soberly. "We're at a turning point now, and you have a choice to make."

She swallowed. "I know."

"You can choose to open up to me, to help me blend our worlds together. There's room for all of it: London, Bellehaven, family, and adventure. Or . . . you can shut me out. It would gut me, Poppy. But if you tell me there's no chance, I'll respect your wishes. If you ask me to, I'll leave Bellehaven and never come back."

"No." She shook her head to erase the image of him walking away for good. "I don't want you to leave. I am willing to walk the narrow plank between both worlds. Even if I must spend mornings fishing in my rowboat and my evenings wearing borrowed gowns."

He exhaled in obvious relief. "Have I mentioned how beautiful you look tonight?"

She shook her head slowly. "Not with words, but I've become rather adept at deciphering your facial expressions."

His gaze dropped to her mouth. "What's my expression telling you right now?"

Her belly fluttered. "It's saying you want to kiss me."

"You *are* good at this." He clasped her wrist, pulled her off the path, and backed her up against an ivy-covered trellis where the moonlight illuminated the sharp angles of his cheekbones and the fullness of his lips.

"Isn't Lady Rufflebum expecting us for charades?" she teased, draping her arms over his shoulders.

His answer was a low, knee-melting growl—just before he covered her mouth with his.

She drank in every detail: the familiar scent of his skin, the springy feel of his hair, the hard wall of his chest. His hands swept down her back, over her hips, and up her sides, claiming her for his own. His tongue traced the seam of her lips, begging entrance, which she gladly granted.

He tasted like a stolen sip of brandy in a moonlit cove. Tangy, heady perfection.

No, she couldn't give him up. She'd made her choice and was now committed to it, even if it upended her life. Even if it broke her heart.

Slowly, she pulled back and gazed into his glowing eyes. "What happens next?"

"There's going to be a ball after the regatta next week."

"Yes, in the new Assembly Rooms. Kitty's been talking about it all summer."

"Everyone in Bellehaven and half of London is going to be in attendance. I think we should go and dance together—more than once. Let everyone know how we feel about each other."

Poppy swallowed. "There will be no going back after that. People will say you've gone mad. They'll call me a fortune hunter and a light-skirt—and worse."

"I don't care what people say about me, but if anyone dares slight you, they'll suffer the consequences."

"What do you intend to do?" she asked. "You can't very well challenge someone like Lady Rufflebum to a duel."

He arched a dark brow and conjured an evil smile. "Maybe I'll hide a dead fish under the seat of her coach or fill her drawers with sand."

Poppy smiled. "I don't really care what people say, either." The real test of their relationship wasn't what other people thought about them. It was whether she could trust someone who'd been raised so differently to understand her, to respect her family and way of life. To love her even in the most difficult of times.

"Then it's settled." He brushed the pad of his thumb across her lower lip. "Even though all I want to do is bustle you into my coach and whisk you away to a private spot overlooking the ocean, I will refrain. Instead, I shall do the honorable thing and escort you back to the countess's drawing room where we will endure a tedious game of charades. I will pretend that I'm not thinking of kissing you or reliving the nights we've spent together."

She shot him a sultry grin. "And I shall pretend I haven't seen you walking naked out of the surf."

"Right," he drawled. More seriously, he added, "But the good news is this: We won't have to pretend for much longer. Soon, everyone at the First Annual Bellehaven Regatta Ball will know how smitten I am with you. And maybe you'll begin to believe it, too."

Just before they reached the house, Keane paused and faced her. "Miss Poppy Summers."

The tender way he said her name made her pulse quicken, and she knew what was coming. "I thought I'd fulfilled all my obligations," she teased.

"Out of the goodness of your heart, will you grant me another question?"

"Are you always this greedy?"

"Where you're concerned, I fear I am."

She softened. "Go on."

"How do you take your tea?"

"Steaming hot, with one sugar cube and a spot of cream." She hesitated, then added, "Poured into a chipped, hand-painted teacup that belonged to my mother."

He smiled as though she'd given him a precious gift. "That is good to know."

On the day before the regatta, there were so many people pouring into Bellehaven Bay that the streets seemed as crowded as London. Every room at the Bluffs' Brew Inn had been let, the boardinghouse was full, and any cottage that had room for an extra guest—or six—was bursting at the seams.

Keane was dragging a straightedge down one lathered side of his face when a knock sounded at the door. "Give me a minute," he grumbled before setting down the razor, striding across his room at the inn, and swinging open the door.

Diggs stood in the doorway, looking uncharacteristically officious. "Your uncle is here," he announced.

Keane blinked. "In Bellehaven?"

"At the Salty Mermaid, to be precise," Diggs replied. "He asked if you would be so kind as to meet him there."

"Of course. I'll can be there in a quarter of an hour." Keane hurried back to the looking glass to finish his shave with Diggs on his heels. His uncle was one of the few people he trusted. One of the few people who'd been kind to Keane when his own father could scarcely stand to look at him. "I wonder what brought him here," he mused. "The regatta, the ball . . . ?"

Diggs chuckled. "If I had to venture a guess, I'd say *you* brought him here."

He patted his chin with a towel. "I guess we'll find out soon, won't we?"

Keane straightened his cravat and exhaled as he walked into the Salty Mermaid a few minutes later. It had been months since he'd seen his uncle, the Viscount Rawlings, but Keane immediately spotted his bald head, dark beard, and twinkling blue eyes at a table across from the bar. Upon seeing Keane, he rose and held out his arms for an embrace. "Andrew," he said, slapping him on the back. "It's been far too long."

"This is a welcome surprise. It's good to see you, Uncle. How is Teddy?"

"Your cousin is fine. He's here in Bellehaven, too. He ran into a friend at the tea shop earlier and was persuaded to join in a game of cricket." He shook his head ruefully.

"Theodore's the same age you are, and yet, I sometimes wonder if he'll ever grow up."

"It's why the ladies find him charming. I assume you're in town for all the festivities," Keane said, taking a seat on the bench opposite his uncle. "I'm surprised you were able to find lodgings."

"We're guests of the mayor," he said with a shrug. "But I didn't come to Bellehaven for the entertainments. I've been worried about you, Andrew. There were rumors that you hadn't been seen for weeks. And now you've reappeared—with the devil of a scar, I see."

Keane ran a finger over the jagged mark. "Aye. Someone blindsided me as I left this pub one night."

"Good God." His uncle threw back the rest of his whiskey and signaled the barmaid for a couple more drinks. "They're not very bloody hospitable toward out-of-towners here, are they?"

Keane scoffed. "The person behind the attack has a personal grudge. He wanted me dead."

His uncle blinked, and some of the color drained out of his face. "I'd assumed it was your standard pub brawl. Are you in some sort of trouble, Andrew?"

"No. That is, I don't think so."

"If you're in debt or caught up in some sort of scandal, I can help. You only need to ask." He reached across the weathered tabletop and squeezed Keane's forearm.

His uncle's eyes contained more affection than his father's ever had, which made Keane both grateful and sad. "Thank you for the kind offer. But I'm not in debt, and I haven't done anything to warrant an attempt on my life."

"Of course you haven't." Rawlings slowly exhaled. "Look, I don't know what precipitated the attack, but I do know this: It's time you came home to London. You have responsibilities . . . and a life there."

"You're right. I do." Keane paused while the barmaid plunked a couple of glasses on the table, then continued. "I've realized I cannot continue to shirk my duties. I have leaned on you for far too long, and it's high time I stepped into my father's boots."

"You're different from him, you know."

"Yes." Keane's chest tightened. "He was fond of reminding me how different I am. In fact, he derived a great deal of pleasure from listing all the ways I fell short of his expectations."

"Don't give any credence to his words. What I meant is that you're better than him." Rawlings took a sip of his whiskey and met Keane's gaze. "He was my brother, and I loved him, but he was not a kind person, Andrew. And he was definitely not a good father."

"No, he wasn't." Keane hated that his throat burned. Hated that the mere mention of his father could still affect him so. "But it's been years. I see no point in dwelling on his shortcomings."

"You can't escape your past until you make peace with it." Rawlings swirled the liquid in his glass. "Your father was bitter. Angry at your mother—and himself, I suppose."

That was putting it mildly. Keane's childhood had been little more than a series of shouting matches echoing through the cavernous house as his parents hurled vases and trinkets, threats and accusations. Their fights were so nasty, so intense that Keane would burrow under his bedcovers to avoid hearing them. But not even his pillow could muffle the worst of it. Mama sobbing, saying his father spent more time with his mistress than her. His father bellowing, accusing Mama of sleeping with half the ton.

Indeed, Keane could still recall the evening that his parents returned home from the opera, yelling at each other as they made their way down the corridor outside his room.

Mama had wanted to peek in on Keane as he slept; his father had asked which of her myriad lovers had sired her son.

Mama gasped and slapped him.

But she didn't contradict him. Or deny the allegation.

It took Keane some time after that to admit the truth to himself. He hadn't been ready to believe it at nine, but by the time he was twelve he understood deep in his bones that he was not his father's son.

And when he was fourteen and his mother turned gravely ill, she told him to be brave and to never cower from his father. She died soon after, and Keane did his best to stand his ground.

His father could yell loud enough to rattle the windows. Keane wouldn't flinch.

His father could take a switch to his backside. Keane gritted his teeth and smiled.

On the outside, he was tough and unbothered. But some of his father's vitriol seeped through the cracks in his armor and took root. A boy couldn't live that way day after day, year after year without wondering. Without thinking that, perhaps, he'd deserved it.

Rawlings cleared his throat, snapping Keane back to the present. "Your father wanted you to believe that your kind soul and generous spirit were weaknesses, but they aren't. You'll run the dukedom differently than he did—and that, Andrew, is a good thing."

"Since my father's death, I've been drifting. Afloat at sea," Keane mused. "I was happy to leave it to others to run the estate and follow the precedents set by my father. But all of that is about to change."

"I'm glad to hear you'll be more involved. You are the duke, and your tenants rely on you."

"My first order of business is to do right by them. To make sure they have safe, comfortable homes, plenty of food on their tables, and a doctor to tend to them when they're sick. My father was a miser who watched over his fortune like a dragon guarding a treasure trove, but that's no way to run an estate."

"Good for you," Rawlings said approvingly. "Are you contemplating other changes?"

Keane looked his uncle in the eyes. "I plan to split my time between London and Bellehaven."

Understanding dawned, and Rawlings smiled sagely. "You've met a woman."

Keane nodded. "I'm embarrassed to say I didn't realize how much I'd been given till I saw the world through her eyes. I was blessed with a title and a fortune. I'm not going to squander the chance to do some good with those things."

"A noble sentiment," Rawlings said, nodding. "I look forward to meeting the woman responsible for your change of heart. I assume you intend to make her your duchess?"

"That is the plan," Keane confirmed. "If I can convince her to go along with it."

"I cannot blame her for having reservations—especially since it seems someone tried to kill you." Rawlings rubbed his jaw, thoughtful. "Solve that mystery first. Maybe then the rest of the pieces will fall into place."

"What pieces?" Teddy sauntered toward them and gave Keane a hearty embrace before sliding onto the bench next to his father.

His cousin had a few new lines around the eyes, but his wry grin was as familiar to Keane as the path from his childhood home to the river where they'd fished. "It's been too long. You're looking well." Teddy's jacket was perfectly tailored, and his waistcoat expertly embroidered, but apparently all the pomade in the world couldn't tame the cowlick he'd had since they were lads running through the fields like a pair of banshees.

"Glad to see you're hale and hearty as well. I told Father he had nothing to fear. You've always been able to take care of yourself."

Rawlings chuckled. "Andrew was just telling me that he's met a woman here in Bellehaven. And he wants to marry her."

"You don't say." Teddy grinned at Keane, flagged down the barmaid, and ordered a pint. "There can't be many local women who are duchess material. Who is the lucky lady?"

"Miss Poppy Summers." Just saying her name felt good. Right. "I can't imagine anyone who'd be a better duchess. And you'll both have the chance to meet her at the Regatta Ball tomorrow night."

Chapter 23

"You look . . . so much like your mother." Papa's voice cracked on the last word, and his eyes shone with emotion.

"Thank you." Poppy had been thinking of Mama all day, too.

She would have adored the prospect of a ball in Belle-haven. She would have beamed as she helped Poppy pin up her hair and lace up her dress and offered her the sort of insightful, heartfelt advice that only a mother can give. And she'd have known just what to say to help Poppy navigate her current predicament, which was figuring out whether she could trust Keane with her heart, her family, and her future.

The shimmering silver ball gown that Poppy had borrowed from Hazel felt frightfully out of place in their humble cottage, but she'd insisted on preparing for the ball there so she could eat dinner with Papa before leaving him for the evening. "Hazel and Blade will be here to pick me up soon. Is there anything you need before I go?"

"Naught but a hug," he said gruffly.

She went to his chair by the fire, leaned over, and pecked him on the forehead. "I shall be out late, so please do not wait up."

He frowned. "I have a strange feeling about tonight."

"How so?" She perched on the footstool in front of him so she could see his beloved, wizened face.

"Same way I always know when a storm's a-coming. It's an unease. A sense that there's going to be a shift—and everything will change."

"Things are always changing, Papa, especially by the sea. But that's not necessarily a bad thing."

He snorted. "Tell that to the legions of sailors who crashed on the rocks and sank to their watery graves."

She reached for his hands and gave them an affectionate squeeze. "Don't fear, Papa. I'm looking out for the rocks. But whatever happens, we will weather it together. No matter where the tide takes us, we will always be family. That is my promise to you."

He nodded silently, as if he didn't trust himself to speak. At last, he cleared his throat and said, "I don't want to be a burden to you, Poppy. I won't be the reason you don't live the life you're meant to lead."

She swallowed a painful lump. "You're not a burden; you're my dear Papa. I know you want what's best for me. I'm trying to sort that out, too."

The cottage door rattled, startling them both. "I didn't hear the carriage pull up," she said, rising.

But before she reached the door, it swung open—and Dane walked through. "Home at l—" he began, then blinked at Poppy, stunned. "Zounds. I almost didn't recognize you."

Papa smiled proudly. "Your sister is going to be the belle of the ball tonight. Welcome home, son."

"Did you know he was coming?" Poppy asked her father.

"Aye. Didn't I mention it?" he said, scratching his head.

"I'd planned to come in time for the regatta, but the mail

coach was delayed," Dane grumbled as he threw his large bag onto the floor. "I heard that bastard Dunmire won."

"Only because Kitty and I didn't enter this year," Poppy said with a grin.

The clop of hooves and crunch of gravel sounded outside. "Expecting someone?" Dane asked.

"Hazel and Blade kindly offered to drive me to the ball. Are you going to go? I'm certain they'd be happy to have you come along. We could wait a few minutes while you change."

Dane scoffed. "You'll not catch me riding in an earl's carriage. I'll clean up, chat with Papa for a spell, and then take Calypso into town."

"Suit yourself. But don't disparage Blade. I consider him a friend. If you sat and had a pint with him, you probably would, too." She pressed another kiss to Papa's forehead, picked up her shawl, and hesitated on her way to the door. "I've recently learned that if you give people a chance, they sometimes surprise you . . . in the best of ways."

Papa and Dane stared at her, as if they expected her to elaborate, but there wasn't really time to tell them about Keane right then, so she simply said, "My carriage awaits," and winked at them as she walked out the cottage door.

The Regatta Ball was the inaugural event hosted in Belle-haven's spacious new Assembly Rooms on Main Street. There was still scaffolding up on one side of the building where carpenters were putting finishing touches on the exterior, but most of the construction had been completed, and the residents looked forward to having their first look at their official gathering place.

The smells of cut wood and fresh paint tickled Poppy's nose as she, Hazel, Kitty, and Blade walked through the doors and joined the already bustling crowd. It seemed that everyone was there. Tradesmen and gentry, townsfolk and Londoners, debutantes and matriarchs all mingled in the airy, rustic hall.

The decorating committee—composed of a dozen of the town's matriarchs and chaired by Lady Rufflebum, of course—had made a valiant attempt to liven up the stark interior with yards of pink bunting over every window and door, sprays of pink flowers in every vase, and strands of pink seashells suspended from the ceiling.

Which made for an overall effect that was quite strikingly . . . pink.

"It's a good thing you chose the silver satin instead of the rose silk," Kitty mused.

Poppy nodded. "I'd have been harder to find than a flounder on the ocean floor."

And she could not fade into the background tonight. This night was important to Keane—and to their relationship. It was their chance to show Bellehaven and the rest of the world that they cared for each other enough to compensate for the dramatic difference in their stations.

"You could never blend in, Poppy," Hazel said affectionately.

"I must agree with my wife," Blade concurred. "All eyes are on us—or rather, you three ladies. I'm the envy of every man here."

"You're both very kind," Poppy said. But she was fairly certain that people were staring for a different reason altogether—namely, that they could not believe that a fisherman's daughter had the audacity to enter the ball with the Earl of Bladenton, his wife, and his niece.

If they thought Poppy's entrance was shocking, they'd likely need smelling salts when Keane asked her to dance. The mere thought made her pulse race and her cheeks flush.

As if she could sense Poppy's discomfort, Hazel

squeezed her elbow. "Keep breathing," she whispered. "This gets easier with time. After a while, you won't even notice the curious glances."

"That seems difficult to imagine," Poppy said. "But since you are a Belle, I shall take your word for it."

Hazel smiled. "Don't look now, but Lady Rufflebum is headed this way."

"Lady Bladenton and Miss Summers," the countess said, toddling toward them with her faithful, silent companion, Miss Whitford, in tow. "What is your opinion of the decorations?" Without pausing, she added, "They are rather understated, are they not? I feel we could have done with more embellishment. Bunches of pink feathers and a carpet of rose petals scattered on the floor would have been most welcome touches, don't you think?"

"You and the decorating committee have outdone yourselves," Hazel said, deftly walking the line between truth and diplomacy.

The countess turned her gaze on Poppy. "You are becoming quite the socialite of late, Miss Summers," she remarked, her sharp tone suggesting that she did not entirely approve of this recent development.

"I am far from a socialite," Poppy said. "But I confess I am fond of trading my fishing nets for a dance card now and again."

"I, for one, could not be more pleased." The voice behind her was so warm, deep, and sure that it tickled the wisps of hair at her nape. *Keane.*

Poppy inclined her head. "Thank you, Your Grace."

He gallantly greeted the countess and the rest of their party as he joined their small circle.

"I could not be more pleased," Lady Rufflebum echoed, "to have a duke attend the first public gathering in our Assembly Rooms. What an auspicious start!"

"The pleasure is all mine." He looked into Poppy's eyes so deeply that for a moment it felt as if only the two of them were there. "In fact, I was hoping to persuade Miss Summers to dance the first set with me—if she is not otherwise engaged."

Lady Rufflebum's mouth opened and closed several times as though she wanted to say something but was incapable of forming actual words.

Poppy shook her head. "I should be delighted to dance with you."

Almost on cue, the three-piece orchestra began to play, and a dozen couples made their way to the dance floor. Keane offered her his arm, and she froze.

Not because she had any reservations about dancing with him, but because she knew there would be no going back after this. Everyone from the baker to the blacksmith would see her dancing with Keane. And she was not so accomplished an actress that she could hide her feelings for him. As he twirled her around the dance floor, it would be plain for all to see that she'd completely lost her head. That she'd fallen for the duke.

"Shall we?" he prompted softly, snapping her back to the present.

She slipped her hand into the crook of his arm and held her chin high as Keane took his time escorting her toward the line of dancers forming down the center of the room.

"How is it possible," he whispered, "that you grow more beautiful every time I see you?"

She shot him a cheeky grin. "Perhaps you've been spending too much time at the Salty Mermaid. Or maybe that bump on your head has impaired your judgment in ways you had not realized."

"Or," he countered, "you're so happy to be with me that you're glowing."

"If I am glowing, it's because I spent several hours on the water in the blazing sun."

"Whatever the cause, it suits you."

"You look quite dashing as well," she said, fully aware that it was the understatement of the century. His dark, neatly trimmed hair shone in the candlelight, and his rakish dimple was out in full force. His broad shoulders were snugly encased in a midnight-blue jacket, and buckskin trousers clung to his muscular legs. The stark white cravat at his throat was fashioned into a waterfall knot that looked effortless but had probably taken Diggs a half hour to perfect. Predictably, Keane drew appreciative glances from scores of female guests as he led her closer to the dance floor.

"You're not having second thoughts, are you?" he asked.

She shook her head. "No. Are you?"

"Not a one." He led her to a spot at the end of the line and took his place, facing her.

For one terrifying moment, she was convinced she'd forgotten all the steps to the country reel and would prove incapable of stepping in time to the music or executing the simplest of turns.

And then Keane looked into her eyes and gave her a smile so blindingly honest, she forgot her fears and began to move.

The reel required her to slide down the line, briefly dancing with various gentlemen before twirling back into Keane's arms. Each time their hands touched, her heart fluttered happily—and she began to believe that perhaps he had been right.

There they were, dancing together in a crowded ballroom for all the world to see. Lightning had not struck; the chandeliers had not crashed down. No one had stopped the orchestra from playing; no one had marched over to publicly reprimand her and order that she return to her cove. As far as she could tell, not a single soul had swooned from the shock of seeing her and Keane together. In fact, most of the onlookers seemed to be . . . smiling.

Poppy shuffled to her left, linked arms with Dr. Gladwell, and spun around, letting the silver silk of her gown billow around her legs.

"You're looking well, Miss Summers," the doctor said, slightly breathless from his exertions. "How is your father faring?"

"Better, thank you," she replied.

"I shall pay him a visit this week," he offered, knowing full well that they could not afford his usual fee.

"That's very generous of you."

As the last strains of the musical number floated through the hall, the dance wound to a close, and Keane glanced over the head of his dance partner, meeting Poppy's gaze.

"Shall I escort you back to Lord and Lady Bladenton?" the doctor asked.

She cast another glance at Keane, who appeared to be in the process of extricating himself from the clutches of a viscountess with three daughters of a marriageable age. "Thank you, but I think I shall wait here for—"

"Poppy," Dane interrupted, and the uncharacteristically urgent note in her brother's voice raised the hairs on the backs of her arms. "I need to speak with you."

"Is Papa all right?"

"He's fine." Dane reached for her wrist and pulled her toward the rear of the room. "We must talk in private."

She shot Dr. Gladwell an apologetic look, then turned back to her brother. "Can this wait, Dane?"

He swallowed. "No."

A frisson of fear skittered down her spine. "Very well." She looked over her shoulder at Keane, but Dane had already pulled her halfway to a pair of French doors that led to a large balcony.

Once they were outside and alone, Dane shut the doors behind them and stared at her as if she'd sprouted fins and a mermaid's tail. "What in the devil are you thinking, dancing with"—he pointed in the direction of the dance floor and sputtered as if he couldn't quite bring himself to speak Keane's name—"*him*?"

Sweet Jesus. She'd known her brother had a deep-seated resentment of the aristocracy because, until recently, she'd felt precisely the same. But she'd never imagined he'd be so adamantly opposed to something as innocuous as a dance.

Of course, she and Keane had done much more than dance, but Dane didn't know that. Thank heaven.

"You are overreacting," she said calmly. "What is the harm in dancing with the duke?"

"The harm?" he repeated, incredulous. "The harm comes when you let down your guard and allow a scoundrel to deceive you. To trick you into thinking he cares for you."

She scoffed. "He is not a scoundrel."

Dane narrowed his eyes. "How would you know?"

"Not that it is any of your concern, but I have had the opportunity to further my acquaintance with the duke."

Her brother snorted. "Do you hear yourself, Poppy? You're even starting to speak like them."

She bristled. "What does that mean?"

"It means you're trying to sound like you're better than the rest of us. Like you want to pretend you're someone you're not."

"That's ridiculous." She'd folded her arms across her chest and stared at the horizon where moonlight danced on distant waves. If there was one thing she could say with certainty, it was that she'd remained true to herself. "I am a grown woman, Dane. You left Bellehaven to pursue your dreams while I remained here, doing my best to take care of Papa and keep our business afloat. You have no right to judge me, and you certainly have no say when it comes to whom I choose as my dance partner."

"Shit," he muttered, pacing the length of the balcony. "I realize I haven't been a good brother or a good son. But I would protect you with my life. I couldn't bear it if someone hurt you."

"I can take care of myself," she retorted. "No one is going to hurt me."

Dane dragged his palms down his face. "There are things you don't know about Hawking."

Poppy's blood turned icy. "What sorts of things?"

"There's a reason he fled London. He seduced a maid at his country estate and got her with child. When she told him about the babe, he sent her away, and she died in a freezing stable while giving birth to a stillborn son."

She shivered and recalled the untrue charges people had made against him. "You should not believe every rumor you hear, Dane."

"This was not a rumor. I heard it directly from the maid's brother. He was intent on seeking revenge, and I'd have done the same bloody thing in his shoes. I can't let you go on thinking that the duke is some kind of white knight."

Poppy blinked, irate. "When and where did you meet this man, the one who purports to be the maid's brother? How did he intend to get revenge?"

"It was weeks ago. I didn't ask his name," he said.

"He lied to you." She said it with conviction, as though through the sheer force of her words she could convince

Dane of the truth. She had a suspicion that the man her brother spoke of was somehow involved with the attack on Keane.

Dane shook his thick head. "What reason would the woman's brother have had to lie?"

"I don't know," she said. "But I do know that the duke is not the type of man who would use and discard a person like that."

Her brother's expression turned wary. "How well do you know the duke?"

She raised her chin. "Well enough."

"Poppy," he said earnestly, "you've always been able to tell a good bloke from a bad one, but this situation . . . it's more complicated than you realize."

"Then enlighten me," she replied. "Tell me why you are so adamant that I keep my distance from the duke, a man you scarcely know?"

"I would tell you, but I don't want to drag you into my mess," he muttered. "The less you know, the better."

Poppy gripped the balcony railing to prevent herself from throttling her brother. "What mess?"

Dane frowned and idly twisted Mama's handkerchief around his wrist. "I landed myself in trouble a few weeks ago. There was a high-stakes card game at the Barking Barnacle. I thought my hand was unbeatable."

She stifled a groan. "These sorts of stories never end well."

"I needed that money for us—and to make up for being away from you and Papa this summer. I didn't want you to have to fish every morning at the crack of dawn or have calluses on your hands from rowing." His shoulders slumped. "I lost everything. I thought I had a way to make it right, but that went sideways, too."

She exhaled, letting the balmy breeze carry away some of her anger. "What does any of this have to do with the duke?"

"I don't know exactly what is going on between you and Hawking," Dane said soberly, "but I'm afraid you're going to have to choose. You can side with him, or you side with us—your family. I would hope it's an easy decision."

Poppy faced Dane, standing toe-to-toe with him. "Listen to me. The duke, Keane, is a good man. He might not dress like you or speak like you, but if you had a drink with him at the Salty Mermaid, I daresay you'd find you have more in common with him than you realized. He'd give you the coat off his back if you needed it, and he'd be the first to back you in a fight. But all of that is really beside the point because the only thing that truly matters is . . . I care for him."

He gulped. "No."

She nodded. "And he cares for me, too."

"You've fallen for the duke," Dane said, in the sort of tone normally reserved for when speaking of grave illnesses and other dire news.

"I have. Utterly and completely. And would you like to know something else? He isn't asking me to choose between him and my family." She paused and let that sink into Dane's thick skull. "If you loved me, you wouldn't be asking me to choose, either."

With that, she turned on her heel and left him standing on the balcony, alone with the distant roar of the ocean—and her words ringing in his ears.

Chapter 24

"You and the duke are causing quite a stir." Kitty's blue eyes sparkled with relish as she handed Poppy a glass of champagne and took a sip from her own.

Poppy arched a brow at her young friend. "Does your uncle know you're drinking that?"

"Yes, but he thinks it's my first glass," she said with a cheeky grin. "Where have you been?"

"Outside, speaking with Dane. Suffice it to say he did not approve of my dance with Keane."

Kitty sniffed. "What a pity that his opinion is entirely irrelevant," she said dryly.

"Agreed," Poppy mused. "But there's something Dane isn't telling me. And if there is to be any sort of a future for me and Keane, we must find a way to bring our families together."

"Don't look now," Kitty said under her breath, "but your handsome duke this way comes—and it seems he has his uncle and cousin in tow."

"I didn't realize he had family in town." Poppy exhaled and resolved to set aside her worries about Dane, at least for now. Keane's uncle was the closest thing he had to a father, which meant this meeting was rather momentous.

Intent on making a good first impression, she smiled warmly at the older man with the bald head and kind face.

"Miss Summers and Miss Beckett," Keane said, his face beaming. "May I take this opportunity to introduce you to my uncle? This is the Viscount Rawlings."

"Better known simply as Uncle." The viscount grinned and gestured to the younger, glassy-eyed man beside him. "This is my son, Theodore. We are so pleased to meet you both."

"It's lovely to meet you as well," Poppy said with a graceful curtsey. "Welcome to Bellehaven Bay."

"My nephew has told me a bit about you," the viscount said with a wink. "I begin to understand why he has spent so much time away from London."

Poppy felt her cheeks heat. "I am flattered that you imagine I have anything to do with it."

"I believe I am seeing the appeal of this provincial town myself," Theodore declared, looking at Kitty with undisguised interest.

Kitty ignored his leering, and Keane clasped his shoulder. "Perhaps we should go for a walk, Teddy. Some fresh air would do us both good."

"I don't need air," Theodore said, slurring as if he'd uttered one long word. "I was going to ask Miss Beckett to dance."

"I'm afraid my dance card is full," Kitty said, unfazed.

The viscount glared at his son before turning his attention to Poppy and Kitty. "I think perhaps Theodore and I should make an early night of it and return to the mayor's house."

Theodore scowled. "Don't spoil your evening on my account, Father. By all means, stay and enjoy the company of your favorite nephew and his—" His gaze flicked to

Poppy, and she could see him search for the insult with the ruthlessness of a man reaching for his pistol.

"Theodore," the viscount snapped.

"Have a care, Cousin." Keane's voice was low and lethal.

Theodore snorted. "No need to make a fuss. I was just leaving." He stormed out of the assembly room like a thunder cloud spurred by gale-force winds.

"That went well," Kitty said under her breath.

"Please, forgive my son's abominable manners," the viscount said. "I fear he is suffering from an excess of brandy and a lack of good sense."

"No apology is necessary," Poppy said.

"It most certainly is," Kitty murmured, "just not from *him*."

Poppy smiled, warmed by Kitty's loyalty. As a handsome young man with dark hair and arresting green eyes approached, Poppy subtly poked an elbow in Kitty's side. "It looks like your next dance partner has come to claim your hand."

Kitty placed her empty champagne glass on the tray of a passing footman, took the arm the young man offered, and inclined her head toward Keane and the viscount. "Enjoy the rest of the evening, Your Grace, my lord."

Keane grinned and held out a hand to Poppy. "Shall we join them, Miss Summers?"

Dancing twice with Keane would create even more of a stir, and if the conversation she'd just had with Dane was any indication, he could very well suffer an attack of apoplexy. But she was fully committed to this path. To trying to make things work with Keane.

It had felt good to tell her brother the truth about Keane.

Now, all that was left to do was to tell *him*.

She gazed into his eyes, and her heart fluttered like a dragonfly's wings. "I'd love to dance, Your Grace."

Keane swept Poppy onto the dance floor, glad to have her to himself for the remainder of the set. All he'd wanted out of the evening was to prove to Poppy that their worlds could mingle. That they could carve out a place of their own.

And then Teddy had insulted her.

"I'm sorry about my cousin," he said. "He is spoiled and mostly harmless, but that does not in any way excuse his behavior toward you."

"Given the difference in our stations, those sorts of comments are to be expected."

"No," he said firmly. "You should not have to expect them or tolerate them."

"Agreed. But it is naïve to imagine we will not have to endure them."

"You will not—as long as I am by your side." He twirled her as they traveled the length of the dance floor, unable to resist holding her a fraction closer than was strictly proper.

"I will defend your honor as well," she said soberly. "In fact, I already have this evening."

He arched a brow, amused. "Have you? I am in your debt, Miss Summers."

"I shall think of a suitable form of repayment." She shot him a sultry smile that hit him south of the belt—in the best possible way.

In a valiant attempt to distract himself from wicked thoughts, he asked, "To whom did you defend me?"

"My brother."

Keane nearly missed a step, then recovered. "Your brother? Is he here tonight?"

"He is." She craned her neck around the ballroom. "I

don't see him at the moment, but I shall introduce you later if you like."

Good God. Keane would have thought that the odds of Dane attending tonight's ball were about as good as the Queen of England strolling into the Salty Mermaid and ordering a pint at the bar.

Keane had hoped to have answers about the motivation for Dane's attack on him before they were formally introduced. But if Poppy was ready for them to meet, Keane wasn't going to pass up the opportunity. In fact, her willingness to let him into her inner circle warmed his chest like a beach bonfire.

"I'd love to meet your brother," he said sincerely, despite the fact that the man had almost succeeded in killing him. "But I confess I'm curious as to why you felt the need to defend me."

Her freckled cheeks pinkened. "He did not approve of me dancing with you."

"Then this set is not likely to improve his mood," Keane said wryly.

"I assured him that the rumors he'd heard about you were untrue."

The back of Keane's neck prickled ominously. "What rumors?"

Poppy frowned. "Idle gossip. It doesn't matter. I told him that I care for you."

Keane blinked. "You did?"

She nibbled at her lower lip and nodded. "The truth is—"

A woman's distant scream pealed through the air, bringing the music and dancing to a screeching halt.

"What the devil was that?" Keane murmured.

"It sounded like it came from outside," Poppy said.

"I thought so, too." He quickly ushered her off the dance

floor toward Lord and Lady Bladenton while the room filled with gasps and speculation. "I'm going to investigate. Will you be all right here?"

She nodded. "Do not worry about me. I don't go anywhere without my knife," she admitted, surreptitiously raising the hem of her skirt to reveal a sheath strapped to one shapely calf.

"As if I could forget." He could barely resist the urge to lean in and kiss her full, pink lips. Instead, he reached for her hand and slid his thumb across her palm. "I shall see you soon."

As he was headed to check on the other, smaller assembly rooms, a stable boy burst through the doors of the ballroom and slid to a stop, chest heaving. "There's a man," he said, pointing to the stairs behind him. "Outside on the scaffolding. And it looks like he's going to jump."

Keane rushed to the stable boy and clasped his shoulder. "Which side of the building?"

"Facing Main Street—to the right of the entrance. There's a crowd gathering, sir. I . . . I think he means to do it." Beneath the dirt smudged on his cheeks, the boy's face was pale with fright.

"Don't worry, lad. I'll stop him."

Keane hurried ahead of the milling guests, most of whom were filing down the stairs. But he didn't want to watch the spectacle from the ground.

He jogged across landing toward the west side of the building where a series of four doors lined the wall. One stood ajar, and a lantern light glowed from within the room.

He peered inside the small office where a utilitarian table in the center of the room was cluttered with pink tulle, silk bows, and a few empty vases. A salty breeze toyed with the flickering flame of the lantern on the desk near the room's lone window, where the sash was wide open.

Keane strode across the office, thrust his chest through the window, and blinked as his eyes adjusted to the darkness. Several feet below him, a man sat on the scaffolding, facing away from the building, his legs dangling over the side of the wooden platform.

Keane cleared his throat softly so as not to startle the man. "Nice night. Mind if I join you?"

"Suit yourself." The voice was familiar, but Keane didn't fully believe his ears until the man turned and glanced up at him, nonchalant. "Hullo, Cousin."

"Teddy?" Keane leaned forward and squinted. "What the devil are you doing out here? I thought you were leaving."

"I did leave," Teddy said dryly.

Keane threw a leg over the sill, angled his body through the window opening, and jumped lightly onto the scaffold, causing it to sway on its tall, spindly legs. "If it's fresh air you were wanting, I would have recommended the balcony," he quipped. "This platform is about as stable as a three-legged horse."

Teddy glanced over the edge at the dozen or so people gathered on the street below them. "Have you no sense of adventure?"

"I'm not fond of heights." Keane cautiously lowered himself onto the platform beside his cousin and avoided looking down.

"I didn't ask you to follow me," Teddy said with a drunken snort. "Why don't you climb back through that window and resume your shameless pursuit of the red-headed chit?"

"Her name is Miss Summers," Keane managed through

a clenched jaw. "As you well know." In any other circumstances he would have laid Teddy out flat, but they were three stories above the ground and Teddy was three sheets to the wind. So, he exhaled and focused on the problem at hand. "What do you say we go inside and find ourselves a proper drink? Maybe sneak a cheroot?"

"No need." Teddy reached into his jacket and thrust a flask at Keane. "Here's your proper drink."

Keane took it and helped himself to a healthy swig, figuring the more he drank, the less there was left for Teddy. He rubbed the back of his neck and looked at his cousin earnestly. "Some people are worried you're going to fall."

"Actually, they're worried I'm going to jump."

Keane hesitated then said, "We did a lot of foolish things when we were boys, didn't we? Rode our horses at breakneck speeds, climbed trees we had no business climbing . . . But we're men now. We can only tempt fate so many times before she makes us pay."

"What would you know about that?" Teddy's voice had a bitter note to it. "Fate has been nothing but kind to you."

"I can see how you'd think that." Teddy obviously didn't know what a monster Keane's father had been. "But you've been dealt a fine hand, too. Your father is one of the best men I know, and I have no doubt you'll follow in his footsteps. He'd be sick with worry if he learned you were out here."

Teddy scoffed. "I doubt that's true."

Keane blinked at his cousin. "Of course it's true."

"Let me ask you this." Teddy shifted suddenly, making the scaffolding wobble as he turned toward Keane. "Suppose my father had to make a choice and could only save one of us—you or me. Who do you think he would choose?"

Unease settled in the pit of Keane's stomach. "Bloody hell, Teddy. What sort of a question is that?"

"The revealing sort."

Damn, but the night had taken a strange turn. Teddy was prying the lid off Pandora's box, and Keane wasn't at all certain he wanted to see what was inside. He shook his head slowly. "I refuse to waste a single minute speculating about something so asinine—especially when we're three bloody stories high, sitting on a platform that was apparently slapped together by an apprentice with two left hands."

Teddy took the flask, tipped it back, and smacked his lips. "You don't have to speculate, Cousin, because I already know. My father would choose *you*. You're the one he prefers to hunt with, joke with, drink with . . . You're the one he prefers. Period."

Keane scoffed. "That"—he wagged a finger at the flask—"has muddled your head. You don't even know what you're saying. You are his *son*. Of course he would put you first."

"You should have seen him," Teddy said flatly. "Throughout the last few weeks when he thought something had happened to you. He wouldn't eat. Wouldn't sleep. Insisted that we come to this godforsaken town so he could assure himself you were well."

Keane peered over the edge of the scaffold. Even in the darkness he could see that the group of ball guests on the street had doubled in size. Snippets of their conversations floated up, carried by the bay breeze. "They're worried," he said to Teddy. "And I don't much like it up here, either. I propose that we remove ourselves to a more civilized place—somewhere with comfortable chairs and a solid floor."

Keane held his breath, hoping he didn't have to drag

Teddy back through the window by his jacket collar. And after several heartbeats, his shoulders sagged.

"Very well. Do me a favor and forget we ever had this conversation." He shook the empty flask, frowned, and hurled it onto the street, barely missing the heads of the horrified onlookers.

"Jesus, Teddy, you could've killed somebody."

He barked a hollow laugh. "Killing somebody isn't as easy as you might think."

Keane clucked his tongue. "You're an expert, are you? Come on now, I'll help you up." He cast a wary eye at a rope coiled on the platform behind them and slid back from the edge. "Careful. Let's do this slowly, shall we?"

Keane exhaled. In a matter of minutes, he'd be back in the ballroom with Poppy, basking in the glow of her sapphire eyes. Making her believe in a future with him.

Only first, he had to succeed in stuffing his inebriated cousin through a chest-high window.

He stood behind Teddy, grabbed his arms beneath the elbows, and grunted as he hoisted him to his feet.

But Teddy staggered backward, slamming Keane against the building wall and knocking the breath from his lungs. Teddy slipped from his grasp, lurched toward the end of the platform, and crashed into the splintered pole at the corner.

An ominous *crack* rang out, prickling the skin at the back of Keane's neck.

The support snapped, the platform tilted, and Teddy lunged toward Keane.

Teddy's face contorted with fear; his hands grasped at air.

Till Keane grabbed him by the wrist. "I've got you," he said with more confidence than he felt.

Teddy looked down at the steep angle of the platform. "I'm going to fall."

"No, you're not." Keane shifted his weight onto his heels so he wouldn't slide. "Trust me, and don't make any sudden moves."

Teddy released a shaky breath. "Don't let go," he begged.

"I won't." But his fingers were already turning numb. "We need a rope. Suspended from the window." The window that was now almost out of reach.

"There's no time," Teddy wailed. "You have to do something. Quick."

His cousin was right. "On the count of three, I'm going to haul you up. Grab my shoulders and hold on. Understand?"

Teddy nodded mutely.

Keane closed his eyes briefly. "One, two . . . three."

He grunted as he lifted Teddy, inch by backbreaking inch. Keane's forearms quivered; his muscles burned. Teddy latched onto him like a frightened child, clutching fistfuls of jacket and wrapping his legs around Keane's torso. He shook like a leaf and reeked of fear.

"You're safe now," Keane said, even as the scaffolding swayed and creaked beneath his feet. "But we've got to get you up to the window."

Teddy clung tighter. "I can't reach it."

"I'll push you up. You grab onto the sill and pull yourself through. Nothing could be easier. Just pretend you're a lad again, climbing an oak at Hawking Manor."

He glanced up, clearly skeptical, and whimpered.

"I'll help you," Keane assured him. "I'll lace my fingers together like a stirrup."

Teddy pressed his lips together and nodded again. He

climbed and clawed his way over Keane, tearing his jacket, kicking his stomach, and stepping on his head.

At last, he slung an arm over the windowsill. "I've got it!" he yelled victoriously, causing the spectators to cheer. "You need to give me one more big shove."

Keane cautiously centered himself under his cousin and reached for his bootheels. "We need to do this easy," he warned. "On three again. One, two . . . three."

He pushed with all his might, launching Teddy through the window.

The crowd below gasped with relief.

Thank heaven. Now all Keane had to do was—

Groan. The scaffolding careened, on the verge of collapse.

His stomach dropped, and hairs on the backs of his arms raised. He wasn't ready to leave this earth. Or Poppy. "Look out!" he shouted, and the crowd below scattered.

Teddy had tumbled into the office, and Keane didn't have time to wait.

He leaped straight up and grabbed the sill by his fingertips. Just as the platform fell away and crashed to the ground.

Chapter 25

"Surely, Keane should have returned by now," Poppy said to Hazel. "I wish I'd gone with him."

Hazel's gaze flicked to the grandfather clock along the wall of the ballroom. "He hasn't been gone long—and I'm certain he wants you to stay safe here, away from the commotion."

"Perhaps." Poppy tapped the toe of her slipper against the parquet dance floor. "But I cannot stand feeling so useless. I'm going to see what's happened." Decision made, she picked up her skirts and rushed toward the exit.

"Wait," Hazel called after her. "I'm coming, too."

But Poppy was already gliding down the stairs. When she dashed outside of the building, she joined the agitated crowd gathered on the pavement. Some were dressed for the ball, some for the pub, but they were all looking up, so she did, too.

And her stomach sank through her knees.

Keane was hanging from a third-story window, his body pressed against the pale-gray stone façade of the building. Tears burned her eyes as she watched him struggle, his body swaying slightly as he clung to the edge.

"No," she whispered, swallowing the awful knot in her

throat. But there was no denying the truth—she would have recognized him anywhere.

Hazel appeared at her side, breathless. "Good heavens. Please tell me that's not . . ."

"It's Keane," Poppy choked out. "I've got to help."

"I could send for Blade," Hazel offered.

"There's no time." Besides, Poppy was accustomed to taking on the world by herself. It was what she'd always done.

Hazel gave her arm a quick squeeze. "Be careful."

Poppy stifled a sob as she ran back toward the Assembly Rooms. Only a quarter of an hour ago, Keane had been holding her hand. Now, he was holding on for his life.

She should have told him everything that was in her heart while she had the chance. That she secretly adored his vexing questions. That she melted whenever he whispered in her ear. That her belly fluttered every time he shot her a lopsided grin.

She should have told him she loved him.

"Hold on, Keane," she murmured. "If you love me half as much as I love you, just . . . hold on."

Keane's fingers had lost all feeling. His body swung wildly as he adjusted his grip. "Teddy!"

"I'm here," Teddy gasped, sagging against the window frame.

Thank God. "Help me."

"Of course, Cousin. Just give me a moment to catch my breath."

A bead of sweat rolled off the tip of Keane's nose. "I don't have a moment. Pull me up."

His cousin stood there mutely, cold and unseeing.

"Teddy! What's wrong with you?"

Holy hell. He was useless as a statue. Maybe in shock.

Keane was going to have to save himself. One arm over the sill. That was all he needed.

He summoned every ounce of strength. Grunted as he pulled himself one inch higher. Then another. And another.

He swung his legs for some momentum, then threw his right arm over the stone threshold—and held on like it was the only thing between him and a grisly death. Which it was.

"Make way, Teddy," Keane managed between gasps. "I'm coming in."

Teddy's blank stare turned sharp. Chillingly sinister. "I wouldn't be so sure about that, Cousin."

"Not funny," he ground out. "Move, or I'll knock you over."

"I want you to know I didn't plan this. Not this time, at any rate." He reached for the lantern and removed the glass cylinder, exposing the flame. "But fate led us here. It's as though she's finishing the job for me."

Teddy wasn't making sense, damn it, unless . . .

No. Teddy had all but confessed, and yet Keane could scarcely wrap his mind around it. Or maybe he just didn't want to believe it.

Teddy was the one who'd tried to kill him.

He shoved the thought to the back of his brain.

Keane dug the toes of his boots into the outside wall to take some weight off his arm. "If you know what's good for you, you'll get out of my way."

Teddy's smile sent a chill down his spine. "That superior attitude, that insufferable arrogance. They're precisely why I did it."

"Did what?" But deep in his gut, he already knew the answer.

Teddy moved the flame underneath Keane's hand and stared into his eyes. "Tried to get rid of you."

Anger flared in Keane's chest; his fingers burned and blistered in the heat of the flame. He waved his palm blindly, trying to snuff it out.

Teddy only laughed. "You, Cousin, are a bastard who never deserved to become a duke. The title should have passed to my father . . . and then to me."

The stench of burnt skin filled Keane's nostrils. The sleeve of his jacket caught fire. Every nerve ending screamed for him to pull away from the flame. But he could not let go.

"Let's discuss this like men," Keane said. "If you want an estate of your own—"

"I want a dukedom." He moved the flame directly beneath Keane's wrist. "And I'll soon have it."

"By killing me?" Keane gasped.

"This will appear to be a terrible accident. You'll come out looking like a hero, of course. You should be grateful for that."

"Grateful? You prick," he spat.

"How dare you." Teddy hurled the lantern against a wall. Closed his hands around Keane's neck. And squeezed.

The world went hazy. His ears buzzed. Teddy's voice echoed in his head.

"The Summers girl is not duchess material. But she'll make a fine mistress."

"Fuck you," Keane mouthed. No sound came out, but he said it over and over in his head.

Teddy growled with rage. "Damn you to hell, Hawking." They were the words Keane had heard weeks ago on the dock, just before he'd been tossed into the ocean. Teddy *had* tried to drown him.

Keane's throat burned. His eyes bulged. His fingers slipped. If this was the end, he had plenty of regrets.

But the biggest was going before he'd had the chance to marry Poppy.

The world turned gray at the edges. Oblivion crept closer, reaching for him with greedy fingers.

Crack. The lantern clocked Teddy in the jaw, launching him halfway across the room.

Air rushed into Keane's lungs. He sputtered and coughed.

A pair of huge hands grabbed him beneath the arms, hauled him through the window, and dropped him face-down onto the floor. Spasms racked his chest. His clothes smoldered and smoked.

Till a large jacket covered his torso, putting out the last of the flames.

Keane rolled over and blinked. *Poppy.*

She stood above him, gorgeously fierce in her ball gown, holding the lantern like a smoking pistol. Her brother was at her side, flexing his fingers as he glared at Teddy, who was slumped against a wall, unconscious.

"Poppy," Keane choked out. "Are you all right?"

She set down the lantern, knelt beside him, and pressed her palm to his cheek. "I am. Are you?"

"You saved my life."

"I had a little help." She glanced over her shoulder. "Allow me to introduce my brother, Dane. He's the one who pulled you up. I must say, it felt good to count on him, especially when it mattered most."

Poppy's brother shuffled his feet. "Hawking."

Keane raised his chin in acknowledgment. "You pulled me off the ledge."

"I suppose I did." He scrubbed the back of his neck. "Look, there's something I need to tell you."

Keane lifted his arm and examined the charred sleeve of his jacket. "I already know what you're going to say."

"I don't think you do. This doesn't have anything to

do with my sister. Although I have plenty to say on that score, too."

"I'm right here, Dane," Poppy said dryly. "And I think I've proven I'm capable of taking care of myself."

Her brother dragged his hands through his hair, chastened. "I'm sorry I haven't been a better brother. But that's going to change."

Keane staggered to his feet. "There will be time for us to talk later."

Poppy clasped his wrist and frowned at his raw palm. "This looks awful. I'm going to fetch Dr. Gladwell." She looked earnestly at Keane, then her brother. "Can I trust you two alone for a few scant minutes?"

"Absolutely," Dane said, as if the very question were absurd.

"Of course," Keane chimed in, pretending to be mildly offended.

"Right." Poppy's brilliant blue eyes narrowed as she headed for the door. "Let's try to avoid any further excitement this evening, shall we?" With a swish of her skirts, she left them alone in the room, standing toe-to-toe.

To his credit, Dane looked Keane directly in the eyes.

Without preamble, he said, "That night I left the Salty Mermaid, I know it was you who attacked me."

Dane nodded and clasped his hands behind his back as if stoically awaiting his sentence.

"I also know that you did it at the request of my cousin."

"He claimed to be the brother of a maid you seduced and abandoned," Dane said sheepishly. "He offered me a large sum if I'd teach you a lesson. I told myself you deserved it. That the money would help Poppy and my father. That I'd finally have something worthwhile to contribute."

"He lied to you," Keane said sadly. "I suppose he lied to me, too."

"It doesn't excuse what I did," Dane said. "I didn't mean to hit you so hard. I—I think I panicked when you started to fight back. And when I saw how much your head was bleeding, I ran for help. I returned to the alley with one of my mates . . . but you were gone."

"That's because Teddy dragged me to the docks, threw me into the bay, and left me to drown."

Dane shook his head, dumbfounded. "Why does he hate you so much?"

The question made Keane flinch. "I have something he wants."

Dane nodded slowly. "Just so you know, your cousin never paid me. He tried to, later in the pub. He said I'd done my job well, but as desperate as we were—as we still are—I couldn't take his blood money. I'm not saying that makes up for what I did," Dane quickly added. "I suppose that what I'm really saying is I'm sorry." He swallowed and raised his chin. "I'm ready to face the consequences of my actions."

"I accept your apology." With his good hand, Keane grasped Dane's shoulder. "Tonight, you saved me from falling to my death. I'd say that makes us even now."

Dane blinked. "I don't know what to say. Are you certain?"

"I'd shake your hand, but . . ." Keane held up his red, blistered palm.

"Thank you," Dane said, disbelieving. "My sister says you're a good man."

"She says you are, too."

Dane cracked a smile. "She might have exaggerated a bit in my case."

Just then, Bladenton ran into the doorway, chest heaving. "Hawking! Thank God. I feared I'd be too late." His gaze flicked to Teddy, sprawled on the floor, and Dane, standing there in his shirtsleeves. "What the devil is going on here?"

"Come in and lock the door behind you," Keane said. "We have some tidying up to do."

Chapter 26

Poppy found Dr. Gladwell in the ballroom, surrounded by a trio of older gentlemen who were animatedly describing their assorted maladies. He looked more than a little relieved when she approached.

"Miss Summers," he said brightly. "A pleasure."

"Forgive me for interrupting," she said, casting an apologetic smile at the older men. "Dr. Gladwell, I wondered if I might have a word?"

He immediately stepped away from the men and, in a hushed tone, asked, "Is everything all right?"

"It will be." She smiled for the benefit of the curious eyes in the room. "But a couple of men down the hall require your attention. Would you mind coming with me?"

The doctor's smooth forehead creased in concern. "Of course not. My bag is in the room next door; I'll pick it up on our way."

Poppy led him toward the office where she'd left Keane, Dane, and Teddy. "They're in there," she said, pointing to the closed door.

"Who's in there?" asked a familiar voice.

Poppy turned toward Kitty, who was assessing the situation with her shrewd gaze.

"I'll explain everything," Poppy said. "When I can."

Dr. Gladwell knocked on the door. "It's best if you stay out here while I tend to them."

Poppy longed to return to Keane's side, but she trusted the doctor. "Please, let me know if you need anything."

"Thank you," he called over his shoulder, then entered the office and shut the door.

"Well?" Kitty blinked at Poppy, expectant.

Poppy exhaled. "What have you heard?"

"Let's see," Kitty said, dramatically tapping an index finger to her lips. "There was mention of scaffolding collapsing, flames coming from a window, and—oh, yes—a man hanging from the sill."

"I can confirm those rumors." Now that Keane was safe, Poppy had a moment to think about what could have happened—what almost did happen—and it made her knees shake.

Kitty arched a brow. "I've also heard that the man in question was your duke."

"*My* duke?"

"You did dance with him twice this evening," she said, blue eyes twinkling. "I assume he'll be all right?"

"Yes." Poppy exhaled, reminding herself that he was, in fact, safe. "At least for tonight."

As if Kitty sensed that Poppy was a bundle of raw emotions, she took her hand, led her to a chair, and made her sit. "I have about a dozen questions I'd like to ask you, but I shall refrain. For now," she added with a wink.

"Thank you."

Poppy was replaying the events of the night in her head when the door opened a crack, and Dane slipped out. His gaze flicked to Poppy, and he walked closer.

Kitty gasped at the sight of him. "Why does his jacket look like it's been trampled by a herd of sheep?" She wrinkled her perfectly sloped nose. "And why does it smell like a bonfire?"

"Add those to your list of questions," Poppy said with a smile.

"Miss Beckett," Dane said, doing his best impression of a gentlemanly bow.

"Hullo, Dane," Kitty replied.

"Could I please have a word with my sister?"

Kitty sighed in resignation. To Poppy she said, "I have a feeling you could use a drink. I'll fetch you one."

"Just lemonade, please," Poppy said.

"Lemonade for you, champagne for me." Kitty tossed her blond curls and grinned as she glided toward the ballroom.

When she and her brother were alone, Poppy asked, "How is Keane?"

"Hawking is fine. He has a plan, which I'm sure he'll share with you—when the time is right."

"When will he be coming out?"

"Soon. But there's something else I need to tell you."

Oh God. Confessions from Dane always seemed to create more work for Poppy. "What is it?" she asked warily.

He dragged both hands down his face. "I jumped the duke on his way home from the pub one night."

"Dane! I can't believe . . ." She fought back a wave of nausea. "I can't believe you hurt him. How could you?"

"It was a stupid thing to do. Beyond stupid. I thought . . . Well, it doesn't matter what I thought. I was dead wrong about Hawking."

"You could have killed him, Dane," she whispered. "You could have committed murder."

Her brother shuddered. "I know. I'm sorry. Look, I need to go back in there. The best thing you can do is to return to the ballroom and assure the other guests that Hawking and his cousin are fine."

"I will do as you ask, but please give the duke a message for me."

Dane made a face and shook his head, adamant. "Please don't ask me to relay lovesick sentiments from my own sister."

Poppy arched a brow. "All things considered it would be the lightest of sentences. Just inform the duke that if he doesn't come out of that room within the next half hour, I shall find a way in—even if it means I must scale the side of the building."

With that, she stood, made her way back into the ballroom, and found both Kitty and Hazel. Poppy's gaze flicked from the grandfather clock to the large entryway and back. Many of the guests had decided not to return to the Assembly Rooms after the harrowing incident, apparently preferring to remove themselves to the Salty Mermaid—much to Lady Rufflebum's dismay.

"I'm gratified to hear that tragedy was avoided, of course," the countess was saying. "However, 'tis a pity that the ball was spoiled." She clucked her tongue. "I do my best to bring some semblance of culture and refinement to Bellehaven Bay, and this is the result."

"On the bright side," Poppy said, "no one is likely to forget the First Annual Regatta Ball. People will be talking about it all year, ensuring that next year's event shall be even more of a success." She marveled at her ability to engage in small talk when she'd just learned that her brother had tried to kill the man she loved.

"I suppose that is true," Lady Rufflebum said, apparently mollified. "And it doesn't hurt that the hero of the tale is a duke."

"Quite right," Hazel agreed, surreptitiously poking Poppy with her elbow. "A young, handsome duke to boot."

Poppy paced the ballroom for several minutes, then paused to check the time. Again. A half hour had passed, and she refused to wait a second longer. Just as she was heading for the door, a striking group of gentlemen strolled into the room. Blade and Dr. Gladwell stood on either side of Keane's cousin, Teddy, who seemed to require their assistance in order to remain upright.

Keane walked in behind the trio, his confident stride at odds with his disheveled appearance. His cravat was tied in a lopsided slipknot. His hair looked like he'd been at sea for days. One of his jacket sleeves appeared to have been scorched. His hand and wrist were bandaged.

And the sight of him still left her breathless.

He walked directly over and grinned at her, giving no sign of having been on the brink of death earlier that evening. "Miss Summers. Thank you for saving me—again."

She wanted to throw her arms around his neck and kiss him. But since all eyes seemed to be on them, she settled for saying, "Your Grace."

"I am glad you are still here," he murmured, his words like the tickle of a feather over her skin.

"I am glad you are still alive despite your apparent proclivity for flirting with Death."

"I am still very much alive—and only interested in flirting with you."

Her belly turned a somersault. "We need to talk."

"Can I see you later tonight?" he whispered.

She nodded. "Come to the shelter. I'll be waiting."

Poppy checked that Papa was sleeping soundly, placed a few provisions in her satchel, and headed to her refuge.

She couldn't bear to take off the beautiful ball gown so soon, but she'd let down her hair and left her stockings and slippers in her loft.

There was something terribly decadent about wearing silk to the beach. The wind frolicked with her hem; the fabric caressed her skin. She ducked through the entrance, lit the lantern, and pushed aside the curtains, but the swirling ocean breeze did little to soothe her nerves. Indeed, her insides were as knotted as an old fishing net.

She'd hoped that tonight would be the night she could finally tell Keane her feelings.

Instead, she had to tell him that his attacker—the person she'd been helping him look for over the last several weeks—was her brother. The more she considered the circumstances, the more distressing she found them. In order for her to have the possibility of a future with Keane, she needed him to fully embrace her family. But considering that Dane had tried to kill Keane and almost succeeded, she wouldn't blame him if he wanted revenge. And she certainly couldn't ask him to trust her brother.

She and Keane had come so close to making their relationship work. They'd navigated their way through treacherous waters only to have their hopes dashed to bits by rocks along the shore.

With a tremulous sigh, she leaned back among the pillows and reached for a book, resolving to pass the time till Keane arrived. But before long, the book dropped against her chest, her eyes fluttered shut, and she drifted to sleep.

"Poppy." Keane's voice, low and rich, filled her head, mingling with her dreams.

His fingers combed through her hair, caressing her scalp till she tingled from head to toe.

His lips brushed over hers, softly at first, before growing

more insistent. He nibbled her lower lip and dipped his tongue into her mouth, kissing her as if his whole world boiled down to this one beautiful moment.

She longed to surrender to the desire that coursed through her body. Wanted nothing more than to give herself entirely to him. Forever.

But above all else, she owed him the truth.

Gradually, she slowed the kiss and pulled away. "Keane."

"I've missed you," he said hoarsely. "I don't want to be without you anymore."

She sat up and blinked, drinking in the sight of him. He'd changed into a fresh shirt and jacket, and his hair was damp, as if he'd gone for a swim before coming to her.

"We have much to discuss," she said. "I want to know everything that happened tonight—why you were hanging from the window, how your jacket was burned, and why your hand is bandaged. But there's something I must tell you first, and I fear you're not going to like it."

His forehead creased. "As long as you are well, nothing can trouble me."

"You should reserve judgment until you've heard what I have to say. And you must let me tell you the whole of it at once. It will be easier for me that way—ripping off the entire bandage, as it were."

He propped himself on one elbow, stretched his legs beside hers, and gazed directly into her eyes.

She swallowed, making a valiant attempt to focus. To blithely ignore the tanned patch of skin above his open collar and the muscled forearm below his rolled-up shirt-sleeve.

"I know the person who tried to kill you," she said.

He went very still. "You do?"

She nodded and opened her mouth, letting the awful

words come out. "I was in the dark until the ball this evening. You must believe me about that. Not in a hundred years did it occur to me that your attacker could be . . ." She gulped and forced herself to continue. ". . . my brother. But it was Dane. He was the one who hit you on the head after you left the Salty Mermaid. I have no idea why he would commit such a heinous crime, nor will I attempt to defend his actions which are . . . well, indefensible."

Her eyes burned with unshed tears. "All I can say is that he is my brother. My hard-headed, protective-to-a-fault, short-tempered brother. And I beg you to have mercy on him. Of course, you have every right to seek justice, but if you care for me in the slightest—and I believe that you do—please do not report him to the authorities. They would, no doubt, hang him, and I do not believe my poor Papa could survive such a thing. Honestly, I don't think I could bear it, either. If you wish, I could persuade him to go away. To make an honest life in another town and never come back to Bellehaven Bay or London again."

She took a shaky breath and continued. "I realize that this development changes everything between us. I will not fault you if you wish to walk away from this place. To wash your hands of me and my family . . . forever."

Her voice cracked on the last word. Her chest ached. But she'd told him the horrific truth.

Oddly enough, he was still there. His green eyes glowed with compassion—and perhaps something else, too.

"Is that all you wished to tell me?" he asked huskily.

She sniffled. "My brother almost killed you. I'd say that's quite enough, wouldn't you?"

"I already knew about Dane," he said with a shrug.

She shook her head, certain she must have misheard him. "What do you mean?"

"I saw your brother walking to the beach one day, and a few more details from that night suddenly came into focus. I recognized the handkerchief he wears on his wrist. I knew he was the one who knocked me out."

"Did you confront him?" she asked, aghast.

"No."

"Did you tell anyone else?"

"Just Diggs. But you don't need to worry about him."

"I know." She frowned. "Why . . . why didn't you tell me?"

Keane exhaled. "Because I know how important your family is to you. I didn't want you to feel torn between loyalty to your brother and your feelings for me. Maybe it was wrong of me not to tell you, but I didn't want to put you in the middle. And perhaps I was afraid."

She blinked at him. "Afraid of what?"

He hesitated, then looked at her, solemn. "That you'd choose your family over me. Over us."

Poppy sat up slowly, letting his words sink in. Warmth blossomed in her chest and radiated through her limbs. "A few weeks ago, before we went to Ascot, we were right here, in this shelter."

"I remember. I remember everything about you."

"Then you might recall something I said. I said that you might know me in your head . . ."

"But that I'd never understand you in my heart," he finished for her.

She took his large, warm hand and laced her fingers through his. "I was wrong," she said simply. "What you did, the way you tried to protect me and Dane . . . No one has ever been willing to sacrifice so much for me."

"It never felt like a sacrifice, Poppy. It felt like love." He raised her hand and pressed a slow, fervent kiss to the inside of her wrist. "You needn't worry that I'll go to the authorities. I don't think Dane is a danger to me or anyone else. And he doesn't need to go into exile either. We've talked, and I think we understand each other. He's a decent bloke."

"Thank you," she said earnestly. "For seeing the good in him. Trust me when I say I know it isn't always easy. If there's anything we can do to make amends, or if there is anything I can do to repay your kindness, you must tell me."

"No." He frowned as if mildly insulted. "All I want is your heart and your trust."

"You already have that," she assured him.

"Do I?" he asked earnestly. "There is a part of you that has always been closed off to me. Like a room that you've locked up and forbidden me to enter."

"If it is any comfort, it's not just you that I keep out. It's everyone."

He shot her a winsome smile. "And here I thought I was special."

"You are," she said soberly. "And it's time I let you in." Even if the prospect terrified her. Her heart was beating triple-time already.

As if he knew, Keane pressed a kiss to her forehead. "Why don't we walk by the water?" he suggested. "I suspect the fresh air and the sound of the waves will do us both good."

"An excellent idea."

Chapter 27

Poppy and Keane ducked through the blanket hanging in the entrance and stretched their arms and legs. Her gaze flicked to his bandaged hand. "Does it hurt?"

"Not really. You are a welcome distraction."

She held his good hand as they wound their way down the path and through the reeds toward the shore. The breeze whipped at her skirts and turned her hair into a cloud of bouncy curls. When they reached the sand, she inhaled deeply, letting the salty sea air work its magic and soothe her nerves.

"You once asked me why I am distrustful of people like you," she began.

"Of the nobility," he said. "You said they hurt someone you loved."

"It was my mother," she said softly.

His eyes shone with compassion. "I take it you were very close?"

A lump formed in Poppy's throat, and she nodded. "When I was five, she taught me to read, and whenever we could steal a few minutes, we would escape into books. Sometimes she read to me; sometimes I read to her. We read books about faraway lands and daring adventure. We read tales about love and loss and redemption."

"That sounds magical."

Poppy managed a smile. "It was the best sort of childhood. But Mama wanted a better life for me. She'd been raised as a lady and was determined to teach me fine manners and social graces. I fear most of her lessons were lost on me."

"You're kind, caring, and confident," he said firmly. "I think your mother would be proud."

Poppy wanted to believe that, but with each year that passed, it was harder and harder to recall the things Mama had taught her. Worse, it was growing more difficult to remember her sparkling eyes and infectious smile. Poppy gazed at the inky black sky and took courage from the twinkle of a distant star.

"The winter I turned nine, Mama took ill. It was a particularly harsh January, and the cottage was so cold that ice formed inside the windows. No matter how many quilts I piled on top of her, no matter how many logs Papa added to the fire, she still shivered. Never before had I felt so helpless or so scared."

Keane wrapped an arm around her shoulders. "There was nowhere you could go?"

Poppy shook her head. "She became very sick, very quickly. Her fever raged; she couldn't drink. She barely had the strength to open her eyes. The doctor told Papa we should try to make her comfortable . . . and say our goodbyes." Poppy had been sitting beside Mama, pressing a damp cloth to her forehead. She'd bitten the inside of her cheek to keep from screaming.

"Do you want to rest for a bit?" Concern was etched on Keane's face. "This must be very difficult to talk about."

"I think I need to keep going." If she didn't, she might well lose her courage and bottle up the truth for another decade. "Mama kept asking for her sister who lived in

London, but the entire family had disowned her when she married my father."

"Because he was a fisherman?"

Poppy nodded. "They met while she and her family were here on holiday one summer. He taught her to fish, and she taught him to read. She would sneak away to the beach to meet him. And they fell in love. She wanted to marry my father, but he said he loved her too much to make a lady like her a fisherman's wife. She was heartbroken when summer ended and she had to return to London. But soon after, she discovered she was with child."

Keane arched a brow. "I imagine that was quite a scandal."

"Her parents hastily arranged for her to marry an earl, but she refused. As soon as she could manage it, she ran away and came to Bellehaven Bay. She told my father about the babe, and they eloped. If Mama ever regretted her decision, she never showed it. She never seemed to long for the niceties of her former life, but she desperately missed her older sister."

"And when your mother became sick, she wanted to see her."

"Yes. I'd never met Aunt Evelyn, but I'd heard plenty of stories about her. According to Mama, she was whip-smart, gracious, and dutiful. She never married and still lived with my grandparents in London."

"Did your father try to find her?"

"No, but I did."

Keane winced. "On your own?"

Poppy nodded. "I knelt next to Mama's bed and promised to fetch Aunt Evelyn and bring her to Mama's side. I kissed her cheek and swore I'd be back soon . . . but I failed her."

"You were a child." Keane reached for her face and

grazed his thumb across her lower lip. "How on earth could you manage a trip like that?"

"I took the mail coach. I'd been to London with Mama before, and we'd driven past her parents' house in Mayfair. I remembered the ivy-covered stones and the glossy black door with the brass knocker. It was raining when I arrived on their doorstep, and I was so relieved when the butler opened the door, even though he scowled at me. I told him who I was, and that Mama was sick, and begged to speak with Lady Evelyn."

"What happened?"

"He said he would see if the family was receiving and told me to wait there. When he came back, he said that I must have been mistaken. That Lady Evelyn did not have a sister, and she most definitely did not have a niece."

"Poppy," Keane rasped. "I'm sorry."

"I stayed there on the doorstep all night, in the rain. I hoped that someone would come or go, giving me a chance to plead my case. But they never did. The next morning, a kindly maid snuck me a sandwich and urged me to go before the earl ordered a footman to toss me on my ear." Poppy shrugged helplessly. "I didn't know what else to do, so I left."

"Who are they?" Keane's voice was low and lethal. "The earl and countess. What are their names?"

"It doesn't matter. By the time I made it back home . . . Mama was gone. I should have been there with her, holding her hand. I should have at least said goodbye. But I was miles away when her soul left this earth . . . and couldn't even grant her dying wish."

Keane hauled her into her his arms and crushed her to his chest, rubbing her back as she sobbed. She cried for Mama, Papa, Dane, herself, and all the years they should have had together.

She cried because when Mama died, all the dreams she'd had for Poppy died, too.

Till now, she'd never told anyone about the events of that night. Not even Dane or Papa knew exactly what had happened. But Keane had listened. He'd understood. And he didn't seem to mind that she'd soaked the front of his shirt with her tears.

"Thank you for confiding in me." He uttered the words soberly—as if she'd given him a rare and precious gift. "It's no wonder you're wary of members of the ton."

She inhaled a shaky breath. "I know that you're not like them, Keane."

"No," he said firmly. "I'm not."

"But that doesn't mean things will be easy for us. Some of your friends won't approve of me. Some of my family won't trust yours."

"That is probably true. But when they see how ridiculously happy we make each other, they'll change their minds—just like you changed yours." He grinned, scooped her into his arms, and held her against his chest.

"What are you doing?" His arresting green eyes were mere inches from hers, and his hungry gaze made her belly flutter.

"Taking you back to the shelter." He raised a questioning brow. "Any objection?"

She opened her mouth to say she was capable of walking, then thought better of it. After years of taking care of everyone around her, it felt odd—but wonderful—to surrender into Keane's strength. To let him take care of her.

"I have no objection," she said, nuzzling her cheek against his shoulder. "Onward."

Keane savored the feel of Poppy's lush curves pressed against his torso and the citrusy scent of her hair tickling his nose. She melted into him as though she was nestling into a pile of pillows—and he loved that she was taking the comfort he'd offered.

He was even more touched that she'd confided in him. His strong, self-sufficient, and courageous Poppy had trusted him. She'd shared her most vulnerable time, her deepest wound, giving him every reason to be hopeful.

It didn't matter that his cousin—the closest thing he had to a brother—had tried to kill him. Twice. Now that Keane was in possession of the facts, he could deal with Teddy accordingly. But that was a matter for tomorrow. Tonight was exclusively for Poppy and him.

On the way back to the shelter, she asked him about all that had happened that evening, and he told her about the faulty scaffolding, Teddy's shocking confession, and his sadistic attempt to send Keane plummeting from the third-story window.

"Why did you let him walk out of the Assembly Rooms?" she asked, aghast. "He should be locked up and made to pay."

"True. That's what Teddy deserves, but imprisoning him would cause my uncle unnecessary shame and heartache . . . so I'm working on another solution."

She sniffed, incensed on Keane's behalf. "I don't trust Teddy. But I suppose that's not fair of me, considering I pleaded with you to have mercy on Dane."

"My cousin lied to your brother. When Dane knocked me out, he thought he was righting a wrong."

"Dane doesn't *think* much at all," she admitted. "Which is why I fully intend to wring his neck at the first opportunity."

Keane chuckled. "Dane and I will discuss it over a pint of ale. By the time the pub closes, we'll probably be the best of friends."

Her freckled nose crinkled adorably. "Men are vexingly mysterious creatures. But I suppose the important thing is that you were mostly unhurt. How is your hand?" she asked. "The bandaged one."

"It's supporting your bottom right now," he said with a grin. "Which may be the reason I'm not feeling even a hint of pain."

He wound his way up the path, then slowly lowered her to the ground in front of the shelter, letting her body slide down his.

"Thank you," she said breathlessly. "For taking care of me. Now I intend to take care of you."

"You do?" He arched a brow, intrigued.

"Mmm." She took him by the hand, led him inside the dimly lit lean-to, and instructed him to sit on the thick quilt. "First, I think we must remove your boots." Refusing the help he offered, she wrestled off his Hessians and placed them outside.

"Next," she continued, "this jacket must go." She knelt behind him and slowly pulled it off his shoulders and down his arms before setting it aside. "That's much better, don't you think?"

"Aye." He looked over his shoulder at her, and she clucked her tongue.

She slid a fingertip along his jaw, turning his head away from her. "It is your turn to trust me," she whispered close to his ear. "Do you trust me, Keane?"

He didn't miss a beat. "With my life."

"Good." She dangled a scarf in front of him, slid it along his cheek, then gently placed it over his eyes and secured it at the back of his head. "Is that comfortable?"

"Aye," he repeated. But in truth, he was more than comfortable. He was totally and utterly enthralled by this game—and by her.

"Excellent," she purred, tugging at the ties of his shirt. "But I feel certain we can do even better." Her nimble fingers loosened his collar and slid beneath the smooth lawn, tracing the contours of his chest. Like a glass of brandy, her touch heated his blood and left him reeling— in the best possible way.

She reached around him, grabbed fistfuls of his shirt, and smoothly hauled it over his head. As the evening air cooled his skin, Poppy shifted behind him and pressed her warm lips to his nape, sending a delicious shiver down his spine.

Then her hands went to work, kneading his shoulders and the sore muscles he'd used to hang on to the window. She seemed to know just where the most tender spots were, and she lingered on them, banishing the knots with her unique blend of skill and determination.

Gradually, she moved downward, massaging the tightness out of his lower back until he sighed from the sheer pleasure of it.

"Better?" she murmured against his neck.

"Better," he confirmed.

"I am glad." She trailed her fingers over his shoulders and down his arms, leaving his skin tingling in her wake. Her mouth followed a similar path, alternately nipping and licking. Her breasts pressed against his back, making his palms itch with the desire to touch her.

"Poppy," he rasped.

"Shh." She brushed a finger across his lips, practically daring him to take it in his mouth. "You must trust me."

"I do, but . . . I need you."

She shifted beside him and pressed a palm against his chest, easing him onto his back. "I know what you need." She leaned over his chest, and the soft ends of her hair tickled his skin. Her tongue flicked at his nipple while her fingers traced the edge of his waistband. His cock strained against his trousers, and he swallowed a curse.

She kissed her way down his torso, over the ridges of his abdomen. When she reached the tops of his trousers, she moved away and began to unbutton them, slowly peeling them away from his body until his hard length was entirely freed. He heard her breath hitch in her throat and smiled.

But she didn't stop there. She wriggled his trousers off his legs, tossed them aside, then sat between his thighs.

"From the first time I saw you, facedown in the surf," she said softly, "I knew you were going to upset all my plans." She swept her fingertips along the outsides of his legs. "I knew you'd be a danger to my heart. And somewhere deep inside, I knew I wanted to make you mine."

"And here we are," he managed.

"Here we are," she repeated, lightly grazing a fingernail from the inside of his knee to the top of his thigh. His cock twitched in response.

She shifted again, and he felt the warm, tentative touch of her lips on his arousal. She began near the base, slowly licked her way north, and swirled her tongue around the top.

He groaned and clutched the quilt beneath him, praying for control.

She drew him into her mouth, inch by inch. Sucking and stroking. Making little moans in her throat that vibrated through him. Driving him mad with desire.

All the while, her hands explored, too. She squeezed his buttocks and raked her nails down his chest. His cock throbbed. His body broke out in a sweat.

"Poppy," he gasped.

She went still, slowly raised her head, leaving him wet and impossibly hard. "You liked that." It was three parts statement, one part question.

"More than you could possibly know," he ground out.

She moved again, and he heard the rustle of silk. Imagined her lifting the ball gown over her head. Felt her straddle his hips. She rose above him and guided his cock between her legs, rubbing the tip against the hot, slick folds at her entrance.

"Fuck."

"Not yet," she said with a mix of breathlessness and amusement. "But soon." She reached for his good hand, uncurled his fingers, and licked the center of his palm, sending an unexpected shot of pleasure through his arm and straight to his groin. Then she lifted his hand to her breast—which was all the invitation he needed.

She was small and firm, perfect in every way. As he caressed the soft underside, the taut tip grazed his palm, and she sighed sweetly. "Even though you touch me here"—she touched the hand he held to her breast—"I feel it here." Deliberately, she moved his hand down her smooth, flat belly to the juncture of her legs.

Jesus, she felt good. Warm, wet, swollen. Pulsing with desire.

He propped himself on an elbow and stroked her, finding the spot that made her breath hitch. Using the pressure that made her whimper.

"Poppy Summers," he growled. "You. Are. Mine."

"Yes." She reached behind his head, removed the blindfold, and gazed at him with heavy-lidded eyes. "And you, Andrew Keane . . . you are mine."

As if they were sealing the oath, she slowly—almost solemnly—lowered herself onto him. They moved together in perfect rhythm. She met him thrust for thrust, drawing him deeper until they were as close as two people could be.

With every sensuous kiss, she healed him.

And with every subtle moan, she tattooed her name, indelibly, on his heart.

He reached between their bodies and touched her as he gazed at her beautiful, freckled face. Her eyes closed, her back arched, and her skin flushed until, at last, her core pulsed all around him.

As her cries of ecstasy filled his head, pleasure gathered behind his eyes like a firework rocketing into the sky.

He hurtled toward the heavens—and burst into a thousand sparks of light. Torrents of pleasure blinded him. Pounded through his body. Left him sated and utterly spent.

Poppy collapsed on top on him, her legs tangled with his. And he knew he'd never forget that moment.

He and Poppy could live on a majestic country estate or own the most elegant town house in all of London. He'd never love any place more than their little lean-to on the beach of Bellehaven Bay.

He wrapped his arms tightly around her and kissed her temple. "I love you, Poppy."

Chapter 28

Poppy sat up. "What . . . what did you say?"

Keane shot her an amused smile. "I love you."

A thousand effervescent champagne bubbles popped in her chest. "Oh."

He pushed himself to sitting, and the sight of him naked, with his hair standing on end, made her heart flutter— even as echoes of pleasure still thrummed in her veins.

"You seem disappointed," he said with an adorable frown. "I realize it wasn't the most eloquent declaration. Shall I try again?"

"No." She cupped his cheek in her palm, savoring the slight prickle of his stubble against her skin. "I'm only disappointed that I didn't get to say it first."

His eyes crinkled at the corners. "You could say it now . . . if you still want to."

She pretended to ponder the idea as she pulled a quilt from her storage basket and spread it over both of them. They lay down, facing each other in the warm glow of the lantern.

"You once asked me if I could ever love someone like you," she began.

"I remember."

"I said I wasn't sure."

"I remember that, too." He lifted a long curl from her shoulder, wound it around his index finger, and gazed at her with a tenderness that made her chest ache.

"I didn't *want* to love you," she said. "I thought that if I did, I'd be betraying my mother's memory. That I'd be discounting all her suffering and heartache. And I did not want to dishonor her."

"What changed?"

"I did," she said honestly. "I realized Mama would not want me to choose who to love based on a title or fortune or lack thereof. When she chose Papa, she followed her heart. And in spite of all the hardships they faced, I know she'd choose him again if she could. She'd want me to listen to my heart, too."

His lazy smile melted her insides like chocolate. "And what's your heart saying?"

"It's saying *I love you,* Keane. It took me a while to admit it to myself, but I think I've loved you for a while now. I love that you were perfectly happy living in this simple shelter. I love that you asked me a million questions and that you've never asked me to be anyone other than who I am."

He chuckled. "Except for when we went to Ascot, and I asked you to be the daughter of a baron."

"My acting skills may have left something to be desired," she conceded. "But I love that you let me play a part in the search for your attacker. That you didn't dismiss me as being too delicate or weak."

"I know better than that." He pretended to shudder. "I'm not completely daft."

"I am fond of your cheeky sense of humor," she mused. "But would you like to know what I love most about you?"

"I think we've established it's not my title." His smile

slowly faded; his eyes turned a deeper shade of green. "But yes, I would very much like to know."

She cradled his bandaged hand in hers, lifted it, and pressed a gentle kiss to the back. "I think what I love most of all is that you refused to give up on us. You believed in us, even when I pushed you away. Even when you discovered that Dane was the one who hurt you. It would have been so easy for you to leave Bellehaven—and me—but you never did. Thank you."

"You are wrong about one thing." He traced the curve of her cheek with a fingertip, sending a delicious shiver through her body. "It would not have been easy to leave you. It would have felt like leaving behind the best part of me. It would have been damned near impossible. Because I love you. I want to marry you, Poppy."

Her throat ached; her eyes burned. "I want to marry you, too." An unexpected tear trickled down her cheek, and she swiped at it, but another followed. And then another, and another.

"Come here." He hauled her against his body, her back to his chest, and lightly rubbed her head while she sobbed.

She cried because her heart was close to bursting with love for Keane and the life they'd have together. But she also cried because Mama would never see the woman her daughter had become or meet the wonderful man who'd captured her heart. Mama wouldn't attend their wedding or play with her grandchildren.

It seemed the greater Poppy's joy, the more she missed Mama.

"I'm going to make you happy," Keane whispered near her ear. "I swear it."

She sniffled and nodded. Tonight was a very good start.

Warm and secure in the comfort of his arms, she drifted off to sleep.

Pale shafts of morning light shone through the curtain opening at the shelter's door. Keane pressed a kiss to Poppy's temple and reluctantly sat up.

"Must you leave already?" The husky note in her voice brought to mind the best parts of the night they'd spent together.

"I look forward to the day when we can lounge in bed, doing wicked things to each other from dawn till dusk," he drawled. "But today is not that day."

She pried open her beautiful eyes and pouted her plump lips, practically begging him to kiss her. But, summoning restraint he didn't even know he possessed, he reached for his trousers and pulled them on.

"Are you certain?" She stretched her supple arms high above her head, and the quilt slipped low, barely covering the tips of her breasts.

He suppressed a groan and stuffed his arms into the sleeves of his shirt. "I have a meeting this morning."

She arched a strawberry brow. "Is it with the king? Because I cannot imagine any other sort of meeting that would drag you away."

"Not with the king." He shot her an apologetic smile. "I'm meeting with my uncle."

"Oh." She held the quilt to her chest and sat up. "What's going to become of your cousin?"

Keane shrugged on his jacket. "That's what we are going to decide. I will tell you the whole of it later today."

Her mouth curled into a sensuous smile. "I'm going to see you later?"

He nodded. "When I speak to your father. Would you inform him that I'll be paying a call this afternoon?"

Her eyes went wide, and she swallowed. "You're coming to the cottage? To talk with Papa?"

"How else would I ask for your hand?"

She bit her lower lip, let the quilt fall away, and sat back on her heels.

Holy hell. "What are you doing?"

She picked up the scarf she'd used to cover his eyes and slid it around her neck. "I was just thinking that you might like having a turn to blindfold me." She swept her fingertips along the insides of her parted thighs, and his mouth went dry.

With a primal growl, he dropped to his knees, reached for the blindfold, and moved behind her to secure it. "I'm definitely going to be late for my meeting."

"I realize I am entirely to blame," she said with mock remorse, even as she pressed her lush bottom against his hard length. "However, I am willing to pay the price. Just name it."

He eased her head back onto a pillow and braced himself above her. "I suppose it's only fair that I exact payment," he teased. He drew a pink nipple into his mouth, then licked a path down her flat belly, taking a detour around her navel.

"And what is it that you demand, Your Grace?" she asked breathlessly.

"Simple." He dipped his head, flicked his tongue over her sex, and smiled at the whimper in her throat. "I want to hear you scream my name."

"Apologies for keeping you waiting." Keane strode into the small but well-appointed library of the mayor's house and sat in a wing chair opposite his uncle. The curtains were drawn, the room was dark, and the mood was somber—almost as if they were in mourning.

Which, in some respects, they were.

"You are not the one who should be making apologies, Andrew."

"He is still here?"

Rawlings nodded wearily; he seemed to have aged a decade since yesterday. "I have a couple of footmen standing guard outside his room."

"I realize this must be difficult." Keane gestured toward the mayor's well-stocked sideboard. "May I pour you a drink?"

"No, thank you." Rawlings gripped the arms of his chair and inhaled deeply. "Theodore confessed to everything. Not that I doubted your word," he added. "I am horrified—sickened—by what he's done."

Keane dragged a hand down his face. "It is difficult to believe."

"Yes, but I should have suspected this could happen," his uncle admitted. "I knew he was jealous of you. And he coveted more than your title. He wanted your wit and your charm. He wanted me to hold him in the same high regard that I hold you."

"This is not your fault, Uncle."

"Trust me when I say I am partly to blame for Theodore's lack of character. After his mother died, I thought I could fill the void with gifts. I gave him everything he asked for. Small things at first—a trinket here, a sweet there. But before long, he was demanding a thoroughbred horse and an exorbitant allowance. Instead of refusing, I indulged every whim. It was the worst thing I could have done."

"You did your best. It was a damned sight better than my father did."

Rawlings scoffed. "I'm not so certain. I love my son, but he has gone too far this time. He must face the consequences of his misdeeds—whatever those consequences might be."

Keane stood and paced behind his chair. "If I were to turn him over to the authorities, he'd likely end up in Newgate."

His uncle swallowed, and above his dark beard, his face turned ghostly pale. "He could hang."

"I don't want that any more than you do." Keane stifled a curse as he rolled his stiff shoulders and flexed the fingers of his bandaged hand. "Despite all he's done, I believe there's some good in him."

"Maybe, but it's buried deep."

"I can offer him an alternative to Newgate, but he's not going to like it."

"Understood." Rawlings rubbed the stubble along his chin, thoughtful. "Shall I summon him here?"

Keane nodded, went directly to the sideboard, and poured himself a drink.

Teddy shuffled into the room a few minutes later dressed in the same clothes he'd worn last night. His bloodshot eyes said he hadn't slept a wink, and his hands trembled like those of a man of eighty years.

Keane pointed to the chair he'd vacated. "Sit."

Teddy did and shot a pleading look at his father. Rawlings remained expressionless.

"You have a choice," Keane said without preamble.

Hope sparked in his cousin's eyes.

"I can take you to the magistrate and let him determine your fate. Given that your crime is attempted murder, I assume you will end up in prison. If I ask the authorities to have mercy on you, you might not hang."

"I . . . I wouldn't survive prison." Teddy stifled a sob and reached for his father, who sat still as a statue.

"Then you might prefer the alternative," Keane continued, "which is to join the British Army as a soldier. Prove that you can behave honorably. Serve your country and make something of yourself. When you eventually return, you'll be a man. You'll have done something you can be proud of."

Teddy gulped. "The Army? For how long? How long must I stay away?"

Keane didn't flinch. "Ten years."

"But I'll be almost forty by that time." Teddy dropped to his knees and put his head on his father's lap. "Don't let him do this to me," he begged.

"This mess is of your own making," Rawlings said, impassive. "Your cousin is generously giving you a second chance, and I suggest you take it."

"Fine," he whimpered pitifully. "But at least purchase me a commission. Don't make me enlist as a lowly soldier."

"I will not purchase a commission," Rawlings replied. "If you want to be an officer, you will have to work your way through the ranks. You will need to earn that distinction."

"Cousin." Teddy swiveled his head, scrambled to his feet, and searched Keane's face with wild, desperate eyes. "Think of all we've been through together. Have some compassion."

Anger so potent he could taste it bubbled in Keane's throat. He itched to grab Teddy by his wrinkled cravat and plant a fist in his face. But he didn't want to cause his uncle any more pain. He didn't want to let hate stain this day—not when he and Poppy had so much to be thankful for.

"Compassion," Keane repeated, chillingly calm. "Where

was your compassion last night when I was hanging by my fingertips?" He held his bandaged hand an inch from Teddy's nose. "When you watched my skin burn and blister?"

Teddy hung his head and clasped the back of the chair as if his legs might buckle. "I made a mistake. You must believe me."

"I'll see you in a decade, Cousin." Keane strode out of the library without looking back, feeling two stone lighter. Like he'd shut the door on the unsavory parts of his past.

Now he was clear-eyed about the future he wanted. But before he could seize it, he had one more challenge to face—the most crucial yet.

Chapter 29

Keane stood on the doorstep of Poppy's cottage cradling a bottle of brandy in one arm. Yes, it was a blatant attempt to curry favor with her father, but Keane needed every advantage if he was to have any hope of securing the older man's blessing.

His heart pounded as he knocked on the weathered wooden door. The last time he'd felt this nervous was when he'd had to confess to his own father that he'd taken the curricle without permission, flipped it on a winding road, and damaged it beyond repair.

Keane hoped to God that this encounter involved a good deal less cursing and threats of violence than the curricle confession.

The door swung open, and Dane's hulking frame filled the doorway. "Hawking," he said, lifting his chin in a subtle but distinct gesture of respect.

"Is your sister at home?"

Dane arched a brow. "She's gone for a walk. She said you wanted to speak with our father."

"I do." Keane cleared his throat.

"Well then, let's get on with it." The gravelly voice came from inside the cottage, and Dane stepped aside, motioning for Keane to enter the main room where a white-haired man sat in a threadbare chair, a quilt draped across his knees.

"Good afternoon, Mr. Summers." Keane quickly removed his hat. "It's a pleasure to meet you."

Dane chuckled under his breath. "I'm going to check the nets. Good luck, old bloke," he said, slapping Keane on the back. "You'll need it." Dane grabbed his gloves and cap, then headed outside, closing the door behind him.

"What have you got there?" Mr. Summers waved a gnarled finger at the brandy.

"Some spirits for you," Keane said, raising the bottle. "Shall I set it on the table?"

"After you pour a splash in here." He held out a mug of steaming tea while Keane filled it to the brim. "A little brandy might help this bathwater go down. Poppy insists I drink the stuff."

"She's only looking after you."

"Aye," he said with a scowl. "She insisted I shave and comb my hair this morning. Fussed over me like the king himself was paying a visit."

Keane shot him a wry smile. "I apologize for the inconvenience. I only require a bit of your time."

Poppy's father scoffed and pointed at a wooden bench opposite him. "You may as well sit down and say your piece."

"Right." Bloody hell, but this meeting was not going according to plan. Keane sat on the wobbly bench, rested his elbows on his knees, and debated the best way to begin. As he looked at the older man's wizened face, he decided to be blunt—and unapologetically honest.

"I love your daughter."

Mr. Summers stared back, unfazed. "I don't doubt that you do. Everyone loves Poppy. The question is: Can you make her happy?"

"That depends," Keane said earnestly. "I can promise you that I will do everything I can. She'll have my respect, my affection, and my heart. I'll wake up every day with the sole purpose of making her smile."

"Sounds like you have everything figured out," the older man grumbled.

"I don't, actually." Keane met the man's icy gaze. "Because nothing I do will be enough to make her happy— if she thinks that choosing me means losing you."

The cottage turned unnaturally still and quiet. So quiet that Keane could hear his heart beating in his ears.

At last, Mr. Summers sighed. "And she'll never be happy here if she thinks that choosing me means losing you."

"Right."

The older man scratched the back of his head, weary. "So, what are we going to do?"

"We work together. We try to never put her in the middle. And we become . . . friends."

"Friends," he repeated, as if the word tasted like fish oil.

"We both think the world of Poppy," Keane said with a smile. "I suspect we'll discover many more things we have in common."

"You could be right. But I can guarantee you'll never see me tied up in one of those neckcloths." The man flicked his gaze to Keane's starched cravat and barely suppressed a shudder.

"I don't blame you. I'd set fire to all of mine if it wouldn't give my valet apoplexy." He inserted a finger between his neck and his cravat, then turned sober. "I want to marry your daughter, Mr. Summers—and I'd like your blessing."

"Much as I hate to admit it, Poppy has been different

lately. There's a light in her eyes, a spring in her step. I didn't realize how sad she'd been . . . or maybe I didn't want to see it."

"Poppy adores you and Dane. She loves this beach."

"But it's not enough," Mr. Summers said wistfully. "She reminds me of how her mother used to be. Full of hope. Full of dreams. You've given those things back to her, and for that I'm grateful." He leaned forward in his chair and extended a hand. "If Poppy wants to marry you, I'll not stand in the way. You have my blessing, Hawking."

"Thank you, sir." Keane shook his hand, and relief coursed through him. "There are a couple of things you should know. First, I will love your daughter until I take my last breath, and probably after. Second, you and Dane will always be welcome in our home, wherever that may be."

"Good to know," Mr. Summers replied gruffly. "But this cottage is where I belong. Taking me out of it would be like trying to yank an old turtle out of its shell."

Keane glanced around at the tiny, well-loved house and arched a brow. "Well, maybe we can find a way to make your shell a bit more comfortable."

Poppy's father pursed his lips, thoughtful. "I'm willing to listen. Why don't you grab that bottle, fill my cup again, and tell me what you're thinking."

They talked for another hour or so, and after his second splash of brandy, Mr. Summers insisted that Keane call him Ollie.

"You're not the sort of man I imagined Poppy would settle down with," he mused, "but I suppose she could do worse."

Keane chuckled. "That's high praise, coming from you."

"Don't go getting a swollen head." Poppy's father settled back in his chair and sipped his brandy-laced tea. "All I'm saying is that you're a fairly decent bloke . . . for a duke."

"Your name is printed in the pages of *The London Hearsay*." Kitty's voice was filled with a mixture of excitement and awe as she gazed across the table at Poppy. She, Kitty, and Hazel were sitting at a corner table in the Tea Shoppe, nibbling on scones and enjoying an unofficial meeting of the Belles.

Kitty placed the newspaper on the table and pointed at the gossip page. "Right here. *'In an entirely unforeseen turn of events, the elusive Duke of Hawking has announced his intention to marry. The future duchess, Miss Poppy Summers of Bellehaven Bay, is the daughter of a local fisherman, and it seems she has managed to catch the biggest prize of all. One wonders what she used for bait . . .'*" Kitty's voice trailed off, and she crinkled her nose. "I've changed my mind about the *Hearsay*," she announced. "I once thought it a reliable source of information, but it's clear they'll print anything in order to sell a few newspapers."

Hazel nodded in agreement. "It's not worth the paper it's printed on."

Poppy shrugged and smiled, warmed by the loyalty of her friends. "It's a gossip column, after all. The author must find some titillating angle to the story. And if I'm going to be a"—she swallowed and forced her mouth to form the word—"duchess, I must learn to have a thick skin."

"You see," Hazel said softly. "That is the sort of graciousness that will make you a fine duchess."

Kitty sighed dreamily. "It's all turned out so wonderfully, hasn't it? You and the duke are going to be so happy.

You'll move into his elegant town house and host lavish dinner parties and extravagant balls. I shall pounce on any excuse to visit you."

Poppy chuckled. "You will always be welcome. But we plan to set up house here in Bellehaven, too—so we can come back whenever I'm feeling homesick." She met Hazel's gaze briefly, then looked back at Kitty. "To that end, I was hoping to consult you on a couple of projects."

Kitty sat up straight and blinked. "Which projects?"

"I showed Keane some of your drawings, and he was beyond impressed. He agreed we should hire you to sketch plans for a modest house overlooking the bay."

"Truly?" She was practically bouncing in her seat.

"More importantly, however, we were hoping you could help design some improvements to my father's cottage."

"Of course, I would do that. It's in such a lovely location." Her bright blue eyes took on a faraway look, as if her mind was already knocking down walls and erecting new ones. "Your father should be able to see ocean sunsets from every room."

"Nothing would make him happier." Poppy had known Kitty would understand just what her father needed. "And since walking has become difficult for him, he needs a smooth floor."

"Yes," Kitty agreed. "We can replace the front step with a gradual incline and add a nice wide porch where he can sit in the evenings and watch the boats and birds."

"Sounds like the perfect spot for a telescope," Hazel added.

Poppy's chest warmed. "He would love that. And though he'll likely balk at the suggestion of adding onto the cottage, he needs more space."

"A larger kitchen?" Kitty asked.

Poppy nodded. "And an additional bedchamber for a

housekeeper or companion—someone who can cook him healthy meals and ensure he takes his medicine."

Hazel pursed her lips and idly tapped the handle of her teacup. "You'll need to find someone who's as stubborn as he is."

"You should consider Mrs. Wallaby," Kitty said casually.

"The widow who lives down the road?"

"The night you were in Ascot and I checked in on your father, Mrs. Wallaby visited." Kitty paused for dramatic effect. "She brought pie."

"Did she?" Poppy mused, incredulous.

"Cupid certainly has been busy." Hazel opened a notepad and picked up her pencil. "But we mustn't forget the primary order of business of today's meeting of the Belles—planning a proper engagement party for you and your duke."

"What are you thinking?" Kitty asked. "Something festive at the Assembly Rooms, perhaps? Or, if you'd prefer a more formal affair, I'm certain that Lady Rufflebum would gladly host the celebration."

"Honestly, I'd rather have a few close friends and family members gather at a bonfire on the beach," Poppy admitted.

"How does Keane feel about that?" Hazel asked.

Heat rushed to Poppy's cheeks. "He says he wants whatever type of party will make me happy."

Kitty grinned. "Then we shall ensure you have the best beach bonfire ever."

"No," Poppy said firmly. "Much as I would love a Bellehaven bonfire, I feel the need to do something different. Keane has gone to great lengths to show me he can live in my world. Now it's my turn to show him I can live in his. I think the party must be in London."

Hazel gave an approving smile. "The best way to face the ton is directly. Allow them to see how bold—how fearless—you are, and they will respect that."

"What if I said I wasn't feeling particularly bold or fearless?"

Hazel shrugged. "All the more reason to make them think you are. Blade and I are going to London next week; you must come and stay with us. We would be honored to throw a ball in your honor. All you must do is say the word."

"I know it is asking a great deal, but if you were to host the party, I'd be forever grateful."

"I shall discuss it with Blade this evening, but I have no doubt he'll agree."

"Then it's all sorted," Kitty said with a toss of her golden curls. "The Belles are going to London at last."

Chapter 30

A week later, Poppy was in London.

The muddy water of the Thames was a poor substitute for the frothy waves of the bay, and the city's skyline couldn't compare to Bellehaven's towering cliffs. But there was much to love about London, too.

She savored the smell of roasted chestnuts and the colorful storefronts along Bond Street. She soaked in the sounds of hooves clopping on cobblestone and newspaper boys shouting on the street corners. The whole city seemed to crackle with energy and sparkle with possibilities.

Which may have been true, in large part, because Keane was there, too.

That afternoon, he'd picked her up from Hazel and Blade's elegant town house in Mayfair, helped her into his curricle, and whisked her away for a drive in Hyde Park. They talked about the plans for her father's cottage and for the house they'd build in Bellehaven. She told him about the annual cricket match on the beach, and he shared updates about his meetings with tenants and his steward.

Best of all, they talked about their future.

Hazel had warned her she'd be on display. That she should expect curious stares and gossipy whispers.

She was correct, of course. But as long as Keane was close, Poppy didn't mind.

Indeed, she found herself thoroughly distracted by the flex of his arm muscles as he worked the reins. The subtle twitch of his biceps as he maneuvered the curricle around a bend. The sure grasp of his long fingers on the leather straps.

"What do you think of the view?"

She blinked guiltily and snapped her gaze to his. "Pardon?"

His deep chuckle vibrated through her, making her insides shimmer. "How do you like the Serpentine? The swans?"

"Lovely." Her voice was a little breathless to her own ears.

He leaned an inch closer. "Have I mentioned how beautiful you look today?"

She swallowed and pressed her knees together in a futile attempt to stop the pulsing in her core. "You did. In Hazel and Blade's foyer."

His gaze flicked over her face and lingered on the column of her neck. She didn't have to be a reader of minds to know that he was thinking of kissing her. "I miss you," he said gruffly.

If they hadn't been rolling past elegant carriages full of fashionable people, she would have made a wicked suggestion. Something along the lines of parking the curricle behind a hedge, removing their clothes, and becoming intimately reacquainted. Instead, she attempted a serene smile. "I miss you, too."

"Times like these I almost wish we had eloped," he grumbled, shifting in his seat.

"Almost?" Gretna Green had much to recommend it at the moment.

"Mmm." He shot her a smoldering look that was half depraved duke, half fallen archangel. "A few weeks isn't long to wait for forever."

An indisputably romantic sentiment, and yet she hoped with every fiber of her being that they wouldn't have to wait weeks. She'd make it her personal mission to ensure that they did not.

"You know, Your Grace," she said, deliberately breezy, "I fear I've had a bit too much sun. Maybe you should return me to Bladenton House . . . and see if you can find some way to revive me."

"I assume you're referring to a cool cloth and a spot of tea?"

She narrowed her eyes and twirled the long curl skimming her neck. "I was hoping you'd employ more creativity."

He turned the curricle around with impressive alacrity and leaned close to her ear. "When it comes to pleasing you, Poppy Summers, my creativity knows no bounds. I am endlessly inspired. Michelangelo and da Vinci," he scoffed, "they have nothing on me."

Poppy picked up the fan that Hazel had insisted she bring and waved it vigorously for reasons that had absolutely nothing to do with the afternoon sun. Perhaps a tiny part of her had worried that she and Keane would be different in London. That the magic of their relationship was inextricably wrapped up in oceanside breezes and moonlit coves.

As it turned out, they could make magic wherever they were.

Her gaze lingered on his handsome face. The scar on his temple was a poignant reminder of how the stars had aligned to bring them together. She had to pinch herself so she wouldn't smile too broadly as they left the green lawns of the park and ventured toward the elegant streets of Mayfair.

The neighborhood seemed like something out of a painting. Stately stone and brick houses lined wide cobblestone roads. Ladies and gentlemen chatted as they strolled along the pavement, waving at passersby. Maids and footmen bustled about, carrying baskets and balancing towers of packages. Barking pups ran circles around giggling children.

This was where she and Keane would spend much of their time, and it didn't seem so terrible. Perhaps one day, she'd be pushing a pram right down the—

Oh God.

"Stop," she heard herself say. "Please, stop."

Keane pulled on the reins, brought the curricle to a halt, and turned to her, his face full of concern. "What's wrong?"

Her mouth refused to form the words, so she swallowed and lifted her eyes to the house directly across from them. The white stone façade was covered by a thick blanket of ivy, and the glossy black door boasted a shiny brass knocker that winked in the sunlight.

No one walking by would notice anything sinister about the front steps, and yet, the mere sight of them swept Poppy's legs out from under her. Made her shiver despite the warmth of the day.

Keane reached for her hand and squeezed. Then, after a few heartbeats, "Your grandparents' house?"

She nodded. But she didn't think of it that way. True grandparents wouldn't have left her outside all night, huddled in the rain, pretending she wasn't their own flesh and blood.

No, the town house wasn't a home but rather the cold, lonely place where she'd been shut out while her mother lay dying. It was the place where she'd had her eyes opened wide to how cruel people could be. And it was the place where she'd transformed from a happy, carefree girl to a cynical, wary young woman.

"Lord and Lady Whitmore live here," Keane said, his voice low and lethal. "Shall we pay them a visit?"

Her stomach clenched. "You know them?"

"Not well. But I'd welcome the chance to confront them—to call them to account for their actions."

"It was so long ago." Poppy exhaled slowly. "They probably don't even remember that night."

The muscle in his jaw twitched. "Then they're even more depraved than I imagined. Besides, it wasn't simply one night. They've denied your existence since the day you were born."

"Yes. But I'd rather not give them the satisfaction of thinking their rejection matters one whit to me."

"I understand," Keane said grudgingly. "And I'll respect your wishes, of course. But all you have to do is say the word, and I'll see that their heartlessness is exposed. A few whispers in the right ears would ensure they're barred from polite society."

Poppy managed a smile. "I love that you want to seek justice on my behalf. But vengeance isn't going to erase the pain they caused my mother. It won't heal the ache that night left in my chest."

"Is there anything I can do?"

She nodded. "Take me home, Keane. Just take me home."

Chapter 31

"Is there any greater anticipation than waking up on the morning of a ball?" Kitty sat up in the bed she and Poppy were sharing, stretched her arms above her head, and hopped to the floor. "I can't believe we slept so late."

Poppy rubbed her eyelids and stifled a yawn as she checked the clock on the mantel in the guest bedchamber. "It is late. Two months ago, I would have had two baskets of fish cleaned and ready for market by this time of the morning. Now, I'll be lucky if they're still serving breakfast downstairs."

"You needed your rest." Kitty sat at the dressing table and began to unwind her thick blond braid from the end up. "Not only do you have a long night of dancing and revelry ahead, but everyone will be eager to lay eyes on the woman who captured the duke's heart. Scores of disappointed matchmaking mamas will scrutinize your every move, wondering what qualities you possess that their precious daughters don't."

Poppy resisted the urge to pull the covers over her head and burrow deep into the feather mattress. "It sounds about as appealing as a tooth extraction."

"No," Kitty said, gesturing with a silver-handled hairbrush. "More like running the gauntlet. Lucky for you, the Belles will be at your side."

Poppy padded across the room, stood behind Kitty, and smiled at her friend's reflection. "I *am* rather lucky, aren't I?"

"The duke's the lucky one," Kitty said firmly. "You know I couldn't be happier for both of you . . ."

"But?" Poppy probed.

"But soon I'll be the only unwed Belle."

Poppy's heart squeezed as she took the brush from Kitty and pulled it through her golden curls. "You're also the youngest. Not even close to spinster territory," she added with a wink.

"Perhaps not. But now that you and Hazel have found your matches, you'll naturally be inclined to talk about"— Kitty waved hand in the air—"whatever secrets married women talk about, and I shall be . . . alone."

"Never." Poppy leaned over to hug her friend. "I'm afraid you are stuck with Hazel and me. And we will keep all the best secrets just for our trio."

"I did learn about your relationship with the duke before the rest of Bellehaven," Kitty said, clearly buoyed by the thought.

"What do you say we dress quickly and make our way to the dining room before they take the eggs and ham away?"

Kitty placed her palms over her belly. "Perhaps we should stick with a bit of toast, just to make sure our ball gowns fit?"

Poppy planted her hands on her hips and frowned. "A bit of toast?" she repeated. "I hope you're jesting."

Kitty's face split into a wide smile. "Of course I am! I intend to make myself a heaping plate, *and* I am fully prepared to fight you for the last scone."

"That, my friend, is a fight you will lose."

They raced each other to the armoire and donned their day gowns in record time.

"There you are," Hazel commented as they rushed into the dining room. "What happened? Did the two of you stay up late last night? Indulge in too much brandy?"

"Alas, no," Kitty said mournfully. "But that sounds like a fine plan for this evening."

Blade lowered his newspaper and affectionately narrowed his eyes at his niece. "Not unless you want your first London ball to be your last."

Kitty sighed. "Then I suppose one glass of champagne will have to do."

Poppy chuckled as she helped herself to a plate from the sideboard. Papa and Dane had stayed in Bellehaven, but thankfully, Blade, Hazel, and Kitty felt a lot like family, too.

Poppy had just begun to eat when Mr. Sandler, the ginger-haired butler, appeared in the doorway and cleared his throat apologetically. "Pardon the interruption, but Miss Summers has a visitor."

Poppy's teacup froze halfway to her mouth. "I do?" she asked, incredulous. She hadn't expected to see Keane before the ball, but her chest warmed at the prospect of a surprise visit. "Would you please tell the duke I'll be with him in a moment?"

"He's welcome to join us here," Hazel said graciously.

The butler shook his head and handed Poppy a calling card. "It's not the duke, miss. It's a lady."

The back of her neck prickled ominously as she turned the card over. The delicate script read *The Lady Evelyn Fielding*.

Good God. Her cup clattered to her saucer, drawing concerned glances from everyone at the breakfast table.

Kitty squeezed her hand. "Who is it?" She spoke softly, but the fire in her eyes said she was prepared to do battle with anyone who threatened Poppy.

Evelyn, Mama's older sister. The one she'd been desperate to see when she was sick.

Poppy swallowed. "I believe it's my"—the word stuck in her throat—"aunt."

Blade, who had only the vaguest sense that Poppy's London relatives had wronged her, grunted loyally. "Sandler can send her away if you'd like."

"Or I can go myself," Hazel offered, "and inform her you're not receiving at this time—or ever."

Kitty leaned forward, meeting Poppy's gaze. "But if you'd like to speak with your aunt, I'll gladly stand by your side. I shall make sure she doesn't dare look at you cross-eyed, much less utter a single rude word."

The fierce, united show of support made Poppy's eyes well, but she quickly composed herself. "I don't know what I did to deserve such generous friends, but I am forever grateful."

The butler shuffled his feet. "Lady Evelyn is in the drawing room. What shall I tell her?"

Poppy shivered at the sound of the name. Wondered if it would forever reduce her to a terrified nine-year-old girl on the brink of losing her mother, desperate to grant her one final wish. ·

"Please tell her I will join her shortly. Thank you, Mr. Sandler."

As the butler strode off, Poppy took a fortifying sip of tea, placed her napkin on the table, and stood. "I don't know why my mother's sister has come here. I cannot imagine what she wants to say to me or what I want to say to her. But I do know that this is something I must face on my own."

For her friends' sake, she managed a tremulous smile before leaving the dining room and heading down the hall. Her heart pounded as though she were in the middle of the road with a carriage and four bearing down on her, seconds away from running her over. Her body buzzed with the sort of fear that could lock up her knees, if she let it.

But that fear was tempered with anger, and she resolved to face Lady Evelyn with her head held high.

Her childish fantasies of being embraced by her mother's family, of being welcomed into their inner, privileged circles, had been squashed years ago. She'd once harbored a secret, foolish notion—that if Mama's family only had the chance to meet her, they'd immediately see what a clever, industrious child she was. That they'd be full of remorse for all the years they'd shunned their daughter's family and for all the heartache they'd caused. They'd fuss over Poppy and invite her and Mama to stay with them in London, and Mama would be truly happy.

But that was a lifetime ago.

Poppy no longer needed her mother's family to approve of her or accept her. She didn't need their money or their influence. She didn't need any sort of favor. Any power or sway they might once have had over her was gone. And the realization filled her with a sense of calm.

Lady Evelyn couldn't hurt her anymore.

More important, she couldn't hurt Mama.

Poppy paused in the drawing room doorway, momentarily stunned by the sight of her aunt sitting on a settee and gazing wistfully at the freshly painted portrait of Hazel and Blade that hung above the fireplace. Lady Evelyn's profile was so strikingly similar to Mama's that an unexpected wave of grief surged through Poppy.

She cleared her throat and lifted her chin. "Lady Evelyn," she said smoothly.

The woman rose quickly and meekly lifted her eyes. On second glance, she was nothing like Mama. She had the same delicate features, but her face was devoid of sparkle and mirth. "Miss Summers. Thank you for receiving me. I would not have blamed you had you turned me away."

Poppy glided across the room and faced her aunt— though she was scarcely deserving of the label. "I confess I am puzzled as to the timing and motivation for your visit."

She swallowed and smoothed a strand of faded brown hair into her simple chignon. "My purpose is threefold, but I promise I will not take much of your time."

Poppy waved a hand at the settee as she sank into a chair opposite her. "Please, have a seat."

Lady Evelyn's eyes welled as she looked at Poppy. She produced a handkerchief from her reticule and dabbed at the corners of her eyes before she spoke. "Forgive me," she said. "I was struck by how much you resemble your mother. She was about your age the last time I saw her, and she was so beautiful—as are you."

Poppy had always prided herself on being immune to idle flattery, but Lady Evelyn seemed sincere, and Poppy could think of no greater compliment than being told she looked like Mama. "Thank you."

Her aunt nodded. "Firstly, I must offer felicitations on your engagement to the Duke of Hawking. I read the news in the *Hearsay* and was delighted to hear you have made such a fine match. You deserve every happiness."

"I confess I am surprised to hear you say such a thing," Poppy said, unable to keep a note of bitterness from her voice. "Especially since you did not extend the same consideration to your sister. You could not even bring yourself to grant her dying wish."

Lady Evelyn hung her head briefly before lifting her chin. "That brings me to the second reason for my visit. I want to sincerely apologize for spurning Lila—and you—when you needed us most. I don't expect you to forgive me," she added quickly. "And trust me when I say that I will never, ever, forgive myself. It is a stain on my soul, one I'll have to live with for the rest of my life. There's not a night when I lay my head on my pillow that I don't regret my actions." Tears spilled down her cheeks, and she chased them with her handkerchief.

"I don't understand," Poppy said helplessly. "It's clear you loved my mother."

Lady Evelyn nodded vehemently. "She was sweet and funny and warm—and I adored her."

"Why, then? Why did you treat her so poorly?"

"Initially, it was the scandal." Her gaze flicked to Poppy's, questioning. "Perhaps you're not aware?"

"I know everything. Mama never hid the details of her and Papa's courtship."

Lady Evelyn smiled fondly. "No, I don't suppose she would have. She made no apologies for following her heart. But our parents were appalled to learn that their unmarried daughter was with child. They were even more distraught when they discovered the father of her babe was a fisherman."

"My father is a good and decent man."

"I don't doubt it," Lady Evelyn replied sincerely. "Even as a girl, Lila had a knack for judging a person's character. She would never have fallen in love with your papa if he wasn't honorable and kind."

Poppy sniffed, mollified. "But he wasn't good enough for your parents?"

"No." She released a remorseful sigh. "They wanted her to cut ties with him, and when she refused . . ."

"My parents were forced to elope."

Her aunt nodded. "I should have stood up for her. I should have begged and pleaded with our parents to accept their marriage and welcome your father into our family. I'm ashamed to say that I didn't. I prided myself on adhering to the rules, even when they made no sense to me. I was so concerned with pleasing our parents, with living up to their image of the ideal, dutiful daughter, that I forgot what it meant to be a good sister."

"My mother wanted to see you one last time," Poppy said hoarsely. "How could you have refused her?"

"The night you came to our door . . . my parents kept me away. They didn't tell me why you came or even that Lila was ill. But from my window, I saw you huddled on our doorstep, and when I caught a glimpse of your hair . . . I knew you must be Lila's daughter."

"Why didn't you intervene?"

"I told myself that you were better off not knowing your grandparents. That you'd be happier if you never knew the full extent of their disdain. But you were still there in the morning, so I snuck you a sandwich and urged you to go home."

"That was you?"

Lady Evelyn stifled a sob. "I'm sorry I didn't listen to you. I'm sorry I wasn't there for Lila when she needed me and that I didn't reach out to you after she was gone. Mostly, I'm sorry that I wasn't a better person."

For several heartbeats, neither of them spoke. Lady Evelyn hiccupped into her handkerchief, but her spine was straight as a rod. She hadn't cast herself as the victim in their family tragedy. Rather, she seemed willing, almost eager, to face Poppy's wrath.

To stoically accept her punishment, however severe.

And, oh, did Poppy want to lash out. To rail at her, to

send her away, to let her suffer for all eternity in the knowledge that she was a horrid, heartless shell of a person.

But deep in her soul, she knew that was not what Mama would have wanted.

She closed her eyes briefly and met her aunt's gaze. "When my mother died, she didn't leave me much in the way of possessions—a few books, a hairbrush, a pair of earrings. But she did give me something precious. Her strength."

Poppy paused, letting that strength swirl inside of her. Its tendrils stretched through her limbs and filled her with warmth. It felt as though Mama was there, hugging her. Telling her she was doing the right thing.

At last, she said, "I was strong enough to take care of my family. I was strong enough to chase my dreams. And I am strong enough to forgive you, Lady Evelyn."

She shot Poppy a grateful, watery smile. "Please, just Evelyn will do. Or even 'Aunt' if you think you could bear it."

Poppy chuckled softly. "I think I might be able to bear it."

"You don't know how much this means to me. Indeed, it is far more than I'd dared hope." She rummaged through her reticule and produced a stack of neatly folded papers bound with a blue satin ribbon. "And this brings me to the third reason for my visit."

An unexpected lump lodged in Poppy's throat. "What's that?"

Evelyn handed the stack to her. "Letters from your mother. She wrote to me several times a year—on my birthday, during Christmastide, and whenever she had special news to share. There are snippets about your first words, your childhood antics, and the bright young woman she knew you'd become. Every page is filled with her love for you, your brother, and your father." She sniffled and waved a hand at the stack. "Anyway, I thought you should have them."

Poppy's eyes flicked to the familiar flourishes and loops of her mother's handwriting. "Thank you," she said, pressing the stack to her chest. "I shall treasure them."

"I should go now," she said, smoothing her skirts and rising to her feet. "You've been so generous with your time. Thank you, Miss Summers."

"Please," she said hoarsely, "you must call me Poppy."

Evelyn pressed her lips together to keep from crying, and the gratitude in her eyes said she couldn't have asked for a greater gift.

"You know, you have her strength, too," Poppy said. "It couldn't have been easy, coming here. But you did. I can't imagine your parents will be pleased."

"It hardly matters. I never married, so I take care of them now," Evelyn said, matter of fact.

"Are they unwell?"

"In a manner of speaking." Evelyn tilted her head, thoughtful. "When Lila left our household, she took all her light and goodness with her. Our parents refused to allow her name to be spoken, but they missed her dearly, and I think the sorrow of losing her made them even more petty and miserable."

"How sad," Poppy mused. "Especially since it needn't have been that way."

"You're quite right. But your grandparents are old and feeble now, and neither one of them is fully in possession of their wits. They frequently forget the year and the season; ironically, though, they have not forgotten Lila. I suppose it is fitting, in a way—a small measure of justice." She inclined her head politely. "Thank you again," she said, before gliding toward the door.

Just as she was about to enter the corridor, Poppy said, "Aunt Evie?"

Her aunt's slippers froze in their tracks. "Evie . . . it's what your mother called me," she said, slowly turning around.

"I know." Poppy went to her, impulsively reached for her hand, and squeezed it. "Would you like to attend my engagement ball this evening?"

Her aunt frowned. "I haven't been to a ball in ages."

"Oh," Poppy said, casually, even as she tamped down her disappointment. "I understand."

"Actually," Evelyn said, her face slowly splitting into a grin, "I can't think of a better reason to dust off my dancing slippers. I shall be there."

Chapter 32

"Does this look lopsided to you?" Keane cast a critical eye at his reflection, or, more specifically, his cravat, which Diggs had already retied twice.

The valet arched an imperious brow. "It does not."

"And you're certain the waistcoat isn't too pretentious?"

Diggs shot him a pained look. "It is a waistcoat. As such, I would not label it as pretentious, humble, or anywhere in between."

"You know what I'm asking, Diggs."

The valet chuckled as he brushed a piece of lint off the shoulder of Keane's evening jacket. "I think that, perhaps, you're wondering if Miss Summers will approve of your appearance, and I can assure you that she will."

Keane dragged a hand through his hair and began pacing the room. "This night is so important to Poppy. I just want it to go smoothly."

"I am certain that the countess has seen to all the particulars. It is sure to be a festive, elegant affair."

"I'm not worried about the flowers or the food," Keane said, scoffing. "This is Poppy's introduction into London's high society, and I want her to feel welcomed. I want her to feel as comfortable as possible."

Diggs clucked his tongue. "You mean you want to

protect her from the petty opinions and outright ugliness of the ton."

Keane could still picture the tormented expression on Poppy's face when they'd passed her grandparents' house. "Yes, damn it. Is that too much to hope for?"

"I'm afraid so." Diggs moved about the room, tidying things with his usual efficiency. "The ton are not inclined to embrace outsiders, especially ones who flout convention. The good news is that Miss Summers is not easily intimidated. She will outshine the rest of them, both in terms of her beauty and wit."

Keane planted his hands on his hips and exhaled. "You're right. She is capable of standing up to anyone, but we're partners now. Which means that from here on out, she shouldn't ever have to face the lions alone."

"A fine sentiment, Your Grace." Diggs arched a sardonic brow. "But perhaps I am not the one to whom you should be voicing it."

Keane chuckled. "As it happens, Diggs, you're the only one in earshot. But after tonight, Poppy will know it, too. This ball is my chance to prove she can always count on me to take her side."

"Good," Diggs said, suspiciously gruff. "It's only natural that she'd be a bit nervous at the ball—her first official foray into polite society."

"Right. And it's bound to set the tone for social events she attends going forward." Keane took one more look in the mirror and decided that one, his cravat was lopsided; and two, he didn't care.

Diggs polished a gold cufflink before tucking it and its match between layers of felt in the bureau drawer. "You won't be able to stop them from throwing their barbs," he said, his eyes full of genuine regret.

"Maybe not. But I can protect Poppy. I can take the barbs myself."

Diggs nodded, thoughtful. "Excellent, Your Grace. But do try to avoid any damage to the new waistcoat."

"That's what you're worried about?" Keane joked. "The bloody waistcoat?"

"You might want to protect your face as well. One facial scar is considered dashing; two or more . . . well, that borders on off-putting."

Keane snorted. "Your concern for my well-being is truly heartwarming. Anything else?"

"Yes, Your Grace." Diggs's wizened face cracked into a smile as he motioned Keane toward the bedchamber door. "Your carriage is out front. Enjoy the evening, and please, give my best to Miss Summers."

"You know that I will." Keane slapped his friend on the back, jogged down the stairs, and headed out the front door into the balmy summer evening. Dusk had painted pink and orange stripes across the western horizon, and the city glowed as if it, too, was seeking to impress on the night of his and Poppy's engagement ball.

He strode down the pavement and gave a cheerful wave to his driver. "Evening, Thomas," he called as he hopped into the polished black cab and pulled the door shut. It was only a short ride to Bladenton House, and he would have walked, but he wanted to arrive in style.

Besides, driving was faster, and he couldn't wait to see Poppy. Couldn't wait to sweep her onto the dance floor and steal her away for a kiss later.

He peered out the window as the town houses slipped by, looking forward to the day when he and Poppy would ride to balls together. He'd hold her hand and try to make her blush by whispering naughty things in her—

Keane blinked as the coach rumbled past the street they should have turned on. It wasn't like Thomas to be careless, but since he didn't seem to realize he should turn around, Keane rapped on the roof of the cab.

Instead of stopping, the coach picked up speed. Keane banged harder, but his driver seemed oblivious. The coach was rolling right through Mayfair, traveling faster than was prudent. Keane banged the roof with his fist. When that had no effect, he opened his window and stuck his head through. "Thomas, pull over!"

The driver craned his head around and looked back at Keane, turning his blood to ice.

The man in the driver's seat wasn't Thomas. It wasn't anyone on Keane's staff.

It was a stranger with an angry scowl who was *definitely* not taking him to Bladenton House, where Poppy was waiting for him.

Holy hell. He should have been walking into his engagement ball.

Instead, he was being kidnapped.

The packed ballroom looked like a painting straight out of a fairy tale. Each of the eight columns flanking the dance floor was wrapped with thick vines of ivy and bright purple bellflowers—a touch that Kitty had insisted on, as a nod to the Belles. A dozen airy tents made of white muslin and trimmed with lavender streamers and silver jingle bells—Hazel's idea—had been erected around the perimeter of the room, adding whimsical little nooks where young couples could escape the watchful eyes of scrupulous elders.

But Poppy's favorite decoration was at the back of the room, near the open French doors: a circular stone fountain with a three-foot geyser of gurgling water at its center. A shell-shaped bowl full of pennies sitting near the base invited guests to toss a coin into the water and make a secret wish.

Taking care not to step on the hem of her lovely new peach gown, Poppy crouched, picked up a shiny penny, and squeezed it in her palm.

Hazel stood at Poppy's left elbow; Kitty was on her right. They'd been shadowing her all evening, as though they feared she'd collapse from the humiliation of apparently being abandoned by her fiancé on the occasion of their engagement ball.

"He's going to walk through those doors any minute," Kitty said, as if the sheer force of her words could make it so.

Hazel gave Poppy's arm a reassuring squeeze. "Blade just left for the duke's house to determine why he's been detained. I am certain there is a logical explanation." A subtle but unmistakable note in her voice said that if there was *not* a logical explanation, Keane would have hell to pay.

Poppy swallowed. She didn't doubt that Keane had a good reason for not being there—and that terrified her more than anything. She knew deep in her soul that he would have walked through fire to be by her side. The fact that it was almost midnight and he still hadn't arrived made a shiver skitter down her spine.

So, she ignored the naked looks of pity on some faces and smugness on others. She ignored the salacious whispers that swirled around her everywhere she went. And she briefly closed her eyes to make a silent plea.

Please, let Keane be safe.

Please let him come back to me—tonight, tomorrow, or the next day.

Just let him be all right.

She laid a hand on her heart as she tossed the penny into

the water. It plunked, then slowly sank to the bottom of the stone basin, one fervent wish amongst scores of others.

"Excuse me, madam." The butler approached Hazel, hesitant. "Given the, er, circumstances, I thought I'd ask about the midnight toast. Would you like us to pass around the champagne, as planned?"

Hazel flicked her gaze to Poppy. "What do you think? No one would notice if we skipped it. Or, if you'd prefer, I could ask Blade to say a few words."

Poppy was tempted—not only to cancel the toast, but to slip out of the ballroom and barricade herself in her bedchamber until the evening was over. But she wasn't going to earn the respect of the ton by slinking away with her tail between her legs.

"Let's proceed with the champagne," she said to Hazel, resolute. "I think I'd like to say something myself."

"Of course." Hazel's eyes shone approvingly, and she nodded to the butler, who hurried off to direct the staff to fill the glasses.

Kitty linked an arm through Poppy's. "One day, I'm going to be just like you," she said. "Fearless."

"If you hadn't noticed, I'm shaking like a leaf."

"You're here," Kitty said. "That's what matters."

Footmen carried huge silver trays through the crowd, offering bubbling flutes to the guests, and Poppy could feel their eyes on her. She caught snippets of their hushed conversations as they scurried past—as though they feared her misery might be contagious.

"This was all quite predictable . . ."

"One cannot help but pity her . . ."

"I told you the engagement was a farce . . ."

Hazel handed a glass to Poppy. "Do not listen to them. Listen to what your heart is telling you and believe it. That's what is true."

The words had barely left her lips when the grandfather clock began to chime.

The orchestra faltered, then lowered their bows.

The dancers ceased their twirling.

Guests turned toward Poppy, their faces expectant.

The low murmur of the crowd faded, till all she could hear was the soft splashing of the fountain behind her and the beating of her heart in her ears.

"You're sure about this?" Hazel whispered.

"I'm sure," she said, even though it felt like her legs had become detached from her body.

"Good." Hazel gently pried Kitty away and swept an arm toward Poppy as she retreated, giving her the floor.

She swallowed, hoping she didn't look half as terrified as she felt. She opened her mouth to speak, but it sounded more like a croak, so she cleared her throat and tried again.

"This evening has been far different than I imagined it," she said. "I had expected that Keane—that is, the duke—and I would be standing here together. Celebrating the start of our lives together."

She inhaled and released her breath slowly—a futile attempt to slow her racing pulse. A sea of unfamiliar faces gaped at her, their open mouths reminding her of the cods she'd pulled from her nets. And she couldn't blame them for staring. This speech was probably ill-advised, and she supposed she was making a spectacle of herself.

She decided then and there that she might as well dedicate herself fully to the task.

"Perhaps I should not be surprised at this latest hiccup," she said, "since our courtship has been unconventional from the start. You see, the duke and I did not meet at a musicale or a dinner party or a ball. We did not fall in love over the course of a waltz or during a sedate stroll through the park . . . but we *did* fall in love."

A few of the women sighed softly.

"I do not know what has kept him away tonight; I cannot say where he is. All I know is that there is a good reason as to why he isn't here right now, and—"

"I think we all know the reason." The words were slurred but laced with venom. Gasps hissed through the crowd.

Poppy whirled around to find Teddy—Keane's cousin—staggering through the French doors behind the fountain, his ascot askew.

"My dear," he bellowed at Poppy, "the reason my cousin isn't here is because he is a *duke*. Dukes do not marry women like you. They simply . . . dally."

Hazel and Kitty would have lunged at him, but Poppy held up a staying hand. This was her fight. Her chance to stand up for herself—and Keane.

Her palms itched to slap the condescension off Theodore's face. Keane had said his cousin was enlisting as a soldier, that he was forbidden to return to London for the next decade at least. Another sinister chill ran down her spine. "Where is he?" she asked. "What have you done to him?"

"*I* have not done anything." Teddy pressed a hand to his chest, all innocence. "Accidents do happen, after all."

"If you've hurt him, you will pay." Poppy stood toe-to-toe with him, seething. If she'd had her knife strapped to her leg beneath her ball gown, the point of it would be at Teddy's throat. "Where . . . is . . . he?"

"If I had to guess, he's in a pub somewhere, deep in his cups and regretting his life choices."

"You know that's a lie," she spat.

"You're right," Teddy drawled menacingly. "It's more likely my cousin is soaking in a bath—trying to scrub the stench of fish off his skin."

"Theodore!" Teddy's father pushed through the crowd and glared at his son. "That's enough."

But the damage had already been done. Scores of guests dressed in their finery and dripping with jewels froze. They blinked at her as though they were seeing right through her borrowed ball gown and her elaborately coiffed hair.

They were seeing the girl in a threadbare dress with a windblown riot of curls.

The girl with the calluses on her palms from casting and hauling in her nets.

The girl with the sunburned nose and fish scales stuck to her shoes.

Heat crept up her chest. Her cheeks flamed. Her tongue turned thick and unwieldy.

Teddy snickered cruelly and leaned in closer. "Did you think you could hide it?"

His snide pomposity was clearly meant to intimidate. To make her feel small and unworthy.

But it had the opposite effect.

She stepped around him like she might a mud puddle and addressed the crowd, forthright. "I *am* a fisherman's daughter," she said, lifting her chin. "I'm a fisherwoman myself. I work with my hands. I support my family. And I won't apologize for who I am."

"Nor should you," piped Aunt Evelyn. The bright blue feather she'd worn in her hair quivered above a sea of heads. "I am proud to call you my niece."

Poppy's chest squeezed at her aunt's show of loyalty.

Hazel came to stand by Poppy's side. "I am proud to call you my dear friend," she declared.

"As am I," Kitty added staunchly.

"And I," came a deep, wonderfully familiar voice from the direction of the French doors, "am both overjoyed and humbled to call you my fiancée."

Chapter 33

"Keane?" Poppy whirled around, hoping her ears hadn't deceived her.

But he *was* really there, standing beside the fountain where she'd made her wish.

The first things she noticed were his heart-stopping smile and his adoring gaze—both of which were focused solely on her.

As she ran to him, she also spotted his torn jacket and trousers, his dusty boots, and an abrasion along his jaw—all of which raised concerning questions. But for now, it was enough to know he was there. He was safe. And he was hers.

She flung her arms around his neck and savored the feel of his hard body pressed against hers. One of his hands cupped the back of her head, the other rubbed soothing circles at the small of her back.

"Sorry I'm late." His gruff whisper made her toes curl. "Did I miss anything?"

"Let's see," she murmured. "Dinner, dancing, and a great deal of speculation as to your whereabouts. The gentlemen were placing bets."

"I love a good wager," he quipped, then more soberly

added, "I hope you know that nothing short of the fires of hell would have kept me away."

"I do know. Are you all right?"

"Never better. I—"

Keane abruptly released Poppy in order to grab Theodore's collar as he attempted to slink toward the doors. "Going somewhere, Cousin?"

Theodore scoffed. "Forgive me if I refuse to be party to this farce of an engagement."

"There's nothing farcical about it." Keane's tone, lethal and low, raised the hairs on the backs of Poppy's arms. "I believe you owe my fiancée an apology."

"I don't owe her anything," Theodore spat. "And I don't owe you anything. Indeed, you should be in *my* debt. By all rights, your title should be my father's . . . and, eventually, mine."

"Theodore," his father said sharply. "You're so foxed you don't know what the devil you're saying."

"Don't I?" Theodore snorted. "You know as well as I that he is *not* the true heir to the dukedom." Turning to Keane, he shouted, "Your mother was nothing but a whore, and you, Cousin, are nothing but a bastard."

The guests murmured in astonishment. Poppy's heart ached for Keane. Surely, there had never been a more disastrous engagement ball.

"Is that why you tried to have me killed outside the Salty Mermaid?" Keane demanded, tightening his grip on Theodore's jacket. "Is that why you wanted me to fall three stories to my death? Why you had someone kidnap me tonight?"

"Forgive me if I tire of watching you sully our family's name," Theodore said, impressively snide for someone who was on the verge of being throttled. "Tonight's ball is a case in point. Everyone knows that woman"—he gestured at Poppy—"is not duchess material. If you had a need to slake your lust, you should have simply made her your mis—"

Thwack. Keane's fist collided with Theodore's jaw. The impact spun him halfway around before he staggered and flopped face-first into the fountain.

A few of the ladies spontaneously cheered. The men grunted in approval. Poppy exhaled.

"My son deserved that," Keane's uncle said. He strode to the fountain, hauled Theodore's head out of the water, and let him slump to the floor, where he sputtered and whimpered. "I fear he's not going to make a very good soldier," the viscount added with a sigh.

"I now have other plans for him," Keane said curtly.

"Understood." His uncle shot Keane an apologetic look. "Please, ignore the rantings of a jealous, drunken fool. You *are* the Duke of Hawking," he said soberly. "And a damn good one, at that."

Keane nodded, appreciative. "I have plenty to learn, Uncle, and lots of work to do. But I'm finally ready to embrace the challenge, especially with Poppy by my side."

He went to her, clasped her hands in his, and stared into her eyes until the rest of the room melted away. "When I washed up on your beach that morning, I was lost. Content to let the tide take me where it would. But you found me. And, without even trying, you helped me find myself."

Poppy felt like she was floating. Would not have been surprised if her slippers left the parquet floor. "You weren't lost. Rather, I think you were precisely where you were meant to be."

He chuckled. "Maybe so. Your kindness humbled me,

your wit captivated me. Your smile made me want to stay with you. Always."

Happy tears stung her eyes. "I want to stay with you, too."

Tenderly, he pressed a kiss to the back of her hand. "I love you, Poppy Summers. I want the ton and all the world to know it. But mostly, I want you to know it. To feel it deep in your soul. I can't wait to begin the rest of our lives together."

"Nor can I," she replied. "Wherever we go—whether we are here, in Bellehaven Bay, or on some new adventure—home will always be with you. I love you, Keane."

The throng surrounding them buzzed with a mixture of excitement and wonder—as if they were already anticipating a detailed recounting of the evening in the next issue of *The London Hearsay*. And then a plump figure wearing a sparkling tiara emerged from the crowd.

"Is that Lady Rufflebum?" Keane whispered, incredulous.

"She made the trip from Bellehaven," Poppy confirmed. "She cannot bear to miss a ball."

The countess lifted the corner of a lacy handkerchief to her eye, delicately patted her nose, then addressed the guests. "I know a love match when I see one, and this is, indeed, a love match. Please, raise your glasses in a toast to His Grace, the Duke of Hawking, and to Miss Poppy Summers, the pride of Bellehaven Bay."

A resounding chorus of "Hear, hear!" rang out among the clink of glasses.

Hazel and Kitty beamed. A misty-eyed Aunt Evelyn pressed a hand to her chest.

Best of all, Keane kissed Poppy softly on the lips. "I'll come to you later tonight," he said, "After I deal with some unfinished business." He threw a glance at his cousin, who sat next to the fountain, wiggling a loose molar.

"I'll ensure that the back entrance of Bladenton House is unlocked and leave a candle lit in my bedchamber."

Keane lifted her hand and pressed a sensuous kiss to the inside of her wrist. "I'll be counting the moments till I see you again."

Keane scaled the wrought iron garden fence and tore his waistcoat on the way down.

But it scarcely mattered.

He'd ruined his jacket and trousers hours before, when he'd crawled out the window of his carriage, climbed onto the roof, and overtaken the driver who'd tried to kidnap him. It hadn't taken long for the brute to confess that Teddy had hired him, but it had taken some time for Keane to drive back to Hawking House and untie his own poor driver, who'd been ruthlessly bound and gagged in the stables.

It was the last straw.

He'd wanted to give his cousin a second chance, but Teddy squandered it, leaving Keane no choice but to choose a permanent solution, and now Teddy was gone. For good.

As Keane wound his way down a brick walkway in the perfectly manicured garden, a blossom caught his gaze. Its bright peach petals were tipped with a hint of deep red—the same rich shade as Poppy's glorious curls. He impulsively plucked the flower from its stem and furtively made his way through the back door of Bladenton House.

Silently, he ascended the stairs and trod lightly down a hallway, grateful for the dimly lit sconces on the walls. He crept past darkened rooms and muted snores till he spotted a light shining beneath a door at the far end of the corridor.

He tentatively turned the handle and eased the door open, revealing a sumptuous bedchamber decorated in rich hues of gold and ivory. In the middle of an enormous four-poster bed, Poppy lay sleeping. Her auburn tresses extended across her silk pillow like the fiery rays of a sunset so perfect it took a man's breath away.

Keane glided to the bed, set the flower on the mattress in front of her, and kissed her forehead.

"You're here." A sleepy smile spread across her face.

"Yes." His chest ached with love for her. "I missed you."

"Then take off your clothes," she purred. "And come to bed."

He almost tripped in his haste to strip off his jacket, boots, and trousers. And when he'd removed everything but his drawers, he slipped beneath the covers and hauled her lithe, naked body against his—her back to his chest.

He breathed in the sultry scent of her skin as his palm skimmed the curve of her hips. With a growl, he swept aside her hair and nipped at the column of her neck. He slipped a hand between her legs, pleasuring her every way he knew how.

And when her whimpers turned to cries of ecstasy, he thrust inside her and licked the shell of her ear. "You're not done yet, love."

"No?" she said breathlessly. "But I . . . *oh.*"

He trailed his fingertips over her shoulders and the swells of her breasts, tracing a spiral near one puckered tip. He rocked his hips against her rounded bottom and when her inner muscles squeezed around him, he held his breath to keep from climaxing.

"This feels too good," she murmured. "Almost like I'm dreaming."

"It's no dream, Poppy." He thrust again, filling her. Savoring the perfect fit of their bodies. "My love for you is as real as the ground we walk on. As vast as the sky above us. As strong as the ocean's currents."

"Will it always be like this?" she asked, panting as she moved against him.

"Always," he said, not a doubt in his mind. "Only better."

"I don't see how it could be—"

He licked his finger and caressed the sensitive spot above her entrance, circling and teasing till her body pulsed around him.

"Oh . . . *Keane.*" Thrilled by the sound of his name as she came apart, he surrendered to pleasure at last. Pure and potent, it pounded through his veins, lighting up every nerve ending and drowning out everything but the sound of his heart, beating in time to hers.

They clung to each other till the last tendrils of pleasure subsided and their breathing slowed.

When Poppy rolled onto her back, her expression was sated, and her eyes brimmed with happiness. "I love you. And I was so worried when you weren't at the ball."

He picked up the peach rose and swept the soft petals over her belly, making her giggle. "I'm sorry I missed most of it. Teddy hired a cretin to tie up my driver, take his place at the reins, and drive me out of town so I'd miss the celebration."

"Why?" she asked, bewildered.

"He's a miserable, wretched excuse for a human," Keane said bluntly. "He thought he could ruin the ball, turn the ton against us, and end our engagement with his tirade. He wanted us to be as miserable as he is."

"His plan failed," Poppy assured him. "I've never been happier. How did you escape?"

"I climbed out the window of the coach and jumped the hired man. We had a bit of a scuffle on the driver's seat. In the end, he was sprawled on the ground, cursing and shaking his fist. I was holding the reins and turning the coach around. Back to you."

"Thank heaven you did," she said. "You must tell me all the details tomorrow."

"And you must tell me what transpired between you and Lady Evelyn."

"Of course I will." She hesitated, then met his gaze. "But there's something I need to ask tonight . . . what did you do to your cousin?"

"He will never harass you again, Poppy. He's gone for good."

"Gone?" she repeated. "You didn't . . ."

"I took him to the docks, put him on a ship to America, and watched as it left the harbor. He'll be an ocean away."

She exhaled, obviously relieved. "Thank God."

He slid the blossom between her breasts and across the taut peaks, and her eyes fluttered shut. He sighed with satisfaction. "All things considered, I'd have to say tonight was an unqualified success."

"Do you think so?" she asked, incredulous.

He swept the flower along her collarbone, lingering near the hollow at the base of her throat. "The gossips have plenty to talk about, we received Lady Rufflebum's endorsement, and you were the undisputed belle of the ball. You've charmed everyone in London."

"That's sweet of you to say. I am happy that my first foray into polite society wasn't a complete failure, and I know we'll make many memories together here, like we have tonight."

"But?" he prompted.

"But do you think we could have our wedding in Belle-haven?"

He kissed her lightly on the tip of her freckled nose. "I would marry you anywhere, Poppy Summers. But I can't think of a better place than Bellehaven Bay—where it all began."

Chapter 34

Two months after the engagement ball, on a balmy fall day, Poppy became the fourth Duchess of Hawking.

"I would have been happy to host a traditional wedding breakfast for you," Lady Rufflebum grumbled, using her fan to fend off a few bits of ash that had floated up to the cliffs from the roaring bonfire on the beach below.

"It was very generous of you to offer," Poppy replied. "But Keane and I wanted a simple ceremony and a party here at home so that Papa could attend. Besides, you must admit that this is a gorgeous backdrop for the celebration." She inhaled a lungful of salty air and sighed as the sun painted the sky orange and pink.

"It's lovely," the countess conceded, "and terribly unconventional. The London folk must think us heathens."

"Perhaps," Poppy said. "But at least they've been enjoying themselves." She gazed down at the shoreline, where children waded in and out of the frothy waves and couples danced gaily in the light of the fire. All the guests had feasted at a long trestle table at the base of the cliffs, enjoying tender roast beef, savory vegetables, ripe fruits, and every sweet imaginable. Two barrels of ale kept the celebration lively.

"The ceremony was beautiful, in any event. I daresay

there wasn't a dry eye in the chapel." The countess cast an approving glance at Poppy's simple, pale green dress. "Now then, I believe I shall retire for the evening and leave the merry-making to you and the rest of the younger set."

"I'm headed for my bed as well," Papa interjected. He shuffled toward Poppy, grinning even as he stifled a yawn. "I don't think I've had so much fun since my own wedding day. I swear I have enough energy to dance a jig."

She chuckled and patted his shoulder. "I'd rather we didn't test that theory."

"Having you here is a gift, Poppy," he said sincerely. "And the changes you've made to the cottage . . . It feels like a palace already."

She waved a dismissive hand. "That was all Kitty's doing, and we've only begun the modifications. Now go, and sleep well. Shall I help you walk home?"

"No need." His cheeks turned ruddy. "Mrs. Wallaby was good enough to offer."

"Did she, now?" Poppy raised a knowing brow as she kissed his cheek. "Good night, Papa."

She made her way down to the beach and found Dane flirting with Lydia—a pretty young woman with a quick smile and a quick wit who worked as a barmaid at the Salty Mermaid. She and Dane had been spending quite a bit of time together of late. Dane had even begun talking about building his own cottage on the shore, not far from Papa's.

"Felicitations, Poppy," Lydia said kindly. "Or should I say, Your Grace?"

"Just Poppy, please. My brother, on the other hand, can address me as Duchess."

He groaned. "I just knew you'd be insufferable."

"I'd say you had it coming," she teased.

Lydia cocked her head at Dane, curious. "Have I missed something?"

"That's a story for another time," he said smoothly. "And, fortunately, we have plenty of time."

"I'm not accustomed to seeing this tender side of my brother," Poppy said. "You don't seem to miss the entertainments of London."

"Not at all," he said, grinning at Lydia. More seriously, he added, "I'm finished with running away, trying to outrun the past. Instead, I'm trying to make peace with it."

"Why the change of heart?" she asked.

Dane hesitated. "I did something pretty awful once, and somebody forgave me. Gave me a second chance when I probably didn't deserve it. I figured it was time I did the same . . . and let go of the hate."

Poppy blinked back tears. "Everyone deserves a second chance."

"I think I'm up to my fourth or fifth," Dane admitted wryly.

Lydia squeezed his arm and beamed at Poppy. "Don't worry. From here on out, I intend to keep a close eye on him."

Poppy chuckled, feeling two stone lighter as she walked through the crowd, looking for Keane. She'd last seen him telling Blade about the parcel of land near the new school building where they hoped to begin construction of their own home soon.

Hazel and Blade had insisted that she and Keane stay with them in the meantime.

"There you are!" Kitty cried, pulling Poppy into an impulsive hug. "Can I tell you a secret?"

"Always," Poppy said, wondering how many glasses of ale Kitty had drunk.

"I am going to miss your hideaway. Whether we were

reading books, stealing an afternoon nap, or simply spending time together, it felt like a little slice of paradise. I felt like it was my sanctuary, too."

"The shelter isn't going anywhere," Poppy said firmly, "and you're welcome there anytime. In fact, I'd appreciate it if you'd stop by whenever you can, just to make certain it doesn't fall into disrepair."

Kitty clasped her hands under her pixie chin. "Do you mean it?"

"I do."

She threw her arms around Poppy again and squeezed. "I'm going to pay a visit now. But don't worry—I'll make sure no one follows me. Least of all my nemesis."

Poppy blinked. *Nemesis?* "Be careful," she called after Kitty, who was already halfway up the path.

As the sun sank into the ocean, some of the revelers began to leave. She spotted Keane chatting with different groups around the fire, and when their eyes met, she felt the same frisson of awareness that she had when she first found him on the beach.

When the last of the guests finally left, he took her hand, lacing his fingers through hers. "Come with me," he said.

They strolled along the shore, gazing up at the sky, where the stars seemed to sparkle just for them.

"You look especially beautiful tonight," he said, eyes aglow with love.

"You look very handsome yourself."

"Ah, Diggs would say that the clothes make the man, but I happen to think it's this scar," he teased, pointing to his temple. "You wouldn't believe the story behind it."

"I think I know that story, and I'm rather fond of it."

"The tale is far from over, you know. It's only just beginning."

Her chest warmed. "Today was like a dream. I wish

Mama could have been here, but in some ways, she is. I feel her presence in the playful ocean breeze and in the moonlight dancing on the water."

"I know you feel her here," he said. "And I know how special this place is to you. I'd never ask you to give it up. I will support you in any endeavor you choose."

"I think I am ready to set aside my nets and try being a duchess."

He chuckled softly. "You don't need to try; you *are* a duchess. And you can be a duchess who fishes if that's what you wish."

"Perhaps I will fish now and then, but mostly for pleasure. I'm turning the business over to Dane. I want to be free to learn new things. To explore the world beyond this beach."

Keane nodded, thoughtful. "I like the sound of that."

"What are you looking forward to?" she asked.

"Beyond spending time with you?"

Poppy grinned. "Yes."

Keane paused, then said, "Being the best duke I can be. Taking care of the estate, helping our tenants, and turning Hawking Manor into a place that feels like . . . home."

"You'll accomplish all of that," she said with confidence. "I'll be there to help you."

He squeezed her hand and stopped in a secluded part of the cove. "I have something for you." He walked to the cliff wall, withdrew a velvet pouch from a deep crevice, and handed it to her.

"What's this?" She loosened the drawstring and turned the pouch over, spilling the contents into her palm. A stunning gold necklace shimmered, and a small pendant sparkled in the moonlight. "A locket?"

"Not quite." He took the necklace, stood behind her, and fastened it at her nape. Suspended from the chain was a tiny glass vial, and she twirled it between her fingertips. "The vial contains sand from this beach," he explained. "So that even when we're in London, you'll have a piece of Bellehaven with you."

Her eyes welled. "I love it." She took a moment to compose herself, then said, "I happen to have something for you, too." She reached into her pocket, pulled out a small jelly jar, and placed it in his hand.

He frowned and held it up to take a closer look at the smooth, colorful pieces inside—then his face split into a wide smile. "Is this . . . ?"

"Sea glass," she confirmed. "I've been collecting it ever since that night we spent on the beach. I've been thinking about what you said. That it takes time to smooth out the rough edges and reveal the beauty within. I can't think of anyone I'd rather tumble through life with."

"I can't either." He swallowed and held the jar reverently, as if she'd given him the most extravagant of gifts. "It's fitting that we're celebrating the start of our life together here—in the precise spot where we first met. You saved me, Poppy. In more ways than one." He leaned closer, touching his forehead to hers, and their breath mingled in the space between them.

"You saved me, too. And you helped me see that you needn't always stray far from home to seek out adventure. Sometimes, adventure comes to us."

He captured her mouth in a slow, sensuous kiss that made her whole body thrum. "I can't wait for our next adventure," he murmured.

She slipped her hands inside his jacket, tracing the sinewy muscles of his back. "I suspect it's just around the corner."

"Do you think so?" he asked huskily.

She took a fortifying breath and looked into his eyes.

"Andrew Keane, Duke of Hawking," she said. "Are you ready for your question?"

A surprised smile lit his face, and he rolled his shoulders, as if preparing himself. "Yes."

"How would you feel about . . . learning to change nappies?"

"I've never really thought ab—" He froze, then swallowed. "Poppy?"

"You have a little time," she said. "About seven months, actually."

He abruptly stepped back and searched her face, unabashedly hopeful. "Truly?"

She nodded, and he picked her up and shouted, twirling her around as the surf licked at her toes.

"We're going to be the happiest family," he said at last. "I would do anything for you—and for our babe."

"I know you would," she said soberly. "I trust you with my heart and my soul. I trust you with our future."

"Let me tell you what our future holds," he murmured, trailing kisses along the column of her neck. "Plenty of nappies, to be sure. But also glorious days like this. Magical nights in each other's arms. Lazy mornings in bed where I bring you steaming hot tea—with one sugar cube and a spot of cream, in your favorite teacup."

She leaned into him, savoring the perfect fit of their bodies. "I can scarcely wait for tomorrow morning."

"We'll have to think of something to pass the time until then." The wicked promise in his words made her shiver in anticipation.

"More questions?" she teased.

"You know the rules, Your Grace," he countered, slowly pulling the pins from her hair. "Only one question is permitted each day. But if it is any consolation, I will tell you what is in my heart right now." His expression turned impossibly tender. "My love for you is boundless. I love you, Poppy Summers. And the day I almost died on your beach was the luckiest day of my life."

"Mine, too," she said, melting at the brush of his lips on her shoulder. "Mine, too."

Don't Miss the Next Book
in the *Rogues to Lovers* Series
by Anna Bennett

IT TAKES A RAKE

Available December 2023 from
St. Martin's Paperbacks

If Leo's calculations were correct—as they usually were—Kitty's shoulder was only three and seven-eighths inches away from his. Her hand rested on the stone wall where they sat, a mere two and five-sixteenths inches away from his thigh. And for the first time in years, they were completely alone. His heartbeat thundered in his chest as if he'd sprinted a mile to get to the countess's terrace.

If he didn't know Kitty so well, he might have misread the flush of her cheeks, the rapid rise and fall of her chest, and the frenetic tapping of her slipper on the flagstone terrace. But he was neither so hopeful nor so foolish as to imagine that those signs had anything to do with him or their closeness.

Kitty was entirely fixated on the mayor's announcement about Bellehaven's building-design contest. She had the same feverish look about her that she'd always had when she was in the throes of envisioning a new project. He'd forgotten how beautiful she looked when she was inspired. How arousing it was when her lips moved—as if she were silently listing the elements she'd incorporate into her creation.

She blinked at him and shook her head as though she'd

almost forgotten he was there. "I know you wished to talk about something," she said. "But may I ask you something first?"

Leo nodded. Clearly, this was not the moment to confess his feelings for her. "I presume this is about the contest?"

She looked into his eyes and blew out a long breath. "Are you going to enter?"

"I don't know," he said truthfully.

She scoffed, incredulous. "How could you not know?"

"I heard about the contest five minutes ago. I haven't had time to weigh the pros and cons, much less consider what sort of building I'd design."

With a frustrated sigh, she stood and paced the terrace in front of him. "Is it necessary to nail down every little detail? Must you be so deliberate about everything?"

He smiled, grateful that he hadn't lost his knack for getting under her skin. "How about if I turn the question around. Do *you* want me to enter the contest?"

"No and yes."

He scratched his head, at a loss. "Care to elaborate?"

"No, I don't want you to enter because, though I'm loath to admit it, you are my strongest competition," she said, and Leo could only imagine what it had cost her.

"And yes because . . . ?"

"Yes, because I don't want to win by default. I want to win knowing that my design was the best. That it outshone every other entry and won on its merits." She exhaled slowly. "You should enter."

"I'm finishing designs for a couple of clients over the next two weeks," he said. "But I'll think about it."

She walked back to the stone wall, sat beside him, and swallowed. "In the meantime, I have a favor to ask of you." She closed her eyes for a moment, then looked deep into his. He'd never seen Kitty Beckett so vulnerable, so exposed.

And in that moment, he would have given her anything. If she'd asked him to rob the next coach that came to town, he'd have donned a mask, hopped on his horse, and found a hiding spot by the road. He was powerless to refuse her when she looked so genuine. So soft.

"What sort of favor?" he asked, his voice a little raspy to his own ears.

"I wondered if you'd help me with my entry in the contest." The words spilled out as if she'd been holding them in for a while. "My technical skills have improved vastly since we last worked together, so I wouldn't be asking you to do everything. I just need someone to come to as questions arise, and to occasionally review my work to make sure my calculations are sound."

"I suppose I could help," he said, trying not to appear too eager.

A warm smile lit her face. "Thank you. I wouldn't have asked, but I've never undertaken a project of this scope before, and this contest is a unique chance for someone like me."

"I understand," he said truthfully. He didn't know any other female architects. Couldn't imagine they'd have the same opportunities he had. "What are you going to design?"

She gazed out at the moonlit garden, and her face took on a dreamy look. "I'm not ready to share quite yet. It's still coming into focus. But it's going to be something the likes of which Bellehaven has never seen."

"I don't doubt it."

"In any event, you mustn't let your involvement with my project prevent you from entering the contest," she said, earnestly. "May the best design win."

He arched a brow in his best villain impersonation. "There could be a conflict of interest. Aren't you afraid I'll try to sabotage your project?"

"Sabotage," she repeated with a chuckle. "That's rich."

"One misplaced decimal could be disastrous," he said, suppressing a shudder at the thought. "Are you certain you trust me?"

"With numbers?" she qualified. "Yes, I do. Besides, you're not capable of carrying out an evil plan. You couldn't be ruthless if you tried."

He sat back, mildly offended. "You don't think I could?"

She patted his knee like she was consoling a schoolboy who'd had his lunch stolen. "Not in a million years. You're far too . . . nice." She winced, as if she'd just delivered news that he had a ghastly illness.

He was still digesting this as she smoothed the skirt of her gown and folded her hands on her lap.

"I'm glad that's settled," she said brightly. "You shall act as a consultant on my contest entry. And now you must tell me what I may do for you in return."

Leo blinked. "You don't need to do anything for me."

"I'm afraid I do," she said firmly. "I wouldn't rest easy otherwise."

"Why? Are you afraid I'd hold the favor over your head? Blackmail you?"

She chuckled again and dabbed the corner of one eye with a fingertip as if some of her mirth had leaked out. "I believe we've already established that you're too honorable to sabotage anything. I'm afraid we must add blackmail to the list of things you're incapable of."

It was true, damn it all. And though he supposed it was a compliment, it sounded more like a fatal flaw. "Very well, Miss Beckett," he drawled. "If you insist on making this an even exchange, tell me: What can you offer me in return for my services?"

She lifted her chin, squared her shoulders, and frowned, thoughtful. "I could sketch a design for you—for one of your current projects or for your contest entry."

He would have loved to have one of her sketches—but not for a job. He'd rather have something she drew just for him. But he couldn't ask her that without revealing his feelings for her, and he wasn't ready to do that. Yet.

He shook his head. "No, thank you. My current clients are accustomed to my dry, functional drawings. If I gave them a glimpse of your talent, I'd only be setting them up for disappointment in the future."

Her mouth quirked adorably. "I take it you still regard the use of watercolors and pastels as frivolous?"

"Not so much frivolous as beyond me," he confessed. "I've come to terms with it."

"Each of us has their cross to bear," she said philosophically. "Let me see. There must be something else you need. Some sort of service I could provide." She tapped the tip of her index finger against her plump lower lip, then her eyes went wide with inspiration. "I could reintroduce you to some of the young ladies in town."

He narrowed his eyes, suspicious. "Why would you do that?"

She shrugged innocently. "I assumed you'd be interested in finding a nice, agreeable woman to settle down with."

Holy hell. "I don't need you to play matchmaker, Kitty."

"It's Kat," she reminded him coolly. "And you needn't sound so offended. I simply thought you could use some assistance in that area. You've been away for a while, after all, and there are some recent newcomers to Bellehaven— eligible young ladies who would suit you."

Leo raked a hand through his hair and took a turn at pacing the terrace. "The idea is ludicrous," he said. "But just out of curiosity, what sort of woman do you think would suit me?"

"That's simple," she said, supremely confident. "Your ideal match would be congenial, sweet, and doting. The sort of woman who lives for the moment when you walk through the door in the evening."

"I can see you've devoted some thought to this," he said wryly. "What else?"

"Well," she said, as if broaching a sticky subject. "Your ideal woman would need to be patient enough to tolerate your meticulous and sometimes moody nature."

"This is extremely enlightening," he quipped. "Is that all?"

"No, of course not. She'll need to be pretty." She smirked, signaling a final jab was coming. "So that there's at least the possibility that you'll produce attractive off-spring."

He glowered at her, and she waved a dismissive hand. "I only tease because you know very well that women find you attractive. I don't want your head to grow too big."

Leo took a moment to digest the compliment—if it could accurately be classified as such. Then he said, "Let me see if I have this correct." He held up a hand, preparing to tick off her list on his fingers. "You think I need a woman who's meek, desperate, and not hideous."

"I was significantly more tactful," Kitty said with a shrug. "But your characterization is also accurate."

Leo started pacing again, beyond frustrated.

"What's wrong?" Kitty asked. She frowned as if she was truly puzzled. "You're not interested in finding a nice woman to court?"

The truth was he didn't want docile or timid. He wanted

spirited and passionate. He wanted obstinate and clever. He wanted Kitty.

But it wasn't as if he could come right out and tell her.

"You have no idea what I'm looking for in a partner," he said flatly.

"Then why don't you inform me?"

He faced her, propped his hands on his hips, and gazed into her eyes, wondering if she'd recognize herself in the description he gave. "I'm looking for someone with a rapier wit and a saucy smile. Someone who knows what she wants and unapologetically goes after it. Someone who challenges me and who occasionally even drives me a bit mad."

Kitty seemed to consider this for a moment, then clucked her tongue in disbelief. "You're quite certain about that?"

"I am."

"I'm afraid I simply can't see that working," she said, her voice laced with regret.

"Why not?" he asked, incredulous.

Kitty gracefully rose from the wall and began to slowly circle him, as if taking his measure. "Would you like me to be honest?"

He tried not to flinch under her scrutiny. "Yes," he said, though he was fairly certain he wasn't going to like her answer.

"We've already established that you're handsome enough. That isn't the problem."

Leo was grateful she was behind him so that she couldn't see him flush. "I sense there's a *but* coming."

"It's the way you dress and carry yourself, the way you interact with people. You're too predictable, principled, and *nice*."

He resisted the urge to grind his teeth. "Those are bad qualities?"

"Not at all!" she assured him. "But they're not going to attract the sort of woman you described."

"Very well. What qualities do I need?"

"I cannot give you a list, Leo. It's more complicated than that." She paused in front of him, lifted her chin, and met his gaze. "If you wish to catch the eye of a daring woman, you must be able to walk into a room and command the attention of everyone in it. You must have a dangerous air about you—the sort that makes a lady's heart flutter."

With each word she spoke, his own heart sank. He was nothing like the man she described. And she wasn't finished. Her expression turned wistful, and her mouth curved into a sensual smile—as if she was imagining the man of *her* dreams.

"You should have a sense of mystery or intrigue. A deliciously disheveled look that makes people wonder whether you've come directly from a high-stakes card game or a lover's bed."

He swallowed, and her words hung in the air between them like the aromatic smoke of a cheroot. Once he'd located his tongue, he asked, "Women truly want that?"

"Not all women," she corrected. "But some do." The faraway look in her eyes left no doubt as to which camp she fell into.

Kitty wanted a rogue. A reprobate. A *rake*.

And he knew exactly what he needed to do.

"Fine," he said, keeping his tone light. "Teach me."

She inhaled sharply—as if someone had splashed her with cold water. "What?"

"You asked what I wanted in exchange for helping you with your contest entry. Show me how to be that kind of man."

She opened her mouth, closed it, and opened it again. As if she was having difficulty making her voice work. At last she managed, "Are you jesting?"

"I'm dead serious."

"But there's nothing wrong with the way you are," she said. "You're perfectly fine."

Fine? He'd have rather she called him "perfectly infuriating" or even "perfectly diabolical." Any adjective would have been preferable to *fine*. Except, perhaps, *nice*.

"That's not the point," he said evenly.

She stalked back to the wall and sat, flouncing her skirts in exasperation. "I don't see why—" Her eyes grew wide and her mouth formed a small O. As if understanding had dawned.

Panic clambered up his chest and skittered around his neck. Kitty knew how he felt about her. She'd finally seen through his façade, and he was totally exposed. As vulnerable as a roofless house in a thunderstorm.

"You needn't be embarrassed," she said earnestly.

"No?" He hadn't dared to believe that she might return his feelings. Especially after everything she'd told him tonight, but maybe . . .

"You're fond of a someone here in Bellehaven," she whispered conspiratorially. "And you want her to believe you're a rake."

Bloody hell.

Her expression was triumphant—as if she'd cracked a secret code. "It's true, isn't it?" she prodded.

"Yes." He saw no point in denying it.

She leaned forward. "Who's the woman you fancy? I must know."

"I'd rather not say." His mouth felt dry as dust. "The question is, can you help me?"

She cast a skeptical glance at his boots, his clothes, his hair. "It would require quite a bit of work, and you'd need to trust me."

"I do trust you," he said evenly.

"I would need to know that you're one hundred percent committed." She crossed her arms, adamant. "I don't do anything by half measures."

"I know." It was one of the things he adored about her. "I'm willing to do whatever you say."

She arched a brow at that. "You must be quite smitten by this mystery woman."

"I suppose I am."

For the space of several heartbeats, she was silent, and Leo wondered if she'd refuse.

At last, she blew out a long breath. "Very well. You will be my consultant for the design contest. In return I shall teach you how to be a rake."

He extended a hand to her. "Deal."

She took his hand, and the touch of their palms sent a rush of heat surging through his body.

"Deal," she confirmed. She didn't release his hand right away, but instead searched his face—as if she longed to know his secrets.

He didn't let go either. When it came to Kitty, he would never be the first to let go. "A fair trade," he said. "I'll help you win the contest. You'll help me win the object of my affections."

She smiled at that, then slowly uncurled her fingers, releasing him. "I should return to the ballroom before the next gentleman listed on my dance card forms a search party and scours every room in Lady Rufflebum's house from the kitchen to the attic."

"Good idea."

As she turned and crossed the flagstone terrace, he

watched the subtle sway of her hips and the swish of her gown around her legs, half mesmerized.

"Oh, and Leo?" she called over her shoulder, mid-stride. "Meet me on the corner of Main Street and Broadneck tomorrow at half past two."

He scratched his head. "What for?"

She paused and rolled her eyes as if praying for patience. "Your first lesson. Don't be late," she instructed. "And be sure to bring your billfold with you."